The Dennis Wheatley Library of the Occult
Volume 20

On the one side his fear drove him onwards;
on the other a Horror faced him. He dared
not recoil, for he understood where security
lay; he longed, like the child screaming in the
dark and beating his hands, to get back to the
warmth and safety of bed; yet there stood
before him a Presence, or at least an Emotion
of some kind, so hostile, so terrible that he
dared not penetrate it. It was not that an
actual restraint lay upon him: he knew, that
is, that the door was open; yet it needed an
effort of the will of which his paralysis of
terror rendered him incapable. . . .

The Dennis Wheatley Library of the Occult

1 *Dracula*
  Bram Stoker

2 *The Werewolf of Paris*
  Guy Endore

3 *Moonchild*
  Aleister Crowley

4 *Studies in Occultism*
  Helena Blavatsky

5 *Carnacki the Ghost-Finder*
  William Hope Hodgson

6 *The Sorcery Club*
  Elliott O'Donnell

7 *Harry Price: The Biography
  of a Ghost-Hunter*
  Paul Tabori

8 *The Witch of Prague*
  F. Marion Crawford

9 *Uncanny Tales 1*
  Selected by Dennis Wheatley

10 *The Prisoner in the Opal*
  A. E. W. Mason

11 *The Devil's Mistress*
  J. W. Brodie-Innes

12 *You and Your Hand*
  Cheiro

13 *Black Magic*
  Marjorie Bowen

14 *Real Magic*
  Philip Bonewits

15 *Faust*
  Goethe

16 *Uncanny Tales 2*
  Selected by Dennis Wheatley

17 *The Gap in the Curtain*
  John Buchan

18 *The Interpretation of Dreams*
  Zolar

19 *Voodoo*
  Alfred Métraux

20 *The Necromancers*
  R. H. Benson

21 *Satanism and Witches*
  Selected by Dennis Wheatley

22 *The Winged Pharaoh*
  Joan Grant

23 *Down There*
  J. K. Huysmans

24 *The Monk*
  Matthew Lewis

The Necromancers
R. H. BENSON

SPHERE BOOKS LIMITED
30/32 Gray's Inn Road, London WCIX 8JL

First published in Great Britain by Hutchinson & Co Ltd 1909
Published by Sphere Books 1974
Introduction copyright © Dennis Wheatley 1974

TRADE
MARK

Set in Intertype Baskerville

Printed in Great Britain by
Hazell Watson & Viney Ltd
Aylesbury, Bucks

ISBN 0 7221 1615 2

I MUST express my gratitude to the Rev. Father Augustine Howard, O.P., who has kindly read this book in manuscript and favoured me with his criticisms

INTRODUCTION

Robert Hugh Benson was a distinguished Roman Catholic priest and his novels were immensely popular in late Victorian times and those of King Edward VII. His death in 1914 was a severe blow, both to his Church and the reading public, for in his writings he displayed the subtle art of attacking evil practices without in the least appearing to preach.

In the present story Father Benson's principal character is a young barrister named Laurie Baxter. He falls in love with the local grocer's daughter, Amy, a pretty but quite brainless young girl. His family naturally disapprove so are not unduly distressed when the girl dies, from natural causes, before Laurie has married her. But his passion for this innocent charmer continues to be intense; so much so that he joins a spiritualist circle in South Kensington in the hope that the medium will enable him to see again, and possibly even touch, his dead love.

Obsessed with this idea he neglects his work and family. His mother, a lazy, shallow woman, is not particularly distressed but her adopted daughter, Margaret Deronnais, who has come down from Oxford to live with her, becomes greatly worried. Margaret is intelligent and courageous. She and Laurie have been brought up together almost as brother and sister, yet both have, subconsciously, a deeper feeling for each other. On Laurie's ever rarer visits to his mother's house in the country, Margaret gradually learns of the hold that Spiritualism is gaining over him; then she starts to fight it, her only weapons being her strong will and fondness for him.

Despite her efforts nothing will deter Laurie from trying to get in touch with Amy's spirit. Encouraged by a medium, whose only interest is to carry out experiments regardless of their consequences, and two credulous women, after several séances the night Laurie has been longing for arrives. A spectre – assumed to be that of Amy raised from the dead –

appears. Laurie attempts to seize it in his arms and chaos ensues.

As a result of this séance Laurie becomes a changed man. His expression, his manner, his attitude to life all alter; although, at times, he seems to be his normal self. To Margaret's horror she realises that he now has a dual personality and is, in part, possessed by an evil spirit that is seeking to gain complete domination over him.

To give further particulars of the story would spoil it for the reader. But, with overwhelming clarity Father Benson makes clear his conviction; and it is the same that has caused the Spiritualist Press to regard my own writings on the occult with considerable hostility.

I maintain that Spiritualism – or to give this practice its proper name – Necromancy, is an evil thing. One has only to consider how every day scores of engaged couples or newly-weds, deeply in love, are suddenly separated by some fatal accident, to realise that it is against the laws of the spiritual world for the dead to return. Otherwise would it not be a common occurrence for the newly-dead to appear to their beloved and comfort them with the assurance that they had not been separated indefinitely?

During the past century countless mediums have been exposed as frauds; and it is notable that in times of war the number of these criminal tricksters increases a hundredfold, to batten unscrupulously on mothers, fathers and fiancées who wish to get in touch with soldiers killed in battle, whom they have loved.

I do not say that all mediums are dishonest. Many genuinely believe that their psychic powers enable them to speak on behalf of the dead. But is the voice of the spirit really that of the dead person called upon – or an evil spirit impersonating the departed? Are the dead in any circumstances allowed to return, or are even ghosts evil entities taking their form for reasons still hidden from us?

One further point. At séances it is assumed by the audiences that the spirit of the medium leaves his or her body, which becomes temporarily the habitation of another spirit. In other words the medium, if honest, is possessed. Can anything possibly justify a person laying themselves open to an unknown force and so imperiling their immortal soul?

Father Benson's book may well arouse such sinister thoughts but, as a novel, it makes excellent reading with great suspense in the final chapter.

Dennis Wheatley

CHAPTER ONE

'I am very much distressed about it all,' murmured Mrs. Baxter.

She was a small, delicate-looking old lady, very true to type indeed, with the silvery hair of the devout widow crowned with an exquisite lace cap, in a filmy black dress, with a complexion of precious china, kind short-sighted blue eyes, and white blue-veined hands busy now upon needle-work. She bore about with her always an atmosphere of piety, humble, tender, and sincere, but as persistent as the gentle sandal-wood aroma which breathed from her dress. Her theory of the universe, as the girl who watched her now was beginning to find out, was impregnable and unap-proachable. Events which conflicted with it were either not events, or they were so exceptional as to be negligible. If she were hard pressed she emitted a pathetic peevishness that rendered further argument impossible.

The room in which she sat reflected perfectly her person-ality. In spite of the early Victorian date of the furniture, there was in its arrangement and selection a taste so ex-quisite as to deprive it of even a suspicion of Philistinism. Somehow the rosewood table on which the September morn-ing sun fell with serene beauty did not conflict as it ought to have done with the Tudor panelling of the room. A tapestry screen veiled the door into the hall, and soft curtains of velvety gold hung on either side of the tall, modern windows leading to the garden. For the rest, the furniture was charm-ing and suitable – low chairs, a tapestry couch, a multitude of little leather-covered books on every table, and two low carved bookshelves on either side of the door filled with poetry and devotion.

The girl who sat upright with her hands on her lap was of another type altogether – of that type of which it is impos-sible to predicate anything except that it makes itself felt in every company. Any respectable astrologer would have had no difficulty in assigning her birth to the sign of the Scorpion. In outward appearance she was not remarkable, though extremely pleasing, and it was a pleasingness that grew upon acquaintance. Her beauty, such as it was, was based upon a good foundation : upon regular features, a slightly cleft rounded chin, a quantity of dark coiled hair, and large, steady, serene brown eyes. Her hands were not small, but beautifully shaped; her figure slender, well made, and always at its ease in any attitude. In fact, she had an air of repose, strength, and all-round competence; and, contrasted with this other, she resembled a well-bred sheep-dog eyeing an Angora cat.

They were talking now about Laurie Baxter.

'Dear Laurie is so impetuous and sensitive,' murmured his mother, drawing her needle softly through the silk, and then patting her material, 'and it is all terribly sad.'

This was undeniable, and Maggie said nothing, though her lips opened as if for speech. Then she closed them again, and sat watching the twinkling fire of logs upon the hearth. Then once more Mrs. Baxter took up the tale.

'When I first heard of the poor girl's death,' she said, 'it seemed to me so providential. It would have been too dreadful if he had married her. He was away from home, you know, on Thursday, when it happened; but he was back here on Friday, and has been like – like a madman ever since. I have done what I could, but—'

'Was she quite impossible?' asked the girl in her slow voice. 'I never saw her, you know.'

Mrs. Baxter laid down her embroidery.

'My dear, she was. Well, I have not a word against her character, of course. She was all that was good, I believe. But, you know, her home, her father – well, what can you expect from a grocer – and a Baptist,' she added, with a touch of vindictiveness.

'What was she like?' asked the girl, still with that meditative air.

'My dear, she was like – like a picture on a chocolate-box. I can say no more than that. She was little and fair-haired, with a very pretty complexion, and a ribbon in her hair always. Laurie brought her up here to see me, you know – in the garden; I felt I could not bear to have her in the house just yet, though, of course, it would have had to have come. She spoke very carefully, but there was an unmistakable accent. Once she left out an aitch, and then she said the word over again quite right.'

Maggie nodded gently, with a certain air of pity, and Mrs. Baxter went on encouraged.

'She had a little stammer that – that Laurie thought very pretty, and she had a restless little way of playing with her fingers as if on a piano. Oh, my dear, it would have been too dreadful; and now, my poor boy—'

The old lady's eyes filled with compassionate tears, and she laid her sewing down to fetch out a little lace-fringed pocket-handkerchief.

Maggie leaned back with one easy movement in her low chair, clasping her hands behind her head; but she still said nothing. Mrs. Baxter finished the little ceremony of wiping her eyes, and, still winking a little, bending over her needlework, continued the commentary.

'Do try to help him, my dear. That was why I asked you to come back yesterday. I wanted you to be in the house for the funeral. You see, Laurie's becoming a Catholic at Oxford has brought you two together. It's no good my talking to him about the religious side of it all; he thinks I know nothing at all about the next world, though I'm sure—'

'Tell me,' said the girl suddenly, still in the same attitude, 'has he been practising his religion? You see, I haven't seen much of him this year, and—'

'I'm afraid not very well,' said the old lady tolerantly. 'He thought he was going to be a priest at first, you remember, and I'm sure I should have made no objection; and then in the spring he seemed to be getting rather tired of it all. I don't think he gets on with Father Mahon very well. I don't think Father Mahon understands him quite. It was he, you know, who told him not to be a priest, and I think that discouraged poor Laurie.'

'I see,' said the girl shortly. And Mrs. Baxter applied herself again to her sewing.

It was indeed a rather trying time for the old lady. She was a tranquil and serene soul; and it seemed as if she were doomed to live over a perpetual volcano. It was as pathetic as an amiable cat trying to go to sleep on a rifle-range; she was developing the jumps. The first serious explosion had taken place two years before, when her son, then in his third year at Oxford, had come back with the announcement that Rome was the only home worthy to shelter his aspiring soul, and that he must be received into the Church in six weeks' time. She had produced little books for his edification, as in duty bound, she had summoned Anglican divines to the rescue; but all had been useless, and Laurie had gone back to Oxford as an avowed proselyte.

She had soon become accustomed to the idea, and indeed, when the first shock was over had not greatly disliked it, since her own adopted daughter, of half French parentage, Margaret Marie Deronnais, had been educated in the same faith, and was an eminently satisfactory person. The next shock was Laurie's announcement of his intention to enter the priesthood, and perhaps the Religious Life as well; but this too had been tempered by the reflection that in that case Maggie would inherit this house and carry on its traditions in a suitable manner. Maggie had come to her, upon leaving her convent school three years before, with a pleasant little income of her own – had come to her by an arrangement made previously to her mother's death – and her manner of life, her reasonableness, her adaptability, her presentableness had reassured the old lady considerably as to the tolerableness of the Roman Catholic religion. Indeed, once she had hoped that Laurie and Maggie might come to an understanding that would prevent all possible difficulty as to the future of his house and estate; but the fourth volcanic storm had once more sent the world flying in pieces about Mrs. Baxter's delicate ears; and, during the last three months she had had to face the prospect of Laurie's bringing home as a bride the rather underbred, pretty, stammering, pink and white daughter of a Baptist grocer of the village.

This had been a terrible affair altogether; Laurie, as is the custom of a certain kind of young male, had met, spoken to, and ultimately kissed this Amy Nugent, on a certain summer evening as the stars came out; but, with a chivalry not so common in such cases, had also sincerely and simply fallen in love with her, with a romance usually reserved for better-matched affections. It seemed, from Laurie's conversation, that Amy was possessed of every grace of body, mind, and soul required in one who was to be mistress of the great house; it was not, so Laurie explained, at all a milkmaid kind of affair; he was not the man, he said, to make a fool of himself over a pretty face. No, Amy was a rare soul, a flower growing on stony soil – sandy perhaps would be the better word – and it was his deliberate intention to make her his wife.

Then had followed every argument known to mothers, for it was not likely that even Mrs. Baxter would accept without a struggle a daughter-in-law who, five years before, had bobbed to her, wearing a pinafore, and carrying in a pair of rather large hands a basket of eggs to her back door. Then she had consented to see the girl, and the interview in the garden had left her more distressed than ever. (It was there that the aitch incident had taken place.) And so the struggle had gone on; Laurie had protested, stormed, sulked, taken refuge in rhetoric and dignity alternately; and his mother had with gentle persistence objected, held her peace, argued, and resisted, conflicting step by step against the inevitable, seeking to reconcile her son by pathos and her God by petition; and then in an instant, only four days ago, it seemed that the latter had prevailed; and to-day Laurie, in a black suit, rent by sorrow, at this very hour at which the two ladies sat and talked in the drawing-room was standing by an open grave in the village churchyard, seeing the last of his love, under a pile of blossoms as pink and white as her own complexion, within four elm-boards with a brass plate upon the cover.

Now, therefore, there was a new situation to face, and Mrs. Baxter was regarding it with apprehension.

It is true that mothers know sometimes more of their sons than their sons know of themselves, but there are certain elements of character that sometimes neither mothers nor sons appreciate. It was one or two of those elements that Maggie Deronnais with her hands behind her head, was now considering. It seemed to her very odd that neither the boy himself nor Mrs. Baxter in the least seemed to realise the astonishing selfishness of this very boy's actions.

She had known him now for three years, though owing to her own absence in France a part of the time, and his absence in London for the rest, she had seen nothing of this last affair. At first she had liked him exceedingly; he had seemed to her ardent, natural, and generous. She had liked his affection for his mother and his demonstrativeness in showing it; she had liked his well-bred swagger, his manner with servants, his impulsive courtesy to herself. It was a real pleasure to her to see him, morning by morning, in his knickerbockers and Norfolk jacket, or his tweed suit; and evening by evening in his swallow-tail coat and white shirt, and the knee-breeches and buckled shoes that he wore by reason of the touch of picturesque and defiant romanticism that was so obvious a part of his nature. Then she had begun, little by little, to perceive the egotism that was even more apparent; his self-will, his moodiness, and his persistence.

Though, naturally, she had approved of his conversion to Catholicism, yet she was not sure that his motives were pure. She had hoped indeed that the Church, with its astonishing peremptoriness, might do something towards a moral conversion, as well as an artistic and intellectual change of view. But this, it seemed, had not happened; and this final mad episode of Amy Nugent had fanned her criticism to indignation. She did not disapprove of romance – in fact she largely lived by it – but there were things even more important, and she was as angry as she could be, with decency, at this last manifestation of selfishness.

For the worst of it was that, as she knew perfectly well, Laurie was rather an exceptional person. He was not at all the Young Fool of Fiction. There was a remarkable virility about him, he was tender-hearted to a degree, he had more than his share of brains. It was intolerable that such a person should be so silly.

She wondered what sorrow would do for him. She had come down from Scotland the night before, and down here to Hertfordshire this morning; she had not then yet seen him; and he was now at the funeral....

Well, sorrow would be his test. How would he take it?

Mrs. Baxter broke in on her meditations.

'Maggie, darling . . . do you think you can do anything? You know I once hoped . . .'

The girl looked up suddenly, with so vivid an air that it was an interruption. The old lady broke off.

'Well, well,' she said. 'But is it quite impossible that—'

'Please, don't. I – I can't talk about that. It's impossible – utterly impossible.'

The old lady sighed; then she said suddenly, looking at

the clock above the oak mantelshelf, 'It is half-past. I expect—'

She broke off as the front door was heard to open and close beyond the hall, and waited, paling a little, as steps sounded on the flags; but the steps went up the stairs outside, and there was silence again.

'He has come back,' she said. 'Oh! my dear.'

'How shall you treat him?' asked the girl curiously.

The old lady bent again over her embroidery.

'I think I shall just say nothing. I hope he will ride this afternoon. Will you go with him?'

'I think not. He won't want anyone. I know Laurie.'

The other looked up at her sideways in a questioning way, and Maggie went on with a kind of slow decisiveness.

'He will be queer at lunch. Then he will probably ride alone and be late for tea. Then tomorrow—'

'Oh! my dear, Mrs. Stapleton is coming to lunch tomorrow. Do you think he'll mind?'

'Who is Mrs. Stapleton?'

The old lady hesitated.

'She's – she's the wife of Colonel Stapleton. She goes in for what I think is called New Thought; at least, so somebody told me last month. I'm afraid she's not a very steady person. She was a vegetarian last year; now I believe she's given that up again.'

Maggie smiled slowly, showing a row of very white, strong teeth.

'I know, auntie,' she said. 'No; I shouldn't think Laurie'll mind much. Perhaps he'll go back to town in the morning, too.'

'No, my dear, he's staying till Thursday.'

There fell again one of those pleasant silences that are possible in the country. Outside the garden, with the meadows beyond the village road, lay in that sweet September hush of sunlight and mellow colour that seemed to embalm the house in peace. From the farm beyond the stable-yard came the crowing of a cock, followed by the liquid chuckle of a pigeon perched somewhere overhead among the twisted chimneys. And within this room all was equally at peace. The sunshine lay on table and polished floor, barred by the mullions of the windows, and stained here and there by the little Flemish emblems and coats that hung across the glass; while those two figures, so perfectly in place in their serenity and leisure, sat before the open fire-place and contemplated the very unpeaceful element that had just walked upstairs incarnate in a pale, drawn-eyed young man in black.

The house, in fact, was one of those that have a personality as marked and as mysterious as of a human character. It affected people in quite an extraordinary way. It took charge of the casual guest, entertained and soothed and sometimes silenced him; and it cast upon all who lived in it an enchantment at once inexplicable and delightful. Externally it was nothing remarkable.

It was a large, square-built house, close indeed to the road, but separated from it by a high wrought-iron gate in an oak paling, and a short, straight garden-path; originally even ante-Tudor, but matured through centuries, with a Queen Anne front of mellow red brick, and back premises of tile, oak, and modern rough-cast, with old brew-houses that almost enclosed a gravelled court behind. Behind this again lay a great kitchen garden with box-lined paths dividing it all into a dozen rectangles, separated from the orchard and yew walk by a broad double hedge down the centre of which ran a sheltered path. Round the south of the house and in the narrow strip westwards lay broad lawns surrounded by high trees completely shading it from all view of the houses that formed the tiny hamlet fifty yards away.

Within, the house had been modernised almost to a commonplace level. A little hall gave entrance to the drawing-room on the right where these two women now sat, a large, stately room, panelled from floor to ceiling, and to the dining-room on the left; and, again, through to the back, where a smoking-room, an inner hall, and the big kitchens and back premises concluded the ground floor. The two more stories above consisted, on the first floor, of a row of large rooms, airy, high, and dignified, and in the attics of a series of low-pitched chambers, white-washed, oak-floored, and dormer-windowed, where one or two of the servants slept in splendid isolation. A little flight of irregular steps leading out of the big room on to the first floor, where the housekeeper lived in state, gave access to the further rooms near the kitchen and sculleries.

Maggie had fallen in love with the place from the instant that she had entered it. She had been warned in her French convent of the giddy gaieties of the world and its temptations; and yet it seemed to her after a week in her new home that the world was very much maligned. There was here a sense of peace and sheltered security that she had hardly known even at school; and little by little she had settled down here, with the mother and the son, until it had begun to seem to her that days spent in London or in other friends' houses were no better than interruptions and failures compared with the leisurely, tender life of this place, where it was so easy to read and pray and possess her soul in peace. This affair of Laurie's was almost the first reminder of what she had known by hearsay, that Love and Death and Pain were the bones on which life was modelled.

With a sudden movement she leaned forward, took up the bellows, and began to blow the smouldering logs into flame.

Meanwhile, upstairs on a long couch beside the fire in his big bed-sitting-room lay a young man on his face motionless.

A week ago he had been one of those men who in almost any company appear easy and satisfactory, and, above all, are satisfactory to themselves. His life was a very pleasant one indeed.

He had come down from Oxford just a year ago, and had determined to take things as they came, to foster acquaintanceships, to travel a little with a congenial friend, to stay about in other people's houses, and, in fact, to enjoy himself entirely before settling down to read law. He had done this most successfully, and had crowned all, as has been related, by falling in love on a July evening with one who, he was quite certain, was the mate designed for him for Time and Eternity. His life, in fact, up to three days ago had developed along exactly those lines along which his temperament travelled with the greatest ease. He was the only son of a widow, he had an excellent income, he made friends wherever he went, and he had just secured the most charming rooms close to the Temple. He had plenty of brains, an exceedingly warm heart, and had lately embraced a religion that satisfied every instinct of his nature. It was the best of all possible worlds, and fitted him like his own well-cut clothes. It consisted of privileges without responsibilities.

And now the crash had come, and all was over.

As the gong sounded for luncheon he turned over and lay on his back, staring at the ceiling.

It should have been a very attractive face under other circumstances. Beneath his brown curls, just touched with gold, there looked out a pair of grey eyes, bright a week ago, now dimmed with tears, and patched beneath with lines of sorrow. His clean-cut, rather passionate lips were set now, with down-turned corners, in a line of angry self-control piteous to see; and his clear skin seemed stained and dull. He had never dreamt of such misery in all his days.

As he lay now, with lax hands at his side, tightening at times in an agony of remembrance, he was seeing vision after vision, turning now and again to the contemplation of a dark future without life or love or hope. Again he saw Amy, as he had first seen her under the luminous July evening, jewelled overhead with peeping stars, amber to the westwards, where the sun had gone down in glory. She was in her sun-bonnet and print dress, stepping towards him across the fresh-scented meadow grass lately shorn of its flowers and growth, looking at him with that curious awed admiration that delighted him with its flattery. Her face was to the west, the reflected glory lay on it as delicate as the light on a flower, and her blue eyes regarded him beneath a halo of golden hair.

He saw her again as she had been one moonlight evening as the two stood together by the sluice of the stream, among the stillness of the woods below the village, with all fairy-land about them and in their hearts. She had thrown a wrap about her head and stolen down there by devious ways, according to the appointment, meeting him, as was arranged, as he came out from dinner with all the glamour of the Great House about him, in his evening dress, buckled shoes, and knee-breeches all complete. How marvellous she had been then – a sweet nymph of flesh and blood, glorified by the moon to an ethereal delicacy, with the living pallor of sun-kissed skin, her eyes looking at him like stars beneath her shawl. They had said very little; they had stood there at the sluice gate, with his arm about her, and herself willingly nestling against him, trembling now and again; looking out at the sheeny surface of the slow-flowing stream from which, in the imperceptible night breeze, stole away wraith after wraith of water mist to float and lose themselves in the sleeping woods.

Or, once more, clearer than all else he remembered how he had watched her, himself unseen, delaying the delight of revealing himself, one August morning, scarcely three weeks ago, as she had come down the road that ran past the house, again in her sun-bonnet and print dress, with the dew shining about her on grass and hedge, and the haze of a summer morning veiling the intensity of the blue sky above. He had called her then gently by name, and she had turned her face to him, alight with love and fear and sudden wonder. . . . He remembered even now with a reflection of memory that was nearly an illusion the smell of yew and garden flowers.

This, then, had been the dream; and to-day the awakening and the end.

That end was even more terrible than he had conceived possible on that horrible Friday morning last week, when he had opened the telegram from her father.

He had never before understood the sordidness of her surroundings, as when, an hour ago, he had stood at the grave-side, his eyes wandering from that long elm box with the silver plate and the wreath of flowers, to the mourners on the other side – her father in his broadcloth, his heavy, smooth face pulled in lines of grotesque sorrow; her mother, with her crimson, tear-stained cheeks, her elaborate black, her intolerable crape, and her jet-hung mantle. Even these people had been seen by him up to then through a haze of love; he had thought them simple honest folk, creatures of the soil, yet wholesome, natural, and sturdy. And now that the jewel was lost the setting was worse than empty. There in the elm-box lay the remnants of the shattered gem. . . . He had seen her in her bed on the Sunday, her fallen face, her sunken eyes, all framed in the detestable whiteness of linen and waxen flowers, yet as pathetic and as appealing as ever, and as necessary to his life. It was then that the supreme fact had first penetrated to his consciousness, that he had lost her – the fact which, driven home by the funeral scene this morning, the rustling crowd come to see the young Squire, the elm-box, the heap of flowers – had now flung him down on this couch, crushed, broken, and hopeless, like young ivy after a thunderstorm.

His moods alternated with the rapidity of flying clouds.

21

At one instant he was furious with pain, at the next broken and lax from the same cause. At one moment he cursed God and desired to die, defiant and raging; at the next he sank down into himself as weak as a tortured child, while tears ran down his cheeks and little moans as of an animal murmured in his throat. God was a hated adversary, a merciless Judge . . . a Blind Fate . . . there was no God . . . He was a Fiend . . . there was nothing anywhere in the whole universe but Pain and Vanity . . .

Yet, through it all, like a throbbing pedal note, ran his need of this girl. He would do anything, suffer anything, make any sacrifice, momentary or lifelong, if he could but see her again, hold her hand for one instant, look into her eyes mysterious with the secret of death. He had but three or four words to say to her, just to secure himself that she lived and was still his, and then . . . then he would say good-bye to her, content and happy to wait till death should reunite them. Ah! he asked so little, and God would not give it him.

All, then, was a mockery. It was only this past summer that he had begun to fancy himself in love with Maggie Deronnais. It had been an emotion of very quiet growth, developing gently, week by week, feeding on her wholesomeness, her serenity, her quiet power, her cool, capable hands, and the look in her direct eyes; it resembled respect rather than passion, and need rather than desire; it was a hunger rather than a thirst. Then had risen up this other, blinding and bewildering; and, he told himself, he now knew the difference. His lips curled into bitter and resentful lines as he contemplated the contrast. And all was gone, shattered and vanished; and even Maggie was now impossible.

Again he writhed over, sick with pain and longing; and so lay.

It was ten minutes before he moved again, and then he only roused himself as he heard a foot on the stairs. Perhaps it was his mother.

He slipped off the couch and stood up, his face lined and creased with the pressure with which he had lain just now, and soothed his tumbled clothes. Yes, he must go down.

He stepped to the door and opened it.

'I am coming immediately,' he said to the servant.

He bore himself at lunch with a respectable self-control, though he said little or nothing. His mother's attitude he found hard to bear, as he caught her eyes once or twice looking at him with sympathy; and he allowed himself internally to turn to Maggie with relief in spite of his meditations just now. She at least respected his sorrow, he told himself. She bore herself very naturally, though with long silences, and never once met his eyes with her own. He made his excuses as soon as he could and slipped across to the stable-yard. At least he would be alone this afternoon. Only, as he rode away half an hour later, he caught a sight of the slender little figure of his mother waiting to have one word with him if she could, beyond the hall-door. But he set his lips and would not see her.

It was one of those perfect September days that fall sometimes as a gift from heaven after the bargain of summer has been more or less concluded. As he rode all that afternoon through lanes and across uplands, his view barred always to the north by the great downs above Royston, grey-blue against the radiant sky, there was scarcely a hint in earth or heaven of any emotion except prevailing peace. Yet the very serenity tortured him the more by its mockery. The birds babbled in the deep woods, the cheerful noise of children reached him now and again from a cottage garden, the mellow light smiled unending benediction, and yet his subconsciousness let go for never an instant of the long elm box six feet below ground, and of its contents lying there in the stifling dark, in the long-grassed churchyard on the hill above his home.

He wondered now and again as to the fate of the spirit that had informed the body and made it what it was; but his imagination refused to work. After all, he asked himself, what were all the teachings of theology but words gabbled to break the appalling silence? Heaven . . . Purgatory. . . . Hell. What was known of these things? The very soul itself – what was that? What was the inconceivable environment, after all, for so inconceivable a thing? . . .

He did not need these things, he said – certainly not now – nor those labels and signposts to a doubtful, unimaginable land. He needed Amy herself, or, at least, some hint or sound or glimpse to show him that she indeed was as she had always been; whether in earth or heaven, he did not care;

that there was somewhere something that was herself, some definite personal being of a continuous consciousness with that which he had known, characterised still by those graces which he thought he had recognised and certainly loved. Ah! he did not ask much. It would be so easy to God! Here out in this lonely lane where he rode beneath the branches, his reins loose on his horse's neck, his eyes, unseeing, roving over copse and meadow across to the eternal hills – a face, seen for an instant, smiling and gone again; a whisper in his ear, with that dear stammer of shyness; a touch on his knee of those rippling fingers that he had watched in the moonlight playing gently on the sluice-gate above the moonlit stream. . . . He would tell no one if God wished it to be a secret; he would keep it wholly to himself. He did not ask now to possess her; only to be certain that she lived, and that death was not what it seemed to be.

'Is Father Mahon at home?' he asked, as he halted a mile from his own house in the village, where stood the little tin church, not a hundred yards from its elder alienated sister, to which he and Maggie went on Sundays.

The housekeeper turned from her vegetable-gathering beyond the fence, and told him yes. He dismounted, hitched the reins round the gatepost, and went in.

Ah! what an antipathetic little room this was in which he waited while the priest was being fetched from upstairs!

Over the mantelpiece hung a large oleograph of Leo XIII, in cope and tiara, blessing with upraised hand and that eternal, wide-lipped smile; a couple of jars stood beneath filled with dyed grasses; a briar pipe, redolent and foul, lay between them. The rest of the room was in the same key; a bright Brussels carpet, pale and worn by the door, covered the floor; cheap lace curtains were pinned across the windows; and over the littered table a painted deal bookshelf held a dozen volumes, devotional, moral, and dogmatic theology; and by the side of that an illuminated address framed in gilt, and so on.

Laurie looked at it all in dumb dismay. He had seen it before, again and again, but had never realised its horror as he realised it now from the depths of his own misery. Was it really true that his religion could emit such results?

There was a step on the stairs – a very heavy one – and

24

Father Mahon came in, a large, crimson-faced man, who seemed to fill the room with a completely unethereal presence, and held out his hand with a certain gravity. Laurie took it and dropped it.

'Sit down, my dear boy,' said the priest, and he impelled him gently to a horsehair-covered armchair.

Laurie stiffened.

'Thank you, father; but I mustn't stay.'

He fumbled in his pocket, and fetched out a little paper-covered packet.

'Will you say Mass for my intention, please?' And he laid the packet on the mantelshelf.

The priest took up the coins and slipped them into his waistcoat pocket.

'Certainly,' he said. 'I think I know—'

Laurie turned away with a little jerk.

'I must be going,' he said. 'I only looked in—'

'Mr. Baxter,' said the other, 'I hope you will allow me to say how much—'

Laurie drew his breath swiftly, with a hiss as of pain, and glanced at the priest.

'You understand, then, what my intention is?'

'Why, surely. It is for her soul, is it not?'

'I suppose so,' said the boy, and went out.

CHAPTER TWO

I

'I have told him,' said Mrs. Baxter, as the two women walked beneath the yews that morning after breakfast. 'He said he didn't mind.'

Maggie did not speak. She had come out just as she was, hatless, but had caught up a spud that stood in the hall, and at that instant had stopped to destroy a youthful plantain that had established himself with infinite pains on the slope of the path. She attacked for a few seconds, extricated what was possible of the root with her strong fingers, tossed the corpse among the ivy, and then moved on.

'I don't know whether to say anything to Mrs. Stapleton or not,' pursued the old lady.

'I think I shouldn't, auntie,' said the girl slowly.

They spoke of it for a minute or two as they passed up and down, but Maggie only attended with one superficies of her mind.

She had gone up as usual to Mass that morning, and had been astonished to find Laurie already in church; they had walked back together, and, to her surprise, he had told her that the Mass had been for his own intention.

She had answered as well as she could; but a sentence or two of his as they came near home had vaguely troubled her.

It was not that he had said anything he ought not, as a Catholic, to have said; yet her instinct told her that something was wrong. It was his manner, his air, that troubled her. What strange people these converts were! There was so much ardour at one time, so much chilliness at another; there was so little of that steady workaday acceptance of religious facts that marked the born Catholic.

'Mrs. Stapleton is a New Thought kind of person,' she said presently.

'So I understand,' said the old lady, with a touch of

peevishness. 'A vegetarian last year. And I believe she was a sort of Buddhist five or six years ago. And then she nearly became a Christian Scientist a little while ago.'

Maggie smiled.

'I wonder what she'll talk about,' she said.

'I hope she won't be very advanced,' went on the old lady. 'And you think I'd better not tell her about Laurie?'

'I'm sure it's best not,' said the girl, 'or she'll tell him about Deep Breathing, or saying Om, or something. No; I should let Laurie alone.'

It was a little before one o'clock that the motor arrived, and that there descended from it at the iron gate a tall, slender woman, hooded and veiled, who walked up the little path, observed by Maggie from her bedroom, with a kind of whisking step. The motor moved on, wheeled in through the gates at the left, and sank into silence in the stable-yard.

'It's too charming of you, dear Mrs. Baxter,' Maggie heard as she came into the drawing-room a minute or two later, 'to let me come over like this. I've heard so much about this house. Lady Laura was telling me how very psychical it all was.'

'My adopted daughter, Miss Deronnais,' observed the old lady.

Maggie saw a rather pretty, *passé* face, triangular in shape, with small red lips, looking at her, as she made her greetings.

'Ah! how perfect all this is,' went on the guest presently, looking about her, 'how suggestive, how full of meaning!'

She threw back her cloak presently, and Maggie observed that she was busy with various very beautiful little emblems – a scarab, a snake swallowing its tail, and so forth – all exquisitely made, and hung upon a slender chain of some green enamel-like material. Certainly she was true to type. As the full light fell upon her it became plain that this other-worldly soul did not disdain to use certain toilet requisites upon her face; and a curious Eastern odour exhaled from her dress.

Fortunately, Maggie had a very deep sense of humour, and she hardly resented all this at all, nor even the tactful hints dropped from time to time, after the conventional part of the conversation was over, to the effect that Christianity was, of course, played out, and that a Higher Light had dawned. Mrs. Stapleton did not quite say this outright, but it amounted to as much. Even before Laurie came downstairs it appeared that the lady did not go to church, yet that, such was her broad-mindedness, she did not at all object to do so. It was all one, it seemed, in the Deeper Unity. Nothing particular was true; but all was very suggestive and significant and symbolical of something else to which Mrs. Stapleton and a few friends had the key.

Mrs. Baxter made more than one attempt to get back to more mundane subjects, but it was useless. When even the weather serves as a symbol, the plain man is done for.

Then Laurie came in.

He looked very self-contained and rather pinched this morning, and shook hands with the lady without a word. Then they moved across presently to the green-hung dining-room across the hall, and the exquisite symbol of Luncheon made its appearance.

Lady Laura, it appeared, was one of those who had felt the charm of Stantons; only for her it was psychical rather than physical, and all this was passed on by her friend. It seemed that the psychical atmosphere of most modern houses was of a yellow tint, but that this one emanated a brown-gold radiance which was very peculiar and exceptional. Indeed, it was this singularity that had caused Mrs. Stapleton to apply for an invitation to the house. More than once during lunch, in a pause of the conversation, Maggie saw her throw back her head slightly as if to appreciate some odour or colour not experienced by coarser-nerved persons. Once, indeed, she actually put this into words.

'Dear Laura was quite right,' cried the lady; 'there is something very unique about this place. How fortunate you are, dear Mrs. Baxter!'

'My dear husband's grandfather bought the place,' observed the mistress plaintively. 'We have always found it very soothing and pleasant.'

'How right you are! And – and have you had any experiences here?' Mrs. Baxter eyed her in alarm. Maggie had an irrepressible burst of internal laughter, which, however, gave no hint of its presence in her steady features. She glanced at Laurie, who was eating mutton with a depressed air.

'I was talking to Mr. Vincent, the great spiritualist,' went on the other vivaciously, 'only last week. You have heard of him, Mrs. Baxter? I was suggesting to him that any place where great emotions have been felt are coloured and stained by them as objectively as old walls are weather-beaten. I had such an interesting conversation, too, with Cardinal Newman on the subject' – she smiled brilliantly at Maggie, as if to reassure her of her own orthodoxy – 'scarcely six weeks ago.'

There was a pregnant silence. Mrs. Baxter's fork sank to her plate.

'I don't understand,' she said faintly. 'Cardinal Newman – surely—'

'Why yes,' said the other gently. 'I know it sounds very startling to orthodox ears; but to us of the Higher Thought all these things are quite familiar. Of course, I need hardly say that Cardinal Newman is no longer – but perhaps I had better not go on.'

She glanced archly at Maggie.

'Oh, please go on,' said Maggie genially. 'You were saying that Cardinal Newman—'

'Dear Miss Deronnais, are you sure you will not be offended?'

'I am always glad to receive new light,' said Maggie solemnly.

The other looked at her doubtfully; but there was no hint of irony in the girl's face.

'Well,' she began, 'of course on the Other Side they see things very differently. I don't mean at all that any religion is exactly untrue. Oh no; they tell us that if we cannot welcome the New Light, that the old lights will do very well for the present. Indeed, when there are Catholics present Cardinal Newman does not scruple to give them a Latin blessing—'

'Is it true that he speaks with an American accent?' asked Maggie gravely. The other laughed with a somewhat shrill geniality.

'That is too bad, Miss Deronnais. Well, of course, the personality of the medium affects the vehicle through which the communications come. That is no difficulty at all when once you understand the principle—'

Mrs Baxter interrupted. She could bear it no longer.

'Mrs. Stapleton. Do you mean that Cardinal Newman really speaks to you?'

'Why yes,' said the other, with a patient indulgence. 'That is a very useful experience, but Mr. Vincent does much more than that. It is quite a common experience not only to hear him, but to see him. I have shaken hands with him more than once . . . and I have seen a Catholic kiss his ring.'

Mrs. Baxter looked helplessly at the girl; and Maggie came to the rescue once more. 'This sounds rather advanced to us,' she said. 'Won't you explain the principles first?'

Mrs. Stapleton laid her knife and fork down, leaned back, and began to discourse. When a little later her plate was removed, she refused sweets with a gesture, and continued.

Altogether she spoke for about ten minutes, uninterrupted, enjoying herself enormously. The others ate food or refused it in attentive silence. Then at last she ended.

'. . . I know all this must sound quite mad and fanatical to those who have not experienced it; and yet to us who have been disciples it is as natural to meet our friends who have crossed over as to meet those who have not. . . . Dear Mrs. Baxter, think how all this enlarges life. There is no longer any death to those who understand. All those limitations are removed; it is no more than going into another room. All are together in the Hands of the All-Father' – Maggie recognised the jetsam of Christian Science. ' "O death!" as Paul says, "where is thy sting? O grave, where is thy victory?" '

Mrs. Stapleton flashed a radiant look of helpfulness round the faces, lingering for an instant on Laurie's, and leaned back.

There followed a silence.

'Shall we go into the drawing-room?' suggested Mrs. Baxter, feebly rising. The guest rose too, again with a brilliant patient smile, and swept out. Maggie crossed herself and looked at Laurie. The boy had an expression, half of disgust, half of interest, and his eyelids sank a little and rose again. Then Maggie went out after the others.

'A dreadful woman,' observed Mrs. Baxter half an hour later, as the two strolled back up the garden path, after seeing Mrs. Stapleton wave a delicately gloved hand encouragingly to them over the back of the throbbing motor.

'I suppose she thinks she believes it all,' said Maggie.

'My dear, that woman would believe anything. I hope poor Laurie was not too much distressed.'

'Oh! I think Laurie took it all right.'

'It was most unfortunate, all that about death and the rest. . . . Why, here comes Laurie; I thought he would be gone out by now.'

The boy strolled towards them round the corner of the house, tossing away the fragment of his cigarette. He was still in his dark suit, bare-headed, with no signs of riding about him.

'So you've not gone out yet, dear boy?' remarked his mother.

'Not yet,' he said, and hesitated as they went on. Mrs. Baxter noticed it.

'I'll go and get ready,' she said. 'The carriage will be round at three, Maggie.'

When she was gone the two moved out together on to the lawn.

'What did you think of that woman?' demanded Laurie with a detached air.

Maggie glanced at him. His tone was a little too much detached.

'I thought her quite dreadful,' she said frankly. 'Didn't you?' she added.

'Oh yes, I suppose so,' said Laurie. He drew out a cigarette and lighted it. 'You know a lot of people think there's something in it,' he said.

'In what?'

'Spiritualism.'

'I daresay,' said Maggie.

She perceived out of the corner of her eye that Laurie looked at her suddenly and sharply. For herself, she loathed what little she knew of the subject, so cordially and completely, that she could hardly have put it into words. Nine-tenths of it she believed to be fraud – a matter of wigs and Indian muslin and cross-lights – and the other tenth, by the most generous estimate, an affair of the dingiest and foulest of all the backstairs of life. The prophetic outpourings of Mrs. Stapleton had not altered her opinion.

'Oh! if you feel like that—' went on Laurie.

She turned on him.

'Laurie,' she said, 'I think it perfectly detestable. I acknowledge I don't know much about it; but what little I do know is enough, thank you.'

Laurie smiled in a faintly patronising way.

'Well,' he said indulgently, 'if you think that, it's not much use discussing it.'

'Indeed it's not,' said Maggie, with her nose in the air.

There was not much more to be said; and the sounds of stamping and whoaing in the stable-yard presently sent the girl indoors in a hurry.

Mrs. Baxter was still mildly querulous during the drive. It appeared to her, Maggie perceived, a kind of veiled insult that things should be talked about in her house which did not seem to fit in with her own scheme of the universe. Mrs. Baxter knew perfectly well that every soul when it left this world went either to what she called Paradise, or in extremely exceptional cases, to a place she did not name; and that these places, each in its own way, entirely absorbed the attention of its inhabitants. Further, it was established in her view that all the members of the spiritual world, apart from the unhappy ones, were a kind of Anglicans, with their minds no doubt enlarged considerably, but on the original lines.

Tales like this of Cardinal Newman therefore were extremely tiresome and upsetting.

And Maggie had her theology also; to her also it appeared quite impossible that Cardinal Newman should frequent the drawing-room of Mr. Vincent in order to exchange impressions with Mrs. Stapleton; but she was more elementary in her answer. For her the thing was simply untrue; and that was the end of it. She found it difficult therefore to follow her companion's train of thought.

'What was it she said?' demanded Mrs. Baxter presently. 'I didn't understand her ideas about materialism.'

'I think she called it materialisation,' explained Maggie patiently. 'She said that when things were very favourable, and the medium a very good one, the soul that wanted to communicate could make a kind of body for itself out of what she called the astral matter of the medium or the sitters.'

'But surely our bodies aren't like that?'

'No; I can't say that I think they are. But that's what she said.'

'My dear, please explain. I want to understand the woman.'

Maggie frowned a little.

'Well, the first thing she said was that those souls want to communicate; and that they begin generally by things like table-rapping, or making blue lights. Then when you know they're there, they can go further. Sometimes they gain control of the medium who is in a trance, and speak through him, or write with his hand. Then, if things are favourable, they begin to draw out this matter, and make it into a kind of body for themselves, very thin and ethereal, so that you can pass your hand through it. Then, as things get better and better, they go further still, and can make this body so solid that you can touch it; only this is sometimes rather dangerous, as it is still, in a sort of way, connected with the medium. I think that's the idea.'

'But what's the good of it all?'

'Well, you see, Mrs. Stapleton thinks that they really are souls from the other world, and that they can tell us all kinds of things about it all, and what's true, and so on.'

'But you don't believe that?'

Maggie turned her large eyes on the old lady; and a spark of humour rose and glimmered in them.

'Of course I don't,' she said.

'Then how do you explain it?'

'I think it's probably all a fraud. But I really don't know. It doesn't seem to me to matter much—'

'But if it should be true?'

Maggie raised her eyebrows, smiling.

'Dear auntie, do put it out of your head. How can it possibly be true?'

Mrs. Baxter set her lips in as much severity as she could.

'I shall ask the Vicar,' she said. 'We might stop at the Vicarage on the way back.'

Mrs. Baxter did not often stop at the Vicarage; as she did not altogether approve of the Vicar's wife. There was a good deal of pride in the old lady, and it seemed to her occasionally as if Mrs. Rymer did not understand the difference between the Hall and the Parsonage. She envied sometimes, secretly, the Romanist idea of celibacy : it was so much easier to get on with your spiritual adviser if you did not have to consider his wife. But here was a matter which a clergyman must settle for her once and for all; so she put on a slight air of dignity which became her very well, and a little after four o'clock the victoria turned up the steep little drive that led to the Vicarage.

3

The dusk was already fallen before Laurie, strolling vaguely in the garden, heard the carriage wheels draw up at the gate outside.

He had ridden again alone, and his mind had run, to a certain extent, as might be expected, upon the recent guest and her very startling conversation. He was an intelligent young man, and he had not been in the least taken in by her pseudo-mystical remarks. Yet there had been something in her extreme assurance that had affected him, as a man may smile sourly at a good story in bad taste. His attitude, in fact, was that of most Christians under the circumstances. He did not, for an instant, believe that such things really and literally happened, and yet it was difficult to advance any absolutely conclusive argument against them. Merely, they had not come his way; they appeared to conflict with experience, and they usually found as their advocates such persons as Mrs. Stapleton.

Two things, however, prevailed to keep the matter before his mind. The first was his own sense of loss, his own experience, sore and hot within him, of the unapproachable emptiness of death; the second, Maggie's attitude. When a plainly sensible and controlled young woman takes up a position of superiority, she is apt, unless the young man in her company happens to be in love with her – and sometimes even when he is – to provoke and irritate him into a camp of opposition. She is still more apt to do so if her relations to him have once been in the line of even greater tenderness.

Laurie then was not in the most favourable of moods to receive the dicta of the Vicar.

They were announced to him immediately after Mrs. Baxter had received from Maggie's hands her first cup of tea.

'Mr. Rymer tells me it's all nonsense,' she said.

Laurie looked up.

'What?' he said.

'Mr. Rymer tells me Spiritualism is all nonsense. He told me about someone called Eglingham, who kept a beard in his portmanteau.'

'Eglinton, I think, auntie,' put in Maggie.

'I daresay, my dear. Anyhow, it's all the same. I felt sure it must be so.' Laurie took a bun, with a thoughtful air.

'Does Mr. Rymer know very much about it, do you think, mother?'

'Dear boy, I think he knows all that anyone need know. Besides, if you come to think of it, how could Cardinal Newman possibly appear in a drawing-room? Particularly when Mrs. Stapleton says he isn't a Christian any longer.'

This had a possible and rather pleasing double interpretation; but Laurie decided it was not worth while to be humorous.

'What about the Witch of Endor?' he asked innocently, instead.

'That was in the Old Testament,' answered his mother rapidly. 'Mr. Rymer said something about that too.'

'Oh! wasn't it really Samuel who appeared?'

'Mr. Rymer thinks that things were permitted then that are not permitted now.'

Laurie drank up his cup of tea. It is a humiliating fact that extreme grief often renders the mourner rather cross. There was a distinct air of crossness about Laurie at this moment. His nerves were very near the top.

'Well, that's very convenient,' he said. 'Maggie, do you know if there's any book on Spiritualism in the house?'

The girl glanced uneasily near the fire-place.

'I don't know,' she said. 'Yes; I think there's something up there. I believe I saw it the other day.'

Laurie rose and stood opposite the shelves.

'What colour is it? (No, no more tea, thanks.)'

'Er . . . black and red, I think,' said the girl. 'I forget.'

She looked up at him, faintly uneasy, as he very deliberately drew down a book from the shelf and turned the pages.

'Yes . . . this is it,' he said. 'Thanks very much. . . . No, really no more tea, thanks, mother.'

Then he went to the door, with his easy, rather long steps, and disappeared. They heard his steps in the inner hall. Then a door closed overhead.

Mrs. Baxter contentedly poured herself out another cup of tea.

'Poor boy,' she said. 'He's thinking of that girl still. I'm glad he's got something to occupy his mind.'

The end room, on the first floor, was Laurie's possession. It was a big place, with two windows, and a large open fire, and he had skilfully masked the fact that it was a bedroom by disposing his furniture, with the help of a screen, in such a manner as completely to hide the bed and the washing arrangements.

The rest of the room he had furnished in a pleasing male kind of fashion, with a big couch drawn across the fire, a writing-table and chairs, a deep easy chair near the door, and a long, high bookcase covering the wall between the door and the windows. His college oar, too, hung here, and there were pleasant groups and pictures scattered on the other walls.

Maggie did not often come in here, except by invitation, but about seven o'clock on this evening, half an hour before she had to go and dress, she thought she would look in on him for a few minutes. She was still a little uncomfortable; she did not quite know why : it was too ridiculous, she told herself, that a sensible boy like Laurie could be seriously affected by what she considered the wicked nonsense of Spiritualism.

Yet she went, telling herself that Laurie's grief was an excuse for showing him a little marked friendliness. Besides, she would like to ask him whether he was really going back to town on Thursday.

She tapped twice before an answer came; and then it seemed a rather breathless voice which spoke.

The boy was sitting bolt upright on the edge of the sofa, with a couple of candles at his side, and the book in his hands. There was a strained and intensely interested look in his eyes.

'May I come in for a few minutes? It's nearly dressing time,' she said.

'Oh – er – certainly.'

He got up, rather stiffly, still keeping his place in the book with one finger, while she sat down. Then he too sat again, and there was silence for a moment.

'Why, you're not smoking,' she said.

'I forgot. I will now, if you don't mind.'

She saw his fingers tremble a little as he put out his hand to a box of cigarettes at his side. But he put the box down, after looking at the page.

She could keep her question in no longer.

'What do you think of that?' she said, nodding at the book.

He filled his lungs with smoke and exhaled again slowly.

'I think it's extraordinary,' he said shortly.

'In what way?'

Again he paused before answering. Then he answered deliberately.

'If human evidence is worth anything, those things happen,' he said.

'What things?'

'The dead return.'

Maggie looked at him, aware of his deliberate attempt at dramatic brevity. He was watching the end of his cigarette with elaborate attention, and his face had that white, rather determined look that she had seen on it once or twice before, in the presence of a domestic crisis.

'Do you really mean you believe that?' she said, with a touch of careful bitterness in her voice.

'I do,' he said, 'or else—'

'Well?'

'Or else human evidence is worth nothing at all.'

Maggie understood him perfectly; but she realised that this was not an occasion to force issues. She still put the tone of faint irony into her voice.

'You really believe that Cardinal Newman comes to Mr. Vincent's drawing-room and raps on tables?'

'I really believe that it is possible to get into touch with those whom we call dead. Each instance, of course, depends on its own evidence.'

'And Cardinal Newman?'

'I have not studied the evidence for Cardinal Newman,' remarked Laurie in a head-voice.

'Let's have a look at that book,' said Maggie impulsively.

He handed it to her; and she began to turn the pages, pausing now and again to read a particular paragraph, and once for nearly a minute while she examined an illustration. Certainly the book seemed interestingly written, and she read an argument or two that appeared reasonably presented. Yet she was extraordinarily repelled even by the dead paper and ink she had in her hands. It was as if it was something obscene. Finally she tossed it back on to the couch.

Laurie waited; but she said nothing.

'Well?' he asked at last, still refraining from looking at her.

'I think it's horrible,' she said.

Laurie delicately adjusted a little tobacco protruding from his cigarette.

'Isn't that a little unreasonable?' he asked. 'You've hardly looked at it yet.'

Maggie knew this mood of his only too well. He reserved it for occasions when he was determined to fight. Argument was a useless weapon against it.

'My dear boy,' she said with an effort, 'I'm sorry. I daresay it is unreasonable. But that kind of thing does seem to me so disgusting. That's all. . . . I didn't come to talk about that. . . . Tell me—'

'Didn't you?' said Laurie.

Maggie was silent.

'Didn't you?'

'Well—yes I did. But I don't want to any more.'

Laurie smiled so that it might be seen.

'Well, what else did you want to say?' (He glanced purposely at the book. Maggie ignored his glance.)

'I just came to see how you were getting on.'

'How do you mean? With the book?'

'No; in every way.'

He looked up at her swiftly and suddenly, and she saw that his agony of sorrow was acute beneath all his attempts at superiority, his courteous fractiousness, and his set face. She was filled suddenly with an enormous pity.

'Oh! Laurie, I'm so sorry,' she cried out. 'Can't I do anything?'

'Nothing, thanks; nothing at all,' he said quietly.

Again pity and misery surged up within her, and she cast all prudence to the winds. She had not realised how fond she was of this boy till she saw once more that look in his eyes.

'Oh! Laurie, you know I didn't like it; but – but I don't know what to do, I'm so sorry. But don't spoil it all,' she said wildly, hardly knowing what she feared.

'I beg your pardon?'

'You know what I mean. Don't spoil it, by – by fancying things.'

'Maggie,' said the boy quietly, 'you must let me alone. You can't help.'

'Can't I?'

'You can't help,' he repeated. 'I must go my own way. Please don't say any more. I can't stand it.'

There followed a dead silence. Then Maggie recovered and stood up. He rose with her.

'Forgive me, Laurie, won't you? I must say this. You'll remember I'll always do anything I can, won't you?'

Then she was gone.

4

The ladies went to bed early at Stantons. At ten o'clock precisely a clinking of bedroom candlesticks was heard in the hall, followed by the sound of locking doors. This was the signal. Mrs. Baxter laid aside her embroidery with the punctuality of a religious at the sound of a bell, and said two words—

'My dears.'

There were occasionally exclamatory expostulations from the two at the picquet-table, but in nine cases out of ten the game had been designed with an eye upon the clock, and hardly any delay followed. Mrs. Baxter kissed her son, and passed her arm through Maggie's. Laurie followed; gave them candles, and generally took one himself.

But this evening there was no piquet. Laurie had stayed later than usual in the dining-room, and had wandered rather restlessly about when he had joined the others. He looked at a London evening paper for a little, paced about, vanished again, and only returned as the ladies were making ready to depart. Then he gave them their candlesticks, and himself came back to the drawing-room.

He was, in fact, in a far more perturbed and excited mood than even Maggie had had any idea of. She had interrupted him half-way through the book, but he had read again steadily until five minutes before dinner, and had, indeed, gone back again to finish it afterwards. He had now finished it; and he wanted to think.

It had had a surprising effect on him, coming as it did upon a state of mind intensely stirred to its depths by his sorrow. Crossness, as I have said, had been the natural psychological result of his emotions; but his emotions were none the less real. The froth of whipped cream is real cream, after all.

Now Laurie had seen perfectly well the extreme unconvincingness of Mrs. Stapleton, and had been genuine enough in his little shrug of disapproval in answer to Maggie's, after lunch; yet that lady's remarks had been sufficient just to ignite the train of thought. This train had smouldered in the afternoon, had been fanned ever so slightly by two breezes – the sense of Maggie's superiority and the faint rebellious reaction which had come upon him with regard to his personal religion. Certainly he had had Mass said for Amy this morning; but it had been by almost a superstitious rather than a religious instinct. He was, in fact, in that state of religious unreality which occasionally comes upon converts within a year or two of the change of their faith. The impetus of old association is absent, and the force of novelty has died.

Underneath all this then, it must be remembered that the one thing that was intensely real to him was his sense of loss of the one soul in whom his own had been wrapped up. Even this afternoon as yesterday, even this morning as he lay awake, he had been conscious of an irresistible impulse to demand some sign, to catch some glimpse of that which was now denied to him.

It was in this mood that he had read the book; and it is not to be wondered at that he had been excited by it.

For it opened up to him, beneath all its sham mysticism, its intolerable affectations, its grotesque parody of spirituality – of all of which he was largely aware – a glimmering avenue of a faintly possible hope of which he had never dreamed – a hope, at least, of that half self-deception which is so tempting to certain characters.

Here, in this book, written by a living man, whose name and address were given, were stories so startling, and theories so apparently consonant with themselves and with other partly known facts – stories and theories, too, which met so precisely his own overmastering desire, that it is little wonder that he was affected by them.

Naturally, even during his reading, a thousand answers and adverse comments had sprung to his mind – suggestions of fraud, of lying, of hallucination – but yet, here the possibility remained. Here were living men and women who, with the usual complement of senses and reason, declared categorically and in detail, that on this and that date, in this place and the other, after having taken all possible precautions against fraud, they had received messages from the dead – messages of which the purport was understood by none but themselves – that they had seen with their eyes, in sufficient light, the actual features of the dead whom they loved, that they had even clasped their hands, and held for an instant the bodies of those whom they had seen die with their own eyes, and buried.

When the ladies' footsteps had ceased to sound overhead, Laurie went to the French window, opened it, and passed on to the lawn.

He was astonished at the warmth of the September night. The little wind that had been chilly this afternoon had dropped with the coming of the dark, and high overhead he could see the great masses of the leaves motionless against the sky. He passed round the house, and beneath the yews, and sat down on the garden bench.

It was darker here than outside on the lawn. Beneath his feet were the soft needles from the trees, and above him, as he looked out, still sunk in his thought, he could see the glimmer of a star or two between the branches.

It was a fragrant kindly night. From the hamlet of half a dozen houses beyond the garden came no sound; and the house, too, was still behind him. An illuminated window somewhere on the first floor went out as he looked at it, like a soul leaving a body; once a sleepy bird somewhere in the shrubbery chirped to its mate and was silent again.

Then as he still laboured in argument, putting this against that, and weighing that against the other, his emotion rose up in an irresistible torrent, and all consideration ceased. One thing remained : he must have Amy, or he must die.

It was five or six minutes before he moved again from that attitude of clenched hands and tensely strung muscles into which his sudden passion had cast him.

During those minutes he had willed with his whole power that she should come to him now and here, down in this warm and fragrant darkness, hidden from all eyes – in this sweet silence, round which sleep kept its guard. Such things had happened before; such things must have happened, for the will and the love of man are the mightiest forces in creation. Surely again and again it had happened; there must be somewhere in the world man after man who had so called back the dead – a husband sobbing silently in the dark, a child wailing for his mother; surely that force had before, in the world's history, willed back again from the mysterious dark of space the dear personality that was all that even heaven could give, and even compelled into a semblance of life some sort of body to clothe it in. These things must have happened – only secrets had been well kept.

So this boy had willed it; yet the dark had remained empty; and no shadow, no faintly outlined face, had even for an instant blotted out the star on which he stared; no touch on his shoulder, no whisper in his ear. It had seemed as he strove there, in the silence, that it must be done; that there was no limit to power concentrated and intense. Yet it had not happened. . . .

Once he had shuddered a little; and the very shudder of fear that had in it a touch of delicious, trembling expectation. Yet it had not happened.

Laurie relaxed his muscles therefore, let his breath exhale in a long sigh, and once more remembered the book he had read and Mrs. Stapleton's feverish, self-conscious thought.

Half an hour later his mother, listening in her bed, heard his footsteps pass her room.

CHAPTER THREE

Lady Laura Bethell, spinster, had just returned to her house in Queen's Gate, with her dearest friend, Mrs. Stapleton, for a few days of psychical orgy. It was in her house, as much as in any in London, that the modern prophets were to be met with – severe-looking women in shapeless dresses, little men and big, with long hair and cloaks; and it was in her drawing-room that tea and Queen cakes were dispensed to inquirers, and papers read and discussed when the revels were over.

Lady Laura herself was not yet completely emancipated from what her friends sometimes called the grave-clothes of so-called Revelation. To her it seemed a profound truth that things could be true and untrue simultaneously – that what might be facts of This Side, as she would have expressed it, might be falsehoods on the Other. She was accustomed, therefore, to attend All Saints', Carlton Gardens, in the morning, and psychical drawing-rooms or halls in the evening, and to declare to her friends how beautifully the one aspect illuminated and interpreted the other.

For the rest, she was a small, fair-haired woman, with pencilled dark eyebrows, a small aquiline nose, gold pince-nez, and an exquisite taste in dress.

The two were seated this Tuesday evening, a week after Mrs. Stapleton's visit to the Stantons, in the drawing-room of the Queen's Gate house, over the remnants of what corresponded to five-o'clock tea. I say 'corresponded', since both of them were sufficiently advanced to have renounced actual tea altogether. Mrs. Stapleton partook of a little hot water out of a copper-jacketed jug; her hostess of boiled milk. They shared their Plasmon biscuits together. These things were considered important for those who would successfully find the Higher Light.

At this instant they were discussing Mr. Vincent.

'Dearest, he seems to me so different from the others,' mewed Lady Laura. 'He is such a man, you know. So often those others are not quite like men at all; they wear such funny clothes, and their hair always is so queer, somehow.'

'Darling, I know what you mean. Yes, there's a great deal of that about James Vincent. Even dear Tom was almost polite to him : he couldn't bear the others : he said that he always thought they were going to paw him.'

'And then his powers,' continued Lady Laura – 'his powers always seem to me so much greater. The magnetism is so much more evident.'

Mrs. Stapleton finished her hot water.

'We are going on Sunday?' she said questioningly.

'Yes; just a small party. And he comes here to-morrow, you remember, just for a talk. I have asked a clergyman I know in to meet him. It seems to me such a pity that our religious teachers should know so little of what is going on.'

'Who is he?'

'Oh, Mr. Jamieson . . . just a young clergyman I met in the summer. I promised to let him know the next time Mr. Vincent came to me.'

Mrs. Stapleton murmured her gratification.

These two had really a great deal in common besides their faith. It is true that Mrs. Stapleton was forty, and her friend but thirty-one; but the former did all that was possible to compensate for this by adroit toilette tactics. Both, too, were accustomed to dress in soft materials, with long chains bearing various emblems; they did their hair in the same way; they cultivated the same kinds of tones in their voices – a purring, mewing manner – suggestive of intuitive kittens. Both alike had a passion for proselytism. But after that the differences began. There was a deal more in Mrs. Stapleton besides the kittenish qualities. She was perfectly capable of delivering a speech in public; she had written some really well-expressed articles in various Higher periodicals; and she had a will-power beyond the ordinary. At the point where Lady Laura began to deprecate and soothe, Mrs. Stapleton began to clear decks for action, so to speak, to be incisive, to be fervent, even to be rather eloquent. She kept 'dear Tom', the Colonel, not crushed or beaten, for that was beyond the power of man to do, but at least silently acquiescent in her programme : he allowed her even to entertain her prophetical friends at his expense, now and then; and, even when among men, refrained from too bitter speech. It was said by the Colonel's friends that

44

Mrs. Colonel had a tongue of her own. Certainly, she ruled her house well and did her duty; and it was only because of her husband's absence in Scotland that during this time she was permitting herself the refreshment of a week or two among the Illuminated.

At about six o'clock Lady Laura announced her intention of retiring for her evening meditation. Opening out of her bedroom was a small dressing-room that she had fitted up for this purpose with all the broad suggestiveness that marks the Higher Thought : decked with ornaments emblematical of at least three religions, and provided with a faldstool and an exceedingly easy chair. It was here that she was accustomed to spend an hour before dinner, with closed eyes, emancipating herself from the fetters of sense; and rising to a due appreciation of the Nothingness that was All, from which All came and to which it retired.

'I must go, dearest; it is time.'

A ring at the bell below made her pause.

'Do you think that can be Mr. Vincent?' she said, pleasantly apprehensive. 'It's not the right day, but one never knows.'

A footman's figure entered.

'Mr. Baxter, my lady. . . . Is your ladyship at home?'

'Mr. Baxter—'

Mrs. Stapleton rose.

'Let me see him instead, dearest. . . . You remember . . . from Stantons.'

'I wonder what he wants?' murmured the hostess. 'Yes, do see him, Maud; you can always fetch me if it's anything.'

Then she was gone. Mrs. Stapleton sank into a chair again; and in a minute Laurie was shaking hands with her.

Mrs. Stapleton was accustomed to deal with young men, and through long habit had learned how to flatter them without appearing to do so. Laurie's type, however, was less familiar to her. She preferred the kind that grow their hair rather long and wear turn-down collars, and have just found out the hopeless banality of all orthodoxy whatever. She even bore with them when they called themselves unmoral. But she remembered Laurie, the silent boy at lunch last week, she had even mentioned him to Lady Laura, and received information about the village girl, more or less correct. She was also aware that he was a Catholic.

She gave him her hand without rising.

'Lady Laura asked me to excuse her absence to you, Mr. Baxter. To be quite truthful, she is at home, but had just gone upstairs for her meditation.'

'Indeed!'

'Yes, you know; we think that so important, just as you do. Do sit down, Mr. Baxter. You have had tea?'

'Yes, thanks.'

'I hope she will be down before you go. I don't think she'll be very long this evening. Can I give her any message, Mr. Baxter, in case you don't see her?'

Laurie put his hat and stick down carefully, and crossed his legs.

'No; I don't think so, thanks,' he said. 'The fact is, I came partly to find out your address, if I might.'

Mrs. Stapleton rustled and rearranged herself.

'Oh! but that's charming of you,' she said. 'Is there anything particular?'

'Yes,' said Laurie slowly; 'at least it seems rather particular to me. It's what you were talking about the other day.'

'Now how nice of you to say that! Do you know, I was wondering as we talked. Now do tell me exactly what is in your mind, Mr. Baxter.'

Mrs. Stapleton was conscious of a considerable sense of pleasure. Usually she found this kind of man very imperceptive and gross. Laurie seemed perfectly at his ease, dressed quite in the proper way, and had an air of presentableness that usually only went with Philistinism. She determined to do her best.

'May I speak quite freely, please?' he asked, looking straight at her.

'Please, please,' she said, with that touch of childish intensity that her friends thought so innocent and beautiful.

'Well, it's like this,' said Laurie. 'I've always rather disliked all that kind of thing, more than I can say. It did seem to me so – well – so feeble, don't you know; and then I'm a Catholic, you see, and so—'

'Yes; yes?'

'Well, I've been reading Mr. Stainton Moses, and one or two other books; and I must say that an awful lot of it seems to me still great rubbish; and then there are any amount of frauds, aren't there, Mrs. Stapleton, in that line?'

46

'Alas! Ah, yes!'

'But then I don't know what to make of some of the evidence that remains. It seems to me that if evidence is worth anything at all, there must be something real at the back of it all. And then, if that is so, if it really is true that it is possible to get into actual touch with people who are dead – I mean really and truly, so that there's no kind of doubt about it – well, that does seem to me about the most important thing in the world. Do you see?'

She kept her eyes on his face for an instant or two. Plainly he was really moved; his face had gone a little white in the lamplight and his hands were clasped tightly enough over his knee to whiten the knuckles. She remembered Lady Laura's remarks about the village girl, and understood. But she perceived that she must not attempt intimacy just yet with this young man : he would resent it. Besides, she was shrewd enough to see by his manner that he did not altogether like her.

She nodded pensively once or twice. Then she turned to him with a bright smile. 'I understand entirely,' she said. '(May I too speak quite freely? Yes?) Well, I am so glad you have spoken out. Of course, we are quite accustomed to being distrusted and feared. After all, it is the privilege of all truth-seekers to suffer, is it not? Well, I will say what is in my heart.

'First, you are quite right about some of our workers being dishonest sometimes. They are, Mr. Baxter. I have seen more than one, myself, exposed. But that is natural, is it not? Why, there have been bad Catholics, too, have there not? And, after all, we are only human; and there is a great temptation sometimes not to send people away disappointed. You have heard those stories, I expect, Mr. Baxter?'

'I have heard of Mr. Eglinton.'

'Ah! Poor Willie. . . . Yes. But he had great powers, for all that. . . . Well, but the point you want to get at is this, is it not? Is it really true, underneath it all? Is that it?'

Laurie nodded, looking at her steadily. She leaned forward.

'Mr. Baxter, by all that I hold most sacred, I assure you that it is, that I myself have seen and touched . . . *touched* . . . my own father, who crossed over twenty years ago. I have received messages from his own lips . . . and communications in other ways too, concerning matters only known to him and to myself. Is that sufficient? No'; (she held up a delicate silencing hand) '. . . no, I will not ask you to take my word. I will ask you to test it for yourself.'

Laurie too learned forward now in his low chair, his hands clasped between his knees.

'You will – you will let me test it?' he said in a low voice.

She sat back easily, pushing her draperies straight. She was in some fine silk that fell straight from her high slender waist to her copper-coloured shoes.

'Listen, Mr. Baxter. To-morrow there is coming to this house certainly the greatest medium in London, if not in Europe. (Of course we cannot compete with the East. We are only children beside them.) Well, this man, Mr. Vincent – I think I spoke of him to you last week – he is coming here just for a talk to one or two friends. There shall be no difficulty if you wish it. I will speak to Lady Laura before you go.'

Laurie looked at her without moving.

'I shall be very much obliged,' he said. 'You will remember that I am not yet in the least convinced? I only want to know.'

'That is exactly the right attitude. That is all we have any right to ask. We do not ask for blind faith, Mr. Baxter – only for believing after having seen.'

Laurie nodded slowly.

'That seems to me reasonable,' he said.

There was silence for a moment. Then she determined on a bold stroke.

'There is someone in particular – Mr. Baxter – forgive me asking – someone who has passed over—?'

She sank her voice to what she had been informed was a sympathetic tone, and was scarcely prepared for the sudden tightening of that face.

'That's my affair, Mrs. Stapleton.'

Ah well, she had been premature. She would fetch Lady Laura, she said; she thought she might venture for such a purpose. No, she would not be away three minutes. Then she rustled out.

Laurie went to the fire to wait, and stood there, mechanically warming his hands and staring down at that sleeping core of red coal.

He had taken his courage in both hands in coming at all. In spite of his brave words to Maggie, he had been conscious of a curious repulsion with regard to the whole matter – a repulsion not only of contempt towards the elaborate affectations of the woman he had determined to consult. Yet he had come.

What he had said just now had been perfectly true. He was not yet in the least convinced, but he was anxious, intensely and passionately anxious, goaded too by desire.

Ah! surely it was absurd and fantastic – here in London, in this century. He turned and faced the lamp-lit room, letting his eyes wander round the picture-hung walls, the blue stamped paper, the Empire furniture, the general appearance of beautiful comfort and sane modern life. It was absurd and fantastic; he would be disappointed again, as he had been disappointed in everything else. These things did not happen – the dead did not return. Step by step those things that for centuries had been deemed evidence of the supernatural, one by one had been explained and discounted. Hypnotism, water-divining, witchcraft, and the rest. All these had once been believed to be indisputable proofs of a life beyond the grave, of strange supernormal personalities, and these, one by one, had been either accounted for or discredited. It was mad of him to be alarmed or excited. No, he would go through with it, expecting nothing, hoping nothing. But he would just go through with it to satisfy himself. . . .

The door opened, and the two ladies came in.

'I am delighted that you called, Mr. Baxter; and on such an errand!'

Lady Laura put out a hand, tremulous with pleasure at welcoming a possible disciple.

'Mrs. Stapleton has explained—' began Laurie.

'I understand everything. You come as a sceptic – no, not as a sceptic, but as an inquirer, that is all that we wish. . . . Then to-morrow, at about half-past four.'

CHAPTER FOUR

I

It was a mellow October afternoon, glowing towards sunset, as Laurie came across the south end of the park to his appointment next day; and the effect of it upon his mind was singularly unsuggestive of supernatural mystery. Instead, rather, the warm sky, the lights beginning to peep here and there, though an hour before sunset, turned him rather in the direction of the natural and the domestic.

He wondered what his mother and Maggie would say if they knew his errand, for he had suffient self-control not to have told them of his intentions. As regards his mother he did not care very much. Of course she would deprecate it and feebly dissuade; but he recognised that there was no particular principle behind, beyond a sense of discomfort at the unknown. But it was necessary for him to argue with himself about Maggie. The angry kind of contempt that he knew she would feel needed an answer; and he gave it by reminding himself that she had been brought up in a convent-school, that she knew nothing of the world, and that, lastly, he himself did not take the matter seriously. He was aware, too, that the instinctive repulsion that she felt so keenly found a certain echo in his own feelings; but he explained this by the novelty of the thing.

In fact, the attitude of mind in which he more or less succeeded in arraying himself was that of one who goes to see a serious conjurer. It would be rather fun, he thought, to see a table dancing. But there was not wholly wanting that inexplicable tendency of some natures deliberately to deceive themselves on what lies nearest to their hearts.

Mr. Vincent had not yet arrived when he was shown upstairs, even though Laurie himself was late. (This was partly deliberate. He thought it best to show a little nonchalance.) There was only a young clergyman in the room with the ladies; and the two were introduced.

'Mr. Baxter – Mr. Jamieson.'

He seemed a harmless young man, thought Laurie, and plainly a little nervous at the situation in which he found himself, as might a greyhound carry himself in a kennel of well-bred foxhounds. He was very correctly dressed, with Roman collar and stock, and obviously had not long left a theological college. He had an engaging kind of courtesy, ecclesiastically cut features, and curly black hair. He sat balancing a delicate cup adroitly on his knee.

'Mr. Jamieson is so anxious to know all that is going on,' explained Lady Laura, with a voluble frankness. 'He thinks it so necessary to be abreast of the times, as he said to me the other day.'

Laurie assented, grimly, pitying the young man for his indiscreet confidences. The clergyman looked priggish in his efforts not to do so.

'He has a class of young men on Sundays,' continued the hostess – '(Another biscuit, Maud darling?) – whom he tries to interest in all modern movements. He thinks it so important.'

Mr. Jamieson cleared his throat in a virile manner.

'Just so,' he said; 'exactly so.'

'And so I told him he must really come and meet Mr. Vincent. . . . I can't think why he is so late; but he has so many calls upon his time, that I am sure I wonder—'

'Mr. Vincent,' announced the footman.

A rather fine figure of a man came forward into the room, dressed in much better taste than Laurie somehow had expected, and not at all like the type of an insane dissenting minister in broadcloth which he had feared. Instead, it was a big man that he saw, stooping a little, inclined to stoutness, with a full curly beard tinged with grey, rather overhung brows, and a high forehead, from which the same kind of curly greyish hair was beginning to retreat. He was in a well-cut frock-coat and dark trousers, with the collar of the period and a dark tie.

Lady Laura was in a flutter of welcome, pouring out little sentences, leading him to a seat, introducing him, and finally pressing refreshments into his hands.

'It is too good of you,' she said; 'too good of you, with all your engagements. . . . These gentlemen are most anxious. . . . Mrs. Stapleton of course you know. . . . And you will just

sit and talk to us . . . like friends . . . won't you. . . . No, no!
no formal speech at all . . . just a few words . . . and you will
allow us to ask you questions. . . .'

And so on.

Meanwhile Laurie observed the high-priest carefully and
narrowly, and was quite unable to see any of the unpleasant
qualities he had expected. He sat easily, without self-consciousness or arrogance or unpleasant humility. He had a
pair of pleasant, shrewd, and rather kind eyes; and his voice,
when he said a word or two in answer to Lady Laura's
volubility, was of that resonant softness that is always a
delight to hear. In fact, his whole bearing and personality
was that of a rather exceptional average man – a publisher,
it might be, or a retired lawyer – a family man with a sober
round of life and ordinary duties, who brought to their
fulfilment a wholesome, kindly, but distinctly strong character of his own. Laurie hardly knew whether he was pleased
or disappointed. He would almost have preferred a wild
creature with rolling eyes, in a cloak; yet he would have
been secretly amused and contemptuous at such a man.

'The sitting is off for Sunday, by the way, Lady Laura,'
said the newcomer.

'Indeed! How is that?'

'Oh! there was some mistake about the rooms; it's the
secretary's fault; you mustn't blame me.'

Lady Laura cried out her dismay and disappointment,
and Mrs. Stapleton played chorus. It was *too* tiresome, they
said, *too* provoking, particularly just now, when 'Annie' was
so complacent. (Mrs. Stapleton explained kindly to the two
young gentlemen that 'Annie' was a spirit who had lately
made various very interesting revelations.) What was to be
done? Were there no other rooms?

Mr. Vincent shook his head. It was too late, he said, to
make arrangements now.

While the ladies continued to buzz, and Mr. Jamieson to
listen from the extreme edge of his chair, Laurie continued
to make mental comments. He felt distinctly puzzled by the
marked difference between the prophet and his disciples.
These were so shallow; this so impressive by the most ordinary of all methods, and the most difficult of imitation, that
is, by sheer human personality. He could not grasp the least

common multiple of the two sides. Yet this man tolerated these women, and, indeed, seemed very kind and friendly towards them. He seemed to possess that sort of competence which rises from the fact of having well-arranged ideas and complete certitude about them.

And at last a pause came. Mr. Vincent set down his cup for the second time, refused buttered bun, and waited.

'Yes, do smoke, Mr. Vincent.'

The man drew out his cigarette-case, smiling, offering it to the two men. Laurie took one; the clergyman refused.

'And now, Mr. Vincent.'

Again he smiled, in a half-embarrassed way.

'But no speeches, I think you said,' he remarked.

'Oh! well, you know what I mean; just like friends, you know. Treat us all like that.'

(Mrs. Stapleton rose, came nearer the circle, rustled down again, and sank into an elaborate silence.)

'Well, what is it these gentlemen wish to hear?'

'Everything – everything,' cried Lady Laura. 'They claim to know nothing at all.'

Laurie thought it time to explain himself a little. He felt he would not like to take this man at an unfair advantage.

'I should just like to say this,' he said. 'I have told Mrs. Stapleton already. It is this. I must confess that so far as I am concerned I am not a believer. But neither am I a sceptic. I am just a real agnostic in this matter. I have read several books; and I have been impressed. But there's a great deal in them that seems to me nonsense; perhaps I had better say which I don't understand. This materialising business, for instance. . . . I can understand that the minds of the dead can affect ours; but I don't see how they can affect matter – in table-rapping, for instance, and still more in appearing, and our being able to touch and see them. . . . I think that's my position,' he ended rather lamely.

The fact was that he was a little disconcerted by the other's eyes. They were, as I have said, kind and shrewd eyes, but they had a good deal of power as well. Mr. Vincent sat motionless during this little speech, just looking at him, not at all offensively, yet with the effect of making the young man feel rather like a defiant and naughty little boy who is trying to explain.

Laurie sat back and drew on his cigarette rather hard.

53

'I understand perfectly,' said the steady voice. 'You are in a very reasonable position. I wish all were as open-minded. May I say a word or two?'

'Please.'

'Well, it is materialisation that puzzles you, is it?'

'Exactly,' said Laurie. 'Our theologians tell us— By the way, I am a Catholic.' (The other bowed a little.) 'Our theologians, I believe, tell us that such a thing cannot be, except under peculiar circumstances, as in the lives of the saints, and so on.'

'Are you bound to believe all that your theologians say?' asked the other quietly.

'Well, it would be very rash indeed—' began Laurie.

'Exactly, I see. But what if you approach it from the other side, and try to find out instead whether these things actually do happen. I do not wish to be rude, Mr. Baxter; but you remember that your theologians – I am not so foolish as to say the Church, for I know that that was not so – but your theologians, you know, made a mistake about Galileo.'

Laurie winced a little. Mr. Jamieson cleared his throat in gentle approval.

'Now I don't ask you to accept anything contrary to your faith,' went on the other gently; 'but if you really wish to look into this matter, you must set aside for the present all other presuppositions. You must not begin by assuming that the theologians are always right, nor even in asking how or why these things should happen. The one point is, *Do they happen?*'

His last words had a curious little effect as of a sudden flame. He had spoken smoothly and quietly; then he had suddenly put an unexpected emphasis into the little sentence at the end. Laurie jumped, internally. Yes, that was the point, he assented internally.

'Now,' went on the other, again in that slow, reassuring voice, flicking off the ash of his cigarette, 'is it possible for you to doubt that these things happen? May I ask you what books you have read?'

Laurie named three or four.

'And they have not convinced you?'

'Not altogether.'

'Yet your accept human evidence for a great many much

more remarkable things than these – as a Catholic.'

'That is Divine Revelation,' said Laurie, sure of his ground.

'Pardon me,' said the other. 'I do not in the least say it is not Divine Revelation – that is another question – but you receive the statement that it is so, on the word of man. Is that not true?'

Laurie was silent. He did not quite know what to say; and he almost feared the next words. But he was astonished that the other did not press home the point.

'Think over that, Mr. Baxter. That is all I ask. And now for the real thing. You sincerely wish to be convinced?'

'I am ready to be convinced.'

The medium paused an instant, looking intently at the fire. Then he tossed the stump of his cigarette away and lighted another. The two ladies sat motionless.

'You seem fond of *a priori* arguments, Mr. Baxter,' he began, with a kindly smile. 'Let us have one or two, then.

'Consider first the relation of your soul to your body. That is infinitely mysterious, is it not? An emotion rises in your soul, and a flush of blood marks it. That is the subconscious mechanism of your body. But to say that, does not explain it. It is only a label. You follow me? Yes? Or still more mysterious is your conscious power. You will to raise your hand, and it obeys. Muscular action? Oh yes; but that is but another label.' (He turned his eyes, suddenly sombre, upon the staring listening young man, and his voice rose a little.) 'Go right behind all that, Mr. Baxter, down to the mysteries. What is that link between soul and body? You do not know! Nor does the wisest scientist in the world. Nor ever will. Yet there the link is!'

Again he paused.

Laurie was aware of a rising half-excited interest far beyond the power of the words he heard. Yet the manner of these too was striking. It was not the sham mysticism he had expected. There was a certain reverence in them, an admitting of mysteries, that seemed hard to reconcile with the ideas he had formed of the dogmatism of these folk.

'Now begin again,' continued the quiet, virile voice. 'You believe, as a Christian, in the immortality of the soul, in the survival of personality after death. Thank God for that! All do not, in these days. Then I need not labour at that.

'Now, Mr. Baxter, imagine to yourself some soul that you have loved passionately, who has crossed over to the other side.' (Laurie drew a long, noiseless breath, steadying himself with clenched hands.) 'She has come to the unimaginable glories according to her measure; she is at an end of doubts and fears and suspicions. She knows because she sees. . . . But do you think that she is absorbed in these things? You know nothing of human love, Mr. Baxter' (the voice trembled with genuine emotion) . . . 'if you can think that! . . . If you can think that her thought turns only to herself and her joys. Why, her life has been lived in your love by our hypothesis – you were at her bedside when she died, perhaps; and she clung to you as to God Himself, when the shadow deepened. Do you think that her first thought, or at least her second, will not be of you? . . . In all that she sees, she will desire you to see it also. She will strive, crave, hunger for you – not that she may possess you, but that you may be one with her in her own possession; she will send out vibration after vibration of sympathy and longing; and you, on this side, will be tuned to her as none other can be – you, on this side, will be empty for her love, for the sight and sound of her. . . . Is death then so strong? – stronger than love? Can a Christian believe that?'

The change in the man was extraordinary. His heavy beard and brows hid half his face, but his whole being glowed passionately in his voice, even in his little trembling gestures, and Laurie sat astonished. Every word uttered seemed to fit his own case, to express by an almost perfect vehicle the vague thoughts that had struggled in his own heart during this last week. It was Amy of whom the man spoke, Amy with her eyes and hair, peering from the glorious gloom to catch some glimpse of her lover in his meaningless light of earthly day.

Mr. Vincent cleared his throat a little, and at the sound the two motionless women stirred and rustled a little. The sound of a hansom, the spanking trot and wintry jingle of bells swelled out of the distance, passed, and went into silence before he spoke again. Then it was in his usual slow voice that he continued.

'Conceive such a soul as that, Mr. Baxter. She desires to communicate with one she loves on earth, with you or me, and it is a human and innocent desire. Yet she has lost that

56

connection, that machinery of which we have spoken – that connection of which we know nothing, between matter and spirit, except that it exists. What is she to do? Well, at least she will do this, she will bend every power that she possesses upon that medium – I mean matter – through which alone the communication can be made; as a man on an island, beyond the power of a human voice, will use any instrument, however grotesque, to signal to a passing ship. Would any decent man, Mr. Baxter, mock at the pathos and effort of that, even if it were some grotesque thing, like a flannel shirt on the end of an oar? Yet men mock at the tapping of a table! . . .

'Well, then, this longing soul uses every means at her disposal, concentrates every power she possesses. Is it so very unreasonable, so very unchristian, so very dishonouring to the love of God, to think that she sometimes succeeds? . . . that she is able, under comparatively exceptional circumstances, to re-establish that connection with material things, that was perfectly normal and natural to her during her earthly life. . . . Tell me, Mr. Baxter.'

Laurie shifted a little in his chair.

'I cannot say that it does,' he said, in a voice that seemed strange in his own ears. The medium smiled a little.

'So much for *a priori* reasoning,' he said. 'There remains only the fact whether such things do happen or not. There I must leave you to yourself, Mr. Baxter.'

Laurie sat forward suddenly.

'But that is exactly where I need your help, sir,' he said.

A murmur broke from the ladies' lips simultaneously, resembling applause. Mr. Jamieson sat back and swallowed perceptibly in his throat.

'You have said so much, sir,' went on Laurie deliberately, 'that you have, so to speak, put yourself in my debt. I must ask you to take me further.'

Mr. Vincent smiled full at him.

'You must take your place with others,' he said. 'These ladies—'

'Mr. Vincent, Mr. Vincent,' cried Lady Laura. 'He is quite right, you must help him. You must help us all.'

'Well, Sunday week,' he began deprecatingly.

Mrs. Stapleton broke in.

'No, no; now, Mr. Vincent, now. Do something now. Surely the circumstances are favourable.'

'I must be gone again at six-thirty,' said the man hesitatingly.

Laurie broke in. He felt desperate.

'If you can show me anything of this, sir, you can surely show it now. If you do not show it now—'

'Well, Mr. Baxter?' put in the voice, sharp and incisive, as if expecting an insult and challenging it.

Laurie broke down.

'I can only say,' he cried, 'that I beg and entreat of you to do what you can – now and here.'

There was a silence.

'And you, Mr. Jamieson?'

The young clergyman started, as if from a daze. Then he rose abruptly.

'I – I must be going, Lady Laura,' he said. 'I had no idea it was so late. I – have a confirmation class.'

An instant later he was gone.

'That is as well,' observed the medium. 'And you are sure, Mr. Baxter, that you wish me to try? You must remember that I promise nothing.'

'I wish you to try.'

'And if nothing happens?'

'If nothing happens, I will promise to – to continue my search. I shall know then that – that it is at least sincere.'

Mr. Vincent rose to his feet.

'A little table just here, Lady Laura, if you please, and a pencil and paper. . . . Will you kindly take your seats? . . . Yes, Mr. Baxter, draw up your chair . . . here. Now, please, we must have complete silence, and, so far as possible, silence of thought.'

2

The table, a small, round rosewood one, stood, bare of any cloth, upon the hearthrug. The two ladies sat, motionless statues once more, upon the side farthest from the fire, with their hands resting lightly upon the surface. Laurie sat on one side and the medium on the other. Mr. Vincent had received his paper and pencil almost immediately, and now sat resting his right hand with the pencil upon the paper as if to write, his left hand upon his knee as he sat, turned away slightly from the centre.

Laurie looked at him closely. . . .

And now he began to be aware of a certain quite indefinable change in the face at which he looked. The eyes were open – no, it was not in them that the change lay, nor in the lines about the mouth, so far as he could see them, nor in any detail, anywhere. Neither was it the face of a dreamer or a sleep-walker, or of the dead, when the lines disappear and life retires. It was a living, conscious face, yet it was changed. The lips were slightly parted, and the breath came evenly between them. It was more like the face of one lost in deep, absorbed, introspective thought. Laurie decided that this was the explanation.

He looked at the hand on the paper – well shaped, brownish, capable – perfectly motionless, the pencil held lightly between the finger and thumb.

Then he glanced up at the two ladies.

They too were perfectly motionless, but there was no change in them. The eyes of both were downcast, fixed steadily upon the paper. And as he looked he saw Lady Laura begin to lift her lids slowly as if to glance at him. He looked himself upon the paper and the motionless fingers.

He was astonished at the speed with which the situation had developed. Five minutes ago he had been listening to talk, and joining in it. The clergyman had been here; he himself had been sitting a yard farther back. Now they sat here as if they had sat for an hour. It seemed that the progress of events had stopped. . . .

Then he began to listen for the sounds of the world outside, for within here it seemed as if a silence of a very strange quality had suddenly descended and enveloped them. It was as if a section – that place in which he sat – had been cut out of time and space. It was apart here, it was different altogether. . . .

He began to be intensely and minutely conscious of the world outside – so entirely conscious that he lost all perception of that at which he stared; whether it was the paper, or the strong, motionless hand, or the introspective face, he was afterwards unaware. But he heard all the quiet roar of the London evening, and was able to distinguish even the note of each instrument that helped to make up that untiring, inconclusive orchestra. Far away to the northwards sounded a great thoroughfare, the rolling of wheels, a myriad hoofs, the pulse of motor vehicles, and the cries of street boys; upon all these his attention dwelt as they came up through the outward windows into that dead silent, lamp-lit room of which he had lost consciousness. Again a hansom came up the street, with the rap of hoofs, the swish of a whip, the wintry jingle of bells. . . .

He began gently to consider these things, to perceive, rather than to form, little inward pictures of what they signified; he saw the lighted omnibus, the little swirl of faces round a news-board.

Then he began to consider what had brought him here; it seemed that he saw himself, coming in his dark suit across the park, turning into the thoroughfare and across it. He began to consider Amy; and it seemed to him that in this intense and living silence he was conscious of her for the first time without sorrow since ten days ago. He began to consider.

Something brought him back in an instant to the room and his perception of it, but he had not an idea what this was, whether a movement or a sound. But on considering it afterwards he remembered that it was as that sound is that wakes a man at the very instant of his falling asleep, a sharp momentary tick, as of a clock. Yet he had not been in the least sleepy.

On the contrary, he perceived now with an extreme and alert attention the hand on the paper; he even turned his head slightly to see if the pencil had moved. It was as motionless as at the beginning. He glanced up, with a touch of surprise, at his hostess's face, and caught her in the very act of turning her eyes from his. There was no impatience in her movement : rather her face was of one absorbed, listening intently, not like the bearded face opposite, intro-spective and intuitive, but eagerly, though motionlessly, observant of the objective world. He looked at Mrs. Staple-ton. She too bore the same expression of intent regarding thought on her usually rather tiresome face.

Then once again the silence began to come down, like a long, noiseless hush.

This time, however, his progress was swifter and more

sure. He passed with the speed of thought through those processes that had been measurable before, faintly conscious of the words spoken before the sitting began –

'... If possible, the silence of thought.'

He thought he understood now what this signified, and that he was experiencing it. No longer did he dwell upon, or consider, with any voluntary activity, the images that passed before him. Rather they moved past him while he simply regarded them without understanding. His perception ran swiftly outwards, as through concentric circles, yet he was not sure whether it were outwards or inwards that he went. The roar of London, with its flight of ocular visions, sank behind him, and without any further sense of mental travel, he found himself perceiving his own home, whether in memory, imagination, or fact he did not know. But he perceived his mother, in the familiar lamp-lit room, over her needlework, and Maggie – Maggie looking at him with a strange, almost terrified expression in her great eyes. Then these two were gone; and he was out in some warm silence, filled with a single presence – that which he desired; and there he stopped.

He was not in the least aware of how long this lasted. But he found himself at a certain moment in time, looking steadily at the white paper on the table, from which the hand had gone, again conscious of the sudden passing of some clear sound that left no echo – as sharp as the crack of a whip. Oh! the paper – that was the important point! He bent a little closer, and was aware of a sharp disappointment as he saw it was stainless of writing. Then he was astonished that the hand and pencil had gone from it, and looked up quickly.

Mr. Vincent was looking at him with a strange expression.

At first he thought he might have interrupted, and wondered with dismay whether this were so. But there was no sign of anger in those eyes – nothing but a curious and kindly interest.

'Nothing happened?' he exclaimed hastily. 'You have written nothing?'

He looked at the ladies.

Lady Laura too was looking at him with the same strange

interest as the medium. Mrs. Stapleton, he noticed, was just folding up, in an unobtrusive manner, several sheets of paper that he had not noticed before.

He felt a little stiff, and moved as if to stand up; but, to his astonishment, the big man was up in an instant, laying his hands on his shoulders.

'Just sit still quietly for a few minutes,' said the kindly voice. 'Just sit still.'

'Why – why—' began Laurie, bewildered.

'Yes, just sit still quietly,' went on the voice; 'you feel a little tired.'

'Just a little,' said Laurie. 'But—'

'Yes, yes; just sit still. No; don't speak.'

Then a silence fell again.

Laurie began to wonder what this was all about. Certainly he felt tired, yet strangely elated. But he felt no inclination to move; and sat back, passive, looking at his own hands on his knees. But he was disappointed that nothing had happened.

Then the thought of time came into his mind. He supposed that it would be about ten minutes past six. The sitting had begun a little before six. He glanced up at the clock on the mantelpiece; but it was one of those bulgy-faced Empire gilt affairs that display everything except the hour. He still waited a moment, feeling all this to be very unusual and unconventional. Why should he sit here like an invalid, and why should these three sit here and watch him so closely?

He shifted a little in his chair, feeling that an effort was due from him. The question of the time of day struck him as a suitably conventional remark with which to break the embarrassing silence.

'What is the time?' he said. 'I am afraid I ought to be—'

'There is plenty of time,' said the grave voice across the table.

With a sudden movement Laurie was on his feet, peering at the clock, knowing that something was wrong somewhere. Then he turned to the company bewildered and suspicious.

'Why, it is nearly eight,' he cried.

Mr. Vincent smiled reassuringly.

'It is about that,' he said. 'Please sit down again, Mr. Baxter.'

'But – but—' began Laurie.

'Please sit down again, Mr. Baxter,' repeated the voice, with a touch of imperiousness that there was no resisting.

Laurie sat down again; but he was alert, suspicious, and intensely puzzled.

'Will you kindly tell me what has happened?' he asked sharply.

'You feel tired?'

'No; I am all right. Kindly tell me what has happened.'

He saw Lady Laura whisper something in an undertone he could not hear. Mr. Vincent stood up with a nod and leaned himself against the mantelpiece, looking down at the rather indignant young man.

'Certainly,' he said. 'You are sure you are not exhausted, Mr. Baxter?'

'Not in the least,' said Laurie.

'Well, then, you passed into trance about five minutes—'

'*What?*'

'You passed into trance about five minutes past six; you came out of it five minutes ago.'

'Trance?' gasped Laurie.

'Certainly. A very deep and satisfactory trance. There is nothing to be frightened of, Mr. Baxter. It is an unusual gift, that is all. I have seldom seen a more satisfactory instance. May I ask you a question or two, sir?'

Laurie nodded vaguely. He was still trying hopelessly to take in what had been said.

'You nearly passed into trance a little earlier. May I ask whether you heard or saw anything that recalled you?'

Laurie shut his eyes tight in an effort to think. He felt dimly rather proud of himself.

'It was quite short. Then you came back and looked at Lady Laura. Try to remember.'

'I remember thinking I had heard a sound.'

The medium nodded.

'Just so,' he said.

'That would be the third,' said Lady Laura, nodding sagely.

'Third what?' said Laurie rather rudely.

No one paid any attention to him.

'Now can you give any account of the last hour and a half?' continued the medium tranquilly.

Laurie considered again. He was still a little confused.

'I remember thinking about the streets,' he said, 'and then of my own home, and then . . .' He stopped.

'Yes; and then?'

'Then of a certain private matter.'

'Ah! We must not pry then. But can you answer one question more? Was it connected with any person who has crossed over?'

'It was,' said Laurie shortly.

'Just so,' said the medium.

Laurie felt suspicious.

'Why do you ask that?' he said.

Mr. Vincent looked at him steadily.

'I think I had better tell you, Mr. Baxter; it is more straightforward, though you will not like it. You will be surprised to hear that you talked very considerably during this hour and a half; and from all that you said I should suppose you were controlled by a spirit recently crossed over – a young girl who on being questioned gave the name of Amy Nugent—'

Laurie sprang to his feet, furious.

'You have been spying, sir. How dare you—'

'Sit down, Mr. Baxter, or you shall not hear a word more,' rang out the imperious, unruffled voice. 'Sit down this instant.'

Laurie shot a look at the two ladies. Then he remembered himself. He sat down.

'I am not at all angry, Mr. Baxter,' came the voice, sauve and kindly again. 'Your thought was very natural. But I think I can prove to you that you are mistaken.'

Mr. Vincent glanced at Mrs. Stapleton with an almost imperceptible frown, then back at Laurie.

'Let me see, Mr. Baxter. . . . Is there anyone on earth besides yourself who knew that you had sat out, about ten days ago or so, under some yew trees in your garden at home, and thought of this young girl – that you—'

Laurie looked at him in dumb dismay; some little sound broke from his mouth.

'Well, is that enough, Mr. Baxter?'

Lady Laura slid in a sentence here.

'Dear Mr. Baxter, you need not be in the least alarmed. All that has passed here is, of course, as sacred as in the confessional. We should not dream, without your leave—'

'One moment,' gasped the boy.

He drove his face into his hands and sat overwhelmed. Presently he looked up.

'But *I* knew it,' he said. '*I* knew it. It was just my own self which spoke.'

The medium smiled.

'Yes,' he said, 'of course that is the first answer.' He placed one hand on the table, leaning forward, and began to play his fingers as if on a piano. Laurie watched the movement, which seemed vaguely familiar.

'Can you account for that, Mr. Baxter? You did that several times. It seemed uncharacteristic of you, somehow.'

Laurie looked at him, mute. He remembered now. He half raised a hand in protest.

'And . . . and do you ever stammer?' went on the man.

Still Laurie was silent. It was beyond belief or imagination.

'Now if those things were characteristic—'

'Stop, sir,' cried the boy; and then, 'But those too might be unconscious imitation.'

'They might,' said the other. 'But then we had the advantage of watching you. And there were other things.'

'I beg your pardon?'

'There was the loud continuous rapping, at the beginning and the end. You were awakened twice by these.'

Laurie remained perfectly motionless without a word. He was still striving to marshal this flood of mad ideas. It was incredible, amazing.

Then he stood up.

'I must go away,' he said. 'I – I don't know what to think.'

'You had better stay a little longer and rest,' said the medium kindly.

The boy shook his head.

'I must go at once,' he said. 'I cannot trust myself.'

He went out without a word, followed by the medium. The two ladies sat eyeing one another.

'It has been astonishing . . . astonishing,' sighed Mrs. Stapleton. 'What a find !'

There was no more said. Lady Laura sat as one in trance herself.

Then Mr. Vincent returned.

'You must not lose sight of that young man,' he said abruptly. 'It is an extraordinary case.'

'I have all the notes here,' remarked Mrs. Stapleton.

'Yes; you had better keep them. He must not see them at present.'

CHAPTER FIVE

I

As the weeks went by Maggie's faint uneasiness disappeared. She was one of those fortunate persons who, possessing what are known as nerves, are aware of the possession, and discount their effects accordingly.

That uneasiness had culminated a few days after Laurie's departure one evening as she sat with the old lady after tea – in a sudden touch of terror at she knew no what.

'What is the matter, my dear?' the old lady had said without warning.

Maggie was reading, but it appeared that Mrs. Baxter had noticed her lower her book suddenly, with an odd expression.

Maggie had blinked a moment.

'Nothing,' she said. 'I was just thinking of Laurie; I don't know why.'

But since then she had been able to reassure herself. Her fancies were but fancies, she told herself; and they had ceased to trouble her. The boy's letters to his mother were ordinary and natural : he was reading fairly hard; his coach was as pleasant a person as he had seemed; he hoped to run down to Stantons for a few days at Christmas. There was nothing whatever to alarm anyone; plainly his ridiculous attitude about Spiritualism had been laid by; and, better still, he was beginning to recover himself after his sorrow in September.

It was an extraordinarily peaceful and uneventful life that the two led together – the kind of life that strengthens previous proclivities and adds no new ones; that brings out the framework of character and motive as dropping water clears the buried roots of a tree. This was all very well for Mrs. Baxter, whose character was already fully formed, it may be hoped; but not so utterly satisfactory for the girl, though the process was pleasant enough.

After Mass and breakfast she spent the morning as she

wished, overseeing little extra details of the house – gardening plans, the poultry, and so forth – and reading what she cared to. The afternoon was devoted to the old lady's airing; the evening till dinner to anything she wished; and after dinner again to gentle conversation. Very little happened. The Vicar and his wife dined there occasionally, and still more occasionally Father Mahon. Now and then there were vague entertainments to be patronised in the village schoolroom, in an atmosphere of ink and hair-oil; and a mild amount of rather dreary and stately gaiety connected with the big houses round. Mrs. Baxter occasionally put in appearances, a dignified and aristocratic old figure with her gentle eyes and black lace veil; and Maggie went with her.

The pleasure of this life grew steadily upon Maggie. She was one of that fraction of the world that finds entertainment to lie, like the kingdom of God, within. She did not in the least wish to be 'amused' or stimulated and distracted. She was perfectly and serenely content with the fowls, the garden, her small selected tasks, her religion, and herself.

The result was, as it always is in such cases, she began to revolve about three or four main lines of thought, and to make a very fair progress in the knowledge of herself. She knew her faults quite well; and she was not unaware of her virtues. She knew perfectly that she was apt to give way to internal irritation, of a strong though invisible kind, when interruptions happened; that she now and then gave way to an unduly fierce contempt of tiresome people, and said little bitter things that she afterwards regretted. She also knew that she was quite courageous, that she had magnificent physical health, and that she could be perfectly content with a life that a good many other people would find narrow and stifling.

Her own character then was one thing that she had studied – not in the least in a morbid way – during her life at Stantons. And another thing she was beginning to study, rather to her own surprise, was the character of Laurie. She began to become a little astonished at the frequency with which, during a silent drive, or some mild mechanical labour in the gardens, the image of that young man would rise before her.

Indeed, as has been said, she had new material to work on. She had not realised till the *affaire* Amy that boy's

68

astonishing selfishness; and it became for her a rather pleasant psychological exercise to build up his characteristics into a consistent whole. It had not struck her, till this specimen came before her notice, how generosity and egotism, for example, so far from being mutually exclusive, can very easily be complements, each of the other.

So then she passed her days – exteriorly a capable and occupied person, interested in half a dozen simple things; interiorly rather introspective, rather scrupulous, and intensely interested in the watching of two characters – her own and her adopted brother's. Mrs. Baxter's character needed no dissection; it was a consistent whole, clear as crystal and as rigid.

It was still some five weeks before Christmas that Maggie became aware of what, as a British maiden, she ought, of course, to have known long before – namely, that she was thinking just a little too much about a young man who, so far as was apparent, thought nothing at all about her. It was true that once he had passed through a period of sentimentality in her regard; but the extreme discouragement it had met with had been enough.

Her discovery happened in this way.

Mrs. Baxter opened a letter one morning, smiling contentedly to herself.

'From Laurie,' she said. Maggie ceased eating toast for a second, to listen.

Then the old lady uttered a small cry of dismay.

'He thinks he can't come, after all,' she said.

Maggie had a moment of very acute annoyance.

'What does he say? Why not?' she asked.

There was a pause. She watched Mrs. Baxter's lips moving slowly, her glasses in place; saw the page turned, and turned again. She took another piece of toast. There are few things more irritating than to have fragments of a letter doled out piecemeal.

'He doesn't say. He just says he's very busy indeed, and has a great deal of way to make up.' The old lady continued reading tranquilly, and laid the letter down.

'Nothing more?' asked Maggie, consumed with annoyance.

'He's been to the theatre once or twice. . . . Dear Laurie! I'm glad he's recovering his spirits.'

69

Maggie was very angry indeed. She thought it abominable of the boy to treat his mother like that. And then there was the shooting – not much, indeed, beyond the rabbits, which the man who acted as occasional keeper told her wanted thinning, and a dozen or two of wild pheasants – yet this shooting had always been done, she understood, at Christmas, ever since Master Laurie had been old enough to hold a gun.

She determined to write him a letter.

When breakfast was over, with a resolved face she went to her room. She would really tell this boy a home-truth or two. It was a – a sister's place to do so. The mother, she knew well enough, would do no more than send a little wail, and would end by telling the dear boy that, of course, he knew best, and that she was very happy to think that he was taking such pains about his studies. Someone must point out to the boy his overwhelming selfishness, and it seemed that no-one was at hand but herself. Therefore she would do it.

She did it, therefore, politely enough, but unmistakably; and as it was a fine morning, she thought that she would like to step up to the village and post it. She did not want to relent; and once the letter was in the post-box, the thing would be done.

It was, indeed, a delicious morning. As she passed out through the iron gate the trees overhead, still with a few brown belated leaves, soared up in filigree of exquisite workmanship into a sky of clear November blue, as fresh as a hedge-sparrow's egg. The genial sound of cock-crowing rose, silver and exultant, from the farm beyond the road, and the tiny street of the hamlet looked as clean as a Dutch picture.

She noticed on the right, just before she turned up to the village on the left, the grocer's shop, with the name 'Nugent' in capitals as bright and flamboyant as on the depot of a merchant king. Mr. Nugent could be faintly descried within, in white shirt-sleeves and an apron, busied at a pile of cheeses. Overhead, three pairs of lace curtains, each decked with a blue bow, denoted the bedrooms. One of them must have been Amy's. She wondered which. . . .

All up the road to the village, some half-mile in length, she pondered Amy. She had never seen her, to her knowledge; but she had a tolerably accurate mental picture of her from Mrs. Baxter's account. . . . Ah! how could Laurie? How could he? . . . Laurie, of all people! It was just one more example. . . .

After dropping her letter into the box at the corner, she hesitated for an instant. Then, with an odd look on her face, she turned sharply aside to where the church tower pricked above the leafless trees.

It was a typical little country church, with that odour of the respectable and rather stuffy sanctity peculiar to the class; she had wrinkled her nose at it more than once in Laurie's company. But she passed by the door of it now, and, stepping among the wet grasses, came down the little slope among the headstones to where a very white marble angel clasped an equally white marble cross. She passed to the front of this, and looked, frowning a little over the intolerable taste of the thing.

The cross, she perceived, was wreathed with a spray of white marble ivory; the angel was a German female, with a very rounded leg emerging behind a kind of button; and there, at the foot of the cross, was the inscription, in startling black—

AMY NUGENT
THE DEAR AND ONLY DAUGHTER
OF
AMOS AND MARIA NUGENT
OF STANTONS
DIED SEPTEMBER 21ST 1901
RESPECTED BY ALL
"I SHALL SEE HER BUT NOT NOW."

Below, as vivid as the inscription, there stood out the maker's name, and of the town where he lived.

So she lay there, reflected Maggie. It had ended in that. A mound of earth, cracking a little, and sunken. She lay there, her nervous fingers motionless and her stammer silent. And could there be a more eloquent monument of what she was? . . . Then she remembered herself, and signed herself with the cross, while her lips moved an instant for the repose of the poor girlish soul. Then she stepped up again on to the path to go home.

It was as she came near the church gate that she understood herself, that she perceived why she had come, and was
conscious for the first time of her real attitude of soul as she
had stood there, reading the inscription, and, in a flash,
there followed the knowledge of the inevitable meaning of
it all.

In a word it was this.

She had come there, she told herself, to triumph, to gloat.
Oh! she spared herself nothing, as she stood there, crimson
with shame, to gloat over the grave of a rival. Amy was
nothing less than that, and she herself – she, Margaret Marie
Deronnais – had given way to jealousy of this grocer's
daughter, because . . . because . . . she had begun to care,
really to care, for the man to whom she had written that
letter this morning, and this man had scarcely said one word
to her, or given her one glance, beyond such as a brother
might give to a sister. There was the naked truth.

Her mind fled back. She understood a hundred things
now. She perceived that that sudden anger at breakfast had
been personal disappointment – not at all that lofty dis-
interestedness on behalf of the mother that she had pretended. She understood too, now, the meaning of those long
contented meditations as she went up and down the garden
walks, alert for plantains, the meaning of the zeal she had
shown, only a week ago, on behalf of a certain hazel which
the gardener wanted to cut down.

'You had better wait till Mr. Laurence comes home,' she
had said. 'I think he once said he liked the tree to be just
there.'

She understood now why she had been so intuitive, so con-
demnatory, so critical of the boy – it was that she was passionately interested in him, that it was a pleasure even to
abuse him to herself, to call him selfish and self-centred, that
all this lofty disapproval was just the sop that her subconsciousness had used to quiet her uneasiness.

Little scenes rose before her – all passed almost in a flash
of time – as she stood with her hand on the medieval-looking
latch of the gate, and she saw herself in them all as a proud,
unmaidenly, pharisaical prig, in love with a man who was
not in love with her.

She made an effort, unlatched the gate, and moved on, a
beautiful, composed figure, with great steady eyes and well-

cut profile, a model of dignity and grace, interiorly a raging, self-contemptuous, abject wretch.

It must be remembered that she was convent-bred.

2

By the time that Laurie's answer came, poor Maggie had arranged her emotions fairly satisfactorily. She came to the conclusion, arrived at after much heart-searching, that after all she was not yet actually in love with Laurie, but was in danger of being so, and that therefore now that she knew the danger, and could guard against it, she need not actually withdraw from her home, and bury herself in a convent or the foreign mission-field.

She arrived at this astonishing conclusion by the following process of thought. It may be presented in the form of a syllogism.

All girls who are in love regard the beloved as a spotless, reproachless hero.

Maggie Deronnais did not regard Laurie Baxter as a spotless, reproachless hero.

Ergo. Maggie Deronnais was not in love with Laurie Baxter.

Strange as it may appear to non-Catholic readers, Maggie did not confide her complications to the ear of Father Mahon. She mentioned, no doubt, on the following Saturday, that she had given way to thoughts of pride and jealousy, that she had deceived herself with regard to a certain action, done really for selfish motives, into thinking she had done it for altruistic motives, and there she left it. And, no doubt, Father Mahon left it there too, and gave her absolution without hesitation.

Then Laurie's answer arrived, and had to be dealt with, that is, it had to be treated interiorly with a proper restraint of emotions.

'My dear Maggie,' he wrote;

'Why all this fury? What have I done? I said to mother that I didn't know for certain whether I could come or not, as I had a lot to do. I don't think she can have given you the letter to read, or you wouldn't have written all that about my being away from home at the one season of the year, etc. Of course I'll come, if you or anybody feels like that. Does mother feel upset too? Please tell me if she ever feels that, or is in the least unwell, or anything. I'll come instantly. As it is, shall we say the 20th of December, and I'll stay at least a week. Will that do?

'Yours,
'L. B.'

This was a little overwhelming, and Maggie wrote off a penitent letter, refraining carefully, however, from any expressions that might have anything of the least warmth, but saying that she was very glad he was coming, and that the shooting should be seen to.

She directed the letter; and then sat for an instant looking at Laurie's – at the neat Oxford-looking hand, the artistic appearance of the paragraphs, and all the rest of it.

She would have liked to keep it – to put it with half a dozen others she had from him; but it seemed better not.

Then as she tore it up into careful strips, her conscience smote her again, shrewdly; and she drew out the top left-hand drawer of the table at which she sat.

There they were, a little pile of them, neat and orderly. She looked at them an instant; then she took them out, turned them quickly to see if all were there, and then, gathering up the strips of the one she had received that morning, went over to the wood fire and dropped them in.

It was better so, she said to herself.

The days went pleasantly enough after that. She would not for an instant allow to herself that any of their smoothness arose from the fact that this boy would be here again in a few weeks. On the contrary, it was because she had detected a weakness in his regard, she told herself, and had resolutely stamped on it, that she was in so serene a peace. She arranged about the shooting – that is to say, she informed the acting keeper that Master Laurie would be home for Christmas as usual – all in an unemotional manner, and went about her various affairs without effort.

She found Mrs. Baxter just a little trying now and then. That lady had come to the conclusion that Laurie was unhappy in his religion – certainly references to it had dropped out of his letters – and that Mr. Rymer must set it right.

'The Vicar must dine here at least twice while Laurie is here,' she observed at breakfast one morning. 'He has a great influence with young men.'

Maggie reflected upon a remark or two, extremely unjust, made by Laurie with regard to the clergyman.

'Do you think – do you think he understands Laurie?' she said.

'He has known him for fifteen years,' remarked Mrs. Baxter.

'Perhaps it's Laurie that doesn't understand him then,' said Maggie tranquilly.

'I daresay.'

'And – and what do you think Mr. Rymer will be able to do?' asked the girl.

'Just settle the boy. . . . I don't think Laurie's very happy. Not that I would willingly disturb his mind again; I don't mean that, my dear. I quite understand that your religion is just the one for certain temperaments, and Laurie's is one of them; but a few helpful words sometimes—' Mrs. Baxter left it at an aposiopesis, a form of speech she was fond of.

There was a grain of truth, Maggie thought, in the old lady's hints, and she helped herself in silence to marmalade. Laurie's letters, which she usually read, did not refer much to religion, or to the Brompton Oratory, as his custom had been at first. She tried to make up her mind that this was a healthy sign; that it showed that Laurie was settling down from that slight feverishness of zeal that seemed the inevitable atmosphere of most converts. Maggie found converts a little trying now and then; they would talk so much about facts, certainly undisputed, and for that very reason not to be talked about. Laurie had been a marked case, she remembered; he wouldn't let the thing alone, and his contempt of Anglican clergy, whom Maggie herself regarded with respect, was hard to understand. In fact she had remonstrated on the subject of the Vicar. . . .

Maggie perceived that she was letting her thoughts run again on disputable lines; and she made a remark about the Balkan crisis so abruptly that Mrs. Baxter looked at her in bewilderment.

'You do jump about so, my dear. We were speaking of Laurie, were we not?'

'Yes,' said Maggie.

'It's the twentieth he's coming on, is it not?'

'Yes,' said Maggie.

'I wonder what train he'll come by?'

'I don't know,' said Maggie.

A few days before Laurie's arrival she went to the greenhouse to see the chrysanthemums. There was an excellent show of them.

'Mrs. Baxter doesn't like them hairy ones,' said the gardener.

'Oh! I had forgotten. Well, Ferris, on the nineteenth I shall want a big bunch of them. You'd better take those – those hairy ones. And some maidenhair. Is there plenty?'

'Yes, miss.'

'Can you make a wreath, Ferris?'

'Yes, miss.'

'Well, will you make a good wreath of them, please, for a grave? The morning of the twentieth will do. There'll be plenty left for the church and house?'

'Oh yes, miss.'

'And for Father Mahon?'

'Oh yes, miss.'

'Very well, then. Will you remember that? A good wreath, with fern, on the morning of the twentieth. If you'll just leave it here I'll call for it about twelve o'clock. You needn't send it up to the house.'

'Very good, miss.'

CHAPTER SIX

I

Laurie was sitting in his room after breakfast, filling his briar pipe thoughtfully, and contemplating his journey to Stantons.

It was more than six weeks now since his experience in Queen's Gate, and he had gone through a variety of emotions. Bewildered terror was the first, a nervous interest the next, a truculent scepticism the third; and lately, to his astonishment, the nervous interest had begun to revive.

At first he had been filled with unreasoning fear. He had walked back as far as the gate of the park, hardly knowing where he went, conscious only that he must be in the company of his fellows; upon finding himself on the south side of Hyde Park Corner, where travellers were few, he had crossed over in nervous haste to where he might jostle human beings. Then he had dined in a restaurant, knowing that a band would be playing there, and had drunk a bottle of champagne; he had gone to his rooms, cheered and excited, and had leapt instantly into bed for fear that his courage should evaporate. For he was perfectly aware that fear, and a sickening kind of repulsion, formed a very large element in his emotions. For nearly two hours, unless three persons had lied consummately, he – his essential being, that sleepless self that underlies all – had been in strange company, had become identified in some horrible manner with the soul of a dead person. It was as if he had been informed some morning that he had slept all night with a corpse under his bed. He woke half a dozen times that night in the pleasant curtained bedroom, and each time with the terror upon him. What if stories were true, and this Thing still haunted the air? It was remarkable, he considered afterwards, how the sign which he had demanded had not had the effect for which he had hoped. He was not at all reassured by it.

77

Then as the days went by, and he was left in peace, his horror began to pass. He turned the thing over in his mind a dozen times a day, and found it absorbing. But he began to reflect that, after all, he had nothing more than he had had before in the way of evidence. An hypnotic sleep might explain the whole thing. That little revelation he had made in his unconsciousness, of his sitting beneath the yews, might easily be accounted for by the fact that he himself knew it, that it had been a deeper element in his experience than he had known, and that he had told it aloud. It was no proof of anything more. There remained the rapping and what the medium had called his 'appearance' during the sleep; but of all this he had read before in books. Why should he be convinced any more now than he had been previously? Besides, it was surely doubtful, was it not, whether the rapping, if it had really taken place, might not be the normal cracks and sounds of woodwork, intensified in the attention of the listeners? or if it was more than this, was there any proof that it might not be produced in some way by the intense will-power of some living person present? This was surely conceivable – more conceivable, that is, than any other hypothesis. . . . Besides, what had it all got to do with Amy?

Within a week of his original experience, scepticism was dominant. These lines of thought did their work by incessant repetition. The normal life he lived, the large, business-like face of the lawyer whom he faced day by day, a theatre or two, a couple of dinners – even the noise of London streets and the appearance of workaday persons – all these gradually reassured him.

When therefore he received a nervous little note from Lady Laura, reminding him of the *séance* to be held in Baker Street, and begging his attendance, he wrote a most proper letter back again, thanking her for her kindness, but saying that he had come to the conclusion that this kind of thing was not good for him or his work, and begging her to make his excuses to Mr. Vincent.

A week or two passed, and nothing whatever happened. Then he heard again from Lady Laura, and again he answered by a polite refusal, adding a little more as to his own state of mind; and again silence fell.

Then at last Mr. Vincent called on him in person one evening after dinner.

Laurie's rooms were in Mitre Court, very convenient to the Temple – two rooms opening into one another, and communicating with the staircase.

He had played a little on his grand piano, that occupied a third of his sitting-room, and had then dropped off to sleep before his fire. He awakened suddenly to see the big man standing almost over him, and sat up confusedly.

'I beg your pardon, Mr. Baxter; the porter's boy told me to come straight up. I found your outer door open.'

Laurie hastened to welcome him, to set him down in a deep chair, to offer whisky and to supply tobacco. There was something about this man that commanded deference.

'You know why I have come, I expect,' said the medium, smiling.

Laurie smiled back, a little nervously.

'I have come to see whether you will not reconsider your decision.'

The boy shook his head.

'I think not,' he said.

'You found no ill effects, I hope, from what happened at Lady Laura's?'

'Not at all, after the first shock.'

'Doesn't that reassure you at all, Mr. Baxter?'

Laurie hesitated.

'It's like this,' he said; 'I'm not really convinced. I don't see anything final in what happened.'

'Will you explain, please?'

Laurie set the results of his meditations forth at length. There was nothing, he said, that could not be accounted for by a very abnormal state of subjectivity. The fact that this . . . this young person's name was in his mind . . . and so forth. . . .

'. . . And I find it rather distracting to my work,' he ended. 'Please don't think me rude or ungrateful, Mr. Vincent.'

(He thought he was being very strong and sensible !)

The medium was silent for a moment.

'Doesn't it strike you as odd that I myself was able to get no results that night?' he said presently.

'How? I don't understand.'

'Why, as a rule, I find no difficulty at all in getting some sort of response by automatic handwriting. Are you aware that I could do nothing at all that night?'

Laurie considered it.

'Well,' he said at last, 'this may sound very foolish to you; but granting that I have got unusual gifts that way – they are your own words, Mr. Vincent – if that is so, I don't see why my own concentration of thought, or hypnotic sleep or trance – or whatever it was – might not have been so intense as to—'

'I quite see,' interrupted the other. 'That is, of course, conceivable from your point of view. It had occurred to me that you might think that. . . . Then I take it that your theory is that the subconscious self is sufficient to account for it all – that in this hypnotic sleep, if you care to call it so, you simply uttered what was in your heart, and identified yourself with . . . with your memory of that young girl.'

'I suppose so,' said Laurie shortly.

'And the rapping, loud, continuous, unmistakable?'

'That doesn't seem to me important. I did not actually hear it, you know.'

'Then what you need is some unmistakable sign?'

'Yes . . . but I see perfectly that this is impossible. Whatever I said in my sleep, either I can't identify it as true, in which case it is worthless as evidence, or I can identify it, because I already know it, and in that case it is worthless again.'

The medium smiled, half closing his eyes.

'You must think us very childish, Mr. Baxter,' he said.

He sat up a little in his chair; then, putting his hand into his breast pocket, drew out a note-book, holding it still closed on his knee.

'May I ask you a rather painful question?' he said gently.

Laurie nodded. He felt so secure.

'Would you kindly tell me – first, whether you have seen the grave of this young girl since you left the country; secondly, whether anyone happens to have mentioned it to you?'

Laurie swallowed in his throat.

'Certainly no one has mentioned it to me. And I have not seen it since I left the country.'

'How long ago was that?'

'That was . . . about September the twenty-seventh.'

'Thank you! . . .' (He opened the note-book and turned the pages a moment or two.) 'And will you listen to this, Mr.

Baxter? – "'Tell Laurie that the ground has sunk a little above my grave; and that cracks are showing at the sides.'"

'What is that book?' said the boy hoarsely.

The medium closed it and returned it to his pocket.

'That book, Mr. Baxter, contains a few extracts from some of the things you said during your trance. The sentence I have read is one of them, an answer given to a demand made by me that the control should give some unmistakable proof of her identity. She . . . you hesitated some time before giving that answer.'

'Who took the notes?'

'Mrs. Stapleton. You can see the originals if you wish. I thought it might distress you to know that such notes had been taken; but I have had to risk that. We must not lose you, Mr. Baxter.'

Laurie sat, dumb and bewildered.

'Now all you have to do,' continued the medium serenely, 'is to find out whether what has been said is correct or not. If it is not correct, there will be an end of the matter, if you choose. But if it is correct—'

'Stop; let me think!' cried Laurie.

He was back again in the confusion from which he thought he had escaped. Here was a definite test, offered at least in good faith – just such a test as had been lacking before; and he had no doubt whatever that it would be borne out by facts. And if it were – was there any conceivable hypothesis that would explain it except the one offered so confidently by this grave, dignified man who sat and looked at him with something of interested compassion in his heavy eyes? Coincidence? It was absurd. Certainly graves did sink, sometimes – but . . . Thought-transference from someone who noticed the grave? . . . But why that particular thought, so vivid, concise, and pointed? . . .

If it were true? . . .

He looked hopelessly at the man, who sat smoking quietly and waiting.

And then again another thought, previously ignored, pierced him like a sword. If it were true; if Amy herself, poor pretty Amy, had indeed been there, were indeed near him now, hammering and crying out like a child shut out at night, against his own sceptical heart . . . if it were indeed true that during those two hours she had had her heart's

81

desire, and had been one with his very soul, in a manner to which no earthly union could aspire . . . how had he treated her? Even at this thought a shudder of repulsion ran through him. . . . It was unnatural, detestable . . . yet how sweet ! . . . What did the Church say of such things? . . . But what if religion were wrong, and this indeed were the satiety of the higher nature of which marriage was but the material expression? . . .

The thoughts flew swifter than clouds as he sat there, bewildering, torturing, beckoning. He made a violent effort. He must be sane, and face things.

'Mr. Vincent,' he cried.

The kindly face turned to him again.

'Mr. Vincent . . .'

'Hush, I quite understand,' said the fatherly voice. 'It is a shock, I know; but Truth is a little shocking sometimes. Wait. I perfectly understand that you must have time. You must think it all over, and verify this. You must not commit yourself. But I think you had better have my address. The ladies are a little too emotional, are they not? I expect you would sooner come to see me without them.'

He laid his card on the little tea-table and stood up.

'Good-night, Mr. Baxter.'

Laurie took his hand, and looked for a moment into the kind eyes. Then the man was gone.

2

That was a little while ago, now, and Laurie sitting over breakfast had had time to think it out, and by an act of sustained will to suspend his judgment.

He had come back again to the state I have described – to nervous interest – no more than that. The terror seemed gone, and certainly the scepticism seemed gone too. Now he had to face Maggie and his mother, and to see the grave. . . .

Somehow he had become more accustomed to the idea that there might be real and solid truth under it all, and familiarity had bred ease. Yet there was nervousness there too at the thought of going home. There were moods in which, sitting or walking alone, he passionately desired it all to be true; other moods in which he was acquiescent; but in both there was a faint discomfort in the thought of meeting Maggie, and a certain instinct of propitiation towards her. Maggie had begun to stand for him as a kind of embodiment of a view of life which was sane, wholesome, and curiously attractive; there was a largeness about her, a strength, a sense of fresh air that was delightful. It was that kind of thing, he thought, that had attracted him to her during this past summer. The image of Amy, on the other hand, more than ever now since those recent associations, stood for something quite contrary – certainly for attractiveness, but of a feverish and vivid kind, extraordinarily unlike the other. To express it in terms of time, he thought of Maggie in the morning, and of Amy in the evening, particularly after dinner. Maggie was cool and sunny; Amy suited better the evening fever and artificial light.

And now Maggie had to be faced.

First he reflected that he had not breathed a hint, either to her or his mother, as to what had passed. They both would believe that he had dropped all this. There would then be no arguing, that at least was a comfort. But there was a curious sense of isolation and division between him and the girl.

Yet, after all, he asked himself indignantly, what affair was it of hers? She was not his confessor; she was just a convent-bred girl who couldn't understand. He would be aloof and polite. That was the attitude. And he would manage his own affairs.

He drew a few brisk draughts of smoke from his pipe and stood up. That was settled.

It was in this determined mood then that he stepped out on to the platform at the close of this wintry day, and saw Maggie, radiant in furs, waiting for him, with her back to the orange sunset.

These two did not kiss one another. It was thought better not. But he took her hand with a pleasant sense of welcome and home-coming.

'Auntie's in the brougham,' she said. 'There's lots of room for the luggage on the top. . . . Oh! Laurie, how jolly this is !'

It was a pleasant two-mile drive that they had. Laurie sat with his back to the horses. His mother patted his knee once or twice under the fur rug, and looked at him with benevolent pleasure. It seemed at first a very delightful home-coming. Mrs. Baxter asked after Mr. Morton, Laurie's coach, with proper deference.

But places have as strong a power of retaining associations as persons, and even as they turned down into the hamlet Laurie was aware that this was particularly true just now. He carefully did not glance out at Mr. Nugent's shop, but it was of no use. The whole place was as full to him of the memory of Amy – and more than the memory, it seemed – as if she was still alive. They drew up at the very gate where he had whispered her name; the end of the yew walk, where he had sat on a certain night, showed beyond the house; and half a mile behind lay the meadows, darkling now, where he had first met her face to face in the sunset, and the sluice of the stream where they had stood together silent. And all was like a landscape seen through coloured paper by a child, it was of the uniform tint of death and sorrow.

Laurie was rather quiet all that evening. His mother noticed it, and it produced a remark from her that for an instant brought his heart into his mouth.

'You look a little peaked, dearest,' she said, as she took her bedroom candlestick from him. 'You haven't been thinking any more about that Spiritualism?'

He handed a candlestick to Maggie, avoiding her eyes.

'Oh, for a bit,' he said lightly, 'but I haven't touched the thing for over two months.'

He said it so well that even Maggie was reassured. She had just hesitated for a fraction of a second to hear his answer, and she went to bed well content.

Her contentment was even deeper next morning when Laurie, calling to her through the cheerful frosty air, made her stop at the turning to the village on her way to church.

'I'm coming,' he said virtuously; 'I haven't been on a weekday for ages.'

They talked of this and that for the half-mile before them. At the church door she hesitated again.

'Laurie, I wish you'd come to the Protestant churchyard with me for a moment afterwards, will you?'

He paled so suddenly that she was startled.

'Why?' he said shortly.

'I want you to see something.'

He looked at her still for an instant with an incomprehensible expression. Then he nodded with set lips.

When she came out he was waiting for her. She determined to say something of regret.

'Laurie, I'm dreadfully sorry if I shouldn't have said that.... I was stupid.... But perhaps—'

'What is it you want me to see?' he said without the faintest expression in his voice.

'Just some flowers,' she said. 'You don't mind, do you?'

She saw him trembling a little.

'Was that all?'

'Why yes.... What else could it be?'

They went on a few steps without another word. At the church gate he spoke again.

'It's awfully good of you, Maggie ... I ... I'm rather upset still, you know; that's all.'

He hurried, a little in front of her, over the frosty grass beyond the church; and she saw him looking at the grave very earnestly as she came up. He said nothing for a moment.

'I'm afraid the monument's rather ... rather awful.... Do you like the flowers, Laurie?'

She was noticing that the chrysanthemums were a little blackened by the frost; and hardly attended to the fact that he did not answer.

'Do you like the flowers?' she said again presently.

He started from his prolonged stare downwards.

'Oh yes, yes,' he said; 'they're ... they're lovely.... Maggie, the grave's all right, isn't it : the mound, I mean?'

At first she hardly understood.

'Oh yes ... what do you mean?'

He sighed, whether in relief or not she did not know.

'Only ... only I have heard of mounds sinking sometimes, or cracking at the sides. But this one—'

'Oh yes,' interrupted the girl. 'But this was very bad yesterday.... What's the matter, Laurie?'

He had turned his face with some suddenness, and there was in it a look of such terror that she herself was frightened.

'What were you saying, Maggie?'

'It was nothing of any importance,' said the girl hurriedly. 'It wasn't in the least disfigured, if that—'

'Maggie, will you please tell me exactly in what condition this grave was yesterday? When was it put right?'

'I ... I noticed it when I brought the chrysanthemums up

yesterday morning. The ground was sunk a little, and cracks were showing at the sides. I told the sexton to put it right. He seems to have done it. . . . Laurie, why do you look like that?'

He was staring at her with an expression that might have meant anything. She would not have been surprised if he had burst into a fit of laughter. It was horrible and unnatural.

'Laurie! Laurie! Don't look like that!'

He turned suddenly away and left her. She hurried after him.

On the way to the house he told her the whole story from beginning to end.

3

The two were sitting together in the little smoking-room at the back of the house on the last night of Laurie's holidays. He was to go back to town next morning.

Maggie had passed a thoroughly miserable week. She had had to keep her promise not to tell Mrs. Baxter – not that that lady would have been of much service, but the very telling would be a relief – and things really were not serious enough to justify her telling Father Mahon.

To her the misery lay, not in any belief she had that the spiritualistic claim was true, but that the boy could be so horribly excited by it. She had gone over the arguments again and again with him, approving heartily of his suggestions as to the earlier part of the story, and suggesting herself what seemed to her the most sensible explanation of the final detail. Graves did sink, she said, in two cases out of three, and Laurie was as aware of that as herself. Why in the world should not this then be attributed to the same subconscious mind as that which, in the hypnotic sleep – or whatever it was – had given voice to the rest of his imaginations? Laurie had shaken his head. Now they were at it once more. Mrs. Baxter had gone to bed half an hour before.

'It's too wickedly grotesque,' she said indignantly. 'You can't seriously believe that poor Amy's soul entered into your mind for an hour and a half in Lady Laura's drawing-room. Why, what's purgatory, then, or heaven? It's so utterly and ridiculously impossible that I can't speak of it with patience.'

Laurie smiled at her rather wearily and contemptuously.

'The point,' he said, 'is this : Which is the simplest hypothesis? You and I both believe that the soul is somewhere; and it's natural, isn't it, that she should want – oh ! dash it all ! Maggie, I think you should remember that she was in love with me – as well as I with her,' he added.

Maggie made a tiny mental note.

'I don't deny for an instant that it's a very odd story,' she said. 'But this kind of explanation is just – oh, I can't speak of it. You allowed yourself that up to this last thing you didn't really believe it; and now because of this coincidence the whole thing's turned upside down. Laurie, I wish you'd be reasonable.'

Laurie glanced at her.

She was sitting with her back to the curtained and shuttered window, beyond which lay the yew-walk; and the lamplight from the tall stand fell full upon her. She was dressed in some rich darkish material, her breast veiled in filmy white stuff, and her round, strong arms lay, bare to the elbow, along the arms of her chair. She was a very pleasant wholesome sight. But her face was troubled, and her great serene eyes were not so serene as usual. He was astonished at the persistence with which she attacked him. Her whole personality seemed thrown into her eyes and gestures and quick words.

'Maggie,' he said, 'please listen. I've told you again and again that I'm not actually convinced. What you say is just conceivably possible. But it doesn't seem to me to be the most natural explanation. The most natural seems to me to be what I have said; and you're quite right in saying that it's this last thing that has made the difference. It's exactly like the grain that turns the whole bottle into solid salt. It needed that. . . . But, as I've said, I can't be actually and finally convinced until I've seen more. I'm going to see more. I wrote to Mr. Vincent this morning.'

'You did?' cried the girl.

'Don't be silly, please. . . . Yes, I did. I told him I'd be at his service when I came back to London. Not to have done that would have been cowardly and absurd. I owe him that.'

'Laurie, I wish you wouldn't,' said the girl pleadingly.

He sat up a little, disturbed by this very unusual air of hers.

'But if it's all such nonsense,' he said, 'what's there to be afraid of?'

'It's – it's morbid,' said Maggie, 'morbid and horrible. Of course it's nonsense; but it's – it's wicked nonsense.'

Laurie flushed a little.

'You're polite,' he said.

'I'm sorry,' she said penitently. 'But you know, really—'

The boy suddenly blazed up a little.

'You seem to think I've got no heart,' he cried. 'Suppose it was true – suppose really and truly Amy was here, and—'

A sudden clear sharp sound like the crack of a whip sounded from the corner of the room. Even Maggie started and glanced at the boy. He was dead white on the instant; his lips were trembling.

'What was that?' he whispered sharp and loud.

'Just the woodwork,' she said tranquilly; 'the thaw has set in to-night.'

Laurie looked at her; his lips still moved nervously.

'But – but—' he began.

'Dear boy, don't you see the state of nerves—'

Again came the little sharp crack, and she stopped. For an instant she was disturbed; certain possibilities opened before her, and she regarded them. Then she crushed them down, impatiently and half timorously. She stood up abruptly.

'I'm going to bed,' she said. 'This is too ridiculous—'

'No, no; don't leave me. . . . Maggie. . . . I don't like it.'

She sat down again, wondering at his childishness, and yet conscious that her own nerves, too, were ever so slightly on edge. She would not look at him, for fear that the meeting of eyes might hint at more than she meant. She threw her head back on her chair and remained looking at the ceiling. But to think that the souls of the dead – ah, how repulsive!

Outside the night was very still.

The hard frost had kept the world iron-bound in a sprinkle of snow during the last two or three days, but this afternoon the thaw had begun. Twice during dinner there had come the thud of masses of snow falling from the roof on to the lawn outside, and the clear sparkle of the candles had seemed a little dim and hazy. 'It would be a comfort to get at the garden again,' she had reflected.

And now that the two sat here in the windless silence the thaw became more apparent every instant. The silence was profound, and the little noises of the night outside, the drip from the eaves slow and deliberate, the rustle of released leaves, and even the gentle thud on the lawn from the yew branches – all these helped to emphasise the stillness. It was not like the murmur of day; it was rather like the gnawing of a mouse in the wainscot of some death-chamber.

It requires almost superhumanly strong nerves to sit at night, after a conversation of this kind, opposite an apparently reasonable person who is white and twitching with terror, even though one resolutely refrains from looking at him, without being slightly affected. One may argue with oneself to any extent, tap one's foot cheerfully on the floor, fill the mind most painstakingly with normal thoughts; yet it is something of a conflict, however victorious one may be.

Even Maggie herself became aware of this.

It was not that now for one single moment she allowed that the two little sudden noises in the room could possibly proceed from any cause whatever except that which she had stated – the relaxation of stiffened wood under the influence of the thaw. Nor had all Laurie's arguments prevailed to shake in the smallest degree her resolute conviction that there was nothing whatever preternatural in his certainly queer story.

Yet, as she sat there in the lamplight, with Laurie speechless before her, and the great curtained window behind, she became conscious of an uneasiness that she could not entirely repel. It was just physical, she said; it was the result of the change of weather; or, at the most, it was the silence that had now fallen and the proximity of a terrified boy.

She looked across at him again.

He was lying back in the old green arm-chair, his eyes rather shadowed from the lamp overhead, quite still and quiet, his hands still clasping the lion-bosses of his chair-arms. Beside him, on the little table, lay his still smouldering cigarette-end in the silver tray. . . .

Maggie suddenly sprang to her feet, slipped round the table, and caught him by the arm.

'Laurie, Laurie, wake up. . . . What's the matter?'

A long shudder passed through him. He sat up, with a bewildered look.

'Eh? What is it?' he said. 'Was I asleep?'

He rubbed his hands over his eyes and looked round.

'What is it, Maggie? Was I asleep?'

(Was the boy acting? Surely it was good acting!)

Maggie threw herself down on her knees by the chair.

'Laurie! Laurie! I beg you not to go to see Mr. Vincent. It's bad for you. . . . I do wish you wouldn't.'

He still blinked at her a moment.

'I don't understand. What do you mean, Maggie?'

She stood up, ashamed of her impulsiveness.

'Only I wish you wouldn't go and see that man. Laurie, please don't.'

He stood up too, stretching. Every sign of nervousness seemed gone.

'Not see Mr. Vincent? Nonsense; of course I shall. You don't understand, Maggie.'

CHAPTER SEVEN

I

'What a relief,' sighed Mrs. Stapleton. 'I thought we had lost him.'

The three were sitting once again in Lady Laura's drawing-room soon after lunch. Mr. Vincent had just looked in with Laurie's note to give the news. It was a heavy fog outside, woolly in texture and orange in colour, and the tall windows seemed opaque in the lamplight; the room, by contrast, appeared a safe and pleasant refuge from the reek and stinging vapour of the street.

Mrs. Stapleton had been lunching with her friend. The Colonel had returned for Christmas, so his wife's duties had recalled her for the present from those spiritual conversations which she had enjoyed in the autumn. It was such a refreshment, she had said with a patient smile, to slip away sometimes into the purer atmosphere.

Mr. Vincent folded the letter and restored it to his pocket.

'We must be careful with him,' he said. 'He is extraordinarily sensitive. I almost wish he were not so developed. Temperaments like his are apt to be thrown off their balance.'

Lady Laura was silent.

For herself she was not perfectly happy. She had lately come across one or two rather deplorable cases. A very promising girl, daughter of a publican in the suburbs, had developed the same kind of powers, and the end of it all had been rather a dreadful scene in Baker Street. She was now in an asylum. A friend of her own, too, had lately taken to lecturing against Christianity in rather painful terms. Lady Laura wondered why people could not be as well balanced as herself.

'I think he had better not come to the public *séances* at present,' went on the medium. 'That, no doubt, will come later; but I was going to ask a great favour from you, Lady Laura.'

She looked up.

'That bother about the rooms is not yet settled, and the Sunday *séances* will have to cease for the present. I wonder if you would let us come here, just a few of us only, for three or four Sundays, at any rate.'

She brightened up.

'Why, it would be the greatest pleasure,' she said. 'But what about the cabinet?'

'If necessary, I would send one across. Will you allow me to make arrangements?'

Mrs. Stapleton beamed.

'What a privilege!' she said. 'Dearest, I quite envy you. I am afraid dear Tom would never consent—'

'There are just one or two things on my mind,' went on Mr. Vincent so pleasantly that the interruption seemed almost a compliment, 'and the first is this. I want him to see for himself. Of course, for ourselves, his trance is the point; but hardly for him. He is tremendously impressed; I can see that; though he pretends not to be. But I should like him to see something unmistakable as soon as possible. We must prevent his going into trance, if possible. . . . And the next thing is his religion.'

'Catholics are supposed not to come,' observed Mrs. Stapleton.

'Just so. . . . Mr. Baxter is a convert, isn't he? . . . I thought so.'

He mused for a moment or two.

The ladies had never seen him so interested in an amateur. Usually his manner was remarkable for its detachment and severe assurance; but it seemed that this case excited even him. Lady Laura was filled again with sudden compunction.

'Mr. Vincent,' she said, 'do you really think there is no danger for this boy?'

He glanced up at her.

'There is always danger,' he said. 'We know that well enough. We can but take precautions. But pioneers always have to risk something.'

She was not reassured.

'But I mean special danger. He is extraordinarily sensitive, you know. There was that girl from Surbiton. . . .'

92

'Oh! she was exceptionally hysterical. Mr. Baxter's not like that. I do not see that he runs any greater risk than we run ourselves.'

'You are sure of that?'

He smiled deprecatingly.

'I am sure of nothing,' he said. 'But if you feel you would sooner not—'

Mrs. Stapleton rustled excitedly, and Lady Laura grabbed at her retreating opportunity.

'No, no,' she cried. 'I didn't mean that for one moment. Please, please come here. I only wondered whether there was any particular precaution—'

'I will think about it,' said the medium. 'But I am sure we must be careful not to shock him. Of course, we don't all take the same view about religion; but we can leave that for the present. The point is that Mr. Baxter should, if possible, see something unmistakable. The rest can take care of itself. . . . Then, if you consent, Lady Laura, we might have a little sitting here next Sunday night. Would nine o'clock suit you?'

He glanced at the two ladies.

'That will do very well,' said the mistress of the house.

'And, about preparations—'

'I will look in on Saturday afternoon. Is there anyone particular you think of asking?'

'Mr. Jamieson came to see me again a few days ago,' suggested Lady Laura tentatively.

'That will do very well. Then we three and those two. That will be quite enough for the present.'

He stood up a big, dominating figure – a reassuring man to look at, with his kindly face, his bushy, square beard, and his appearance of physical strength. Lady Laura sat vaguely comforted.

'And about my notes,' asked Maud Stapleton.

'I think they will not be necessary. . . . Good-day. . . . Saturday afternoon.'

The two sat on silently for a minute or two after he was gone.

'What is the matter, dearest?'

Lady Laura's little anxious face did not move. She was staring thoughtfully at the fire. Mrs. Stapleton laid a sympathetic hand on the other's knee.

'Dearest—' she began.

'No; it is nothing, darling,' said Lady Laura.

Meanwhile the medium was picking his way through the foggy streets. Figures loomed up, sudden and enormous, and vanished again. Smoky flares of flame shone like spots of painted fire, bright and unpenetrating, from windows overhead; and sounds came to him through the woolly atmosphere, dulled and sonorous. It would, so to speak, have been a suitably dramatic setting for his thoughts if he had been thinking in character, vaguely suggestive of presences and hints and peeps into the unknown.

But he was a very practical man. His spiritualistic faith was a reality to him, as unexciting as Christianity to the normal Christian; he entertained no manner of doubt as to its truth.

Beyond all the fraud, the self-deception, the amazing feats of the sub-conscious self, there remained certain facts beyond doubting – facts which required, he believed, an objective explanation, which none but the spiritualistic thesis offered. He had far more evidence, he considered sincerely enough, for his spiritualism than most Christians for their Christianity.

He had no very definite theory as to the spiritual world beyond thinking that it was rather like this world. For him it was peopled with individualities of various characters and temperaments, of various grades and achievements; and of these a certain number had the power of communicating under great difficulties with persons on this side who were capable of receiving such communications. That there were dangers connected with this process, he was well aware; he had seen often enough the moral sense vanish and the mental powers decay. But these were to him no more than the honourable wounds to which all who struggle are liable. The point for him was that here lay the one certain means of getting into touch with reality. Certainly that reality was sometimes of a disconcerting nature, and seldom of an illuminating one; he hated, as much as anyone, the tambourine business, except so far as it was essential; and he deplored the fact that, as he believed, it was often the most degraded and the least satisfactory of the inhabitants of the other world that most easily got into touch with the inhabitants of this. Yet, for him, the main tenets of spiritualism were as the

94

bones of the universe; it was the only religion which seemed to him in the least worthy of serious attention.

He had not practised as a medium for longer than ten or a dozen years. He had discovered, by chance as he thought, that he possessed mediumistic powers in an unusual degree, and had begun then to take up the life as a profession. He had suffered, so far as he was aware, no ill effects from this life, though he had seen others suffer; and, as his fame grew, his income grew with it.

It is necessary, then, to understand that he was not a conscious charlatan; he loathed mechanical tricks such as he occasionally came across; he was perfectly and serenely convinced that the powers which he possessed were genuine, and that the personages he seemed to come across in his mediumistic efforts were what they professed to be; that they were not hallucinatory, that they were not the products of fraud, that they were not necessarily evil. He regarded this religion as he regarded science; both were progressive, both liable to error, both capable of abuse. Yet as a scientist did not shrink from experiment for fear of risk, neither must the spiritualist.

As he picked his way to his lodgings on the north of the park, he was thinking about Laurie Baxter. That this boy possessed in an unusual degree what he would have called 'occult powers' was very evident to him. That these powers involved a certain risk was evident too. He proposed, therefore, to take all reasonable precautions. All the catastrophes he had witnessed in the past were due, he thought, to a too rapid development of those powers, or to inexperience. He determined, therefore, to go slowly.

First, the boy must be convinced; next, he must be attached to the cause; thirdly, his religion must be knocked out of him; fourthly, he must be trained and developed. But for the present he must not be allowed to go into trance if it could be prevented. It was plain, he thought, that Laurie had a very strong 'affinity,' as he would have said, with the disembodied spirit of a certain 'Amy Nugent.' His communication with her had been of a very startling nature in its rapidity and perfection. Real progress might be made, then, through this channel.

(Yes; I am aware that this sounds grotesque nonsense.)

95

Laurie came back to town in a condition of interior quietness that rather astonished him. He had said to Maggie that he was not convinced; and that was true so far as he knew. Intellectually, the spiritualistic theory was at present only the hypothesis that seemed the most reasonable; yet morally he was as convinced of its truth as of anything in the world. And this showed itself by the quietness in which he found his soul plunged.

Moral conviction – that conviction on which a man acts – does not always coincide with the intellectual process. Occasionally it outruns it; occasionally lags behind; and the first sign of its arrival is the cessation of strain. The intellect may still be busy, arranging, sorting, and classifying; but the thing itself is done, and the soul leans back.

A certain amount of excitement made itself felt when he found Mr. Vincent's letter waiting for his arrival to congratulate him on his decision, and to beg him to be at Queen's Gate not later than half-past eight o'clock on the following Sunday; but it was not more than momentary. He knew the thing to be inevitably true now; the time and place at which it manifested itself was not supremely important.

Yes, he wrote in answer; he would certainly keep the appointment suggested.

He dined out at a restaurant, returned to his rooms, and sat down to arrange his ideas.

These, to be frank, were not very many, nor very profound.

He had already, in the days that had passed since his shock, no lighter because expected, when he had learned from Maggie that the test was fulfilled, and that a fact known to no one present, not even himself, in Queen's Gate, had been communicated through his lips – since that time the idea had become familiar that the veil between this world and the next was a very thin one. After all, a large number of persons in the world believe that, as it is, and they are not, in consequence, in a continuous state of exaltation. Laurie had learned this, he thought, experimentally. Very well, then, that was so; there was no more to be said.

Next, the excitement of the thought of communicating with Amy in particular had to a large extent burned itself out. It was nearly four months since her death; and in his very heart of hearts he was beginning to be aware that she had not been so entirely his twin-soul as he would still have maintained. He had reflected a little, in the meantime, upon the grocer's shop, the dissenting tea-parties, the odour of cheeses. Certainly these things could not destroy an 'affinity' if the affinity were robust; but it would need to be. . . .

He was still very tender towards the thought of her; she had gained too, inevitably, by dying, a dignity she had lacked while living, and it might well be that intercourse with her in the manner proposed would be an extraordinarily sweet experience. But he was no longer excited – passionately and overwhelmingly – by the prospect. It would be delightful? Yes. But . . .

Then Laurie began to look at his religion and at that view he stopped dead. He had no ideas at all on the subject; he had not a notion where he stood. All he knew was that it had become uninteresting. True? Oh, yes, he supposed so. He retained it still as many retain faith in the supernatural – a reserve that could be drawn upon in extremities.

He had not yet missed hearing Mass on Sunday; in fact, he proposed to go even next Sunday. 'A man must have a religion,' he said to himself; and, intellectually, there was at present no other possible religion for him except the Catholic. Yet as he looked into the future he was doubtful.

He drew himself up in his chair and began to fill his pipe. . . . In three days he would be seated in a room with three or four persons, he supposed. Of these two – and certainly the two strongest characters – had no religion except that supplied by spiritualism, and he had read enough to know this was, at any rate in the long run, non-Christian. And these three or four persons, moreover, believed with their whole hearts that they were in relations with the invisible world, far more evident and sensible than those claimed by any other believers on the face of the earth. And, after all, Laurie reflected, there seemed to be justice in their claim. He would be seated in that room, he repeated to himself, and it might be that before he left it he would have seen with his own eyes, and possibly handled, living persons who had, in the common phrase, 'died' and been buried. Almost certainly, at the very least, he would have received from such intelligences unmistakable messages. . . .

He was astonished that he was not more excited. He asked himself again whether he really believed it; he compared his belief in it with his belief in the existence of New Zealand. Yes, if that were belief, he had it. . . . But the excitement of doubt was gone, as no doubt it was gone when New Zealand became a geographical expression.

He was astonished at its naturalness – at the extraordinary manner in which, when once the evidence had been seen and the point of view grasped, the whole thing fell into place. It seemed to him as if he must have known it all his life; yet, he knew, six months ago he had hardly known more than that there were upon the face of the earth persons called Spiritualists, who believed, or pretended to believe, what he then was quite sure was fantastic nonsense. And now he was, to all intents, one of them. . . .

He was being drawn forward, it seemed, by a process as inevitable as that of spring or autumn; and, once he had yielded to it, the conflict and the excitement were over. Certainly this made very few demands. Christianity said that those were blessed who had not seen and yet believed; Spiritualism said that the only reasonable belief was that which followed seeing.

So then Laurie sat and meditated.

Once or twice that evening he looked round him tranquilly without a touch of that terror that had seized him in the smoking-room at home.

If all this were true – and he repeated to himself that he knew it was true – these presences were about him now, why was it that he was no longer frightened?

He looked carefully into the dark corner behind him, beyond the low jutting bookshelf, in the angle between the curtained windows, at his piano, glossy and mysterious in the gloom, at the door half-open into his bedroom. All was quiet here, shut off from the hum of Fleet Street; circumstances were propitious. Why was he not frightened? . . . Why, what was there to frighten him? These presences were natural and normal; even as a Catholic he believed in them. And if they manifested themselves, what was there to fear in that?

He looked steadily and serenely; and as he looked, like the kindling of a fire, there rose within him a sense of strange exaltation.

'Amy,' he whispered.

But there was no movement or hint.

Laurie smiled a little, wearily. He felt tired; he would sleep a little. He beat out his pipe, crossed his feet before the fire, and closed his eyes.

2

There followed that smooth rush into gulfs of sleep that provides perhaps the most exquisite physical sensation known to man, as the veils fall thicker and softer every instant, and the consciousness gathers itself inwards from hands and feet and limbs, like a dog curling himself up for rest; yet retains itself in continuous being, and is able to regard its own comfort. All this he remembered perfectly half an hour later; but there followed in his memory that inevitable gap in which self loses itself before emerging into the phantom land of dreams, or returning to reality.

But that into which he emerged, he remembered afterwards, was a different realm altogether from that which is usual – from that country of grotesque fancy and jumbled thoughts, of thin shadows of truth and echoes from the common world where most of us find ourselves in sleep.

This dream was as follows :—

He was still in his room, he thought, but no longer in his chair. Instead, he stood in the very centre of the floor, or at least poised somewhere above it, for he could see at a glance, without turning, all that the room contained. He directed his attention – for it was this, rather than sight, through which he perceived – to the piano, the chiffonier, the chairs, the two doors, the curtained windows; and finally, with scarcely even a touch of surprise, to himself still sunk in the chair before the fire. He regarded himself with pleased interest, remembering even in that instant that he had never before seen himself with closed eyes. . . .

All in the room was extraordinarily vivid and clear-cut. It was true that the firelight still wavered and sank again in billows of soft colour about the shadowed walls, but the changing light was no more an interruption to the action of that steady medium through which he perceived than the movement of summer clouds across the full sunlight. It was at that moment that he understood that he was no longer with eyes, but with the faculty of perception to which sight is only analogous – that facility which underlies and is common to all the senses alike.

His reasoning powers, too, at this moment, seemed to have gone from him like a husk. He did not argue or deduce; simply he understood. And, in a flash, **si**multaneous with the whole vision, he perceived that he was behind all the slow processes of the world, by which this is added to that, and a conclusion drawn; by which light travels, and sounds resolve themselves and emotions run their course. He had reached, he thought, the ultimate secret. . . . It was This that lay behind everything.

Now it is impossible to set down, except progressively, all this sum of experiences that occupied for him one interminable instant. Neither did he remember afterwards the order in which they presented themselves; for it seemed to him that there was no order; all was simultaneous.

But he understood plainly by intuition that all was open to him. Space no longer existed for him; nothing, to his perception, separated this from that. He was able, he saw, without stirring from his attitude to see in an instant any place or person towards which he chose to exercise his attention. It seemed a marvellously simple point, this – that space was little more than an illusion; that it was, after all, nothing else but a translation into rather coarse terms of what may be called 'differences'. 'Here' and 'There' were but relative terms; certainly they correspond to facts, but they were not those facts themselves. . . . And since he now stood behind them he saw them on their inner side, as a man standing in the interior of a globe may be said to be equally present to every point upon its surface.

The fascination of the thought was enormous; and, like a child who begins to take notice and to learn the laws of extension and distance, so he began to learn their reverse. He saw, he thought (as he had seen once before, only, this time, without the sense of movement), the interior of the lighted drawing-room at home, and his mother nodding in her chair; he directed his attention to Maggie, and perceived her passing across the landing toward the head of the stairs with a candle in her hand. It was this sight that brought him to a further discovery, to the effect that time also was of very nearly no importance either; for he perceived that by bending his attention upon her he could restrain her, so to speak, in her movement. There she stood, one foot outstretched, the candle flame leaning motionless backward; and he knew too that it was not she who was thus restrained, but that it was the intensity and directness of his thought that fixed, so to say, in terms of eternity, that instant of time. . . .

So it went on; or, rather, so it was with him. He pleased himself by contemplating the London streets outside, the darkness of the garden in some square, the interior of the Oratory where a few figures kneeled – all seen beyond the movements of light and shadow in this clear invisible radiance that was to his perception as common light to common eyes. The world of which he had had experience – for he found himself unable to see that which he had never experienced – lay before his will like a movable map : this or that person or place had but to be desired, and it was present.

And then came the return; and the Horror. . . .

He began in this way.

He understood that he wished to awake, or, rather, to be reunited with the body that lay there in deep sleep before the fire. He observed it for a moment or two, interested and pleased, the face sunk a little on the hand, the feet lightly crossed on the fender. He looked at his own profile, the straight nose, the parted lips through which the breath came evenly. He attempted even to touch the face, wondering with gentle pleasure what would be the result. . . .

Then, suddenly, an impulse came to him to enter the body, and with the impulse the process, it seemed, began.

That process was not unlike that of falling asleep. In an instant perception was gone; the lighted room was gone, and that obedient world which he had contemplated just now. Yet self-consciousness for a while remained; he still had the power of perceiving his own personality, though this dwindled every moment down to that same gulf of nothingness through which he had found his way.

But at the next instant in which consciousness was passing there met him an emotion so fierce and overwhelming that he recoiled in terror back from the body once more and earth-perceptions; and a panic seized him.

It was such a panic as seizes a child who, fearfully courageous, has stolen at night from his room, and turning in half-simulated terror finds the door fast against him, or is aware of a malignant presence come suddenly into being, standing between himself and the safety of his own bed.

On the one side his fear drove him onwards; on the other a Horror faced him. He dared not recoil, for he understood where security lay; he longed, like the child screaming in the dark and beating his hands, to get back to the warmth and safety of bed; yet there stood before him a Presence, or at the least an Emotion of some kind, so hostile, so terrible, that he dared not penetrate it. It was not that an actual restraint lay upon him : he knew, that is, that the door was open; yet it needed a effort of the will of which his paralysis of terror rendered him incapable. . . .

The tension became intolerable.

'Oh God . . . God . . . God . . .' he cried.

And in an instant the threshold was vacated; the swift rush asserted itself, and the space was passed.

Laurie sat up abruptly in his chair.

4

Mr. Vincent was beginning to think about going to bed. He had come in an hour before, had written half a dozen letters, and was smoking peacefully before the fire.

His rooms were not remarkable in any way, except for half a dozen objects standing on the second shelf of his bookcase, and the selection of literature ranged below them. For the rest, all was commonplace enough; a mahogany knee-hole table, a couple of easy chairs, much worn, and a long, extremely comfortable sofa standing by itself against the wall with evident signs, in its tumbled cushions and rubbed fabric, of continual and frequent use. A second door gave entrance to his bedroom.

He beat out his pipe slowly, yawned, and stood up.

It was at this instant that he heard the sudden tingle of the electric bell in the lobby outside, and, wondering at the interruption at this hour, went quickly out and opened the door on the stairs.

'Mr Baxter ! Come in, come in; I'm delighted to see you.'

Laurie came in without a word, went straight up to the fire-place, and faced about.

'I'm not going to apologise,' he said, 'for coming at this time. You told me to come and see you at any time, and I've taken you at your word.'

The young man had an odd embarrassed manner, thought the other; an air of having come in spite of uneasiness; he was almost shame-faced.

The medium impelled him gently into a chair.

'First a cigarette,' he said; 'next a little whisky; and then I shall be delighted to listen. . . . No; please do as I say.'

Laurie permitted himself to be managed; there was a strong, almost paternal air in the other's manner that was difficult to resist. He lit his cigarette, he sipped his whisky; but his movements were nervously quick.

'Well, then . . .' and he interrupted himself. 'What are those things, Mr. Vincent?' (He nodded towards the second shelf in the bookcase.)

Mr. Vincent turned on the hearthrug.

'Those? Oh! those are a few rather elementary instruments for my work.'

He lifted down a crystal ball on a small black polished wooden stand and handed it over.

'You have heard of crystal-gazing? Well, that is the article.'

'Is that crystal?'

'Oh no : common glass. Price three shillings and sixpence.'

Laurie turned it over, letting the shining globe run on to his hand.

'And this is—' he began.

'And this,' said the medium, setting a curious windmill-shaped affair, its sails lined with looking-glass, on the little table by the fire, 'this is a French toy. Very elementary.'

'What's that?'

'Look.'

Mr. Vincent wound a small handle at the back of the windmill to a sound of clockwork, set it down again, and released it. Instantly the sails began to revolve, noiseless and swift, producing the effect of a rapidly flashing circle of light across which span lines, waxing and waning with extra-ordinary speed.

'What the—'

'It's a little machine for inducing sleep. Oh! I haven't used that for months. But it's useful sometimes. The hypnotic subject just stares at that steadily. . . . Why, you're looking dazed yourself, already, Mr. Baxter,' smiled the medium.

He stopped the mechanism and pushed it on one side.

'And what's the other?' asked Laurie, looking again at the shelf.

'Ah!'

The medium, with quite a different air, took down and set before him an object resembling a tiny heart-shaped table on three wheeled legs, perhaps four or five inches across. Through the centre ran a pencil perpendicularly of which the point just touched the table-cloth on which the thing rested. Laurie looked at it, and glanced up.

'Yes, that's Planchette,' said the medium.

'For . . . for automatic writing?'

The other nodded.

'Yes,' he said. 'The experimenter puts his fingers lightly upon that, and there's a sheet of paper beneath. That is all.'

Laurie looked at him, half curiously. Then with a sudden movement he stood up.

'Yes,' he said. 'Thank you. But—'

'Please sit down, Mr. Baxter. . . . I know you haven't come about that kind of thing. Will you kindly tell me what you have come about?'

He, too, sat down, and, without looking at the other, began slowly to fill his pipe again, with his strong capable fingers. Laurie stared at the process, unseeing.

'Just tell me simply,' said the medium again, still without looking at him.

Laurie threw himself back.

'Well, I will,' he said. 'I know it's absurdly childish; but I'm a little frightened. It's about a dream.'

'That's not necessarily childish.'

'It's a dream I had tonight – in my chair after dinner.'

'Well?'

Then Laurie began.

For about ten minutes he talked without ceasing. Mr. Vincent smoked tranquilly, putting what seemed to Laurie quite unimportant questions now and again, and nodding gently from time to time.

'And I'm frightened,' ended Laurie; 'and I want you to tell me what it all means.'

The other drew a long inhalation through his pipe, expelled it, and leaned back.

'Oh, it's comparatively common,' he said; 'common, that is, with people of your temperament, Mr. Baxter – and mine. . . . You tell me that it was prayer that enabled you to get through at the end? That is interesting.'

'But – but – was it more than fancy – more, I mean, than an ordinary dream?'

'Oh, yes; it was objective. It was a real experience.'

'You mean—'

'Mr. Baxter, just listen to me for a minute or two. You can ask any questions you like at the end. First, you are a Catholic, you told me; you believe, that is to say, among other things, that the spiritual world is a real thing, always present more or less. Well, of course, I agree with you; though I do not agree with you altogether as to the geography and – and other details of that world. But you believe, I take it, that the world is continually with us – that this room, so to speak, is a great deal more than that of which our senses tell us; that there are with us, now and always, a multitude of influences, good, bad, and indifferent, really present to our spirits?'

'I suppose so,' said Laurie.

'Now begin again. There are two kinds of dreams. (I am just stating my own belief, Mr. Baxter. You can make what comments you like afterwards.) The one kind of dream is entirely unimportant; it is merely a hash, a *réchauffée*, of our own thoughts, in which little things that we have experienced reappear in a hopeless sort of confusion. It is the kind of dream that we forget altogether, generally, five minutes after waking, if not before. But there is another kind of dream that we do not forget. It leaves as vivid an impression upon us as if it were a waking experience – an actual incident. And that is exactly what it is.'

'I don't understand.'

'Have you ever heard of the subliminal consciousness, Mr. Baxter?'

'No.'

The medium smiled.

'That is fortunate,' he said. 'It's being run to death just now. . . . Well, I'll put in in an untechnical way. There is a part of us (is there not?) that lies below our ordinary waking thoughts – that part of us in which our dreams reside, our habits take shape, our instincts, intuitions, and all the rest, are generated. Well, in ordinary dreams, when we are asleep, it is this part that is active. The pot boils, so to speak, all by itself, uncontrolled by reason. A madman is a man in whom this part is supreme in his waking life as well. Well, it is through this part of us that we communicate with the spiritual world. There are, let us say, two doors in it – that which leads up to our senses, through which come down our waking experiences to be stored up; and – and the other door. . . .'

'Yes?'

The medium hesitated.

'Well,' he said, 'in some natures – yours, for instance, Mr. Baxter – this door opens rather easily. It was through that door that you went, I think, in what you call your "dream". You yourself said it was quite unlike ordinary dreams.'

'Yes.'

'And I am the more sure that this is so, since your experience is exactly that of so many others under the same circumstances.'

Laurie moved uncomfortably in his chair.

'I don't quite understand,' he said sharply. 'You mean it was not a dream?'

'Certainly not. At least, not a dream in the ordinary sense. It was an actual experience.'

'But – but I was asleep.'

'Certainly. That is one of the usual conditions – an almost indispensable condition, in fact. The objective self – I mean the ordinary workaday faculties – was lulled; and your subjective self – call it what you like – but it is your real self, the essential self that survives death – this self, simply went through the inner door, and – saw what was to be seen.'

Laurie looked at him intently. But there was a touch of apprehension in his face, too.

'You mean,' he said slowly, 'that – that all I saw – the limitations of space, and so forth – that these were facts and not fancies?'

'Certainly. Doesn't your theology hint at something of the kind?'

Laurie was silent. He had no idea of what his theology told him on the point.

'But why should I – I of all people – have such an experience?' he asked suddenly.

The medium smiled.

'Who can tell that?' he said. 'Why should one man be an artist, and another not? It is a matter of temperament. You see you've begun to develop that temperament at last; and it's a very marked one to begin with. As for—'

Laurie interrupted him.

'Yes, yes,' he said. 'But there's another point. What about that fear I had when I tried to – to awaken?'

There passed over the medium's face a shade of gravity. It was no more than a shade, but it was there. He reached out rather quickly for his pipe which he had laid aside, and blew through it carefully before answering.

'That?' he said, with what seemed to the boy an affected carelessness, 'That? Oh, that's a common experience. Don't think about that too much, Mr. Baxter. It's never very healthy—'

'I am sorry,' said Laurie deliberately. 'But I must ask you to tell me what you think. I must know what I'm doing.'

The medium filled his pipe again. Twice he began to speak, and checked himself; and in the long silence Laurie felt his fears gather upon him tenfold.

'Please tell me at once, Mr. Vincent,' he said. 'Unless I know everything that is to be known, I will not go another step along this road. I really mean that.'

The medium paused in his pipe-filling.

'And what if I do tell you?' he said in his slow virile voice. 'Are you sure you will not be turned back?'

'If it is a well-known danger, and can be avoided with prudence, I certainly shall not turn back.'

'Very well, Mr. Baxter, I will take you at your word. . . . Have you ever heard the phrase, "The Watcher on the Threshold"?'

Laurie shook his head.

'No,' he said. 'At least I don't think so.'

'Well,' said the medium quietly, 'that is what we call the

Fear you spoke of. . . . No; don't interrupt. I'll tell you all we know. It's not very much.'

He paused again, stretched his hand for the matches, and took one out. Laurie watched him as if fascinated by the action.

Outside roared Oxford Street in one long rolling sound as of the sea; but within here was that quiet retired silence which the boy had noticed before in the same company. Was that fancy, too, he wondered? . . .

The medium lit his pipe and leaned back.

'I'll tell you all we know,' he said again quietly. 'It's not very much. Really the phrase I used just now sums it up pretty well. We who have tried to get beyond this world of sense have become aware of certain facts of which the world generally knows nothing at all. One of these facts is that the door between this life and the other is guarded by a certain being of whom we know really nothing at all, except this his presence causes the most appalling fear in those who experience it. He is set there – God only knows why – and his main business seems to be to restrain, if possible, from re-entering the body those who have left it. Just occasionally his presence is perceived by those on this side, but not often. But I have been present at death-beds where he has been seen—'

'Seen?'

'Oh! yes. Seen by the dying person. It is usually only a glimpse; it might be said to be a mistake. For myself I believe that that appalling terror that now and then shows itself, even in people who do not fear death itself, who are perfectly resigned, who have nothing on their conscience, – well, personally, I believe the fear comes from a sight of this – this Personage.'

Laurie licked his dry lips. He told himself that he did not believe one word of it.

'And . . . and he is evil?' he asked.

The other shrugged his shoulders.

'Isn't that a relative term?' he said. 'From one point of view, certainly; but not necessarily from all.'

'And . . . and what's the good of it?'

The medium smiled a little.

'That's a question we soon cease to ask. You must remember that we hardly know anything at all yet. But one thing seems more and more certain the more we investigate, and that is that our point of view is not the only one, nor even the principal one. Christianity, I fancy, says the same thing, does it not? The "glory of God", whatever that may be, comes before even the "salvation of souls".'

Laurie wrenched his attention once more to a focus.

'Then I was in danger?' he said.

'Certainly. We are always in danger—'

'You mean, if I hadn't prayed—'

'Ah! that is another question. . . . But, in short, if you hadn't succeeded in getting past – well, you'd have failed.'

Again there fell a silence.

It seemed to Laurie as if his world was falling about him. Yet he was far from sure whether it were not all an illusion. But the extreme quietness and confidence of the man in enunciating these startling theories had their effect. It was practically impossible for the boy to sit here, still nervous from his experience, and hear, unmoved, this apparently reasonable and connected account of things that were certainly incomprehensible on any other hypothesis. His remembrance of the very startling uniqueness of his dream was still vivid. . . . Surely it all fitted in . . . yet . . .

'But there is one thing,' broke in the medium's quiet voice. 'Should you ever experience this kind of thing again, I should recommend you not to pray. Just exercise your own individuality; assert yourself; don't lean on another. You are quite strong enough.'

'You mean—'

'I mean exactly what I say. What is called Prayer is really an imaginative concession to weakness. Take the short cut, rather. Assert your own – your own individuality.'

Laurie changed his attitude. He uncrossed his feet and sat up a little.

'Oh! pray if you want to,' said the medium. 'But you must remember, Mr. Baxter, that you are quite an exceptional person. I assure you that you have no conception of your own powers. I must say that I hope you will take the strong line.' (He paused.) 'These *séances*, for instance. Now that you know a little more of the dangers, are you going to turn back?'

His overhung kindly eyes looked out keenly for an instant at the boy's restless face.

'I don't know,' said Laurie; 'I must think....'

He got up.

'Look here, Mr. Vincent,' he said, 'it seems to me you're extraordinarily – er – extraordinarily plausible. But I'm even now not quite sure whether I'm not going mad. It's like a perfectly mad dream – all these things one on the top of the other.'

He paused, looking sharply at the elder man, and away again.

'Yes?'

Laurie began to finger a pencil that lay on the chimney-shelf.

'You see what I mean, don't you?' he said. 'I'm not disputing – er – your point of view, nor your sincerity. But I do wish you would give me another proof or two.'

'You haven't had enough?'

'Oh! I suppose I have – if I were reasonable. But, you know, it all seems to me as if you suddenly demonstrated to me that twice two made five.'

'But then, surely no proof—'

'Yes; I know. I quite see that. Yet I want one – something quite absolutely ordinary. If you can do all these things – spirits and all the rest – can't you do something ever so much simpler, that's beyond mistake?'

'Oh, I daresay. But wouldn't you ask yet another after that?'

'I don't know.'

'Or wouldn't you think you'd been hypnotised?'

Laurie shook his head.

'I'm not a fool,' he said.

'Then give me that pencil,' said the medium, suddenly extending his hand.

Laurie stared a moment. Then he handed over the pencil.

On the little table by the arm-chair, a couple of feet from Laurie, stood the whisky apparatus and a box of cigarettes. These the medium, without moving from his chair, lifted off and set on the floor beside him, leaving the woven-glass surface of the table entirely bare. He then laid the pencil gently in the centre – all without a word. Laurie watched him carefully.

'Now kindly do not speak one word or make one movement,' said the man peremptorily. 'Wait! You're perfectly sure you're not hypnotised, or any other nonsense?'

'Certainly not.'

'Just go round the room, look out of the window, poke the fire – anything you like.'

'I'm satisfied,' said the boy.

'Very good. Then kindly watch that pencil.'

The medium leaned a little forward in his chair, bending his eyes steadily upon the little wooden cylinder lying, like any other pencil, on the top of the table. Laurie glanced once at him, then back again. There it lay, common and ordinary.

For at least a minute nothing happened at all, except that from the intentness of the elder man there seemed once more to radiate out that curious air of silence that Laurie was beginning to know so well – that silence that seemed impenetrable to the common sounds of the world and to exist altogether independent of them. Once and again he glanced round at the ordinary-looked room, the curtained windows, the dull furniture; and the second time he looked back at the pencil he was almost certain that some movement had just taken place with it. He resolutely fixed his eyes upon it, bending every faculty he possessed into one tense attitude of attention. And a moment later he could not resist a sudden movement and a swift indrawing of breath; for there, before his very eyes, the pencil tilted, very hesitatingly and quiveringly, as if pulled by a spider's thread. He heard, too, the tiny tap of its fall.

He glanced at the medium, who jerked his head impatiently, as if for silence. Then once more the silence came down.

A minute later there was no longer the possibility of a doubt.

There before the boy's eyes, as he stared, whitefaced, with parted, lips, the pencil rose, hesitated, quivered; but, instead of falling back again, hung so for a moment on its point, forming with itself an acute angle with the plane of the table in an entirely impossible position; then, once more rising higher, swung on its point in a quarter circle, and after one more pause and quiver, rose to its full height, remained poised one instant, then fell with a sudden movement, rolled across the table and dropped on the carpet.

The medium leaned back, drawing a long breath.

'There,' he said; and smiled at the bewildered young man.

'But – but—' began the other.

'Yes, I know,' said the man. 'It's startling, isn't it? and indeed it's not as easy as it looks. I wasn't at all sure—'

'But, good Lord, I saw—'

'Of course you did; but how do you know you weren't hypnotised?'

(Laurie sat down suddenly, unconscious that he had done so.)

The medium put out his hand for his pipe once more.

'Now, I'm going to be quite honest,' he said. 'I have quite a quantity of comments to make on that. First, it doesn't prove anything whatever, even if it really happened—'

'Even if it—!'

'Certainly. . . . Oh, yes; I saw it too; and there's the pencil on the floor' (he stooped and picked it up).

'But what if we were both hypnotised – both acted upon by self-suggestion? We can't prove we weren't.'

Laurie was dumb.

'Secondly, it doesn't prove anything, in any case, as regards the other matters we were speaking of. It only shows – if it really happened, as I say – that the mind has extraordinary control over matter. It hasn't anything to do with immortality, or – or spiritualism.'

'Then why did you do it?' gasped the boy.

'Merely fireworks . . . only to show off. People are convinced by such queer things.'

Laurie sat regarding, still with an unusual pallor in his face and brightness in his eyes. He could not in the last degree put into words why it was that the tiny incident of the pencil affected him so profoundly. Vaguely, only, he perceived that it was all connected somehow with the ordinariness of the accessories, and more impressive therefore than all the paraphernalia of planchette, spinning mirrors, or even his own dreams.

He stood up again suddenly.

'It's no good, Mr. Vincent,' he said, putting out his hand, 'I'm knocked over. I can't imagine why. It's no use talking now. I must think. Good night.'

'Good night, Mr. Baxter,' said the medium serenely.

CHAPTER EIGHT

I

'Her ladyship told me to show you in here, sir,' said the footman at half-past eight on Sunday evening.

Laurie put down his hat, slipped off his coat, and went into the dining-room.

The table was still littered with dessert-plates and napkins. Two people had dined there he observed. He went round to the fire, wondering vaguely as to why he had not been shown upstairs, and stood, warming his hands behind him, and looking at the pleasant gloom of the high picture-hung walls.

In spite of himself he felt slightly more excited than he had thought he would be; it was one thing to be philosophical at a prospect of three days' distance; and another when the gates of death actually rise in sight. He wondered in what mood he would see his own rooms again. Then he yawned slightly – and was a little pleased that it was natural to yawn.

There was a rustle outside; the door opened, and Lady Laura slipped in.

'Forgive me, Mr. Baxter,' she said. 'I wanted to have just a word with you first. Please sit down a moment.'

She seemed a little anxious and upset, thought Laurie, as he sat down and looked at her in her evening dress with the emblematic chain more apparent than ever. Her frizzled hair sat as usual on the top of her head, and her pince-nez glimmered at him across the hearthrug like the eyes of a cat.

'It is this,' she said hurriedly. 'I felt I must just speak to you. I wasn't sure whether you quite realised the . . . the dangers of all this. I didn't want you to . . . to run any risks in my house. I should feel responsible, you know.'

She laughed nervously.

'Risks? Would you mind explaining?' said Laurie.

'There . . . there are always risks, you know.'

'What sort?'

'Oh . . . you know . . . nerves, and so on. I . . . I have seen people very much upset at *séances*, more than once.'

Laurie smiled.

'I don't think you need be afraid, Lady Laura. It's awfully kind of you; but, do you know, I'm ashamed to say that, if anything, I'm rather bored.'

The pince-nez gleamed.

'But – but don't you believe it? I thought Mr. Vincent said—'

'Oh yes, I believe it; but, you know, it seems to me so natural now. Even if nothing happens to-night, I don't think I shall believe it any the less.'

She was silent an instant.

'You know there are other risks,' she said suddenly.

'What? Are things thrown about?'

'Please don't laugh at it, Mr. Baxter. I am quite serious.'

'Well – what kind do you mean?'

Again she paused.

'It's very awful,' she said; 'but, you know, people's nerves do break down entirely sometimes, even though they're not in the least afraid. I saw a case once—'

She stopped.

'Yes?'

'It – it was a very awful case. A girl – a sensitive – broke down altogether under the strain. She's in an asylum.'

'I don't think that's likely for me,' said Laurie, with a touch of humour in his voice. 'And, after all, you run these risks, don't you – and Mrs. Stapleton?'

'Yes; but you see we're not sensitives. And even I—'

'Yes?'

'Well, even I feel sometimes rather overcome. . . . Mr. Baxter, do you quite realise what it all means?'

'I think so. To tell the truth—'

He stopped.

'Yes; but the thing itself is really overwhelming. . . . There's – there's an extraordinary power sometimes. You know I was with Maud Stapleton when she saw her father—'

She stopped again.

'Yes?'

'I saw him too, you know. . . . Oh! there was no possibility of fraud. It was with Mr. Vincent. It – it was rather terrible.'

'Yes?'

'Maud fainted. . . . Please don't tell her I told you, Mr. Baxter; she wouldn't like you to know that. And then other things happen sometimes which aren't nice. Do you think me a great coward? I – I think I've got a fit of nerves to-night.'

Laurie could see that she was trembling.

'I think you're very kind,' he said, 'to take the trouble to tell me all this. But indeed I was quite ready to be startled. I quite understand what you mean – but—'

'Mr. Baxter, you can't understand unless you've experienced it. And, you know, the other day here you knew nothing at all : you were not conscious. Now to-night you're to keep awake; Mr. Vincent's going to arrange to do what he can about that. And – and I don't quite like it.'

'Why, what on earth can happen?' asked Laurie, bewildered.

'Mr. Baxter, I suppose you realise that it's you that they – whoever they are – are interested in? There's no kind of doubt that you'll be the centre to-night. And I did just want you to understand fully that there are risks. I shouldn't like to think—'

Laurie stood up.

'I understand perfectly,' he said. 'Certainly, I always knew there were risks. I hold myself responsible, and no one else. Is that quite clear?'

The wire of the front-door bell suddenly twitched in the hall, and a peal came up the stairs.

'He's come,' said the other. 'Come upstairs, Mr. Baxter. Please don't say a word of what I've said.'

She hurried out, and he after her, as the footman came up from the lower regions.

The drawing-room presented an unusual appearance to Laurie as he came in. All the small furniture had been moved away to the side where the windows looked into the street, and formed there what looked like an amateur barricade. In the centre of the room, immediately below the electric light, stood a solid small round table with four chairs set round it as if for Bridge. There was on the side further from the street a kind of ante-room communicating with the main room by a high, wide archway nearly as large as the room to which it gave access; and within this, full in sight, stood a curious erection, not unlike a confessional, seated within for one, roofed, walled, and floored with thin wood. The front of this was open, but screened partly by two curtains that seemed to hang from a rod within. The rest of the little extra room was entirely empty except for the piano that stood closed in the corner.

There were two persons standing rather disconsolately on the vacant hearthrug – Mrs. Stapleton and the clergyman whom Laurie had met on his last visit here. Mr. Jamieson wore an expression usually associated with funerals, and Mrs. Stapleton's face was full of suppressed excitement.

'Dearest, what a time you've been! Was that Mr. Vincent?'

'I think so,' said Lady Laura.

The two men nodded to one another, and an instant later the medium came in.

He was in evening clothes; and, more than ever, Laurie thought how average and conventional he looked. His manner was not in the least pontifical, and he shook hands cordially and naturally, but gave one quick glance of approval at Laurie.

'It struck me as extraordinarily cold,' he said. 'I see you have an excellent fire.' And he stooped, rubbing his hands together to warm them.

'We must screen that presently,' he said.

Then he stood up again.

'There's no use in wasting time. May I say a word first, Lady Laura?'

She nodded, looking at him almost apprehensively.

'First, I must ask you gentlemen to give me your word on a certain point. I have not an idea how things will go, or whether we shall get any results; but we are going to attempt materialisation. Probably, in any case, this will not go very far; we may not be able to do more than to see some figure or face. But in any case, I want you two gentlemen to give me your word that you will attempt no violence. Anything in the nature of seizing the figure may have very disastrous results indeed to myself. You understand that what you will see, if you see anything, will not be actual flesh or blood; it will be formed of a certain matter of which we understand very little at present, but which is at any rate intimately connected with myself or with someone present. Really we know no more of it than that. We are all of us inquirers equally. Now will you gentlemen give me your words of honour that you will obey me in this; and that in all other matters you will follow the directions of . . . (he glanced at the two ladies) – 'of Mrs. Stapleton, and do nothing without her consent?'

He spoke in a brisk, matter-of-fact way, and looked keenly from face to face of the two men as he ended.

'I give you my word,' said Laurie.

'Yes; just so,' said Mr. Jamieson.

'Now there is one matter more,' went on the medium. 'Mr. Baxter, you are aware that you are a sensitive of a very high order. Now I do not wish you to pass into trance to-night. Kindly keep your attention fixed upon me steadily. Watch me closely : you will be able to see me quite well enough, as I shall explain presently. Mrs. Stapleton will sit with her back to the fire, Lady Laura opposite, Mr. Jamieson with his back to the cabinet, and you, Mr. Baxter, facing it. (Yes, Mr. Jamieson, you may turn round freely, so long as you keep your hands upon the table.) Now, if you feel anything resembling sleep or unconsciousness coming upon you irresistibly, Mr. Baxter, I wish you just lightly to tap Mrs. Stapleton's hand. She will then, if necessary, break up the circle. Give the signal directly you feel the sensation is really coming on, or if you find it very difficult to keep your attention fixed. You will do this?'

'I will do it,' said Laurie.

'Then that is really all.'

He moved a step away from the fire. Then he paused.

'By the way, I may as well just tell you our methods. I shall take my place within the cabinet, drawing the curtains partly across at the top so as to shade my face. But you will be able to see the whole of my body, and probably even my face as well. You four will please to sit at the table in the order I have indicated, with your hands resting upon it. You will not speak unless you are spoken to, or until Mrs. Stapleton gives the signal. That is all. You then wait. Now it may be ten minutes, half and hour, an hour – anything up to two hours before anything happens. If there is no result, Mrs. Stapleton will break up the circle at eleven o'clock, and awaken me if necessary.'

He broke off.

'Kindly just examine the cabinet and the whole room first, gentlemen. We mediums must protect ourselves.'

He smiled genially and nodded to the two.

Laurie went straight across the open floor to the cabinet. It was raised on four feet, about twelve inches from the ground. Heavy green curtains hung from a bar within. Laurie took these, and ran them to and fro; then he went into the cabinet. It was entirely empty except for a single board that formed the seat. As he came out he encountered the awe-struck face of the clergyman who had followed him in dead silence, and now went into the cabinet after him. Laurie passed round behind : the little room was empty except for the piano at the back, and two low bookshelves on either side of the fireless hearth. The window looking presumably into the garden was shuttered from top to bottom, and barred, and the curtains were drawn back so that it could be seen. A cat could not have hidden in the place. It was all perfectly satisfactory.

He came back to where the others were standing silent, and the clergyman followed him.

'You are satisfied, gentlemen?' said the medium, smiling.

'Perfectly,' said Laurie, and the clergyman bowed.

'Well, then,' said the other, 'it is close upon nine.'

He indicated the chairs, and himself went past towards the cabinet, his heavy step making the room vibrate as he went. As he came near the door, he fumbled with the button, and all the lights but one went out.

The four sat down. Laurie watched Mr. Vincent step up into the cabinet, jerk the curtains this way and that, and at last sit easily back, in such a way that his face could be seen in a kind of twilight, and the rest of his body perfectly visible.

Then silence came down upon the room.

2

The cat of the next house decided to go a-walking after an excellent supper of herring-heads. He had an appointment with a friend. So he cleaned himself carefully on the landing outside the pantry, evaded a couple of caresses from the young footman lately come from the country, and finally leapt on the window-sill, and sat there regarding the back garden, the smoky wall beyond seen in the light of the pantry window, and the chimney-pots high and forbidding against the luminous night sky. His tail moved with a soft ominous sinuousness as he looked.

Presently he climbed cautiously out beneath the sash, gathered himself for a spring, and the next instant was seated on the boundary wall between his own house and that of Lady Laura's.

Here again he paused. That which served him for a mind, that mysterious bundle of intuitions and instincts by which he reckoned time, exchanged confidences, and arranged experiences, informed him that the night was yet young, and that his friend would not yet be arrived. He sat there so still and so long, that if it had not been for his resolute head and the blunt spires of his ears, he would have appeared to an onlooker below as no more than a humpy finial on an otherwise regularly built wall. Now and again the last inch of his tail twitched slightly, like an independent member, as he contemplated his thoughts.

Overhead the last glimmer of day was utterly gone, and in the place of it the mysterious glow of night over a city hung high and luminous. He, a town-bred cat, descended from generation of town-bred cats, listened passively to the gentle roar of traffic that stood, to him, for the running of brooks and the sighing of forest trees. It was to him the auditory background of adventure, romance, and bitter war.

The energy of life ran strong in his veins and sinews. Once and again as that, which was for him imaginative vision and anticipation, asserted itself, he crisped his strong claws into the crumbling mortar, shooting them, by an unconscious muscular action, from the padded sheaths in which they lay. Once a furious yapping sounded from a lighted window far beneath; but he scorned to do more than turn a slow head in the direction of it : then once more he resumed his watch.

The time came at last, conveyed to him as surely as by a punctual clock, and he rose noiselessly to his feet. Then again he paused, and stretched first one strong foreleg and then the other to its furthest reach, shooting again his claws, conscious with a faint sense of well-being of those tightly-strung muscles rippling beneath his loose striped skin. They would be in action presently. And, as he did so, there looked over the parapet six feet above him, at the top of the trellis up which presently he would ascend, another resolute little head and blunt-spired ears, and a soft indescribable voice spoke a gentle insult. It was his friend . . . and, he knew well enough, on some high ridge in the background squatted a young female beauty, with flattened ears and waving tail, awaiting the caresses of the victor.

As he saw the head above him, to human eyes a shapeless silhouette, to his eyes a grey-pencilled picture perfect in all its details, he paused in his stretching. Then he sat back, arranged his tail, and lifted his head to answer. The cry that came from him, not yet *fortissimo*, sounded in human ears beneath no more than a soft broken-hearted wail, but to him who sat above it surpassed in insolence even his own carefully modulated offensiveness.

Again the other answered, this time lifting himself to his full height, sending a message along the nerves of his back that prickled his own skin and passed out along the tail with an exquisite ripple of movement. And once more came the answer from below.

So the preliminary challenge went on. Already in the voice of each there had begun to show itself that faint note of hysteria that culminates presently in a scream of anger and a torrent of spits, leading again in their turn to an ominous silence and the first fierce clawing blows at eyes and ears. In another instant the watcher above would recoil for a moment as the swift rush was made up the trellis, and then the battle would be joined : but that instant never came. There fell a sudden silence; and he, peering down into the grey gloom, chin on paws, and tail twitching eighteen inches behind, saw an astonishing sight. His adversary had broken off in the midst of a long crescendo cry, and was himself crouched flat upon the narrow wall staring now not upwards, but downwards, diagonally, at a certain curtained window eight feet below.

This was all very unusual and contrary to precedent. A dog, a human hand armed with a missile, a furious minatory face – these things were not present to account for the breach of etiquette. Vaguely he perceived this, conscious only on inexplicability; but he himself also ceased, and watched for developments.

Very slowly they came at first. That crouching body beneath was motionless now; even the tail had ceased to twitch and hung limply behind, dripping over the edge of the narrow wall into the unfathomable pit of the garden; and as the watcher stared, he felt himself some communication of the horror so apparent in the other's attitude. Along his own spine, from neck to flank, ran the paralysing nervous movement; his own tail ceased to move; his own ears drew back instinctively, flattening themselves at the sides of the square strong head. There was a movement near by, and he turned quick eyes to see the lithe young love of his heart stepping softly into her place beside him.

When he turned again his adversary had vanished.

Yet he still watched. Still there was no sound from the window at which the other had stared just now : no oblong of light shone out into the darkness to explain that sudden withdrawal from the fray.

All was as silent as it had been just now; on all sides windows were closed; now and then came a human voice, just a word or two, spoken and answered from one of those pits beneath, and the steady rumble of traffic went on far away across the roofs; but here, in the immediate neighbourhood, all was at peace. He knew well enough the window in question; he had leapt himself upon the sill once and again and seen the foodless waste of floor and carpet and furniture within.

Yet as he watched and waited his own horror grew. That for which in men we have as yet no term was strong within him, as in every beast that lives by perception rather than reason; and he too by this strange faculty knew well enough that something was abroad, raying out from that silent curtained unseen window – something of an utterly different order from that of dog or flung shoe and furious vituperation – something that affected certain nerves within his body in a new and awful manner. Once or twice in his life he had been conscious of it before, once in an empty room, once in a room tenanted by a mere outline beneath a sheet and closed by a locked door.

His heart too seemed melted within him; his tail too hung limply behind the stucco parapet, and he made no answering movement to the tiny crooning note that sounded once in his ears.

And still the horror grew. . . .

Presently he withdrew one claw from the crumbling edge,

raising his head delicately; and then the other. For an instant longer he waited, feeling his back heave uncontrollably. Then, dropping noiselessly on to the lead, he fled beneath the sheltering parapet, a noiseless shadow in the gloom; and his mate fled with him.

CHAPTER NINE

I

Laurie turned slowly over in bed, drew a long breath, expelled it, and, releasing his arms from the bed-clothes, sat up. He switched on the light by his bed, glanced at his watch, switched off the light, and sank down again into the sheets. He need not get up just yet.

Then he remembered.

When an event of an entirely new order comes into experience, it takes a little time to be assimilated. It is as when a large piece of furniture is brought into a room; all the rest of the furniture takes upon itself a different value. A picture that did very well up to then over the fire-place must perhaps be moved. Values, relations, and balance all require readjustment.

Now up to last night Laurie had indeed been convinced, in one sense, of spiritualistic phenomena; but they had not yet for him reached the point of significance when they affected everything else. The new sideboard, so to speak, had been brought into the room, but it had been put temporarily against the wall in a vacant space to be looked at; the owner of the room had not yet realised the necessity of rearranging the whole. But last night something had happened that changed all this. He was now beginning to perceive the need of a complete review of everything.

As he lay there, quiet indeed, but startlingly alert, he first reviewed the single fact.

About an hour or so had passed away before anything particular happened. They had sat there, those four, in complete silence, their hands upon the table, occasionally shifting a little, hearing the sound of one another's breathing or the faint rustle of one of the ladies' dresses, in sufficient light from the screened fire and the single heavily shaded electric burner to recognise faces, and even, after the first few minutes, to distinguish even small objects, or to read large print.

For the most part Laurie had kept his eyes upon the medium in the cabinet. There the man had leaned back, plainly visible for the most part, with even the paleness of his face and the dark blot of his beard clearly discernible in the twilight. Now and then the boy's eyes had wandered to the other faces, to the young clergyman's opposite downcast and motionless, with a sort of apprehensive look and a determination not to give way – to the three-quarter profiles of the two women, and the gleam of the pince-nez below Lady Laura's frizzled hair.

So he had sat, the thoughts at first racing through his brain, then, as time went on, moving more and more slowly, with his own brain becoming ever more passive, until at last he had been compelled to make a little effort against the drowsiness that had begun to envelop him. He had had to do this altogether three or four times, and had even begun to wonder whether he should be able to resist much longer, when a sudden trembling of the table had awakened him, alert and conscious in a moment, and he had sat with every faculty violently attentive to what should follow.

That trembling was a curious sensation beneath his hands. At first it was no more than might be caused by the passing of a heavy van in the street; only there was no van. But it had increased, with spasms and recoils, till it resembled a continuous shudder as of a living rigid body. It began also to tilt slightly this way and that.

Now all this, Laurie knew well, meant nothing at all – or rather, it need not. And when the movement passed again through all the reverse motions, sinking at last into complete stillness, he was conscious of disappointment. A moment later, however, as he glanced up again at the medium in the cabinet, he drew his breath sharply, and Mr. Jamieson, at the sound, wheeled his head swiftly to look.

There, in the cabinet, somewhere overhead behind the curtain, a faint but perfectly distinct radiance was visible. It was no more than a diffused glimmer, but it was unmistakable, and it shone out faintly and clearly upon the medium's face. By its light Laurie could make out every line and every feature, the drooping clipped moustache, the strong jutting nose, the lines from nostril to mouth, and the closed eyes. As he watched the light deepened in intensity, seeming to concentrate itself in the hidden corner at the top. Then, with a smooth, steady motion it emerged into full sight, in appearance like a softly luminous globe of a pale bluish colour, undefined at the edges, floating steadily forward with a motion like that of an air balloon, out into the room. Once outside the cabinet it seemed to hesitate, hanging at about the height of a man's head – then, after an instant, it retired once more, re-entered the cabinet, disappeared in the direction from which it had come, and once more died out.

Well, there it had been; there was no doubt about it. . . . And Laurie was unacquainted with any mechanism that could produce it.

The clergyman too had seemed affected. He had watched, with turned-back head, the phenomenon from beginning to end, and at the close, with a long indrawing of breath, had looked once at Laurie, licked his dry lips with a motion that was audible in that profound silence, and once more dropped his eyes. The ladies had been silent, and all but motionless throughout.

Well, the rest had happened comparatively quickly.

Once more, after the lapse of a few minutes, the radiance had begun to re-form; but this time it had emerged almost immediately, diffused and misty like a nebula; had hung again before the cabinet, and then, with a strange, gently whirling motion, had seemed to arrange itself in lines and curves.

Gradually, as he stared at it, it had begun to take the shape and semblance of a head, swathed in drapery, with that same drapery, hanging, as it appeared in folds, dripping downwards to the ground, where it lost itself in vagueness. Then, as he still stared, conscious of nothing but the amazing fact, features appeared to be forming – first blots and lines as of shadow, finally eyes, nose, mouth, and chin as of a young girl. . . .

A moment later there was no longer a doubt. It was the face of Amy Nugent that was looking at him, grave and steady – as when he had seen it in the moonlight above the sluice – and behind, seen half through the strange drapery, and half apart from it, a couple of feet behind, the face of the sleeping medium.

At that sight he had not moved nor spoken. It was enough that the fact was there. Every power he possessed was concentrated in the one effort of observation. . . .

He heard from somewhere a gasping sigh, and there rose up between him and the face the figure of the clergyman, with his head turned back staring at the apparition, and one hand only on the table, yet with that hand so heavy upon it that the whole table shuddered with his shudder.

There was a movement on the left, and he heard a fierce feminine whisper—

'Sit down, sir; sit down this instant. . . .'

When the clergyman had again sunk down into his seat with that same strong shudder, the luminous face was already incoherent; the features had relapsed again into blots and shadows, the drapery was absorbing itself upwards into the centre from which it came. Once more the nebula trembled, moved backwards, and disappeared. The next instant the radiance went out, as if turned off by a switch. The medium groaned gently and awoke.

Well, that had ended it. Laurie scarcely remembered the talking that followed, the explanations, the apologies, the hardly concealed terror of the young clergyman. The medium had come out presently, dazed and confused. They had talked . . . and so forth. Then Laurie had come home, still trying to assimilate the amazing fact, of which he said that it could make no difference – that he had seen with his own eyes the face of Amy Nugent four months after her death.

Now here he was in bed on the following morning, trying to assimilate it once more.

It seemed to him as if sleep had done its work – that the sub-conscious intelligence had been able to take the fact in – and that henceforth it was an established thing in his experience. He was not excited now, but he was intensely and overwhelmingly interested. There the thing was. Now what difference did it make?

First, he understood that it made an enormous difference to the value of the most ordinary things. It really was true – as true as tables and chairs – that there was a life after this, and that personality survived. Never again could he doubt that for one instant, even in the gloomiest mood. So long as a man walks by faith, by the acceptance of authority, human or Divine, there is always psychologically possible the assertion of self, the instinct that what one has not personally experienced may just conceivably be untrue. But when one has seen – so long as memory does not disappear – this agnostic instinct is an impossibility. Every single act therefore has a new significance. There is no venture about it any more; there is, indeed, very little opportunity for heroism. Once it is certain, by the evidence of the senses, that death is just an interlude, this life becomes merely part of a long process. . . .

Now as to the conduct of that life – what of religion? And here, for a moment or two, Laurie was genuinely dismayed. For, as he looked at the Catholic religion, he perceived that the whole thing had changed. It no longer seemed august and dominant. As he contemplated himself as he had been at Mass on the previous morning, he seemed to have been rather absurd. Why all this trouble, all this energy, all these innumerable acts and efforts of faith? It was not that his religion seemed necessarily untrue; it was certainly possible for a man to hold simultaneously Catholic and spiritualistic beliefs; there had not been a hint last night against Christianity, and yet, in the face of this evidence of the senses, Catholicism seemed a very shadowy thing. It might well be true, as any philosophy may be true, but – did it matter very much? To be enthusiastic about it was the frenzy of an artist, who loves the portrait more than the original – and possibly a very misleading and inadequate portrait. Laurie had seen for himself the original last night; he had seen a disembodied soul in a garb assumed for the purpose of identification. . . . Did he need, then, a 'religion'? Was not his experience all-sufficing? . . .

Then suddenly all speculation fled away in the presence of the personal element.

Three days ago he had contemplated the thought of Amy with comparative indifference. She had been to him lately little more than a 'test case' of the spiritual world, clothed about with the memory of sentiment. Now once more she sprang into vivid vital life as a person. She was not lost; his relations with her were not just incidents of the past; they were as much bound up with the present as courtship has a continuity with married life. She existed – her very self – and communication was possible between them. . . .

Laurie rolled over on to his back. The thought was violently overwhelming; there was a furious, absorbing fascination in it. The gulf had been bridged; it could be bridged again. Even if tales were true, it could be bridged far more securely yet. It was possible that the phantom he had seen could be brought yet more forward into the world of sense, that he could touch again with his very hand a tabernacle enclosing her soul. So far spiritualism had not failed him; why should he suspect it of failure in the future? It had been done before; it could, and should, be done again. Besides, there was the pencil incident. . . .

He threw off the clothes and sprang out of bed. It was time to get up; time to begin again this fascinating, absorbingly interesting earthly life, which now had such enormous possibilities.

2

The rooms of Mr. James Morton were conveniently situated up four flights of stairs in one of those blocks of buildings, so mysterious to the layman, that lie not a very long way from Charing Cross. There is a silence always here as of college life, and the place is frequented by the same curious selections from the human race as haunt University courts. Here are to be seen cooks, aged and dignified men, errand-boys, and rather shabby old women.

The interior of the rooms, too, is not unlike that of an ordinary rather second-rate college; and Mr. James Morton's taste did not redeem the chambers in which he sat. From roof to floor the particular apartment in which he sat was lined with bookshelves filled with unprepossessing volumes and large black tin boxes. A large table stood in the middle of the room, littered with papers, with bulwarks of the same kind of tin boxes rising at either end.

Mr. Morton himself was a square-built man of some forty years, clean-shaven, and rather pale and stout, with strongly marked features, a good loud voice, and the pleasant, brusque manners that befit a University and public school man who has taken seriously to business.

Laurie and he got on excellently together. The younger man had an admiration for the older, whose reputation as a rather distinguished barrister certainly deserved it, and was sufficiently in awe of him to pay attention to his directions in all matters connected with law. But they did not meet much on other planes. Laurie had asked the other down to Stantons once, and had dined with him three or four times in return. And there their acquaintance found its limitations.

This morning, however, the boy's interested air, with its hints of suppressed excitement and his marked inattention to the books and papers which were his business, at last caused the older man to make a remark. It was in his best manner.

'What's the matter, eh?' he suddenly shot at him, without prelude of any kind.

Laurie's attention came back with a jump, and he flushed a little.

'Oh! – er – nothing particular,' he murmured. And he set himself down to his books again in silence, conscious of the watchful roving eye on the other side of the table.

About half-past twelve Mr. Morton shut his own book with a slap, leaned back, and began to fill his pipe.

'Nothing seems very important,' he said.

As the last uttered word had been spoken an hour previously, Laurie was bewildered, and looked it.

'It won't do, Baxter,' went on the other. 'You haven't turned a page an hour this morning.'

Laurie smiled doubtfully, and leaned back too. Then he had a spasm of confidence.

'Yes. I'm rather upset this morning,' he said. 'The fact is, last night . . .'

Mr. Morton waited.

'Well?' he said. 'Oh! don't tell me if you don't want to.'

Laurie looked at him.

'I wonder what you'd say,' he said at last.

The other got up with an abrupt movement, pushed his books together, selected a hat, and put it on.

'I'm going to lunch,' he said. 'Got to be in the Courts at two; and . . .'

'Oh! wait a minute,' said Laurie. 'I think I want to tell you.'

'Well, make haste.' He stood, in attitude to go.

129

'What do you think of spiritualism?'

'Blasted rot,' said Mr. Morton. 'Anything more I can do for you?'

'Do you know anything about it?'

'No. Don't want to. Is that all?'

'Well, look here,' said Laurie. . . . 'Oh! sit down for two minutes.'

Then he began. He described carefully his experiences of the night before, explaining so much as was necessary of antecedent events. The other during the course of it tilted his hat back, and half leaned, half sat against a side-table, watching the boy at first with a genial contempt, and finally with the same curious interest that one gives to a man with a new disease.

'Now, what d'you make of that?' ended Laurie, flushed and superb.

'D'you want to know?' came after a short silence.

Laurie nodded.

'What I said at the beginning, then.'

'What?'

'Blasted rot,' said Mr. Morton again.

Laurie frowned sharply, and affected to put his books together.

'Of course, if you take it like that,' he said. 'But I don't know what respect you can possibly have for any evidence, if . . .'

'My dear chap, that isn't evidence. No evidence in the world could make me believe that the earth was upside down. These things don't happen.'

'Then how do you explain . . . ?'

'I don't explain,' said Mr. Morton. 'The thing's simply not worth looking into. If you really saw that, you're either mad or else there was a trick. . . . Now come along to lunch.'

'But I'm not the only one,' cried Laurie hotly.

'No, indeed you're not. . . . Look here, Baxter, that sort of thing plays the devil with nerves. Just drop it once and for all. I knew a chap once who went in for all that. Well, the end was what everybody knew would happen. . . .'

'Yes?' said Laurie.

'Went off his chump,' said the other briefly. 'Nasty mess all over the floor. Now come to lunch.'

'Wait a second. You can't argue from particulars to universals. Was he the only one you ever knew?'

The other paused a moment.

'No,' he said. 'As it happens, he wasn't. I knew another chap – he's a solicitor. . . . Oh! by the way, he's one of your people – a Catholic, I mean.'

'Well, what about him?'

'Oh! he's all right,' admitted Mr. Morton, with a grudging air. 'But he gave it up and took to religion instead.'

'Yes? What's his name?'

'Cathcart.'

He glanced up at the clock.

'Good Lord,' he said, 'ten to one.'

Then he was gone.

Laurie was far too exalted to be much depressed by this counsel's opinion; and had, indeed, several minutes of delightful meditation on the crass complacency of a clever man when taken off his ground. It was deplorable, he said to himself, that men should be so content with their limitations. But it was always the way, he reflected. To be a specialist in one point involved the pruning of all growth on every other. Here was Morton, almost in the front rank of his particular subject, and, besides, very far from being a bookworm; yet, when taken an inch out of his rut, he could do nothing but flounder. He wondered what Morton would make of these things if he saw them himself.

In the course of the afternoon Morton himself turned up again. The case had ended unexpectedly soon. Laurie waited till the closing of the shutters offered an opportunity for a break in the work, and once more returned to the charge.

'Morton,' he said, 'I wish you'd come with me one day.'

The other looked up.

'Eh?'

'To see for yourself what I told you.'

Mr. Morton snorted abruptly.

'Lord!' he said, 'I thought we'd done with that. No, thank you : Egyptian Hall's all I need.'

Laurie sighed elaborately.

'Oh! of course, if you won't face facts, one can't expect . . .'

'Look here, Baxter,' said the other almost kindly, 'I advise you to give this up. It plays the very devil with nerves, as I told you. Why, you're as jumpy as a cat yourself. And it isn't worth it. If there was anything in it, why it would be another thing; but . . .'

'I . . . I wouldn't give it up for all the world,' stammered Laurie in his zeal. 'You simply don't know what you're talking about. Why . . . why, I'm not a fool . . . I know that. And do you think I'm ass enough to be taken in by a trick? And as if a trick could be played like that in a drawing-room! I tell you I examined every inch. . . .'

'Look here,' said Morton, looking curiously at the boy – for there was something rather impressive about Laurie's manner – 'look here; you'd better see old Cathcart. Know him? . . . Well, I'll introduce you any time. He'll tell you another tale. Of course, I don't believe all the rot he talks; but, at any rate, he's sensible enough to have given it all up. Says he wouldn't touch it with a pole. And he was rather a big bug at it in his time, I believe.'

Laurie sneered audibly.

'Got frightened, I suppose,' he said. 'Of course, I know well enough that it's rather startling—'

'My dear man, he was in the thick of it for ten years. I'll acknowledge his stories are hair-raising, if one believed them; but then, you see—'

'What's his address?'

Morton jerked his head towards the directories in the bookshelf.

'Find him there,' he said. 'I'll give you an introduction if you want it. Though, mind you, I think he talks as much rot as anyone—'

'What does he say?'

'Lord! – I don't know. Some theory or other. But at any rate, he's given it up.'

Laurie pursed his lips.

'I daresay I'll ask you some time,' he said. 'Meanwhile—'

'Meanwhile, for the Lord's sake, get on with that business you've got there.'

Mr. Morton was indeed, as Laurie had reflected, extra-ordinarily uninterested in things outside his beat; and his beat was not a very extended one. He was a quite admirable barrister, competent, alert, merciless and kindly at the proper times, and, while at his business, thought of hardly anything else at all. And when he was not at his business, he threw himself with equal zest into two or three other occupations – golf, dining out, and the collection of a particular kind of chairs. Beyond these things there was for him really nothing of value.

But, owing to circumstances, his beat had been further extended to include Laurie Baxter, whom he was beginning to like extremely. There was an air of romance about Laurie, a pleasant enthusiasm, excellent manners, and a rather delightful faculty of hero-worship. Mr. Morton himself, too, while possessing nothing even resembling a religion, was, like many other people, not altogether unattracted towards those who had, though he thought religiousness to be a sign of a slightly incompetent character; and he rather liked Laurie's Catholicism, such as it was. It must be rather pleasant, he considered (when he considered it at all), to believe 'all that,' as he would have said.

So this new phase of Laurie's interested him far more than he would have allowed, so soon as he became aware that it was not merely superficial; and, indeed, Laurie's constant return to the subject, as well as his air of enthusiastic conviction, soon convinced him that this was so.

Further, after a week or two, he became aware that the young man's work was suffering; and he heard from his lips the expression of certain views that seemed to the elder man extremely unhealthy.

For example, on a Friday evening, not much afterwards, as Laurie was putting his books together, Mr. Morton asked him where he was going to spend the week-end.

'Stopping in town,' said the boy briefly.

'Oh! I'm going to my brother's cottage. Care to come? Afraid there's no Catholic church near.'

Laurie smiled.

'That wouldn't deter me,' he said. 'I've made up my mind—'

'Yes?'

'Oh, it doesn't matter,' said Laurie. 'No – thanks awfully, but I've got to stop in town.'

'Lady Laura's again?'

'Yes.'

'Same old game?'

Laurie sat down.

'Look here,' he said, 'I know you don't mean anything; but I wish you'd understand.'

'Well?'

The boy's face flushed with sudden nervous enthusiasm.

'Do you understand,' he said, 'that this is just everything to me? Do you know it's beginning to seem to me just the only thing that matters? I'm quite aware that you think it all the most utter bunkum; but, you see, I *know* it's true. And the whole thing is just like heaven opening. . . . Look here . . . I didn't tell you half the other day. The fact is, that I was just as much in love with this girl as – as a man could be. She died; and now—'

'Look here, what were you up to last Sunday?'

Laurie quieted a little.

'You wouldn't understand,' he said.

'Have you done any more of that business?'

'What business?'

'Well – thinking you saw her— All right, seeing her, if you like.'

The boy shook his head.

'No. Vincent's away in Ireland. We've been going on other lines.'

'Tell me; I swear I won't laugh.'

'All right; I don't care if you do. . . . Well, automatic handwriting.'

'What's that?'

Laurie hesitated.

'Well, I go into trance, you see, and—'

'Good Lord, what next?'

'And then this girl writes through my hand,' said Laurie deliberately, 'when I'm unconscious. See?'

'I see you're a damned young fool,' said Morton seriously.

'But if it's all rot, as you think?'

'Of course it's all rot! Do you think I believe for one instant—' He broke off. 'And so's a nervous breakdown all rot, isn't it, and D.T.? They aren't real snakes, you know.'

Laurie smiled in a superior manner.

'And you're getting yourself absorbed in all this—'

Laurie looked at him with a sudden flash of fanaticism.

'I tell you,' he said, 'that it's all the world to me. And so would it be to you, if—'

'Oh, Lord! don't become Salvation Army. . . . Seen Cathcart yet?'

'No. I haven't the least wish to see Cathcart.'

Morton rose, put his pens in the drawer, locked it; slid half a dozen papers into a black tin box, locked that too, and went towards his coat and hat, all in silence.

As he went out he turned on the threshold.

'When's that man coming back from Ireland?' he said.

'Who? Vincent? Oh! another month yet. We're going to have another try when he comes.'

'Try? What at?'

'Materialisation,' said Laurie. 'That's to say—'

'I don't want to know what the foul thing means.'

He still paused, looking hard at the boy. Then he sniffed.

'A young fool,' he said. 'I repeat it. . . . Lock up when you come. . . . Good night.'

CHAPTER TEN

I

Mrs. Baxter possessed one of the two secrets of serenity. The other need not be specified; but hers arose from the most pleasant and most human form of narrowmindedness. As has been said before, when things did not fit with her own scheme, either they were not things, but only fancies of somebody inconsiderable, or else she resolutely disregarded them. She had an opportunity of testing her serenity on one day early in February.

She rose as usual at a fixed hour – eight o'clock – and when she was ready knelt down at her *prie-Dieu*. This was quite an elaborate structure, far more elaborate than the devotions offered there. It was a very beautiful inlaid Florentine affair, and had a little shelf above it filled with a number of the little leather-bound books in which her soul delighted. She did not use these books very much; but she liked to see them there. It would not be decent to enter the sanctuary of Mrs. Baxter's prayers; it is enough to say that they were not very long. Then she rose from her knees, left her large comfortable bedroom, redolent with soap and hot water, and came downstairs, a beautiful slender little figure in black lace veil and rich dress, through the sunlight of the staircase, into the dining-room.

There she took up her letters and packets. They were not exciting. There was an unimportant note from a friend, a couple of bills, and a *Bon Marché* catalogue; and she scrutinised these through her spectacles, sitting by the fire. When she had done she noticed a letter lying by Maggie's place, directed in a masculine hand. An instant later Maggie came in herself, in her hat and furs, a charming picture, fresh from the winter sunlight and air, and kissed her.

While Mrs. Baxter poured out tea she addressed a remark or two to the girl, but only got back those vague inattentive murmurs that are the sign of a distracted mind; and, looking up presently with a sense of injury, noticed that Maggie was reading her letter with extraordinary diligence.

'My dear, I am speaking to you,' said Mrs. Baxter, with an air of slightly humorous dignity.

'Er – I am sorry,' murmured Maggie, and continued reading.

Mrs. Baxter put out her hand for the *Bon Marché* catalogue in order to drive home her sense of injury, and met Maggie's eyes, suddenly raised to meet her own, with a curious strained look in them.

'Darling, what is the matter?'

Maggie still stared at her a moment, as if questioning both herself and the other, and finally handed the letter across with an abrupt movement.

'Read it,' she said.

It was rather a business to read it. It involved spectacles, a pushing aside of a plate, and a slight turning to catch the light. Mrs. Baxter read it, and handed it back, making three or four times the sound written as 'Tut.'

'The tiresome boy!' she said querulously, but without alarm.

'What are we to do? You see, Mr. Morton thinks we ought to do something. He mentions a Mr. Cathcart.'

Mrs. Baxter reached out for the toast-rack.

'My dear, there's nothing to be done. You know what Laurie is. It'll only make him worse.'

Maggie looked at her uneasily.

'I wish we could do something,' she said.

'My dear, he'd have written to me – Mr. Morton, I mean – if Laurie had been really unwell. You see he only says he doesn't attend to his work as he ought.'

Maggie took up the letter, put it carefully back into the envelope, and went on with breakfast. There was nothing more to be said just then.

But she was uneasy, and after breakfast went out into the garden, spud in hand, to think it all over, with the letter in her pocket.

Certainly the letter was not alarming *per se,* but *per accidens* – that is to say, taking into account who it was that had written, she was not so sure. She had met Mr. Morton but once, and had formed of him the kind of impression that a girl would form of such a man in the hours of a week-end – a brusque, ordinary kind of barrister without much imagination and a good deal of shrewd force. It was surely rather an extreme step for a man like this to write to a girl in such a condition of things, asking her to use her influence to dissuade Laurie from his present course of life. Plainly the man meant what he said; he had not written to Mrs. Baxter, as he explained in the letter, for fear of alarming her unduly, and, as he expressly said, there was nothing to be alarmed about. Yet he had written.

Maggie stopped at the lower end of the orchard path, took out the letter, and read the last three or four sentences again :

'Please forgive me if you think it was unnecessary to write. Of course I have no doubt whatever that the whole thing is nothing but nonsense; but even nonsense can have a bad effect, and Mr. Baxter seems to me to be far too much wrapt up in it. I enclose the address of a friend of mine in case you would care to write to him on the subject. He was once a Spiritualist, and is now a devout Catholic. He takes a view of it that I do not take; but at any rate his advice could do no harm. You can trust him to be absolutely discreet.

'Believe me,

'Yours sincerely,

'JAMES MORTON.'

It really was very odd and unconventional; and Mr. Morton had not seemed at all an odd or unconventional person. He mentioned, too, a particular date, February 25, as the date by which the medium would have returned, and some sort of further effort was going to be made; but he did not attempt to explain this, nor did Maggie understand it. It only seemed to her rather sinister and unpleasant.

She turned over the page, and there was the address he had mentioned – a Mr. Cathcart. Surely he did not expect her to write to this stranger. . . .

She walked up and down with her spud for another half-hour before she could come to any conclusion. Certainly she agreed with Mr. James Morton that the whole thing was nonsense; yet, further, that this nonsense was capable of doing a good deal of harm to an excitable person. Besides,

Laurie obviously had a bad conscience about it, or he would have mentioned it.

She caught sight of Mrs. Baxter presently through the thick hedge, walking with her dainty, dignified step along the paths of the kitchen garden; and a certain impatience seized her at the sight. This boy's mother was so annoyingly serene. Surely it was her business, rather than Maggie's own, to look after Laurie; yet the girl knew perfectly well that if Laurie was left to his mother nothing at all would be done. Mrs. Baxter would deplore it all, of course, gently and tranquilly, in Laurie's absence, and would, perhaps, if she were hard pressed, utter a feeble protest even in his presence; and that was absolutely all. . . .

'Maggie! Maggie!' came the gentle old voice, calling presently; and then to some unseen person, 'Have you seen Miss Deronnais anywhere?'

Maggie put the letter in her pocket and hurried through from the orchard.

'Yes?' she said, with a half hope.

'Come in, my dear, and tell me what you think of those new teacups in the *Bon Marché* catalogue,' said the old lady. 'There seem some beautiful new designs, and we want another set.'

Maggie bowed to the inevitable. But as they passed up the garden her resolution was precipitated.

'Can you let me go by twelve,' she said. 'I rather want to see Father Mahon about something.'

'My dear, I shall not keep you three minutes,' protested the old lady.

And they went in to talk for an hour and threequarters.

2

Father Mahon was a conscientious priest. He said his mass at eight o'clock; he breakfasted at nine; he performed certain devotions till half-past ten; read the paper till eleven, and theology till twelve. Then he considered himself at liberty to do what he liked till his dinner at one. (The rest of his day does not concern us just now.)

He, too, was looking round his garden this morning – a fine, solid figure of a man, in rather baggy trousers, short coat, and expansive waistcoat, with every button doing its duty. He too, like Mr. James Morton, had his beat, an even narrower one than the barrister's, and even better trodden, for he never strayed off it at all, except for four short weeks in the summer, when he hurried across to Ireland and got up late, and went on picnics with other ecclesiastics in straw hats, and joined in cheerful songs in the evening. He was a priest, with perfectly defined duties, and of admirable punctuality and conscientiousness in doing them. He disliked the English quite extraordinarily; but his sense of duty was such that they never suspected it; and his flock of Saxons adored him as people only can adore a brisk, business-like man with a large heart and peremptory ways, who is their guide and father, and is perfectly aware of it. His sermons consisted of cold-cut blocks of dogma taken perseveringly from sermon outlines and served up Sunday by Sunday with a sauce of a slight and delightful brogue. He could never have kindled the Thames, nor indeed any river at all, but he could bridge them with solid stones; and this is, perhaps, even more desirable.

Maggie had begun by disliking him. She had thought him rather coarse and stupid; but she had changed her mind. He was not what may be called subtle; he had no patience at all with such things as scruples, *nuances*, and shades of tone and meaning; but if you put a plain question to him plainly, he gave you a plain answer, if he knew it; if not, he looked it up then and there; and that is always a relief in this intricate world. Maggie therefore did not bother him much; she went to him only on plain issues; and he respected and liked her accordingly.

'Good morning, my child,' he said in his loud, breezy voice, as he came in to find her in his hideous little sitting-room. 'I hope you don't mind the smell of tobacco-smoke.'

The room indeed reeked; he had started a cigar, according to rule, as the clock struck twelve, and had left it just now upon a stump outside when his housekeeper had come to announce a visitor.

'Not in the least, thanks, father. . . . May I sit down? It's rather a long business, I'm afraid.'

The priest pulled out an arm-chair covered with horsehair and an antimacassar.

'Sit down, my child.'

Then he sat down himself, opposite her, in his trousers at

once tight and baggy, with his rather large boots cocked one over the other, and his genial red face smiling at her.

'Now then,' he said.

'It's not about myself, father,' she began rather hurriedly. 'It's about Laurie Baxter. May I begin at the beginning?'

He nodded. He was not sorry to hear something about this boy, whom he didn't like at all, but for whom he knew himself at least partly responsible. The English were bad enough, but English converts were indescribably trying; and Laurie had been on his mind lately, he scarcely knew why.

Then Maggie began at the beginning, and told the whole thing, from Amy's death down to Mr. Morton's letter. He put a question or two to her during her story, looking at her with pressed lips, and finally put out his hand for the letter itself.

'Mrs. Baxter doesn't know what I've come about,' said the girl. 'You won't give her a hint, will you, father?'

He nodded reassuringly to her, absorbed in the letter, and presently handed it back, with a large smile.

'He seems a sensible fellow,' he said.

'Ah! that's what I wanted to ask you, father. I don't know anything at all about spiritualism. Is it – is it really all nonsense? Is there nothing in it at all?'

He laughed loud.

'I don't think you need be afraid,' he said. 'Of course we know that souls don't come back like that. They're somewhere else.'

'Then it's all fraud?'

'It's practically all fraud,' he said, 'but it's very superstitious, and is forbidden by the Church.'

This was straight enough. It was at least a clear issue to begin to attack Laurie upon.

'Then – then that's the evil of it?' she said. 'There's no real power underneath? That's what Mr. Rymer said to Mrs. Baxter; and it's what I've always thought myself.'

The priest's face became theological.

'Let's see what Sabetti says,' he said. 'I fancy—'

He turned in his chair and fetched out a volume behind him.

'Here we are. . . .'

He ran his finger down the heavy paragraphs, turned a page or two, and began a running comment and translation:

' "*Necromantia ex*" . . . "Necromancy arising from invocation of the dead." . . . Let's see . . . yes, "Spiritism, or the consulting of spirits in order to know hidden things, especially that pertain to the future life, certainly is divination properly so called, and is . . . is full of even more impiety than is magnetism, or the use of turning tables. The reason is, as the Baltimore fathers testify, that such knowledge must necessarily be ascribed to Satanic intervention, since in no other manner can it be explained." '

'Then—' began Maggie.

'One moment, my child . . . Yes . . . just so. "Express divination." . . . No, no. Ah! here we are, "Tacit divination, . . . even if it is openly protested that no commerce with the Demon is intended, is *per se* grave sin; but it can sometimes be excused from mortal sin, on account of simplicity or ignorance or a lack of certain faith." You see, my child' — (he set the book back in its place) — 'so far as it's not fraud it's diabolical. And that's an end of it.'

'But do you think it's not all fraud, then?' asked the girl, paling a little.

He laughed again, with a resonance that warmed her heart.

'I should pay just no attention to it all. Tell him, if you like, what I've said, and that it's grave sin for him to play with it; but don't get thinking that the devil's in everything.'

Maggie was puzzled.

'Then it's not the devil?' she asked — 'at least not in this case, you think?'

He smiled again reassuringly.

'I should suspect it was a clever trick,' he said. 'I don't think Master Laurie's likely to get mixed up with the devil in that way. There's plenty of easier ways than that.'

'Do you think I should write to Mr. Cathcart?'

'Just as you like. He's a convert, isn't he? I believe I've heard his name.'

'I think so.'

'Well, it wouldn't do any harm; though I should suspect not much good.'

Maggie was silent.

'Just tell Master Laurie not to play tricks,' said the priest. 'He's got a good, sensible friend in Mr. Morton. I can see that. And don't trouble your head too much about it, my child.'

When Maggie was gone, he went out to finish his cigar, and found to his pleasure that it was still alight, and after a puff or two it went very well.

He thought about his interview for a few minutes as he walked up and down, taking the bright winter air. It explained a good deal. He had begun to be a little anxious about this boy. It was not that Laurie had actually neglected his religion while at Stantons; he was always in his place at mass on Sundays, and even, very occasionally, on weekdays as well. And he had had a mass said for Amy Nugent. But even as far back as the beginning of the previous year, there had been an air about him not altogether reassuring.

Well, this at any rate was a small commentary on the present situation. . . .

(The priest stopped to look at some bulbs that were coming up in the bed beside him, and stooped, breathing heavily, to smooth the earth round one of them with a large finger.)

. . . And as for this Spiritualistic nonsense – of course the whole thing was a trick. Things did not happen like that. Of course the devil could do extraordinary things : or at any rate had been able to do them in the past; but as for Master Laurie Baxter – whose home was down there in the hamlet, and who had been at Oxford and was now reading law – as for the thought that this rather superior Saxon young man was in direct communication with Satan at the present time – well, that needed no comment but loud laughter.

Yet it was very unwholesome and unhealthy. That was the worst of these converts; they could not be content with the sober workaday facts of the Catholic creed. They must be always running after some novelty or other. . . . And it was mortal sin anyhow, if the sinner had the faintest idea—

A large dinner-bell pealed from the back door; and the priest went in to roast beef with Yorkshire pudding, apple dumplings, and a single glass of port-wine to end up with.

It was strange how Maggie felt steadied and encouraged in the presence of something at least resembling danger. So long as Laurie was merely tiresome and foolish, she distrusted herself, she made little rules and resolutions, and deliberately kept herself interiorly detached from him. But now that there was something definite to look to, her sensitiveness vanished.

As to what that something was, she did not trust herself to decide. Father Mahon had given her a point to work at — the fact that the thing, as a serious pursuit, was forbidden; as to what the reality behind was, whether indeed there were any reality at all, she did not allow herself to consider. Laurie was in a state of nerves sufficiently troublesome to bring a letter from his friend and guide; and he was in that state through playing tricks on forbidden ground; that was enough.

Her interview with Father Mahon precipitated her half-formed resolution; and after tea she went upstairs to write to Mr. Cathcart.

It was an unconventional thing to do, but she was sufficiently perturbed to disregard that drawback, and she wrote a very sensible letter, explaining first who she was; then, without any names being mentioned, she described her adopted brother's position, and indicated his experiences : she occupied the last page in asking two or three questions, and begging for general advice.

Mrs. Baxter displayed some symptoms after dinner which the girl recognised well enough. They comprised a resolute avoidance of Laurie's name, a funny stiff little air of dignity, and a touch of patronage. And the interpretation of these things was that the old lady did not wish the subject to be mentioned again, and that, interiorly, she was doing her best to ignore and forget it. Maggie felt, again vaguely comforted ; it left her a freer hand.

She lay awake a long time that night.

Her room was a little square one on the top of the stairs, above the smoking-room where she had that odd scene with

Laurie a month or so before, and looking out upon the yew walk that led to the orchard. It was a cheerful little place enough, papered in brown, hung all over with water colours, with her bed in one corner; and it looked a reassuring familiar kind of place in the firelight, as she lay open-eyed and thinking.

It was not that she was at all frightened; it was no more than a little natural anxiety; and half a dozen times in the hour or two that she lay thinking, she turned resolutely over in bed, dismissed the little pictures that her mind formed in spite of herself, and began to think of pleasant, sane subjects.

But the images recurred. They were no more than little vignettes — Laurie talking to a severe-looking tall man with a sardonic smile; Laurie having tea with Mrs. Stapleton; Laurie in an empty room, looking at a closed door. . . .

It was this last picture that recurred three or four times at the very instant that the girl was drowsing off into sleep; and it had therefore that particular vividness that characterises the thoughts when the conscious attention is dormant. It had too a strangely perturbing effect upon her; and she could not imagine why.

After the third return of it her sense of humour came to the rescue : it was too ridiculous, she said, to be alarmed at an empty room and Laurie's back. Once more she turned on her side, away from the firelight, and resolved, if it recurred again, to examine the details closely.

Again the moments passed : thought followed thought, in those quiet waves that lull the mind towards sleep; finally once more the picture was there, clear and distinct.

Yes; she would look at it this time.

It was a bare room, wainscoted round the walls a few inches up, papered beyond in some common palish pattern. Laurie stood in the centre of the uncarpeted boards, with his back turned to her, looking, it seemed, with an intense expectation at the very dull door in the wall opposite him. He was in his evening dress, she saw, knee-breeches and buckles all complete; and his hands were clenched, as they hung, held out a little from his sides, as he himself, crouching a little, stared at the door.

She, too, looked at the door, at its conventional panels, and its brass handle; and it appeared to her as if both he and she were expectant of some visitor. The door would open presently, she perceived; and the reason why Laurie was so intent upon the entrance, was that he, no more than she, had any idea as to the character of the person who was to come in. She became quite interested as she watched – it was a method she followed sometimes when wooing sleep – and she began, in her fancy, to go past Laurie as if to open the door. But as she passed him she was aware that he put out a hand to check her, as if to hold her back from some danger; and she stopped, hesitating, still looking, not at Laurie, but at the door.

She began then, with the irresponsibility of deepening sleep, to imagine instead what lay beyond the door – to perceive by intuitive vision the character of the house. She got so far as understanding that it was all as unfurnished as this room, that the house stood solitary among trees, and that even these, and the tangled garden that she determined must surround the house, were as listening and as expectant as herself and the waiting figure of the boy. Once more, as if to verify her semi-passive imaginative excursion, she moved to the door. . . .

Ah! what nonsense it was. Here she was, wide awake again, in her own familiar room, with the firelight on the walls.

. . . Well, well; sleep was a curious thing; and so was imagination . . .

. . . At any rate she had written to Mr. Cathcart.

CHAPTER ELEVEN

I

The 'Cock Inn' is situated in Fleet Street, not twenty yards from Mitre Court and scarcely fifty from the passage that leads down to the court where Mr. James Morton still has his chambers.

It was a convenient place, therefore, for Laurie to lunch in, and he generally made his appearance there a few minutes before one o'clock to partake of a small rump steak and a pewter mug of beer. Sometimes he came alone, sometimes in company; and by a carefully thought out system of tips he usually managed to have reserved for him at least until one o'clock a particular seat in a particular partition in that row of stable-like shelters that run the length of the room opposite the door on the first floor.

On the twenty-third of February, however – it was a Friday, by the way, and boiled plaice would have to be eaten instead of rump steak – he was a little annoyed to find his seat already occupied by a small, brisk-looking man with a grey beard and spectacles, who, with a newspaper propped in front of him, was also engaged in the consumption of boiled plaice.

The little man looked up at him sharply, like a bird disturbed in a meal, and then down again upon the paper. Laurie noticed that his hat and stick were laid upon the adjoining chair as if to retain it. He hesitated an instant; then he slid in on the other side, opposite the stranger, tapped his glass with his knife, and sat down.

When the waiter came, a familiarly deferential man with whiskers, Laurie, with a slight look of peevishness, gave his order, and glanced reproachfully at the occupied seat. The waiter gave the ghost of a shrug with his shoulders, significant of apologetic helplessness, and went away.

A minute later Mr. Morton entered, glanced this way and

that, nodding imperceptibly to Laurie, and was just moving off to a less occupied table when the stranger looked up.

'Mr. Morton,' he cried, 'Mr. Morton!' in an odd voice that seemed on the point of cracking into falsetto. (Certainly he was very like a portly bird, thought Laurie.)

The other turned round, nodded with short geniality, and slid into the chair from which the old man moved his hat and stick with zealous haste.

'And what are you doing here?' said Mr. Morton.

'Just taking a bite like yourself,' said the other. 'Friday – worse luck.'

Laurie was conscious of a touch of interest. This man was a Catholic, then, he supposed.

'Oh, by the way,' said Mr. Morton, 'have you – er—' and he indicated Laurie. 'No? . . . Baxter, let me introduce Mr. Cathcart.'

For a moment the name meant nothing to Laurie; then he remembered; but his rising suspicions were quelled instantly by his friend's next remark.

'By the way, Cathcart, we were talking of you a week or two ago.'

'Indeed! I am flattered,' said the old man perkily. (Yes, 'perky' was the word, thought Laurie.)

'Mr. Baxter here is interested in Spiritualism – (rump steak, waiter, and pint of bitter) – and I told him you were the man for him.'

Laurie interiorly drew in his horns.

'A – er – an experimenter?' asked the old man, with courteous interest, his eyes giving a quick gleam beneath his glasses.

'A little.'

'Yes. Most dangerous – most dangerous. . . . And any success, Mr. Baxter?'

Laurie felt his annoyance deepen.

'Very considerable success,' he said shortly.

'Ah, yes – you must forgive me, sir; but I have had a good deal of experience, and I must say— You are a Catholic, I see,' he said, interrupting himself. 'Or a High Churchman.'

'I am a Catholic,' said Laurie.

'So'm I. But I gave up spiritualism as soon as I became

148

one. Very interesting experiences, too; but – well, I value my soul too much, Mr. Baxter.'

Mr. Morton put a large piece of potato into his mouth with a detached air.

It was really rather trying, thought Laurie, to be catechised in this way; so he determined to show superiority.

'And you think it all superstition and nonsense?' he asked.

'Indeed, no,' said the old man shortly.

Laurie pushed his plate on one side, and drew the cheese towards him. This was a little more interesting, he thought, but he was still far from feeling communicative.

'What then?' he asked.

'Oh, very real indeed,' said the old man. 'That is just the danger.'

'The danger?'

'Yes, Mr. Baxter. Of course there's plenty of fraud and trickery; we all know that. But it's the part that's not fraud that's— May I ask what medium you go to?'

'I know Mr. Vincent. And I've been to some public *séances*, too.'

The old man looked at him with sudden interest, but said nothing.

'You think he's not honest?' said Laurie, with cool offensiveness.

'Oh, yes; he's perfectly honest,' said the other deliberately. 'I'll trouble you for the sugar, Mr. Morton.'

Laurie was determined not to begin the subject again. He felt that he was being patronised and lectured, and did not like it. And once again the suspicion crossed his mind that this was an arranged meeting. It was so very neat – two days before the *séance* – the entry of Morton – his own seat occupied. Yet he did not feel quite courageous enough to challenge either of them. He ate his cheese deliberately and waited, listening to the talk between the two on quite irrelevant subjects, and presently determined on a bit of bravado.

'May I look at the *Daily Mirror*, Mr. Cathcart?' he asked.

'There is no doubt of his guilt,' the old man said, as he handed the paper across (the two were deep in a law case now). 'I said so to Markham a dozen times—' and so on.

But there was no more word of spiritualism. Laurie propped the paper before him as he finished his cheese, and waited for coffee, and read with unseeing eyes. He was resenting as hard as he could the abruptness of the opening and closing of the subject, and the complete disregard now shown to him. He drank his coffee, still leisurely, and lit a cigarette; and still the two talked.

He stood up at last and reached down his hat and stick. The old man looked up.

'You are going, Mr. Baxter? . . . Good day. . . . Well then; and as I was waiting in court—'

Laurie passed out indignantly, and went down the stairs.

So that was Mr. Cathcart. . . . Well, he was thankful he hadn't written to him, after all. He was not his kind in the least.

2

The moment he passed out of the door the old man stopped his fluent talking and waited, looking after the boy. Then he turned again to his friend.

'I'm a blundering idiot,' he said.

Mr. Morton sniffed.

'I've put him against me now – Lord knows how; but I've done it; and he won't listen to me.'

'Gad!' said Mr. Morton; 'what funny people you all are! And you really meant what you said?'

'Every word,' said the old man cheerfully. . . . 'Well; our little plot's over.'

'Why don't you ask him to come and see you?'

'First,' said the old man, with the same unruffled cheerfulness, 'he wouldn't have come. We've muddled it. We'd much better have been straightforward. Secondly, he thinks me an old fool – as you do, only more so. No; we must set to work some other way now. . . . Tell me about Miss Deronnais : I showed you her letter?'

The other nodded, helping himself to cheese.

'I told her that I was at her service, of course; and I haven't heard again. Sensible girl?'

'Very sensible, I should say.'

'Sort of girl that wouldn't scream or faint in a crisis?'

'Exactly the opposite, I should say. But I've hardly seen her, you know.'

'Well, well. . . . And the mother?'

'No good at all,' said Mr. Morton.

'Then the girl's the sheet anchor. . . . In love with him, do you know?'

'Lord! How d'you expect me to know that?'

The old man pondered in silence, seeming to assimilate the situation.

'He's in a devil of a mess,' he said, with abrupt cheerfulness. 'That man Vincent—'

'Well?'

'He's the most dangerous of the lot. Just because he's honest.'

'Good God!' broke in the other again suddenly. 'Do all Catholics believe this rubbish?'

'My dear friend, of course they don't. Not one in a thousand. I wish they did. That's what's the matter. But they laugh at it – laugh at it!' . . . (His voice cracked into shrill falsetto.) . . . 'Laugh at hell-fire. . . . Is Sunday the day, did you say?'

'He told me the twenty-fifth.'

'And at that woman's in Queen's Gate, I suppose?'

'Expect so. He didn't say. Or I forget.'

'I heard they were at their games there again,' said Mr. Cathcart with meditative geniality. 'I'd like to blow up the stinking hole.'

Mr. Morton chuckled audibly.

'You're the youngest man of your years I've ever come across,' he said. 'No wonder you believe all that stuff. When are you going to grow up, Cathcart?'

The old man paid no attention at all.

'Well – that plot's over,' he said again. 'Now for Miss Deronnais. But we can't stop this Sunday affair; that's certain. Did he tell you anything about it? Materialisation? Automatic—'

'Lord, I don't know all that jargon. . . .'

'My dear Morton, for a lawyer, you're the worst witness I've ever— Well, I'm off. No more to be done to-day.'

The other sat on a few minutes over his pipe.

It seemed to him quite amazing that a sensible man like Cathcart could take such rubbish seriously. In every other department of life the solicitor was an eminently shrewd and sane man, with, moreover, a youthful kind of brisk humour that is perhaps the surest symptom of sanity that it is possible to have. He had seen him in court for years past under every sort of circumstance, and if it had been required of him to select a character with which superstition and morbid humbug could have had nothing in common, he would have laid his hand upon the senior partner of Cathcart and Cathcart. Yet here was this sane man, taking this fantastic nonsense as if there were really something in it. He had first heard him speak of the subject at a small bachelor dinner party of four in the rooms of a mutual friend; and, as he had listened, he had had the same sensation as one would have upon hearing a Cabinet Minister, let us say, discussing stump-cricket with enthusiasm. Cathcart had said all kinds of things when once he was started – all with that air of business-like briskness that was so characteristic of him and so disconcerting in such a connection. If he had apologised for it as an amiable weakness, if he had been in the least shamefaced or deprecatory, it would have been another matter; one would have forgiven it as one forgives any little exceptional eccentricity. But to hear him speak of materialisation as of a process as normal (though unusual) as the production of radium, and of planchette as of wireless telegraphy – as established, indubitable facts, though out of the range of common experience – this had amazed this very practical man. Cathcart had hinted too of other things – things which he would not amplify – of a still more disconcertingly impossible nature – matters which Morton had scarcely thought had been credible even to the darkest medievalists; and all this with that same sharp, sane humour that lent an air of reality to all that he said.

For romantic young asses like Laurie Baxter such things were not so hopelessly incongruous, though obviously they were bad for him; they were all part of the wild credulousness of a religious youth; but for Cathcart, aged sixty-two, a solicitor in good practice, with a wife and two grown-up daughters, and a reputation for exceptionally sound shrewdness—! But it must be remembered he was a Catholic!

So Mr. James Morton sat in the 'Cock' and pondered. He was not sorry he had tried to take steps to choke off this young fool, and he was just a little sorry that so far they had failed. He had written to Miss Deronnais in an impulse, after an unusually feverish outburst from the boy; and she, he had learnt later, had written to Mr. Cathcart. The rest had been of the other's devising.

Well, it had failed so far. Perhaps next week things would be better.

He paid his bill, left twopence for the waiter, and went out. He had a case that afternoon.

3

Laurie left chambers as it was growing dark that afternoon, and went back to his rooms for tea. He had passed, as was usual now, an extremely distracted couple of hours, sitting over his books with spasmodic efforts only to attend to them. He was beginning, in fact, to be not quite sure whether Law after all was his vocation. . . .

His kettle was singing pleasantly on the hob, and a tray glimmered in the firelight on the little table, as the woman had left it; and it was not until he had poured himself out a cup of tea that he saw on the white cloth an envelope, directed to him, inscribed 'By hand,' in the usual handwriting of persons engaged in business. Even then he did not open it at once; it was probably only some note connected with his chief's affairs.

For half an hour more he sat on, smoking after tea, pondering that which was always in his mind now, and dwelling with a vague pleasant expectancy on what Sunday night should bring forth. Mr. Vincent, he knew, was returning to town that afternoon. Perhaps, even, he might look in for a few minutes, if there were any last instructions to be given.

The effect of the medium on the young man's mind had increased enormously during these past weeks. That air of virile masterfulness, all the more impressive because of its extreme quiet assurance, had proved even more deep than had at first appeared.

It is very hard to analyse the elements of a boy's adoration for a solid middle-aged gentleman with a 'personality'; yet the thing is an enormously potent fact, and plays at least as big a part in the sub-currents that run about the world as any more normal human emotions. Psychologists of the materialistic school would probably say that it was a survival of the tribe-and-war instinct. At any rate, there it is.

Added to all this was the peculiar relation in which the

medium stood to the boy; it was he who had first opened the door towards that strange other-world that so persistently haunts the imaginations of certain temperaments; it was through him that Laurie had had brought before the evidence of his senses, as he thought, the actuality of the things of which he had dreamed – an actuality which his religion had somehow succeeded in evading. It was not that Laurie had been insincere in his religion; there had been moments, and there still were, occasionally, when the world that the Catholic religion preached by word and symbol and sacrament, became apparent; but the whole thing was upon a different plane. Religion bade him approach in one way, spiritualism in the other. The senses had nothing to do with one; they were the only ultimate channels of the other. And it is extraordinarily easy for human beings to regard as more fundamentally real the evidence of the senses than the evidence of faith. . . .

Here then were the two choices – a world of spirit, to be taken largely on trust, to be discerned only in shadow and outline upon rare and unusual occasions of exaltation, of a particular quality which had almost lost its appeal; and a world of spirit that took shape and form and practical intelligibility, in ordinary rooms and under very nearly ordinary circumstances – a world, in short, not of a transcendent God and the spirits of just men made perfect, of vast dogmas and theories, but of a familiar atmosphere, impregnated with experience, inhabited by known souls who in this method or that made themselves apparent to those senses which, Laurie believed, could not lie. . . . And the point of contact was Amy Nugent herself. . . .

As regards his exact attitude to this girl it is more difficult to write. On the one side the human element – those associations directly connected with the senses – her actual face and hands, physical atmosphere and surroundings – those had disappeared; they were dispersed, or they lay underground; and it had been with a certain shock of surprise, in spite of the explanations given to him, that he had seen what he believed to be her face in the drawing-room in Queen's Gate. But he had tried to arrange all this in his imagination, and it had fallen into shape and proportion again. In short, he thought he understood now that it is character which gives unity to the transient qualities of a person on earth, and that, when those qualities disappear, it is as unimportant as the wasting of tissue : when, according to the spiritualists' gospel that character manifests itself from the other side, it naturally reconstitutes the form by which it had been recognised on earth.

Yet, in spite of this sense of familiarity with what he had seen, there had fallen between Amy and himself the august shadow that is called Death. . . . And in spite of the assurances he had received, even at the hands of his own senses, that this was indeed the same girl that he had known on earth, there was a strange awe mingled with his old, rather shallow passion. There were moments, as he sat alone in his rooms at night, when it rose almost to terror; just as there were other moments when awe vanished for a while, and his whole being was flooded with an extraordinary ecstatic semi-earthly happiness at the thought that he and she could yet speak with one another. . . . Imagine, if you please, a child who on returning home finds that his mother has become Queen, and meets her in the glory of ermine and diadem. . . .

But the real deciding point – which, somehow, he knew must come – the moment at which these conflicting notes should become a chord, was fixed for Sunday evening next. Up to now he had had evidence of her presence, he had received intelligible messages, though fragmentary and half stammered through the mysterious veil, he had for an instant or two looked upon her face; but the real point, he hoped, would come in two days. The public *séances* had not impressed him. He had been to three or four of these in a certain road off Baker Street, and had been astonished and disappointed. The kind of people that he had met there – sentimental bourgeois with less power of sifting evidence than the average child, with a credulity that was almost supernatural – the medium, a stout woman who rolled her eyes and had damp fat fingers; the hymn-singing, the wheezy harmonium, the amazing pseudo-mystical oracular messages that revealed nothing which a religiose fool could not invent – in fact the whole affair, from the sham stained-glass lamp-shade to the ghostly tambourines overhead, the puerility of the tricks played on the inquirers, and all the rest of it – this seemed as little connected with what he had experienced with Mr. Vincent as a dervish dance with High Mass. He had reflected with almost ludicrous horror upon the impression it would make on Maggie, and the remarks it would elicit.

But this other engagement was a very different matter.

They were going to attempt a further advance. It had, indeed, been explained to him that these attempts were but tentative and experimental; it was impossible to dictate exactly what should fall; but the object on Sunday night was to go a step farther, and to bring about, if possible, the materialisation process to such a point that the figure could be handled, and could speak. And it seemed to Laurie as if this would be final indeed. . . .

So he sat this evening, within forty-eight hours of the crisis, thinking steadily. Half a dozen times, perhaps, the thought of Maggie recurred to him; but he was learning how to get rid of that.

Then he took up the note and opened it. It was filled with four pages of writing. He turned to the end and read the signature. Then he turned back and read the whole letter.

It was very quiet as he sat there thinking over what he had read. The noise of Fleet Street came up here only as the soothing murmur of the sea upon a beach; and he himself sat motionless, the firelight falling upwards upon his young face; his eyes, and his curly hair. About him stood his familiar furniture, the grand piano a pool of glimmering dark wood in the background, the tall curtained windows suggestive of shelter and warmth and protection.

Yet, if he had but known it, he was making an enormous choice. The letter was from the man he had met at midday, and he was deciding how to answer it. He was soothed and quieted by his loneliness, and his irritation had disappeared : he regarded the letter from a youthfully philosophical standpoint, pleased with his moderation, as the work of a fanatic; he was considering only whether he would yield, for politeness' sake, to the importunity, or answer shortly and decisively. It seemed to him remarkable that a mature and experienced man could write such a letter.

At last he got up, went to his writing-table, and sat down. Still he hesitated for a minute; then he dipped his pen and wrote.

When he had finished and directed it, he went back to

the fire. He had an hour yet in which to think before he need dress. He had promised to dine with Mrs. Stapleton at half-past seven. He had a touch of headache, and perhaps might sleep it off.

CHAPTER TWELVE

I

Lady Laura crossed the road by Knightsbridge Barracks and turned again homewards through the Park.

It was one of those days that occasionally fall in late February which almost cheer the beholder into a belief that spring has really begun. Overhead the sky was a clear pale blue, flecked with summer-looking clouds, gauzy and white; beneath, the whole earth was waking drowsily from a frost so slight as only to emphasise the essential softness of the day that followed : the crocuses were alight in the grass, and an indescribable tint lay over all that had life, like a flush in the face of an awakening child. But these days are too good to last, and Lady Laura, who had looked at the forecast of a Sunday paper, had determined to take her exercise immediately after church.

She had come out not long before from All Saints'; she had listened to an excellent though unexciting sermon and some extremely beautiful singing; and even now, saturated with that atmosphere and with the soothing physical air in which she walked, her anxieties seemed less acute. There were enough of her acquaintances, too, in groups here and there – she had to bow and smile sufficiently often – to prevent these anxieties from reasserting themselves too forcibly. And it may be supposed that not a creature who observed her, in her exceedingly graceful hat and mantle, with her fair head a little on one side, and her gold-rimmed pince-nez delicately gleaming in the sunlight, had the very faintest suspicion that she had any anxieties at all.

Yet she felt strangely unwilling even to go home.

The men were to set about clearing the drawing-room while she was at church; and somehow the thought that it would be done when she got home, that the temple would, so to speak, be cleared for sacrifice, was a distasteful one.

She did not quite know when the change had begun; in

fact, she was scarcely yet aware that there was a change at all. Upon one point only her attention fixed itself, and that was the increasing desire she felt that Laurie Baxter should go no further in his researches under her auspices.

Up to within a few weeks ago she had been all ardour. It had seemed to her, as has been said, that the apparent results of spiritualism were all to the good, that they were in no point contrary to the religion she happened to believe – in fact, that they made real, as does an actual tree in the foreground of a panorama, the rather misty sky and hills of Christianity. She had even called them very 'teaching'.

It was about eighteen months since she had first taken this up under the onslaught of Mrs. Stapleton's enthusism; but things had not been as satisfactory as she wished, until Mr. Vincent had appeared. Then indeed matters had moved forward; she had seen extraordinary things, and the effect of them had been doubled by the medium's obvious honesty and his strong personality. He was to her as a resolute priest to a timid penitent; he had led her forward, supported by his own conviction and his extremely steady will, until she had begun to feel at home in this amazing new world, and eager to make proselytes.

Then Laurie had appeared, and almost immediately a dread had seized her that she could neither explain nor understand. She had attempted a little tentative conversation on the point with dearest Maud, but dearest Maud had appeared so entirely incapable of understanding her scruples that she had said no more. But her inexplicable anxiety had already reached such a point that she had determined to say a word to Laurie on the subject. This had been done, without avail; and now a new step forward was to be made.

As to of what this step consisted she was perfectly aware. The 'controls', she believed – the spirits that desired to communicate – had a series of graduated steps by which the communications could be made, from mere incoherent noises (as a man may rap a message from one room to another), through appearances, also incoherent and intangible, right up to the final point of assuming visible tangible form, and of speaking in an audible voice. This process, she believed, consisted first in a mere connection between spirit and matter, and finally passed into an actual assumption of matter, moulded into the form of the body once worn by the spirit on earth. For nearly all of this process she had had the evidence of her own senses; she had received messages, inexplicable to her except on the hypothesis put forward, from departed relations of her own; she had seen lights, and faces, and even figures formed before her eyes, in her own drawing-room; but she had not as yet, though dearest Maud had been more fortunate, been able to handle and grasp such figures, to satisfy the sense of touch, as well as of sight, in proof of the reality of the phenomenon.

Yes; she was satisfied even with what she had seen; she had no manner of doubt as to the theories put before her by Mr. Vincent; yet she shrank (and she scarcely knew why) from that final consummation which it was proposed to carry out if possible that evening. But the shrinking centred round some half-discerned danger to Laurie Baxter rather than to herself.

It was these kinds of thoughts that beset her as she walked up beneath the trees on her way homewards – checked and soothed now somewhat by the pleasant air and the radiant sunlight, yet perceptible beneath everything. And it was not only of Laurie Baxter that she thought; she spared a little attention for herself.

For she had begun to be aware, for the first time since her initiation, of a very faint distaste – as slight and yet as suggestive as that caused by a half-perceived consciousness of a delicately disagreeable smell. There comes such a moment in the life of cut flowers in water, when the impetus of growing energy ceases, and a new tone makes itself felt in their scent, of which the end is certain. It is not sufficient to cause the flowers to be thrown away; they still possess volumes of fragrance; yet these decrease, and the new scent increases, until it has the victory.

So it was now to the perceptions of this lady. Oh! yes; spiritualism was very 'teaching' and beautiful; it was perfectly compatible with orthodox religion; it was undeniably true. She would not dream of giving it up. Only it would be better if Laurie Baxter did not meddle with it : he was too sensitive. . . . However, he was coming that evening again. . . . There was the fact.

As she turned southwards at last, crossing the road again towards her own street, it seemed to her that the day even now was beginning to cloud over. Over the roofs of Kensington a haze was beginning to make itself visible, as impalpable as a skein of smoke; yet there it was. She felt a little languid, too. Perhaps she had walked too far. She would rest a little after lunch, if dearest Maud did not mind; for dearest Maud was to lunch with her, as was usual on Sundays when the Colonel was away.

As she came, slower than ever, down the broad opulent pavement of Queen's Gate, through the silence and emptiness of Sunday – for the church bells were long ago silent – she noticed coming towards her, with a sauntering step, an old gentleman in frock coat and silk hat of a slightly antique appearance, spatted and gloved, carrying his hands behind his back, as if he were waiting to be joined by some friend from one of the houses. She noticed that he looked at her through his glasses, but thought no more of it till she turned up the steps of her own house. Then she was startled by the sound of quick footsteps and a voice.

'I beg your pardon, madam . . .'

She turned, with her key in the door, and there he stood, hat in hand.

'Have I the pleasure of speaking to Lady Laura Bethell?'

There was a pleasant brisk ring about his voice that inclined her rather favourably towards him.

'Is there anything . . . Did you want to speak to me? . . . Yes, I am Lady Laura Bethell.'

'I was told you were at church, madam, and that you were not at home to visitors on Sunday.'

'That is quite right. . . . May I ask . . . ?'

'Only a few minutes, Lady Laura, I promise you. Will you forgive my persistence?'

(Yes; the man was a gentleman; there was no doubt of that.)

'Would not to-morrow do? I am rather engaged to-day.'

He had his card-case ready, and without answering her at once, he came up the steps and handed it to her.

The name meant nothing at all to her.

'Will not to-morrow . . . ?' she began again.

'To-morrow will be too late,' said the old gentleman. 'I

beg of you Lady Laura. It is on an extremely important matter.'

She still hesitated an instant; then she pushed the door open and went in.

'Please come in,' she said.

She was so taken aback by the sudden situation that she forgot completely that the drawing-room would be upside down, and led the way straight upstairs; and it was not till she was actually within the door, with the old gentleman close on her heels, that she saw that, with the exception of three or four chairs about the fire and the table set out near the hearthrug, the room was empty of furniture.

'I forgot,' she said; 'but will you mind coming in here. . . . We . . . we have a meeting here this evening.'

She led the way to the fire, and at first did not notice that he was not following her. When she turned round she saw the old gentleman, with his air of antique politeness completely vanished, standing and looking about him with a very peculiar expression. She also noticed, to her annoyance, that the cabinet was already in place in the little ante-room, and that his eyes almost immediately rested upon it. Yet there was no look of wonder in his face; rather it was such a look as a man might have on visiting the scene of a well-known crime – interest, knowledge, and loathing.

'So it is here—' he said in quite a low voice.

Then he came across the room towards her.

2

For an instant his bearded face looked so strangely at her that she half moved towards the bell. Then he smiled, with a little reassuring gesture.

'No, no,' he said. 'May I sit down a moment?'

She began hastily to cover her confusion.

'It is a meeting,' she said, 'for this evening. I am sorry—'

'Just so,' he said. 'It is about that that I have come.'

'I beg your pardon . . . ?'

'Please sit down, Lady Laura. . . . May I say in a sentence what I have come to say?'

(This seemed a very odd old man.)

'Why, yes—' she said.

'I have come to beg you not to allow Mr. Baxter to enter

the house. . . . No, I have no authority from anyone, least of all from Mr. Baxter. He has no idea that I have come. He would think it an unwarrantable piece of impertinence.'

'Mr. Cathcart . . . I – I cannot—'

'Allow me,' he said, with a little compelling gesture that silenced her. 'I have been asked to interfere by a couple of people very much interested in Mr. Baxter; one of them, if not both, completely disbelieves in spiritualism.'

'Then you know—'

He waved his hand towards the cabinet.

'Of course I know,' he said. 'Why, I was a spiritualist for ten years myself. No, not a medium; not a professional, that is to say. I know all about Mr. Vincent; all about Mrs. Stapleton and yourself, Lady Laura. I still follow the news closely; I know perfectly well—'

'And you have given it up?'

'I have given it up for a long while,' he said quietly. 'And I have come to ask you to forbid Mr. Baxter to be present this evening, for – for the same reason for which I have given it up myself.'

'Yes? And that—'

'I don't think we need go into that,' he said. 'It is enough, is it not, for me to say that Mr. Baxter's work, and, in fact, his whole nervous system, is suffering considerably from the excitement; that one of the persons who have asked me to do what I can is Mr. Baxter's own law-coach : and that even if he had not asked me, Mr. Baxter's own appearance—'

'You know him?'

'Practically, no. I lunched at the same table with him on Friday; the symptoms are quite unmistakable.'

'I don't understand. Symptoms?'

'Well, we will say symptoms of nervous excitement. You are aware, no doubt, that he is exceptionally sensitive. Probably you have seen for yourself—'

'Wait a moment,' said Lady Laura, her own heart beating furiously. 'Why do you not go to Mr. Baxter himself?'

'I have done so. I arranged to meet him at lunch, and somehow I took a wrong turn with him : I have no tact whatever, as you perceive. But I wrote to him on Friday night, offering to call upon him, and just giving him a hint. Well, it was useless. He refused to see me.'

'I don't see what I—'

'Oh yes,' chirped the old gentleman almost gaily. 'It would be quite unusual and unconventional. I just ask you to send him a line – I will take it myself, if you wish it – telling him that you think it would be better for him not to come, and saying that you are making other arrangements for to-night.'

He looked at her with that odd little air of birdlike briskness that she had noticed in the street; and it pleasantly affected her even in the midst of the uneasiness that now surged upon her again tenfold more than before. She could see that there was something else behind his manner; it had just looked out in the glance he had given round the room on entering; but she could not trouble at this moment to analyse what it was. She was completely bewildered by the strangeness of the encounter, and the extraordinary coincidence of this man's judgment with her own. Yet there were a hundred reasons against her taking his advice. What would the others say? What of all the arrangements . . . the expectation? . . .

'I don't see how it's possible now,' she began. 'I think I know what you mean. But—'

'Indeed, I trust you have no idea,' cried the old gentleman, with a queer little falsetto note coming into his voice – 'no idea at all. I come to you merely on the plea of nervous excitement; it is injuring his health, Lady Laura.'

She looked at him curiously.

'But—' she began.

'Oh, I will go further,' he said. 'Have you never heard of – of insanity in connection with all this? We will call it insanity, if you wish.'

For a moment her heart stood still. The word had a sinister sound, in view of an incident she had once witnessed; but it seemed to her that some meaning behind, unknown to her, was still more sinister. Why had he said that it might be 'called insanity' only? . . .

'Yes. . . . I – I have once seen a case,' she stammered.

'Well,' said the old gentleman, 'is it not enough when I tell you that I – I who was a spiritualist for ten years – have never seen a more dangerous subject than Mr. Baxter? Is the risk worth it? . . . Lady Laura, do you quite understand what you are doing?'

He leaned forward a little; and again she felt anxiety,

sickening and horrible, surge within her. Yet, on the other hand. . . .

The door opened suddenly, and Mr. Vincent came in.

3

There was silence for a moment; then the old gentleman turned round, and in an instant was on his feet, quiet, but with an air of bristling about his thrust-out chin and his tense attitude.

Mr. Vincent paused, looking from one to the other.

'I beg your pardon, Lady Laura,' he said courteously. 'Your man told me to wait here; I think he did not know you had come in.'

'Well – er – this gentleman . . .' began Lady Laura. 'Why, do you know Mr. Vincent?' she asked suddenly, startled by the expression in the old gentleman's face.

'I used to know Mr. Vincent,' he said shortly.

'You have the advantage of me,' smiled the medium, coming forward to the fire.

'My name is Cathcart, sir.'

The other started, almost imperceptibly.

'Ah! yes,' he said quietly. 'We did meet a few times, I remember.'

Lady Laura was conscious of distinct relief at the interruption : it seemed to her a providential escape from a troublesome decision.

'I think there is nothing more to be said, Mr. Cathcart. . . . No, don't go, Mr. Vincent. We had finished our talk.'

'Lady Laura,' said the old gentleman with a rather determined air, 'I beg of you to give me ten minutes more private conversation.'

She hesitated, clearly foreseeing trouble either way. Then she decided.

'There is no necessity to-day,' she said. 'If you care to make another appointment for one day next week, Mr. Cathcart—'

'I am to understand that you refuse me a few minutes now?'

'There is no necessity that I can see—'

'Then I must say what I have to say before Mr. Vincent—'

'One moment, sir,' put in the medium, with that sudden

slight air of imperiousness that Lady Laura knew very well by now. 'If Lady Laura consents to hear you, I must take it on myself to see that nothing offensive is said.' He glanced as if for leave towards the woman.

She made an effort.

'If you will say it quickly,' she began. 'Otherwise—'

The old gentleman drew a breath as if to steady himself. It was plain that he was very strongly moved beneath his self-command : his air of cheerful geniality was gone.

'I will say it in one sentence,' he said. 'It is this : You are ruining that boy between you, body and soul; and you are responsible before his Maker and yours. And if—'

'Lady Laura,' said the medium, 'do you wish to hear any more?'

She made a doubtful little gesture of assent.

'And if you wish to know my reasons for saying this,' went on Mr. Cathcart, 'you have only to ask for them from Mr. Vincent. He knows well enough why I left spiritualism – if he dares to tell you.'

Lady Laura glanced at the medium. He was perfectly still and quiet – looking, watching the old man curiously and half humorously under his heavy eyebrows.

'And I understand,' went on the other, 'that to-night you are to make an attempt at complete materialisation. Very good; then after to-night it may be too late. I have tried to appeal to the boy : he will not hear me. And you too have refused to hear me out. I could give you evidence, if you wished. Ask this gentleman how many cases he has known in the last five years, where complete ruin, body and soul—'

The medium turned a little to the fire, sighing as if for weariness : and at the sound the old man stopped, trembling. It was more obvious than ever that he only held himself in restraint by a very violent effort : it was as if the presence of the medium affected him in an extraordinary degree.

Lady Laura glanced again from one to the other.

'That is all, then?' she said.

His lips worked. Then he burst out—

'I am sick of talking,' he cried – 'sick of it ! I have warned you. That is enough. I cannot do more.'

He wheeled on his heel and went out. A minute later the two heard the front door bang.

She looked at Mr. Vincent. He was twirling softly in his

strong fingers a little bronze candlestick that stood on the mantelpiece: his manner was completely unconcerned; he even seemed to be smiling a little.

For herself she felt helpless. She had taken her choice, impelled to it, though she scarcely recognised the fact, by the entrance of this strong personality; and now she needed reassurance once again. But before she had a word to say, he spoke – still in his serene manner.

'Yes, yes,' he said. 'I remember now. I used to know Mr. Cathcart once. A very violent old gentleman.'

'What did he mean?'

'His reasons for leaving us? Indeed I scarcely remember. I suppose it was because he became a Catholic.'

'Was there nothing more?'

He looked at her pleasantly.

'Why, I daresay there was. I really can't remember, Lady Laura. I suppose he had his nerves shaken. You can see for yourself what a fanatic he is.'

But in spite of his presence, once more a gust of anxiety shook her.

'Mr. Vincent, are you sure it's safe – for Mr. Baxter, I mean?'

'Safe? Why, he's as safe as any of us can be. We all have nervous systems, of course.'

'But he's particularly sensitive, isn't he?'

'Indeed, yes. That is why even this evening he must not go into trance. That must come later, after a good training.'

She stood up, and came herself to stand by the mantelpiece.

'Then really there's no danger?'

He turned straight to her, looking at her with kind, smiling eyes.

'Lady Laura,' he said, 'have I ever yet told you that there was no danger? I think not. There is always danger, for every one of us, as there is for the scientist in the laboratory, and the engineer in his machinery. But what we can do is to reduce that danger to a minimum, so that, humanly speaking, we are reasonably and sufficiently safe. No doubt you remember the case of that girl? Well, that was an accident: and accidents will happen; but do me the justice to remember that it was the first time that I had seen her. It was absolutely impossible to foresee. She was on the very edge of a nervous breakdown before she entered the room. But with regard to Mr. Baxter, I have seen him again and again; and I tell you that I consider him to be running a certain risk – but a perfectly justifiable one, and one that is reduced to a minimum. If I did not think that we were taking every precaution, I would not have him in the room for all the world. . . . Are you satisfied, Lady Laura?'

Every word he said helped her back to assurance. It was all so reasonable and well weighed. If he had said there was no danger, she would have feared the more; but his very recognition of it gave her security. And above all, his tranquillity and his strength were enormous assets on his side.

She drew a breath, and decided to go forward.

'And Mr. Cathcart?' she asked.

He smiled again.

'You can see what he is,' he said. 'I should advise you not to see him again. It's of no sort of use.'

CHAPTER THIRTEEN

I

The weather forecasts had been in the right; and the few that struggled homewards that night from church fought against a south-west wind that tore, laden with driving rain, up the streets and across the open spaces, till the very lights were dimmed in the tall street lamps and shone only through streaming panes that seemed half opaque with mist and vapour. In Queen's Gate hardly one lighted window showed that the houses were inhabited. So fierce was the clamour and storm of the broad street that men made haste to shut out every glimpse of the night, and the fanlights above the doors, or here and there a line of brightness where some draught had tossed the curtains apart, were the only signs of human life. Outside the broad pavements stared like surfaces of some canal, black and mirror-like, empty of passengers, catching every spark or hint of light from house and lamp, transforming it to a tall streak of glimmering wetness.

The housekeeper's room in this house on the right was the more delightful from the contrast. It was here that the august assembly was held every evening after supper, set about with rigid etiquette and ancient rite. Its windows looked on to the little square garden at the back, but were now tight shuttered and curtained; and the room was a very model of comfort and warmth. Before the fire a square table was drawn up, set out with pudding and fruit, for it was here that the upper servants withdrew after the cold meat and beer of the servants' hall, to be waited upon by the butler's boy: and it was round this that the four sat in state – housekeeper, butler, lady's maid, and cook.

It was already aften ten o'clock; and Mr. Parker was permitted to smoke a small cigar. They had discussed the weather, the sermon that Miss Baker had heard in the morning, and the prospects of a Dissolution; and they had once more returned to the mysteries that were being enacted upstairs. They were getting accustomed to them now, and there was not a great deal to say, unless they repeated themselves, which they had no objection to do. Their attitude was one of tolerant scepticism, tempered by an agreeable tendency on the part of Miss Baker to become agitated after a certain point. Mr. Vincent, it was generally conceded, was a respectable sort of man, with an air about him that could hardly be put into words, and it was thought to be a pity that he lent himself to such superstition. Mrs. Stapleton had been long ago dismissed as a silly sort of woman, though with a will of her own; and her ladyship, of course, must have her way; it could not last long, it was thought.

But young Mr. Baxter was another matter, and there was a deal to say about him. He was a gentleman – that was certain; and he seemed to have sense; but it was a pity that he was so often here now on this business. He had not said one word to Mr. Parker this evening as he took off his coat; Mr. Parker had not thought that he looked very well.

'He was too quiet-like,' said the butler.

As to the details of the affair upstairs – these were considered in a purely humorous light. It was understood that tables danced a hornpipe, and that tambourines were beaten by invisible hands; and it was not necessary to go further into principles, particularly since all these things were done by machinery at the Egyptian Hall. Faces also, it was believed, were seen looking out of the cabinet which Mr. Parker had once more helped to erect this morning; but these, it was explained, were 'done' by luminous paint. Finally, if people insisted on looking into causes, Electricity was a sufficient answer for all the rest. No one actually suggested water-power.

As for human motives, these were not called in question at all. It appeared to amuse some people to do this kind of thing, as others might collect old china or practise the *cotillon*. There it was, a fact, and there was no more to be said about it. Old Lady Carraden, where Mr. Parker had once been under-butler, had gone in for pouter pigeons; and Miss Baker had heard tell of a nobleman who had a carpenter's shop of his own.

These things were so, then; and meantime here was a

cigar to be smoked by Mr. Parker, and a little weak tea to be taken by the three ladies.

It was about a quarter-past ten when a reversion was made of the weather. Within here all was supremely comfortable. A black stuff mat, with a red fringed border, lay before the blazing fire, convenient to the feet; the heavy red curtains shut out the darkness, and where the glass cases of china permitted it, large photographs of wedding groups and the houses of the nobility hung upon the walls. A King Charles' spaniel, in another glass case, looked upon the company with an eternal snarl belied by the mildness of his brown eyes; and, corresponding to him on the other side of the fire, a numerous family of humming-birds, a little dusty and dim, poised perpetually above the flowers of a lichened tree, with a flaming sunset to show them up.

But, without, the wind tore unceasingly, laden with rain, through the gusty darkness of the little garden, and, in the pauses, the swift dripping from the roof splashed and splashed upon the paved walk. It was a very wild night, as Mr. Parker observed four times : he only hoped that no one would require a hansom cab. He had been foolish enough to take the responsibility to-night of letting the guests out himself, and of allowing William to go to bed when he wished. And these were late affairs, seldom over before eleven, and often not till nearly midnight.

Mrs. Martin, in her blouse, moved a little nearer the fire, and said she must be off soon to bed; Mrs. Mayle, in her black silk, added that there was no telling when her ladyship would get to bed, what with Mrs. Stapleton and all, and commiserated Miss Baker; Miss Baker moaned a little in self-pity; and Mr. Parker remarked for the fifth time that it was a wild night. It was an astonishingly serene and domestic atmosphere : no effort of imagination or wit was required from anybody; it was enough to make observations when they occurred to the brain and they would meet with a tranquil response.

As half-past ten tingled out from the little yellow marble clock on the mantelpiece – it had been won by Mrs. Mayle's deceased husband in a horticultural exhibition – Mrs. Martin said that she must go and have a look at the scullery to see that all was as it should be; there was no knowing with these girls nowadays what they might not leave undone;

and Mrs. Mayle preened herself gently with the thought that her responsibilities were on a higher plane. Mr. Parker made a courteous movement as if to rise, and remained seated, as the cook rustled out. Miss Baker sighed again as she contemplated the long conversation that might take place between the two ladies upstairs before she could get her mistress to bed.

Once more the tranquil atmosphere settled down on the warm room; the brass lamp burned brightly with a faint and reassuring smell of paraffin; the fire presented a radiant cavern of red coals fringed by dancing flames; and Mr. Parker leaned forwards to shake off the ash of his cigar.

Then, on a sudden, he paused, for from the passage outside came the passionless tingle of an electric bell – then another, and another, and another, as if some person overhead strove by reiteration on that single note to cry out some overwhelming need.

2

Overhead in the great empty drawing-room the noise of the wind and rain, the almost continuous spatter on the glass, and the long hooting of the gusts, had been far more noticeable than in the basement beneath. Below stairs the company had been natural and normal, talking of this and that, in a brightly lighted room, dwelling only on matters that fell beneath the range of their senses, lulled by warmth and food and cigar-smoke into a kind of rapt self-contemplation. But up here, in the gloom, lighted only on this occasion by a single shaded candle, in a complete interior silence, three persons had sat round a table for more than an hour, striving by passivity and a kind of indescribable concentration to ignore all that was presented by the senses, and to await some movement from that which lies beyond them.

Lady Laura had sat down that night in a state of mind which she could not analyse. It was not that her anxieties had been lulled so much as counter-balanced; they were still there, at once poignant and heavy, but on the other side there had been the assured air of the medium, his reasonableness and his personality, as well as the enthusiasm of her friend, and her astonished remonstrances. She had decided to acquiesce, not because she was satisfied, but because on the whole anxiety was outweighed by confidence. She could not have taken action under such circumstances, but she could at least refrain from it.

Laurie, as Mr. Parker had noticed, had been 'quiet-like'; he had said very little indeed, but a nervous strain was evident in the brightness of his eyes; but in answer to a conventional inquiry he had declared himself extremely well. Mr. Vincent had looked at him for just an instant longer than usual as he shook hands, but he said nothing. Mrs. Stapleton had made an ecstatic remark or two on the envy with which she regarded the boy's sensitive faculties.

At the beginning of the *séance* the medium had repeated his warnings as to Laurie's avoiding of trance, and had added one or two other precautions. Then he had gone into the cabinet; the fire had been pressed down under ashes, and a single candle lighted and placed behind the angle of the little adjoining room in such a position that its shaded light fell upon the cabinet only and the figure of the medium within.

When the silence became fixed, Lady Laura for the first time perceived the rage of wind and rain outside. The very intensity of the interior stillness and the rapture of attention emphasised to an extraordinary degree the windy roar without. Yet the silence seemed to her, now as always, to have a peculiar faculty of detaching the psychical from the physical atmosphere. In spite of the batter of rain not ten feet away, the sighing between the shutters, and even the lift now and again of the heavy curtains in the draught, she seemed to herself as remote from it as a man crouching in the dark under some ruin feels himself at an almost infinite distance from the pick and the hammer of the rescuers. These were in one world, she in another.

For over an hour no movement was made. She herself sat facing the fire, Laurie on her left looking towards the cabinet and his back to the windows, Mrs. Stapleton opposite to her.

An endless procession of thoughts defiled before her as she sat, yet these too were somewhat remote – far up, so to speak, on the superficies of consciousness : they did not approach that realm of the will poised now and attentive on another range of existence. Once and again she glanced up without moving her head at the three-quarter profile on her left, at the somewhat Zulu-like outline opposite to her; then down again at the polished little round table and the six hands laid upon it. And meanwhile her brain revolved images rather than thoughts, memories rather than reflections – vignettes, so to speak, – old Mr. Cathcart in his spats and frock-coat, the look on the medium's face, there and gone again in an instant as he had heard the stranger's name; the carved oak stalls of the chancel towards which she had faced this morning, the look of the park, the bloom upon the still leafless trees, the radiance of the blue spring sky. . . .

It must have been, she thought, after a little over an hour that the first expected movement made itself felt – a long trembling shudder through the wood beneath her hands, followed by a strange sensation of lightness, as if the whole table rose a little from the floor. Then, almost before the movement subsided, a torrent of little taps poured itself out, as delicate and as swift and, it seemed, as perfectly calculated, as the rapping of some minute electric hammer. This was new to her, yet not so unlike other experiences as to seem strange or perturbing in any way. . . . Again she bent her attention to the table as the vibration ceased.

There followed a long silence.

It must have been about ten minutes later that she became aware of the next phenomenon; and her attention had been called to it by a sudden noiseless uplifting of the profile on her left. She turned her face to the cabinet and looked; and there, perfectly discernible, was some movement going on between the curtains. For the moment she could see the medium clearly, his arms folded, indicated by the white lines of his cuffs across his breast, his head sunk forward in deep sleep; and at the next instant the curtains flapped two or three times, as if jerked from within and finally rested completely closed.

She glanced quickly at the boy on her left, and in the diffused light from the other room could see him distinctly, his eyes open and watching, his lips compressed as if in some tense effort of self-control.

When she looked at the cabinet again she could see that some movement had begun again behind the curtains, for these swayed and jerked convulsively, as if some person with but little room was moving there. And she could hear now, as the gusts outside lulled for a moment, the steady rather stertorous breathing of the medium. Then once again the wind gathered strength outside; the rain tore at the glass like a streaming handful of tiny pebbles, and the great curtains at her side lifted and sighed in the draught through the shutters.

When it quieted again the breathing had become a measured moaning, as that which a dreaming dog emits at the end of each expiration; and she herself drew a long trembling breath, overwhelmed by the sense of some struggle in the room such as she had not experienced before.

It was impossible for her to express this even to herself; yet the perception was clear – as clear as some presentiment of the senses. She knew during those moments, as she watched the swaying curtains of the cabinet in the shaded light that fell upon them, and heard now and again that low moan from behind them, that some kind of stress lay upon something that was new to her in this connection. For the time she forgot her undertone of anxiety as to this boy at her side, and a curious terrified excitement took its place. Once, even then, she glanced at him again, and saw the motionless profile watching, always watching. . . .

Then in an instant the climax came, and this is what she saw.

The commotion of the curtains ceased suddenly, and they hung in straight folds from roof to floor of the little cabinet. Then they gently parted – she saw the long fingers that laid hold of them – and the form of a person came out, descended the single step, and stood on the floor before her eyes, in the plain candle-light, not four steps away.

It was the figure of a young girl, perfectly formed in all its parts, swathed in some light stuff resembling muslin that fell almost to the feet and shrouded the upper part of the head. Her hands were clasped across her breast, her bare feet were visible against the dark floor, and her features were unmistakably clear. There was a certain beauty in the face – in the young lips, the open eyes, and the dark lines of the brows over them; and the complexion was waxen, clear as of a blonde. But, as the observer had noticed before on the three or four occasions on which she had seen these phenomena, there was a strange mask-like set of the features, as if the life that lay behind them had not perfectly saturated that which expressed it. It was something utterly different from the face of a dead person, yet also not completely alive, though the eyes turned a little in their sockets, and the young down-curved lips smiled. Behind her, plain between the tossed-back curtains, was the figure of the medium sunk in sleep.

And so for a few seconds the apparition remained.

It seemed to the watcher that during those seconds the whole world was still. Whether in truth the wind had dropped, or whether the absorbed attention perceived nothing but the marvel before it, yet so it seemed. Even the breathing of the medium had stopped; Lady Laura heard only the ticking of the watch upon her own wrist.

Then, as once more a gust tore up from the south-west, the figure moved forward a step nearer the table, coming with a motion as of a living person, causing, it even appeared, that faint vibration on the floor as of a living body.

She stood so near now, though with her back to the diffused light of the ante-room, that her features were more plain than before – the stained lips, the open eyes, the shadow beneath the nostrils and chin, even the white fingers clasped across the breast. There was none of that vague mistiness that had been seen once before in that room; every line was as clear-cut as in the face of a living person; even the swell of the breast beneath the hands, the slender sloping shoulders, the long curved line from hip to ankle, all were real and discernible. And once again the staring eyes of the watcher took in, and her mind perceived, that slight mask-like look on the pretty appealing face.

Once again the figure came forward, straight on to the table; and then, so swift that not a motion or a word could check it, the catastrophe fell.

There was a violent movement on Lady Laura's left hand, a chair shot back and fell, and with a horrible tearing cry from the throat, the boy dashed himself face forwards across the table, snatched at and for an instant seized something real and concrete that stood there; and as the two women sprang up, losing sight for an instant of the figure that had been there a moment ago, the boy sank forward, moaning and sobbing, and a crash as of a heavy body falling sounded from the cabinet.

For a space of reckonable time there was complete silence. Then once more a blast of wind tore up from the south-west, rain shattered against the window, and the house vibrated to the shock.

CHAPTER FOURTEEN

I

As the date approached Maggie felt her anxieties settle down, like a fire, from turbulence to steady flame. On the Sunday she had with real difficulty kept it to herself, and the fringe of the storm of wind and rain that broke over Hertfordshire in the evening had not been reassuring. Yet on one thing her will kept steady hold, and that was that Mrs. Baxter must not be consulted. No conceivable good could result, and there might even be harm : either the old lady would be too much or not enough concerned : she might insist on Laurie's return to Stantons, or might write him a cheering letter encouraging him to amuse himself in any direction that he pleased. So Maggie passed the evening in fits of alternate silence and small conversation, and succeeded in making Mrs. Baxter recommend a good long night.

Monday morning, however, broke with a cloudless sky, an air like wine, and the chatter of birds; and by the time that Maggie went to look at the crocuses immediately before breakfast, she was all but at her ease again. Enough, however, of anxiety remained to make her hurry out to the stable-yard when she heard the postman on the way to the back door.

There was one letter for her, in Mr. Cathcart's handwriting; and she opened it rather hastily as she turned in again to the garden.

It was reassuring. It stated that the writer had approached – (that was the word) – Mr. Baxter, though unfortunately with ill-success, and that he proposed on the following day – (the letter was dated on Saturday evening) – also to approach Lady Laura Bethell. He felt fairly confident, he said, that his efforts would succeed in postponing, at any rate, Mr. Baxter's visit to Lady Laura; and in that case he would write further as to what was best to be done. In the meanwhile Miss Deronnais was not to be in the least anxious. Whatever happened, it was extremely improbable that one visit more or less to a *séance* would carry any great harm : it was the habit, rather than the act, that was usually harmful to the nervous system. And the writer begged to remain her obedient servant.

Maggie's spirits rose with a bound. How extraordinarily foolish she had been, she told herself, to have been filled with such forebodings last night ! It was more than likely that the *séance* had taken place without Laurie; and, even at the worst, as Mr. Cathcart said, he was probably only a little more excited than usual this morning.

So she began to think about future arrangements; and by the time that Mrs. Baxter looked benignantly out at her from beneath the Queen Anne doorway to tell her that breakfast was waiting, she was conceiving of the possibility of going up herself to London in a week or two on some shopping excuse, and of making one more genial attempt to persuade Laurie to be a sensible boy again.

During her visit to the fowl-yard after breakfast she began to elaborate these plans.

She was clear now, once again, that the whole thing was a fantastic delusion, and that its sole harm was that it was superstitious and nerve-shaking. (She threw a large handful of maize, with a meditative eye.) It was on that ground and that only that she would approach Laurie. Perhaps even it would be better for her not to go and see him; it might appear that she was making too much of it : a good sensible letter might do the work equally well. . . . Well, she would wait at least to hear from Mr. Cathcart once more. The second post would probably bring a letter from him. (She emptied her bowl.)

She was out again in the spring sunshine, walking up and down before the house with a book by the time that the second post was due. But this time, through the iron gate, she saw the postman go past the house without stopping. Once more her spirits rose, this time, one might say, to par; and she went indoors.

Her window looked out on to the front; and she moved her writing-table to it to catch as much as possible of the radiant air and light of the spring day. She proposed to begin to sketch out what she would say to Laurie, and suggest, if he wished it, to come up and see him in a week or two. She would apologise for her fussiness, and say that the reason why she was writing was that she did not want his mother to be made anxious.

'My dear Laurie . . .'

She bit her pen gently, and looked out of the window to catch inspiration for the particular frame of words with which she should begin. And as she looked an old gentleman suddenly appeared beyond the iron gate, shook it gently, glanced up in vain for a name on the stone posts, and stood irresolute. It was an old trap, that of the front gate; there was no bell, and it was necessary for visitors to come straight in to the front door.

Then, so swiftly that she could not formulate it, an anxiety leapt at her, and she laid her pen down, staring. What was this?

She went quickly to the bell and rang it; standing there waiting, with beating heart and face suddenly gone white. . . .

'Susan,' she said, 'there is an old gentleman at the gate. Go out and see who it is. . . . Stop : if it is anyone for me . . . if – if he gives the name of Mr. Cathcart, ask him to be so kind as to go round the turn to the village and wait for me. . . . Susan, don't say anything to Mrs. Baxter; it may just possibly be bad news.'

From behind the curtain she watched the maid go down the path, saw a few words pass between her and the stranger, and then the maid come back. She waited breathless.

'Yes, miss. It is a Mr. Cathcart. He said he would wait for you.'

Maggie nodded.

'I will go,' she said. 'Remember, please do not say a word to anyone. It may be bad news, as I said.'

As she walked through the hamlet three minutes later, she began to recognise that the news must be really serious; and that beneath all her serenity she had been aware of its possibility. So intense now was that anxiety – though perfectly formless in its details – that all other faculties seemed absorbed into it. She could not frame any imagination as to what it meant; she could form no plan, alternative or absolute, as to what must be done. She was only aware that something had happened, and that she would know the facts in a few seconds.

About fifty yards up the turning she saw the old gentleman waiting. He was in his London clothes, silk-hatted and spatted, and made a curiously incongruous picture there in the deep-banked lane that led upwards to the village. On either side towered the trees, still leafless, yet bursting with life; and overhead chattered the birds against the tender midday sky of spring.

He lifted his hat as she came to him; but they spoke no word of greeting.

'Tell me quickly,' she said. 'I am Maggie Deronnais.'

He turned to walk by her side, saying nothing for a moment.

'The facts or the interpretation?' he asked in his brisk manner. 'I will just say first that I have seen him this morning.'

'Oh! the facts,' she said. 'Quickly, please.'

'Well, he is going to Mr. Morton's chambers this afternoon; he says . . .'

'What?'

'One moment, please. . . . Oh! he is not seriously ill, as the world counts illness. He thought he was just very tired this morning. I went round to call on him. He was in bed at half-past ten when I left him. Then I came straight down here.'

For a moment she thought the old man mad. The relief was so intense that she flushed scarlet, and stopped dead in the middle of the road.

'You came down here,' she repeated. 'Why I thought—'

He looked at her gravely, in spite of the incessant twinkle in his eyes. She perceived that this old man's eyes would twinkle at a death-bed. He stroked his grey beard smoothly down.

'Yes; you thought that he was dead, perhaps? Oh, no. But for all that, Miss Deronnais, it is just as serious as it can be.'

She did not know what to think. Was the man a madman himself?

'Listen, please. I am telling you simply the facts. I was anxious, and I went round this morning first to Lady Laura Bethell. To my astonishment she saw me. I will not tell you all that she said, just now. She was in a terrible state, though she did not know one-tenth of the harm— Well, after what she told me I went round straight to Mitre Court. The porter was inclined not to let me in. Well, I went in, and straight into Mr. Baxter's bedroom; and I found there—'

He stopped.

'Yes?'

'I found exactly what I had feared, and expected.'

'Oh! tell me quickly,' she cried, wheeling on him in anger.

He looked at her as if critically for a moment. Then he went on abruptly.

'I found Mr. Baxter in bed. I made no apology at all. I said simply that I had come to see how he was after the *séance*.'

'It took place, then—'

'Oh! yes. . . . I forgot to mention that Lady Laura would pay no attention to me yesterday. . . . Yes, it took place . . . Well, Mr. Baxter did not seem surprised to see me. He told me he felt tired. He said that the *séance* had been a success. And while he talked I watched him. . . . Then I came away and caught the ten-fifty.'

'I don't understand in the least,' said Maggie.

'So I suppose,' said the other drily. 'I imagine you do not believe in spiritualism at all – I mean that you think that the whole thing is fraud or hysteria?'

'Yes, I do,' said Maggie bravely.

He nodded once or twice.

'So do most sensible people. . . . Well, Miss Deronnais, I have come to warn you. I did not write, because it was impossible to know what to say until I had seen you and heard your answer to that question. At the same time, I wanted to lose no time. Anything may happen now at any moment. . . . I wanted to tell you this : that I am at your service now altogether. When—' he stopped; then he began again, 'If you hear no further news for the present, may I ask when you expect to see Mr. Baxter again?'

'In Easter week.'

'That is a fortnight off. . . . Do you think you could persuade him to come down here next week instead? I should like you to see him for yourself; or even sooner.'

She was still hopelessly confused with these apparent alternations. She still wondered whether Mr. Cathcart were as mad as he seemed. They turned, as the village came in sight ahead, up the hill.

'Next week? I could try,' she said mechanically. 'But I don't understand—'

He held up a gloved hand.

'Wait till you have seen him,' he said. 'For myself, I shall make a point of seeing Mr. Morton every day to hear the news. . . . Miss Deronnais, I tell you plainly that you alone will have to bear the weight of all this, unless Mrs. Baxter—'

'Oh, do explain,' she said almost irritably.

He looked at her with those irresistibly twinkling eyes, but she perceived a very steady will behind them.

'I will explain nothing at all,' he said, 'now that I have seen you, and heard what you think, except this single point. What you have to be prepared for is the news that Mr. Baxter has suddenly gone out of his mind.'

It was said in exactly the same tone as his previous sentences, and for a moment she did not catch the full weight of its meaning. She stopped and looked at him, paling gradually.

'Yes, you took that very well,' he said, still meeting her eyes steadily. 'Stop . . . Keep a strong hold on yourself. That is the worst you have to hear, for the present. Now tell me immediately whether you think Mrs. Baxter should be informed or not.'

Her leaping heart slowed down into three or four gulping blows at the base of her throat. She swallowed with difficulty.

'How do you know—'

'Kindly answer my question,' he said. 'Do you think Mrs. Baxter—'

'Oh, God! Oh, God!' sobbed Maggie.

'Steady, steady,' said the old man. 'Take my arm, Miss Deronnais.'

She shook her head, keeping her eyes fixed on his.

He smiled in his grey beard.

'Very good,' he said, 'very good. And do you think—'

She shook her head again.

'No: not one word. She is his mother. Besides – she is not the kind – she would be of no use.'

'Yes: it is as I thought. Very well, Miss Deronnais; you

will have to be responsible. You can wire for me at any moment. You have my address?'

She nodded.

'Then I have one or two things to add. Whatever happens, do not lose heart for one moment. I have seen these cases again and again. . . . Whatever happens, too, do not put yourself into a doctor's hands until I have seen Mr. Baxter for myself. The thing may come suddenly or gradually. And the very instant you are convinced it is coming, telegraph to me. I will be here two hours after. . . . Do you understand?'

They halted twenty yards from the turning into the hamlet. He looked at her again with his kindly humorous eyes.

She nodded slowly and deliberately, repeating in her own mind his instructions; and beneath, like a whirl of waters, questions surged to and fro, clamouring for answer. But her self-control was coming back each instant.

'You understand, Miss Deronnais?' he said again.

'I understand. Will you write to me?'

'I will write this evening. . . . Once more, then. Get him down next week. Watch him carefully when he comes. Consult no doctor until you have telegraphed to me, and I have seen him.'

She drew a long breath, nodding almost mechanically.

'Good-bye, Miss Deronnais. Let me tell you that you are taking it magnificently. Fear nothing; pray much.'

He took her hand for a moment. Then he raised his hat and left her standing there.

2

Mrs. Baxter was exceedingly absorbed just now in a new pious book of meditations written by a clergyman. A nicely bound copy of it, which she had ordered specially, had arrived by the parcels post that morning; and she had been sitting in the drawing-room ever since looking through it, and marking it with a small silver pencil. Religion was to this lady what horticulture was to Maggie, except of course that it was really important, while horticulture was not. She often wondered that Maggie did not seem to understand : of course she went to mass every morning, dear girl; but religion surely was much more than that; one should be able to sit for two or three hours over a book in the drawing-room, before the fire, with a silver pencil.

So at lunch she prattled of the book almost continuously, and at the end of it thought Maggie more unsubtle than ever : she looked rather tired and strained, thought the old lady, and she hardly said a word from beginning to end.

The drive in the afternoon was equally unsatisfactory. Mrs. Baxter took the book with her, and the pencil, in order to read aloud a few extracts here and there; and she again seemed to find Maggie rather vacuous and silent.

'Dearest child, you are not very well, I think,' she said at last.

Maggie roused herself suddenly.

'What, Auntie?'

'You are not very well, I think. Did you sleep well?'

'Oh ! I slept all right,' said Maggie vaguely.

But after tea Mrs. Baxter did not feel very well herself. She said she thought she must have taken a little chill. Maggie looked at her with unperceptive eyes.

'I am sorry,' she said mechanically.

'Dearest, you don't seem very overwhelmed. I think perhaps I shall have dinner in bed. Give me my book, child. . . . Yes, and the pencil-case.'

Mrs. Baxter's room was so comfortable, and the book so fascinatingly spiritual, that she determined to keep her resolution and go to bed. She felt feverish, just to the extent of being very sleepy and at her ease. She rang her bell and issued her commands.

'A little of the *volaille*,' she said, 'with a spoonful of soup before it. . . . No, no meat; but a custard or so, and a little fruit. Oh ! yes, Charlotte, and tell Miss Maggie not to come and see me after dinner.'

It seemed that the message had roused the dear girl at last, for Maggie appeared ten minutes later in quite a different mood. There was really some animation in her face.

'Dear Auntie, I am so very sorry. . . . Yes; do go to bed, and breakfast there in the morning too. I'm just writing to Laurie, by the way.'

Mrs. Baxter nodded sleepily from her deep chair.

'He's coming down in Easter week, isn't he?'

'So he says, my dear.'

'Why shouldn't he come next week instead, Auntie, and be with us for Easter? You'd like that, wouldn't you?'

'Very nice indeed, dear child; but don't bother the boy.'

'And you don't think it's influenza?' put in Maggie swiftly, laying a cool hand on the old lady's.

She maintained it was not. It was just a little chill, such as she had had this time last year : and it became necessary to rouse herself a little to enumerate the symptoms. By the time she had done, Maggie's attention had begun to wander again : the old lady had never known her so unsympathetic before, and said so with gentle peevishness.

Maggie kissed her quickly.

'I'm sorry, Auntie,' she said. 'I was just thinking of something. Sleep well; and don't get up in the morning.'

Then she left her to a spoonful of soup, a little *volaille*, a custard, some fruit, her spiritual book and contentment.

Downstairs she dined alone in the green-hung dining-room; and she revolved for the twentieth time the thoughts that had been continuously with her since midday, moving before her like a kaleidoscope, incessantly changing their relations, their shapes, and their suggestions. These tended to form themselves into two main alternative classes. Either Mr. Cathcart was a harmless fanatic, or he was unusually sharp. But these again had almost endless subdivisions, for at present she had no idea of what was really in his mind – as to what his hints meant. Either this curious old gentleman with shrewd, humorous eyes was entirely wrong, and Laurie was just suffering from a nervous strain, not severe enough to hinder him from reading law in Mr. Morton's chambers; and this was all the substratum of Mr. Cathcart's mysteries : or else Mr. Cathcart was right, and Laurie was in the presence of some danger called insanity which Mr. Cathcart interpreted in some strange fashion she could not understand. And beneath all this again moved the further questions as to what spiritualism really was – what it professed to be, or mere superstitious nonsense, or something else.

She was amazed that she had not demanded greater explicitness this morning; but the thing had been so startling, so suggestive at first, so insignificant in its substance, that her ordinary commonsense had deserted her. The old gentleman had come and gone like a wraith, had uttered a few

186

inconclusive sentences, and promised to write, had been disappointed with her at one moment and enthusiastic the next. Obviously their planes ran neither parallel nor opposing; they cut at unexpected points; and Maggie had no notion as to the direction in which his lay. All she saw plainly was that there was some point of view other than hers.

So, then, she revolved theories, questioned, argued, doubted with herself. One thing only emerged – the old lady's feverish cold afforded her exactly the opportunity she wished; she could write to Laurie with perfect truthfulness that his mother had taken to her bed, and that she hoped he would come down next week instead of the week after.

After dinner she sat down and wrote it, pausing many times to consider a phrase.

Then she read a little, and soon after ten went upstairs to bed.

3

It was a little before sunset on that day that Mr. James Morton turned down on to the Embankment to walk up to the Westminster underground to take him home. He was a great man on physical exercise, and it was a matter of principle with him to live far from his work. As he came down the little passage he found his friend waiting for him, and together they turned up towards where in the distance the Westminster towers rose high and blue against the evening sky.

'Well?' said the old man.

Mr. Morton looked at him with a humorous eye.

'You are a hopeless case,' he said.

'Kindly tell me what you noticed.'

'My dear man,' he said, 'there's absolutely nothing to say. I did exactly what you said : I hardly spoke to him at all : I watched him very carefully indeed. I really can't go on doing that day after day. I've got my own work to do. It's the most utter bunkum I ever—'

'Tell me anything odd that you saw.'

'There was nothing odd at all, except that the boy looked tired, as you saw for yourself this morning.'

'Did he behave exactly as usual?'

'Exactly, except that he was quieter. He fidgeted a little with his fingers.'

'Yes?'

'And he seemed very hard at work. I caught him looking at me once or twice.'

'Yes? How did he look?'

'He just looked at me – that was all. Good Lord! what do you want—'

'And there was nothing else – absolutely nothing else?'

'Absolutely nothing else.'

'He didn't complain of . . . of anything?'

'Lord! . . . Oh, yes; he did say something about a headache.'

'Ah!' (The old man leaned forward.) 'A headache? What kind?'

'Back of his head.'

The old man sat back with pursed lips.

'Did he talk about last night?' he went on again suddenly.

'Not a word.'

'Ah!'

Mr. Morton burst into a rude uproarious laugh.

'Upon my word!' he said. 'I think, Cathcart, you're the most amazingly—'

The other held up a gloved hand in deprecation; but he did not seem at all ruffled.

'Yes, yes; we can take all that as said. . . . I'm accustomed to it, my dear fellow. Well, I saw Miss Deronnais, as I told you I should in my note. . . . You're quite right about her.'

'Pleased to hear it, I'm sure,' said Mr. Morton solemnly.

'She's one in a thousand. I told her right out, you know, that I feared insanity.'

'Oh! you did! That's tactful! How did she—'

'She took it admirably.'

'And did you tell her your delightful theories?'

'I did not. She will see all that for herself, I expect. Mean-time—'

'Oh, you didn't tell me about your interview with Lady Laura.'

The old face grew a little grim.

'Ah! that's not finished yet,' he said. 'I'm on my way to her now. I don't think she'll play with the thing again just yet.'

'And the others – the medium, and so on?'

'They will have to take their chance. It's absolutely useless going to them.'

'They're as bad as I am, I expect.'

The old man turned a sharp face to him

'Oh! you know nothing whatever about it,' he said. 'You don't count. But they do know quite enough.'

In the underground the two talked no more; but Mr. Morton, affecting to read his paper, glanced up once or twice at the old shrewd face opposite that stared so steadily out of the window into the roaring darkness. And once more he reflected how astonishing it was that anyone in these days – anyone, at least, possessing common sense – and common sense was written all over that old bearded face – could believe such fantastic rubbish as that which had been lately discussed. It was not only the particular points that regarded Laurie Baxter – all these absurd, though disquieting hints about insanity and suicide and the rest of it – but the principles that old Cathcart declared to be beneath – those principles which he had, apparently, not confided to Miss Deronnais. Here was the twentieth century; here was an electric railway, padded seats, and the *Pall Mall!* . . . Was further comment required?

The train began to slow up at Gloucester Road; and old Cathcart gathered up his umbrella and gloves.

'Then to-morrow,' he said, 'at the same time?'

Mr. Morton made a resigned gesture.

'But why don't you go and have it out with him yourself?' he asked.

'He would not listen to me – less than ever now. Good night.'

The train slid on again into the darkness; and the lawyer sat for a moment with pursed lips. Yes, of course the boy was overwrought : anyone could see that : he had stammered a little – a sure sign. But why make all this fuss? A week in the country would set him right.

Then he opened the *Pall Mall* again resolutely.

CHAPTER FIFTEEN

I

Mr. and Mrs. Nugent were enjoying their holiday exceedingly. On Good Friday they had driven laboriously in a waggonette to Royston, where they had visited the hermit's cave in company with other grandees of their village, and held a stately picnic on the downs. They had returned, the gentlemen of the party slightly flushed with brandy and water from the various hostelries on the home journey, and the ladies severe, with watercress on their laps. Accordingly, on the Saturday, Mrs. Nugent had thought it better to stay indoors and despatch her husband to the scene of the first cricket match of the season, a couple of miles away.

At about five o'clock she made herself a cup of tea, and did not wake up from the sleep which followed until the evening was closing in. She awoke with a start, remembering that she had intended to give a good look between the spare bedroom that had been her daughter's, and possibly make a change or two of the furniture. There was a mahogany wardrobe . . . and so forth.

She had not entered this room very often since the death. It had come to resemble to her mind a sort of melancholy sanctuary, symbolical of glories that might have been; for she and her husband were full of the glorious day that had begun to dawn when Laurie, very constrained though very ardent, had called upon them in state to disclose his intentions. Well, it had been a false dawn; but at least it could be, and was, still talked about in sad and suggestive whispers.

It seemed full then of a mysterious splendour when she entered it this evening, candle in hand, and stood regarding it from the threshold. To the outward eye it was nothing very startling. A shrouded bed protruded from the wall opposite with the words 'The Lord preserve thee from all evil' illuminated in pink and gold by the girl's own hand. An oleograph of Queen Victoria in coronation robes hung on one side and the painted photograph of a Nonconformist divine, Bible in hand, whiskered and cravatted, upon the other. There was a small cloth-covered table at the foot of the bed, adorned with an almost continuous line of brass-headed nails as a kind of beading round the edge, in the centre of which rested the plaster image of a young person clasping a cross. A hymn-book and a Bible stood before this, and a small jar of wilted flowers. Against the opposite wall, flanked by dejected-looking wedding-groups, and another text or two, stood the great mahogany wardrobe, whose removal was vaguely in contemplation.

Mrs. Nugent regarded the whole with a tender kind of severity, shaking her head slowly from side to side, with the tin candlestick slightly tilted. (She was a full-bodied lady, in clothes rather too tight for her, and panted a little after the ascent of the stairs.) It seemed to her once more a strangely and inexplicably perverse act of Providence, to whom she had always paid deference, by which so incalculable a rise in the social scale had been denied to her.

Then she advanced a step, her eyes straying from the shrouded bed to the wardrobe and back again. Then she set the candlestick upon the table and turned round.

It must now be premised that Mrs. Nugent was utterly without a trace of what is known as superstition; for the whole evidential value of what follows, such as it is, depends upon that fact. She would not, by preference, sleep in a room immediately after a death had taken place in it, but solely for the reason of certain ill-defined physical theories which she would have summed up under the expression that 'it was but right that the air should be changed.' Her views on human nature and its component parts were undoubtedly practical and common-sense. To put it brutally, Amy's body was in the churchyard and Amy's soul, crowned and robed, in heaven; so there was no more to account for. She knew nothing of modern theories, nothing of the revival of ancient beliefs; she would have regarded with kindly compassion, and met with practical comments, that unwilling shrinking from scenes of death occasionally manifested by certain kind of temperaments.

She turned, then, and looked at the wardrobe, still full of Amy's belongings, with her back to the bed in which Amy had died, without even the faintest premonitory symptom of the unreasoning terror that presently seized upon her.

It came about in this way.

She kneeled down, after a careful scrutiny of the polished surface of the mahogany, pulled out a drawer filled to brimming over with linen of various kinds and uses, and began to dive among these with careful housewifely hands to discover their tale. Simultaneously, as she remembered afterwards, there came from the hill leading down from the direction of the station, the sound of a trotting horse.

She paused to listen, her mind full of that faint gossipy surmise that surges so quickly up in the thoughts of village dwellers, her hands for an instant motionless among the linen. It might be the doctor, or Mr. Paton, or Mr. Grove. Those names flashed upon her; but an instant later were drowned again in a kind of fear of which she could give afterwards no account.

It seemed to her, she said, that there was something coming towards her that set her a-tremble; and when, a moment later, the trotting hoofs rang out sharp and near, she positively relapsed into a kind of sitting position on the floor, helpless and paralysed by a furious up-rush of terror.

For it appeared, so far as Mrs. Nugent could afterwards make it out, as if a sort of double process went on. It was not merely that Fear, full-armed, rushed upon with the approaching wheels, outside and therefore harmless; but that the room itself in which she crouched, itself filled with some atmosphere, swift as water in a rising lock, that held her there motionless, blind and dumb with horror, unable to move, even to lift her hands or turn her head. As one approached, the other rose.

Again sounded the hoofs and wheels, near now and imminent. Again they hushed as the corner approached. Then once more, as they broke out, clear and distinct, not twenty yards away at the turning into the village, Mrs. Nugent, no longer able even to keep that rigid position of fear, sank gently backwards and relapsed in a huddle on the floor.

2

Mr. Nugent was astonished and even a little peevish when, on arriving home after dark, he found the parlour lamp a-smoke and his wife absent.

He inquired for her; the mistress had slipped upstairs scarcely ten minutes ago. He shouted at the bottom of the stairs, but there was no response. And after he had taken his boots off, and his desire for supper had become poignant, he himself stepped upstairs to see into the matter. . . .

It was several minutes, even after the conveyal of an apparently inanimate body downstairs, that his wife first made clear signs of intelligence; and even these were little more than grotesque expressions of fear – rolling eyes and exclamations. It was another quarter of an hour before any kind of connected story could be got out of her. One conclusion only was evident, that Mrs. Nugent did not propose to fetch the forgotten candle still burning on the cloth-covered, brass-nailed table, but that it must be fetched instantly; the door locked on the outside, and the key laid before her on that tablecloth. These were the terms that must be conceded before any further details were gone into.

Plainly there was but one person to carry out these instructions, for the little servant-maid was already all eyes and mouth at the few pregnant sentences that had fallen from her mistress's lips. So Mr. Nugent himself, cloth cap and all, stepped upstairs once more.

He paused at the door and looked in.

All was entirely as usual. In spite of the unpleasant expectancy roused, in spite of himself and his godliness, by the words of his wife and her awful head-nodding, the room gave back to him no echo or lingering scent of horror. The little bed stood there, white and innocent in the candlelight, the drawer still gaped, showing its pathetic contents; the furniture, pictures, texts, and all the rest remained in their places, harmless and undefiled as when Amy herself had set them there.

He looked carefully round before entering; then, stepping forward, he took the candle, closed the drawer, not without difficulty, glanced round once more, and went out, locking the door behind him.

'A pack of nonsense!' he said, as he tossed the key on to the table before his wife.

The theological discussion waxed late that night, and by ten o'clock Mrs. Nugent, under the influence of an excellent supper and a touch of stimulant, had begun to condemn her own terrors, or rather to cease to protest when her husband condemned them for her. A number of solutions had been proposed for the startling little incident, to none of which did she give an unqualified denial. It was the stooping that had done it; there had been a rush of blood to the head that had emptied the heart and caused the sinking feeling. It was the watercress eaten in such abundance on the previous afternoon. It was the fact that she had passed an unoccupied morning, owing to the closing of the shop. It was one of those things, or all of them, or some other like one of them. Even the little maid was reassured, when she came to take away the supper things, by the cheerful conversation of the couple, though she registered a private vow that for no consideration under heaven would she enter the bedroom on the right at the top of the stairs.

About half-past ten Mrs. Nugent said that she would step up to bed; and in that direction she went, accompanied by her husband, whose programme it was presently to step round to the 'Wheatsheaf' for an hour with the landlord after the bar was shut up.

At the door on the right hand he hesitated, but his wife passed on sternly; and as she passed into their own bedroom a piece of news came to his mind.

'That was Mr. Laurie you heard, Mary,' said he. 'Jim told me he saw him go past just after dark. . . . Well; I'll take the house-key with me.'

CHAPTER SIXTEEN

I

'When is he coming?' asked Mrs. Baxter with a touch of peevishness, as she sat propped up in her tall chair before the bedroom fire.

'He will be here about six,' said Maggie. 'Are you sure you have finished?'

The old lady turned away her head from the rice pudding in a kind of gesture of repulsion. She was in the fractious period of influenza, and Maggie had had a hard time with her.

Nothing particular had happened for the last ten days. Mrs. Baxter's feverish cold had developed, and she was but now emerging from the nightdress and flannel-jacket stage to that of the petticoat and dressing-gown. It was all very ordinary and untragic, and Maggie had had but little time to consider the events on which her sub-conscious attention still dwelt. Mr. Cathcart had had no particular news to give her. Laurie, it seemed, was working silently with his coach, talking little. Yet the old man did not for one instant withdraw one word that he had said. Only, in answer to a series of positive inquiries from the girl two days before, he had told her to wait and see him for herself, warning her at the same time to show no signs of perturbation to the boy.

And now the day was come – Easter Eve, as it happened – and she would see him before night. He had sent no answer to her first letter; then, finally, a telegram had come that morning announcing his train.

She was wondering with all her might that afternoon as to what she would see. In a way she was terrified; in another way she was contemptuous. The evidence was so extraordinarily confused. If he were in danger of insanity, how was it that Mr. Cathcart advised her to get him down to a house with only two women and a few maids? Who was there besides this old gentleman who ever dreamed that such a danger was possible? How, if it was so obvious that she would see the change for herself, was it that others – Mr. Morton, for example – had not seen it too? More than ever the theory gained force in her mind that the whole thing was grossly exaggerated by this old man, and that all that was the matter with Laurie was a certain nervous strain.

Yet, for all that, as the afternoon closed in, she felt her nerves tightening. She walked a little in the garden while the old lady took her nap; she came in to read to her again from the vellum-bound little book as the afternoon light began to fade. Then, after tea, she went under orders to see for herself whether Laurie's room was as it should be.

It struck her with an odd sense of strangeness as she went in; she scarcely knew why; she told herself it was because of what she had heard of him lately. But all was as it should be. There were spring flowers on the table and mantelshelf, and a pleasant fire on the hearth. It was even reassuring after she had been there a minute or two.

Then she went to look at the smoking-room where she had sat with him and heard the curious noise of the cracking wood on the night of the thaw, when the boy had behaved so foolishly. Here, too, was a fire, a tall porter's chair drawn on one side with its back to the door, and a deep leather couch set opposite. There was a box of Laurie's cigarettes set ready on the table – candles, matches, flowers, the illustrated papers – yes, everything.

But she stood looking on it all for a few moments with an odd emotion. It was familiar, homely, domestic – yet it was strange. There was an air of expectation about it all. . . . Then on a sudden the emotions precipitated themselves in tenderness. . . . Ah! poor Laurie. . . .

'It is all perfectly right,' she said to the old lady.
'Are the cigarettes there?'
'Yes : I noticed them particularly.'
'And flowers?'
'Yes, flowers too.'
'What time is it, my dear? I can't see.'
Maggie peered at the clock.
'It's just after six, Auntie. Will you have the candles?'
The old lady shook her head.

'No, my dear : my eyes can't stand the light. Why hasn't the boy come?'

'Why, it's hardly time yet. Shall I bring him up at once?'

'Just for two minutes,' sighed the old lady. 'My head's bad again.'

'Poor dear,' said Maggie.

'Sit down, my dearest, for a few minutes. You'll hear the wheels from here. . . . No, don't talk or read.'

There, then, the two women sat waiting.

Outside the twilight was falling, layer on layer, over the spring garden, in a great stillness. The chilly wind of the afternoon had dropped, and there was scarcely a sound to be heard from the living things about the house that once more were renewing their strength. Yet over all, to the Catholic's mind at least, there lay a shadow of death, from associations with that strange anniversary that was passing, hour by hour. . . .

As to what Maggie thought during those minutes of waiting, she could have given afterwards no coherent description. Matters were too complicated to think clearly; she knew so little; there were so many hypotheses. Yet one emotion dominated the rest – expectancy with a tinge of fear. Here she sat, in this peaceful room, with all the homely paraphernalia of convalescence about her – the fire, the bed laid invitingly open with a couple of books, and a reading-lamp on the little table at the side, the faint smell of sandal-wood; and before the fire dozed a peaceful old lady full too of gentle expectation of her son, yet knowing nothing whatever of the vague perils that were about him, that had, indeed, whatever they were, already closed in on him. . . . And that son was approaching nearer every instant through the country lanes. . . .

She rose at last and went on tiptoe to the window. The curtains had not yet been drawn, and she could see in the fading light the elaborate ironwork of the tall gate in the fence, and the common road outside it, gleaming here and there in puddles that caught the green colour from the dying western sky. In front, on the lawn on this side, burned tiny patches of white where the crocuses sprouted.

As she stood there, there came a sound of wheels, and a

carriage came in sight. It drew up at the gate, and the door opened.

2

'He is come,' said the girl softly, as she saw the tall ulstered figure appear from the carriage. There was no answer, and as she went on tiptoe to the fire, she saw that the old lady was asleep. She went noiselessly out of the room, and stood for an instant, every pulse racing with horrible excitement, listening to the footsteps and voices in the hall. Then she drew a long trembling breath, steadied herself with a huge effort of the will, and went downstairs.

'Mr. Laurie's gone into the smoking-room, miss,' said the servant, looking at her oddly.

He was standing by the table as she went in; so much she could see : but the candles were unlighted, and no more was visible of him than his outline against the darkening window.

'Well, Laurie?' she said.

'Well, Maggie,' said his voice in answer. And their hands met.

Then in an instant she knew that something was wrong. Yet at the moment she had not an idea as to what it was that told her that. It was Laurie's voice surely !

'You're all in the dark,' she said.

There was no movement or word in answer. She passed her hand along the mantelpiece for the matches she had seen there just before; but her hand shook so much that some little metal ornament fell with a crash as she fumbled there, and she drew a long almost vocal breath of sudden nervous alarm. And still there was no movement in answer. Only the tall figure stood watching her it seemed – a pale luminous patch showing her his face.

Then she found the matches and struck one; and, keeping her face downcast, lighted, with fingers that shook violently, the two candles on the little table by the fire. She must just be natural and ordinary, she kept on telling herself. Then with another fierce effort of will she began to speak, lifting her eyes to his face as she did so.

'Auntie's just fallen . . .' (her voice died suddenly for an instant, as she saw him looking at her) – Then she finished –

'just fallen asleep. Will . . . you come up presently . . . Laurie?'

Every word was an effort, as she looked steadily into the eyes that looked so steadily into hers.

(It was Laurie – yes – but, good God ! . . .)

'You must just kiss her and come away,' she said, driving out the words with effort after effort.

'She has a bad headache this evening . . . Laurie – a bad headache.'

With a sudden twitch she turned away from those eyes.

'Come, Laurie,' she said. And she heard his steps following her.

They passed so through the inner hall and upstairs : and, without turning again, holding herself steady only by the consciousness that some appalling catastrophe was imminent if she did not, she opened the door of the old lady's room.

'Here he is,' she said. 'Now, Laurie, just kiss her and come away.'

'My dearest,' came the old voice from the gloom, and two hands were lifted.

Maggie watched, as the tall figure came obediently forward, in an indescribable terror. It was as when one watches a man in a tiger's den. . . . But the figure bent obediently, and kissed.

Maggie instantly stepped forward.

'Not a word,' she said. 'Auntie's got a headache. Yes, Auntie, he's very well; you'll see him in the morning. Go out at once, please, Laurie.'

Without a word he passed out, and, as she closed the door after him, heard him stop irresolute on the landing.

'My dearest child,' came the peevish old voice, 'you might have allowed my own son—'

'No, no, Auntie, you really mustn't. I know how bad your head is. . . . Yes, yes; he's very well. You'll see him in the morning.'

(And all the while she was conscious of the figure that must be faced again presently, waiting on the landing.)

'Shall I go and see that everything's all right in his room?' she said. 'Perhaps they've forgotten—'

'Yes, my dearest, go and see. And send Charlotte to me.'

The old voice was growing drowsy again.

Maggie went out swiftly without a word. There again stood the figure waiting. The landing lamp had been forgotten. She led the way to his room.

'Come, Laurie,' she said. 'I'll just see that everything's all right.'

She found the matches again, lighted the candles, and set them on his table, still without a look at that face that turned always as she went.

'We shall have to dine alone,' she said, striving to make her voice natural, as she reached the door.

Then once more she raised her eyes to his, and looked him bravely in the face as he stood by the fire.

'Do just as you like about dressing,' she said. 'I expect you're tired.'

She could bear it no more. She went out without another word, passed steadily across the length of the landing to her own room, locked the door, and threw herself on her knees.

3

She was roused by a tap on the door – how much later she did not know. But the agony was passed for the present – the repulsion and the horror of what she had seen. Perhaps it was that she did not yet understand the whole truth. But at least her will was dominant; she was as a man who has fought with fear alone, and walks, white and trembling, yet perfectly himself, to the operating table.

She opened the door; and Susan stood there with a candle in one hand and a scrap of white in the other.

'For you, miss,' said the maid.

Maggie took it without a word, and read the name and the pencilled message twice.

'Just light the lamp out here,' she said. 'Oh . . . and, by the way, send Charlotte to Mrs. Baxter at once.'

'Yes, miss. . . .'

The maid still paused, eyeing her, as if with an unspoken question. There was terror too in her eyes.

'Mr. Laurie is not very well,' said Maggie steadily. 'Please take no notice of anything. And . . . and, Susan, I think I shall dine alone this evening. Just a tray up here will do. If Mr. Laurie says anything, just explain that I am looking after Mrs. Baxter. And . . . Susan—'

'Yes, miss.'

'Please see that Mrs. Baxter is not told that I am not dining downstairs.'

'Yes, miss.'

Maggie still stood an instant, hesitating. Then a thought recurred again.

'One moment,' she said.

She stepped across the room to her writing-table, beckoning the maid to come inside and shut the door; then she wrote rapidly for a minute or so, enclosed her note, directed it, and gave it to the girl.

'Just send up someone at once, will you, with this to Father Mahon — on a bicycle.'

When the maid was gone, she waited still for an instant looking across the dark landing, expectant of some sound or movement. But all was still. A line of light showed only under the door where the boy who was called Laurie Baxter stood or sat. At least he was not moving about. There in the darkness Maggie tested her power of resisting panic. Panic was the one fatal thing: so much she understood. Even if that silent door had opened, she knew she could stand there still.

She went back, took a wrap from the chair where she had tossed it down on coming in from the garden that afternoon, threw it over her head and shoulders, passed down the stairs and out through the garden once more in the darkness of the spring evening.

All was quiet in the tiny hamlet as she went along the road. A blaze of light shone from the tap-room window where the fathers of families were talking together, and within Mr. Nugent's shuttered shop she could see through the doorway the grocer himself in his shirt-sleeves, shifting something on the counter. So great was the tension to which she had strung herself that she did not even envy the ordinariness of these people : they appeared to be in some other world, not attainable by herself. These were busied with domestic affairs, with beer or cheese or gossip. Her task was of another kind : so much she knew; and as to what that task was, she was about to learn.

As she turned the corner, the figure she expected was waiting there; and she could see in the deep twilight that he lifted his hat to her. She went straight up to him.

'Yes,' she said, 'I have seen for myself. You are right so far. Now tell me what to do.'

It was no time for conventionality. She did not ask why the solicitor was there. It was enough that he had come.

'Walk this way then with me,' he said. 'Now tell me what you have seen.'

'I have seen a change I cannot describe at all. It's just someone else – not Laurie at all. I don't understand it in the least. But I just want to know what to do. I have written to Father Mahon to come.'

He was silent for a step or two.

'I cannot tell you what to do. I must leave that to yourself. I can only tell you what not to do.'

'Very well.'

'Miss Deronnais, you are magnificent! . . . There, it is said. Now then. You must not get excited or frightened whatever happens. I do not believe that you are in any danger – not of the ordinary kind, I mean. But if you want me, I shall be at the inn. I have taken rooms there for a night or so. And you must not yield to him interiorly. I wonder if you understand.'

'I think I shall understand soon. At present I understand nothing. I have said I cannot dine with him.'

'But—'

'I cannot . . . before the servants. One of them at least suspects something. But I will sit with him afterwards, if that is right.'

'Very good. You must be with him as much as you can. Remember, it is not the worst yet. It is to prevent that worst happening that you must use all the power you've got.'

'Am I to speak to him straight out? And what shall I tell Father Mahon?'

'You must use your judgment. Your object is to fight on his side, remember, against this thing that is obsessing him. Miss Deronnais, I must give you another warning.'

She bowed. She did not wish to use more words than were necessary. The strain was frightful.

'It is this : whatever you may see – little tricks of speech or movement – you must not for one instant yield to the thought that the creature that is obsessing him is what he thinks it is. Remember the thing is wholly evil, wholly evil; but it may, perhaps, do its utmost to hide that, and to keep up the illusion. It is intelligent, but not brilliant; it has the intelligence only of some venomous brute in the slime. Or it may try to frighten you. You must not be frightened.'

(She understood hints here and there of what the old man said – enough, at any rate, to act.)

'And you must keep up to the utmost pitch your sympathy with *him* himself. You must remember that he is somewhere there, underneath, in chains; and that, probably, he is struggling too, and needs you. It is not Possession yet : he is still partly conscious . . . Did he know you?'

'Yes; he just knew me. He was puzzled, I think.'

'Has he seen anyone else he knows?'

'His mother . . . yes. He just knew her too. He did not speak to her. I would not let him.'

'Miss Deronnais, you have acted admirably. . . . What is he doing now?'

'I don't know. I left him in his room. He was quite quiet.'

'You must go back directly. . . . Shall we turn? I don't think there's much more to say just now.'

Then she noticed that he had said nothing about the priest.

'And what about Father Mahon?' she said.

The old man was silent a moment.

'Well?' she said again.

'Miss Deronnais, I wouldn't rely on Father Mahon. I've hardly ever met a priest who takes these things seriously. In theory – yes, of course; but not in concrete instances. However, Father Mahon may be an exception. And the worst of it is that the priesthood has enormous power, if they only knew it.'

The tinkle of a bicycle bell sounded down the road behind them. Maggie wheeled on the instant, and caught the profile she was expecting.

'Is that you?' she said, as the rider passed.

The man jumped off, touched his hat, and handed her a note. She tore it open, and glanced through it in the light of the bicycle lamp. Then she crumpled it up and threw it into the ditch with a quick, impatient movement.

'All right,' she said. 'Good night.'

The gardener mounted his bicycle again and moved off.

'Well?' said the old man.

'Father Mahon's called away suddenly. It's from his

housekeeper. He'll only be back in time for the first mass
to-morrow.'

The other nodded, three or four times, as if in assent.

'Why do you do that?' asked the girl suddenly.

'It is what I should have expected to happen.'

'What! Father Mahon? – Do you mean it . . . it is
arranged?'

'I know nothing. It may be coincidence. Speak no more of
it. You have the facts to think of.'

About them as they walked back in silence lay the quiet
spring night. From the direction of the hamlet came the
banging of a door, then voices wishing good night, and the
sound of footsteps. The steps passed the end of the lane and
died away again. Over the trees to the right were visible the
high twisted chimney of the old house where the terror
dwelt.

'Two points then to remember,' said the voice in the
darkness – 'Courage and Love. Can you remember?'

Maggie bowed her head again in answer.

'I will call and ask to see you as soon as the household is
up. If you can't see me, I shall understand that things are
going well – or you can send out a note to me. As for Mrs.
Baxter—'

'I shall not say one word to her until it becomes absolutely necessary. And if—'

'If it becomes necessary I will wire for a doctor from
town. I will undertake all the preliminary arrangements, if
you will allow me.'

Ten steps before the corner they stopped.

'God bless you, Miss Deronnais. Remember I am at the
inn if you need me.'

4

Mrs. Baxter dined placidly in bed at about half-past
seven; but she was more sleepy than ever when she had done.
She was rash enough to drink a little claret and water.

'It always goes straight to my head, Charlotte,' she explained. 'Well, set the book – no, not that one – the one
bound in white parchment. . . . Yes, just so, down here; and
turn the reading lamp so that I can read if I want to. . . .
Oh! ask Miss Maggie to tap at my door very softly when she

comes out from dinner. Has she gone down yet?'

'I think I heard her step just now, ma'am.'

'Very well; then you can just tell Susan to let her know. How was Mr. Laurie looking, Charlotte?'

'I haven't seen him, ma'am.'

'Very well. Then that is all, Charlotte. You can just look in here after Miss Maggie and settle me for the night.'

Then the door closed, and Mrs. Baxter instantly began to doze off.

She was one of those persons whose moments between sleeping and waking, especially during a little attack of feverishness, are occupied in contemplating a number of little vivid pictures of all kinds that present themselves to the mental vision; and she saw as usual a quantity of these, made up of tiny details of the day that was gone, and of other details markedly unconnected with it. She saw for example little scenes in which Maggie and Charlotte and medicine bottles and Chinese faces and printed pages of a book all moved together in a sort of convincing incoherence; and she was just beginning to lose herself in the depths of sleep, and to forget her firm resolution of reading another page or so of the book by her side, when a little sound came, and she opened, as she thought, her eyes.

Her reading lamp cast a funnel of light across her bed, and the rest of the room was lit only by the fire dancing in the chimney. Yet this was bright enough, she thought at the time, to show her perfectly distinctly, though with shadows fleeting across it, her son's face peering in at the door. She thought she said something; but she was not sure afterwards. At any rate, the face did not move; and it seemed to her that it bore an expression of such extraordinary malignity that she would hardly have known it for her son's. In a sudden panic she raised herself in bed, staring; and as the shadows came and went, as she stared, the face was gone again. Mrs. Baxter drew a quick breath or two as she looked; but there was nothing. Yet again she could have sworn that she heard the faint jar of the closing door.

She reached out and put her hand on the bell-string that hung down over her bed. Then she hesitated. It was too ridiculous, she told herself. Besides, Charlotte would have gone to her room.

But the fear did not go immediately; though she told

herself again and again that it was just one of those little waking visions that she knew so well.

She lay back on the pillow, thinking. . . . Why, they would have reached the fish by now. No; she would tell Maggie when she came up. How Laurie would laugh to-morrow! Then, little by little, she dozed off once more.

The next thing of which she was aware was Maggie bending over her.

'Asleep, Auntie dear?' said the girl softly.

The old lady murmured something. Then she sat up, suddenly.

'No, my dear. Have you finished dinner?'

'Yes, Auntie.'

'Where's Laurie? I should like to see him for a minute.'

'Not to-night, Auntie; you're too tired. Besides, I think he's gone to the smoking-room.'

She acquiesced placidly.

'Very well, dearest. . . . Oh! Maggie, such a queer thing happened just now – when you were at dinner.'

'Yes?'

'I thought I saw Laurie look in, just for an instant. But he looked awful, somehow. It was just one of my little waking visions I've told you of, I suppose.'

The girl was silent; but the old lady saw her suddenly straighten herself.

'Just ask him whether he did look in, after all. It may just have been the shadow of his face.'

'What time was it?'

'About ten past eight, I suppose, dearest. You'll ask him, won't you?'

'Yes, Auntie. . . . I think I'd better lock your door when I go out. You won't fancy such things then, will you?'

'Very well, dearest. As you think best.'

The old voice was becoming sleepy again : and Maggie stood watching a moment or two longer.

'Send Charlotte to me, dearest . . . Good night, my pet. . . . I'm too sleepy again. My love to Laurie.'

'Yes, Auntie.'

The old lady felt the girl's warm lips on her forehead. They seemed to linger a little. Then Mrs. Baxter lost herself once more.

The public bar of the Wheatsheaf Inn was the scene this evening of a lively discussion. Some thought the old gentleman, arrived that day from London, to be a new kind of commercial traveller, with designs upon the gardens of the gentry; others that he was a sort of scientific collector; others, again, that he was a private detective; and since there was no evidence at all, good or bad, in support of any one of these suggestions, a very pretty debate became possible.

A silence fell when his step was heard to pass down the stairs and out into the street, and another half an hour later when he returned. Then once more the discussion began.

At ten o'clock the majority of the men moved out into the moonlight to disperse homewards, as the landlord began to put away the glasses and glance at the clock. Overhead the lighted blind showed where the mysterious stranger still kept vigil; and over the way, beyond the still leafless trees, towered up the twisted chimneys of Mrs. Baxter's house. No word had been spoken connecting the two, yet one or two of the men glanced across the way in vague surmise.

Nearly a couple of hours later the landlord himself came to the door to give the great Mr. Nugent himself, with whom he had been sitting in the inner parlour, a last good-night, and he too noticed that the bedroom window was still lighted up. He jerked his finger in the direction of it.

'A late old party,' he said in an undertone.

Mr. Nugent nodded. He was still a little flushed with whisky and with his previous recountings of what would have happened if his poor daughter had lived to marry the young squire, of his (Mr. Nugent's) swift social advancement and its outward evidences, and of the hobnobbing with the gentry that would have taken place. He looked reflectively across at the silhouette of the big house, all grey and silver in the full moon. The landlord followed the direction of his eyes; and for some reason unknown to them both, the two stood there silent for a full half-minute. Yet there was nothing exceptional to be seen.

Immediately before them, across the road, rose the high oak paling that enclosed the lawn on this side, and the immense limes that towered, untrimmed and unclipped, in delicate soaring filigree against the peacock sky of night. Behind them showed the chimneys, above the dusky front of red-brick and the parapet. The moon was not yet full upon the house, and the windows glimmered only here and there, in lines and sudden patches where they caught the reflected light.

Yet the two looked at it in silence. They had seen such a sight fifty times before, for the landlord and the other at least twice a week spent such an evening together, and usually parted at the door. But they stood here on this evening and looked.

All was as still as a spring night can be. Unseen and unheard the life of the earth streamed upwards in twig and blade and leaf, pushing on the miracle of the prophet Jonas, to be revealed in wealth of colour and scent and sound a fortnight later. The wind had fallen; the last doors were shut, and the two figures standing here were as still as all else. To neither of them occurred even the thinnest shadow of a suspicion as to the cause that held them here – two plain men – in silence, staring at an old house – not a thought of any hidden life beyond that of matter, that life by which most men reckon existence. For them this was but one more night such as they had known for half a century. There was a moon. It was fine. That was Mrs. Baxter's house. This was the village street :—that was the sum of the situation. . . .

Mr. Nugent moved off presently with a brisk air, bidding his friend good night, and the landlord, after another look, went in. There came the sound of bolts and bars, the light in the window of the parlour beside the bar suddenly went out, footsteps creaked upstairs; a door shut, and all was silence.

Half an hour later a shadow moved across the blind upstairs : an arm appeared to elongate itself; then, up went the blind, the window followed it, and a bearded face looked out into the moonlight. Behind was the table littered with papers, for Mr Cathcart, laborious even in the midst of anxiety, had brought down with him for the Sunday a quantity of business that could not easily wait; and had sat there patiently docketing, correcting, and writing ever since his interview in the lane nearly five hours before.

Even now his face seemed serene enough; it jerked softly

this way and that, up the street and down again; then once more settled down to stare across the road at the grey and silver pile beyond the trees. Yet even he saw nothing there beyond what the landlord had seen. It stood there, uncrossed by lights or footsteps or sounds, keeping its secret well, even from him who knew what it contained.

Yet to the watcher the place was as sinister as a prison. Behind the solemn walls and the superficial flash of the windows, beneath the silence and the serenity, lay a life more terrible than death, engaged now in some drama of which he could not guess the issue. A conflict was proceeding there, more silent than the silence itself. Two souls fought for one against a foe of unknown strength and unguessed possibilities. The servants slept apart, and the old mistress apart, yet in one of those rooms (and he did not know which) a battle was locked in which the issue was more stupendous than that of any struggle with disease. Yet he could do nothing to help, except what he already did, with his fingers twisting and gripping a string of beads beneath the window-sill. Such a battle as this must be fought by picked champions; and since the priesthood in this instance could not help, a girl's courage and love must take its place.

From the village above the hill came the stroke of a single bell; a bird in the garden-walk beyond the paling chirped softly to his mate; then once more silence came down upon the moonlit street, the striped shadows, the tall house and trees, and the bearded face watching at the window.

CHAPTER SEVENTEEN

I

The little inner hall looked very quiet and familiar as Maggie Deronnais stood on the landing, passing through her last struggle for herself before the shock of battle. The stairs went straight down, with the old carpet, up and down which she had gone a thousand times, with every faint patch and line where it was a little worn at the edges, visible in the lamp-light from overhead; and she stared at these, standing there silent in her white dress, bare-armed and bare-necked, with her hair in great coils on her head, as upright as a lance. Beneath lay the little hall, with the tiger-skin, the red-papered walls, and a few miscellaneous things – an old cloak of hers she used on rainy days in the garden, a straw hat of Laurie's, and a cap or two, hanging on the pegs opposite. In front was the door to the outer hall, to the left, that of the smoking-room. The house was perfectly quiet. Dinner had been cleared away already through the hatch into the kitchen passage, and the servants' quarters were on the other side of the house. No sound of any kind came from the smoking-room; not even the faint whiff of tobacco-smoke that had a way of stealing out when Laurie was smoking really seriously within.

She did not know why, she had stopped there, half-way down the stairs.

She had dined from a tray in her own room, as she had said; and had been there alone ever since, for the most part at her *prie-Dieu*, in dead silence, conscious of nothing connected, listening to the occasional tread of a maid in the hall beneath, passing to and from the dining-room. There she had tried to face the ordeal that was coming – the ordeal, at the nature of which even now she only half guessed, and she had realised nothing, formed no plan, considered no eventuality. Things were so wholly out of her experience that she had no process whereby to deal with them. Just two

words came over and over again before her consciousness —
Courage and Love.

She looked again at the door.

Laurie was there, she said. Then she questioned herself.
Was it Laurie? . . .

'He is there, underneath,' she whispered to herself softly;
'he is waiting for me to help him.' She remembered that she
must make that act of faith. Yet was it Laurie who had
looked in at his mother's door? . . . Well, the door was
locked now. But that secretive visit seemed to her terrible.

What, then, did she believe?

She had put that question to herself fifty times, and found
no answer. The old man's solution was clear enough now :
he believed no less than that out of that infinitely mysterious
void that lies beyond the veils of sense there had come a
Personality, strong, malignant, degraded, and seeking to de-
grade, seizing upon this lad's soul, in the disguise of a dead
girl, and desiring to possess it. How fantastic that sounded !
Did she believe it? She did not know. Then there was the
solution of a nervous strain, rising to a climax of insanity.
This was the answer of the average doctor. Did she believe
that? Was that enough to account for the look in the boy's
eyes? She did not know.

She understood perfectly that the fact of herself living
under conditions of matter made the second solution the
more natural; yet that did not content her. For her religion
informed her emphatically that discarnate Personalities
existed which desired the ruin of human souls, and, indeed,
forbade the practices of spiritualism for this very reason. Yet
there was hardly a Catholic she knew who regarded the
possibility in these days as more than a theoretical one. So
she hesitated, holding her judgment in suspense. One thing
only she saw clearly, and that was that she must act as if
she believed the former solution : she must treat the boy as
one obsessed, whether indeed he were so or not. There was
no other manner in which she could concentrate her force
upon the heart of the struggle. If there were no evil Personality in the affair, it was necessary to assume one.

And still she waited.

There came back to her an old childish memory.

Once, as a child of ten, she had had to undergo a small
operation. One of the nuns had taken her to the doctor's

house. When she had understood that she must come into the next room and have it done, she had stopped dead. The nun had encouraged her.

'Leave me quite alone, please, Mother, just for one minute. Please don't speak. I'll come in a minute.'

After a minute's waiting, while they looked at her, she had gone forward, sat down in the chair and behaved quite perfectly. Yes; she understood that now. It was necessary first to collect forces, to concentrate energies, to subdue the imagination : after that almost anything could be borne.

So she stood here now, without the thought of flight, not arguing, not reassuring herself, not analysing anything; but just gathering strength, screwing the will tight, facing things.

And there was yet another psychological fact that astonished her, though she was only conscious of it in a parenthetical kind of way, and that was the strength of her feeling for Laurie himself. It seemed to her curious, when she considered it, how the horror of that which lay over the boy seemed, like death itself, to throw out as on a clear background the best of himself. His figure appeared to her memory as wholly good and sweet; the shadows of his character seemed absorbed in the darkness that lay over him; and towards this figure she experienced a sense of protective love and energy that astonished her. She desired with all her power to seize and rescue him.

Then she drew a long steady breath, thrust out her strong white hand to see if the fingers trembled; went down the stairs, and, without knocking, opened the smoking-room door and went straight in, closing it behind her. There was a screen to be passed round.

She passed round it.

And he sat there on the couch looking at her.

2

For the first instant she remained there standing motionless; it was like a declaration of war. In one or two of her fragmentary rehearsals upstairs she had supposed she would say something conventional to begin with. But the reality struck conventionality clean out of the realm of the possible. Her silent pause there was as significant as the crouch of a hound; and she perceived that it was recognised to be so by the other that was there. There was in him that quick, silent alertness she had expected : half defiant, half timid, as of a fierce beast that expects a blow.

Then she came a step forward and sideways to a chair, sat down in it with a swift, almost menacing motion, and remained there still looking.

This is what she saw :

There was the familiar background, the dark panelled wall, the engraving, and the shelf of books convenient to the hand; the fire was on her right, and the couch opposite. Upon the couch sat the figure of the boy she knew so well.

He was in the same suit in which he had travelled; he had not even changed his shoes; they were splashed a little with London mud. These things she noticed in the minutes that followed, though she kept her eyes upon his face.

The face itself was beyond her power of analysis. Line for line it was Laurie's features, mouth, eyes and hair; yet its signification was not Laurie's. One that was akin looked at her from out of those windows of the soul – scrutinised her cautiously, questioningly, and suspiciously. It was the face of an enemy who waits. And she sat and looked at it.

A full minute must have passed before she spoke. The face had dropped its eyes after the first long look, as if in a kind of relaxation, and remained motionless, staring at the fire in a sort of dejection. Yet beneath, she perceived, plainly, there was the same alert hostility; and when she spoke the eyes rose again with a quick furtive attentiveness. The semi-intelligent beast was soothed, but not yet re-reassured.

'Laurie?' she said.

The lips moved a little in answer; then again the face glanced down sideways at the fire; the hands dangled almost helplessly between the knees.

There was an appearance of weakness about the attitude that astonished and encouraged her; it appeared as if matters were not yet consummated. Yet she had a sense of nausea at the sight. . . .

'Laurie?' she said again suddenly.

Again the lips moved as if speaking rapidly, and the eyes looked up at her quick and suspicious.

'Well?' said the mouth; and still the hands dangled.

'Laurie,' she said steadily, bending all her will at the words, 'you're very unwell. Do you understand that?'

Again the noiseless gabbling of the lips, and again a little commonplace sentence, 'I'm all right.'

His voice was unnatural – a little hoarse, and quite toneless. It was as a voice from behind a mask.

'No,' said Maggie carefully, 'you're not all right. Listen, Laurie. I tell you you're all wrong; and I've come to help you as well as I can. Will you do your best? I'm speaking to *you*, Laurie . . . to *you*.'

Every time he answered, the lips flickered first as in rapid conversation – as of a man seen talking through a window; but this time he stammered a little over his vowels.

'I – I – I'm all right.'

Maggie leaned forward, her hands clasped tightly, and her eyes fixed steadily on that baffling face.

'Laurie; it's you I'm speaking to – *you*. . . . Can you hear me? Do *you* understand?'

Again the eyes rose quick and suspicious; and her hands knit yet more closely together as she fought down the rising nausea. She drew a long breath first; then she delivered a little speech which she had half rehearsed upstairs. As she spoke he looked at her again.

'Laurie,' she said, 'I want you to listen to me very carefully, and to trust me. I know what is the matter with you; and I think you know too. You can't fight – fight him by yourself. . . . Just hold on as tightly as you can to me – with your mind, I mean. Do you understand?'

For a moment she thought that he perceived something of what she meant : he looked at her so earnestly with those odd questioning eyes. Then he jerked ever so slightly, as if some string had been suddenly pulled, and glanced down again at the fire. . . .

'I . . . I . . . I'm all right,' he said.

It was horrible to see that motionlessness of body. He sat there as he had probably sat since entering the room. His eyes moved, but scarcely his head; and his hands hung down helplessly.

'Laurie . . . attend . . .,' she began again. Then she broke off.

'Have you prayed, Laurie? . . . Do you understand what has happened to you? You aren't really ill – at least, not exactly; but—'

Again those eyes lifted, looked, and dropped again.

It was piteous. For the instant the sense of nausea vanished, swallowed up in emotion. Why . . . why, he was there all the while – Laurie . . . dear Laurie. . . .

With one motion, swift and impetuous, she had thrown herself forward on to her knees, and clasped at the hanging hands.

'Laurie! Laurie!' she cried. 'You haven't prayed . . . you've been playing, and the machinery has caught you. But it isn't too late! Oh, God! it's not too late. Pray with me! Say the Our Father. . . .'

Again slowly the eyes moved round. He had started ever so little at her rush, and the seizing of his hands; and now she felt those hands moving weakly in her own, as of a sleeping child who tries to detach himself from his mother's arms.

'I . . . I . . . I'm all—'

She grasped his hands more fiercely, staring straight up into those strange piteous eyes that revealed so little, except formless commotion and uneasiness.

'Say the Our Father with me. "Our Father—"'

Then his hands tore loose, with a movement as fierce as her own, and the eyes blazed with an unreal light. She still clung to his wrists, looking up, struck with a paralysis of fear at the change, and the furious hostility that flamed up in the face. The lips writhed back, half snarling, half smiling. . . .

'Let go! let go!' he hissed at her. 'What are you—'

'The Our Father, Laurie . . . the Our—'

He wrenched himself backwards, striking her under the chin with his knee. The couch slid backwards a foot against the wall, and he was on his feet. She remained terror-stricken, shocked, looking up at the dully flushed face that glared down on her.

'Laurie! Laurie! . . . Don't you understand? Say one prayer—'

'How dare you?' he whispered; 'how dare you—'

She stood up suddenly – wrenching her will back to self-command. Her breath still came quick and panting; and she waited until once more she breathed naturally. And all the while he stood looking down at her with eyes of extraordinary malevolence.

'Well, will you sit quietly and listen?' she said. 'Will you do that?'

Still he stared at her, with lips closed, breathing rapidly through his nostrils. With a sudden movement she turned and went to her chair, sat down and waited.

He still watched her; then, with his eyes on her, with movements as of a man in the act of self-defence, wheeled out the sofa to its place, and sat down. She waited till the tension of his figure seemed to relax again, till the quick glances at her from beneath drooping eyelids ceased, and once more he settled down with dangling hands to look at the fire. Then she began again, quietly and decisively.

'Your mother isn't well,' she said. 'No . . . just listen quietly. What is going to happen to-morrow? I'm speaking to *you*, Laurie . . . to *you*. Do you understand?'

'I'm all right,' he said dully.

She disregarded it.

'I want to help you, Laurie. You know that, don't you? . . . I'm Maggie Deronnais. You remember?'

'Yes – Maggie Deronnais,' said the boy, staring at the fire.

'Yes, I'm Maggie. You trust me, don't you, Laurie? You can believe what I say? Well, I want you to fight too. You and I together. Will you let me do what I can?'

Again the eyes rose, with that odd questioning look. Maggie thought she perceived something else there too. She gathered her forces quietly in silence an instant or two, feeling her heart quicken like the pulse of a moving engine. Then she sprang to her feet.

'Listen, then – in the name of Jesus of Nazareth—'

He recoiled violently with a movement so fierce that the words died on her lips. For one moment she thought he was going to spring. And again he was on his feet, snarling. There was silence for an interminable instant; then a stream of words, scorching and ferocious, snarled at her like the furious growling of a dog – a string of blasphemies and filth.

Just so much she understood. Yet she held her ground, unable to speak, conscious of the torrent of language that swirled against her from that suffused face opposite, yet not understanding a tenth part of what she heard.

'. . . In the name of . . .'

On the instant the words ceased; but so overpowering was the venom and malice of the silence that followed that again she was silent, perceiving that the utmost she could do was to hold her ground. So the two stood. If the words were horrible to hear, the silence was more horrible a thousand times; it was as when a man faces the suddenly opened door of a furnace and sees the white cavern within.

He was the first to speak.

'You had better take care,' he said.

3

She scarcely knew how it was that she found herself again in her chair, with the figure seated opposite.

It seemed that the direct assault was useless. And indeed she was no longer capable of making it. The nausea had returned, and with it a sensation of weakness. Her knees still were lax and useless; and her hand, as she turned it on the chair-arm, shook violently. Yet she had a curious sense of irresponsibility : there was no longer any terror – nothing but an overpowering weakness of reaction.

She sat back in silence for some minutes, looking now at the fire too, now at the figure opposite, noticing, however, that the helplessness seemed gone. His hands dangled no longer; he sat upright, his hands clasped, yet with a curious look of stiffness and unnaturalness.

Once more she began deliberately to attempt to gather her forces; but the will, it appeared, had lost its nervous grasp of the faculties. It had no longer that quick grip and command with which she had begun. Passivity rather than activity seemed her strength. . . .

Then suddenly and, as it appeared, inevitably, without movement or sound, she began internally to pray, closing her eyes, careless, and indeed unfearing. It seemed her one hope. And behind the steady movement of her will – sufficient at least to elicit acts of petition – her intellect observed a thousand images and thoughts. She perceived the silence of the house and of the breathless spring night outside; she considered Mr. Cathcart in the inn across the road, Mrs. Baxter upstairs : she contemplated the future as it would be on the morrow – Easter Day, was it not? – the past, and scarcely at all the present. She relinquished all plans, all intentions and hopes : she leaned simply upon the supernatural, like a tired child, and looked at pictures

In remembering it all afterwards, she recalled to herself

the fact that this process of prayer seemed strangely tranquil; that there had been in her a consciousness of rest and recuperation as marked as that which a traveller feels who turns into a lighted house from a stormy night. The presence of that other in the room was not even an interruption; the nervous force that the other had generated just now seemed harmless and ineffective.

For a time, at least, that was so. But there came a moment when it appeared as if her almost mechanical and rhythmical action of internal effort began to grip something. It was as when an engine after running free clenches itself again upon some wheel or cog.

The moment she was aware of this, she opened her eyes; and saw that the other was looking straight at her intently and questioningly. And in that moment she perceived for the first time that her conflict lay, not externally, as she had thought, but in some interior region of which she was wholly ignorant. It was not by word or action, but by something else which she only half understood that she was to struggle.

. . .

She closed her eyes again with quite a new kind of determination. It was not self-command that she needed, but a steady interior concentration of forces.

She began again that resolute wordless play of the will – dismissing with a series of efforts the intellectual images of thought – that play of the will which, it seemed, had affected the boy opposite in a new way. She had no idea of what the crisis would be, or how it would come. She only saw that she had struck upon a new path that led somewhere. She must follow it.

Some little sound roused her; she opened her eyes and looked up.

He had shifted his position, and for a moment her heart leapt with hope. For he sat now leaning forward, his elbows on his knees, and his head in his hands, and in the shaded lamplight it seemed that he was shaking.

She too moved, and the rustle of her dress seemed to reach him. He glanced up, and before he dropped his head again she caught a clear sight of his face. He was laughing, silently and overpoweringly, without a sound. . . .

For a moment the nausea seized her so fiercely that she gasped, catching at her throat; and she stared at that bowed head and shaking shoulders with a horror that she had not felt before. The laughter was worse than all : and it was a little while before she perceived its unreality. It was like a laughing machine. And the silence of it gave it a peculiar touch.

She wrestled with herself, driving down the despair that was on her. Courage and love.

Again she leaned back without speaking, closing her eyes to shut out the terror, and began desperately and resolutely to bend her will again to the task.

Again a little sound disturbed her.

Once more he had shifted his position, and was looking straight at her with a curious air of detached interest. His face looked almost natural, though it was still flushed with that forced laughter; but the mirth itself was gone. Then he spoke abruptly and sharply, in the tone of a man who speaks to a tiresome child; and a little conversation followed, in which she found herself taking a part, as in an unnatural dream.

'You had better take care,' he said.

'I am not afraid.'

'Well – I have warned you. It is at your own risk. What are you doing?'

'I am praying.'

'I thought so. . . . Well; you had better take care.'

She nodded at him; closed her eyes once more with new confidence, and set to work.

After that a series of little scenes followed, of which, a few days later, she could only give a disconnected account.

She had heard the locking of the front door a long while ago; and she knew that the household was gone to bed. It was then that she realised how long the struggle would be. But the next incident was marked in her memory by her hearing the tall clock in the silent hall outside beat one. It was immediately after this that he spoke once more.

'I have stood it long enough,' he said, in that same abrupt manner.

She opened her eyes.

'You are still praying?' he said.

She nodded.

He got up without a word and came over to her, leaning forward with his hands on his knees to peer into her face.

Again, to her astonishment, she was not terrified. She just waited, looking narrowly at the strange person who looked through Laurie's eyes and spoke through his mouth. It was all as unreal as a fantastic dream. It seemed like some abominable game or drama that had to be gone through.

'And you mean to go on praying?'

'Yes.'

'Do you think it's the slightest use?'

'Yes.'

He smiled unnaturally, as if the muscles of his mouth were not perfectly obedient.

'Well, I have warned you,' he said.

Then he turned, went back to his couch, and this time lay down on it flat, turning over on his side, away from her, as if to sleep. He settled himself there like a dog. She looked at him a moment; then closed her eyes and began again.

Five minutes later she understood.

The first symptom of which she was aware was a powerlessness to formulate her prayers. Up to that point she had leaned, as has been said, on an enormous Power external to herself, yet approached by an interior way. Now it required an effort of the will to hold to that Power at all. In terms of space, let it be said that she had rested, like a child in the dark, upon Something that sustained her : now she was aware that it no longer sustained her; but that it needed a strong continuous effort to apprehend it at all. There was still the dark about her; but it was of a different quality – it cannot be expressed otherwise – it was as the darkness of an unknown gulf compared to the darkness of a familiar room. It was of such a nature that space and form seemed meaningless. . . .

The next symptom was a sense of terror, comparable only to that which she had succeeded in crushing down as she stood on the stairs four or five hours before. That, however, had been external to her; she had entered it. Now it had entered her, and lay, heavy as pitch, upon the very springs of her interior life. It was terror of something to come. That which it heralded was not yet come : but it was approaching.

The third symptom was the approach itself – swift and silent, like the running of a bear; so swift that it was upon her through the dark before she could stir or act. It came upon her, in a flash at the last; and she understood the whole secret.

It is possible only to describe it as, afterwards, she described it herself. The powerlessness and the terror were no more than the far-off effect of its approach; the Thing itself was the centre.

Of that realm of being from which it came she had no previous conception : she had known evil only in its effects – in sins of herself and others – known it as a man passing through a hospital ward sees flushed or pale faces, or bandaged wounds. Now she caught some glimpse of its essence, in the atmosphere of this bear-like thing that was upon her. As aches and pains are to Death, so were sins to this Personality – symptoms, premonitions, causes, but not Itself. And she was aware that the Thing had come from a spiritual distance so unthinkable and immeasurable, that the very word distance meant little.

Of the Presence itself and its mode she could use nothing better than metaphors. But those to whom she spoke were given to understand that it was not this or that faculty of her being that, so to speak, pushed against it; but that her entire being was saturated so entirely, that it was just possible to distinguish her inmost self from it. The understanding no longer moved; the emotions no longer rebelled; memory simply ceased. Yet through the worst there remained one minute, infinitesimally small spark of identity that maintained 'I am I and I am not that'. There was an analysis or consideration; scarcely even a sense of disgust. In fact for a while there was a period when to that tiny spot of identity it appeared that it would be an incalculable relief to cease from striving, and to let self itself be merged in that Personality so amazingly strong and compelling, that had precipitated itself upon the rest. . . . Relief? Certainly. For though emotion as most men know it was crushed out – that emotion stirred by human love or hatred – there remained an instinct which strove, which, by one long continuous tension, maintained itself in being.

For the malignity of the thing was overwhelming. It was not mere pressure; it had a character of its own for which the girl afterwards had no words. She could only say that, so far from being negation, or emptiness, or non-being, it had an air, hot as flame, black as pitch, and hard as iron.

That then was the situation for a time which she could only afterwards reckon by guesswork; there was no development or movement – no measurable incidents; there was but the state that remained poised; below all those comparatively superficial faculties with which men in general carry on their affair – that state in which two Personalities faced one another, welded together in a grip that lay on the very brink of fusion. . . .

CHAPTER EIGHTEEN

The cocks were crowing from the yards behind the village when Maggie opened her eyes, clear shrill music, answered from the hill as by their echoes and the yews outside were alive with the dawn-chirping of the sparrows.

She lay there quite quietly, watching under her tired eyelids, through the still unshuttered windows, the splendid glow, seen behind the twisted stems in front and the slender fairy forest of birches on the further side of the garden. Immediately outside the window lay the path, deep in yew-needles, the ground-ivy beyond, and the wet lawn glistening in the strange mystical light of morning.

She had no need to remember or consider. She knew every step and process of the night. That was Laurie who lay opposite in a deep sleep, his head on his arm, breathing deeply and regularly; and this was the little smoking-room where she had seen the cigarettes laid ready against his coming, last night.

There was still a log just alight on the hearth, she noticed. She got out of her chair, softly and stiffly, for she felt intolerably languid and tired. Besides, she must not disturb the boy. So she went down on her knees, and, with infinite craft, picked out a coal or two from the fender and dropped them neatly into the core of red-heat that still smouldered. But a fragment of wood detached itself and fell with a sharp sound; and she knew, even without turning her head, that the boy had awakened. There was a faint inarticulate murmur, a rustle and a long sigh.

Then she turned round.

Laurie was lying on his back, his arms clasped behind his head, looking at her with a quiet meditative air. He appeared no more astonished or perplexed than herself. He was a little white-looking and tired in the light of dawn, but his eyes were bright and sure.

She rose from her knees again, still silent, and stood looking down on him, and he looked back at her. There was no

223

need of speech. It was one of those moments in which one does not even say that there are no words to use; one just regards the thing, like a stretch of open country. It is contemplation, not comment, that is needed.

Her eyes wandered away presently, with the same tranquillity, to the brightening garden outside; and her slowly awakening mind, expanding within, sent up a little scrap of quotation to be answered.

'While it was yet early . . . there came to the sepulchre.' How did it run? 'Mary . . .' Then she spoke.

'It is Easter Day, Laurie.'

The boy nodded gently; and she saw his eyes slowly closing once more; he was not yet half awake. So she went past him on tiptoe to the window, turned the handle, and opened the white tall framework-like door. A gush of air, sweet as wine, laden with the smell of dew and spring flowers and wet lawns, stole in to meet her; and a blackbird, in the shrubbery across the garden, broke into song, interrupted himself, chattered melodiously, and scurried out to vanish in a long curve behind the yews. The very world itself of beast and bird was still but half awake, and from the hamlet outside the fence, beyond the trees, rose as yet no skein of smoke and no sound of feet upon the cobbles.

For the time no future presented itself to her. The minutes that passed were enough. She regarded indeed the fact of the old man asleep in the inn, of the old lady upstairs, but she rehearsed nothing of what should be said to them by and by. She did not even think of the hour, or whether she should go to bed presently for a while. She traced no sequence of thought; she scarcely gave a glance at what was past; it was the present only that absorbed her; and even of the present no more than a fraction lay before her attention – the wet lawn, the brightening east, the cool air – those with the joy that had come with the morning were enough.

Again came the long sigh behind her; and a moment afterwards there was a step upon the floor, and Laurie himself stood by her. She glanced at him sideways, wondering for an instant whether his mood was as hers; and his grave, tired, boyish face was answer enough. He met her eyes, and then again let his own stray out to the garden.

He was the first to speak.

'Maggie,' he said, 'I think we had best never speak of this again to one another.' She nodded, but he went on –

'I understand very little. I wish to understand no more. I shall ask no questions, and nothing need be said to anybody. You agree?'

'I agree perfectly,' she said.

'And not a word to my mother, of course.'

'Of course not.'

The two were silent again.

And now reality – or rather, the faculties of memory and consideration by which reality is apprehended – were once more coming back to the girl and beginning to stir in her mind. She began, gently now, and without perturbation, to recall what had passed, the long crescendo of the previous months, the gathering mutter of the spiritual storm that had burst last night – even the roar and flare of the storm itself, and the mad instinctive fight for the conscious life and identity of herself through which she had struggled. And it seemed to her as if the storm, like others in the material plane, had washed things clean again, and discharged an oppression of which she had been but half conscious. Neither was it herself alone who had emerged into this 'clear shining after rain'; but the boy that stood by her seemed to her to share in her joy. They stood here together now in a spiritual garden, of which this lovely morning was no more than a clumsy translation into another tongue. There stirred an air about them which was as wine to the soul, a coolness and clearness that was beyond thought, in a radiance that shone through all that was bathed within it, as sunlight that filtered through water. She perceived that the experience had been an initiation for them both, that here they stood, one by the other, each transparent to the other, or, a least, he transparent to her; and she wondered, not whether he would see it as she did, for of that she was confident, but when. For this space of silence she perceived him through and through, and understood that perception was everything. She saw the flaws in him as plainly as in herself, the cracks in the crystal; yet these did not matter, for the crystal was crystal. . . .

So she waited, confident, until he should understand it too.

'But that is only one fraction of what is in my mind—' He broke off.

Then for the first time since she had opened her eyes just now her heart began to beat. That which had lain hidden for so long – that which she had crushed down under stone and seal and bidden lie still – yet that which had held her resolute, all unknown to herself, through the night that was gone – once more asserted itself and waited for liberation.

'Yet how dare I—' began Laurie.

Again she glanced at him, terrified lest that which was in her heart should declare itself too plainly by her eyes and lips; and she saw how he still looked across the garden, yet seeing nothing but his own thought written there against the glory of sky and leaf and grass. His face caught the splendour from the east, and she saw in it the lines that would tell always of the anguish through which he was come; and again the terror in her heart leapt to the other side, in spite of her confidence, and bade her fear lest through some mistake, some conventional shame, he should say no more.

Then he turned his troubled eyes and looked her in the face, and as he looked the trouble cleared.

'Why – Maggie !' he said.

EPILOGUE

'The worst of it all is,' said Maggie, four months later, to a very patient female friend who adored her, and was her *confidante* just then – 'the worst of it is that I'm not in the least sure of what it is that I believe even now.'

'Tell me, dear,' said the girl.

The two were sitting out in a delightfully contrived retreat cut out at the lower end of the double hedge. Above them and on two sides rose masses of August greenery, hazel and beech, as close as the roof and walls of a summer-house : the long path ran in green gloom up to the old brick steps beneath the yews : and before the two girls rested the pleasant apparatus of tea – silver, china and damask, all the more delightful from its barbaric contrast with its surroundings.

Maggie looked marvellously well, considering the nervous strain that had come upon her after Eastertime. She had collapsed altogether, it seemed, in Easter week itself, and had been for a long rest – one at her own dear French convent until a week ago, being entirely forbidden by the nuns to speak of her experiences at all, so soon as they had heard the rough outline. Mrs. Baxter had spent the time in rather melancholy travel on the Continent, and was coming back this evening.

'It seems to me now exactly like a very bad dream,' said Maggie pensively, beginning to measure in the tea with a small silver scoop. 'Oh ! Mabel; may I tell you exactly what is in my mind : and then we won't talk of it any more at all ?'

'Oh ! do,' said the girl, with a little comfortable movement.

When the tea had been poured out and the plates set ready to hand, Maggie began.

'It seems perfectly dreadful to me to have any doubts at all, after all this; but . . . but you don't know how queer it seems. There's a kind of thick hedge—' she waved a hand illustratively to the hazels beside her – ' a kind of thick hedge between me and Easter – I suppose it's the illness: the nuns tell me so. Well, it's like that. I can see myself, and Laurie, and Mr. Cathcart, and all the rest of them, like figures moving beyond; and they all seem to me to be behaving rather madly, as if they saw something that I can't see. . . . Oh! it's hopeless. . . .

'Well, the first theory I have is that these little figures, myself included, really see something that I can't now: that there really was something, or somebody, which makes them dance about like that. (Yes: that's not grammar; but you understand, don't you?) Well, I'll come back to that presently.

'And my next theory is this . . . is this' – (Maggie sipped her tea meditatively) – 'my next theory is that the whole thing was simple imagination, or, rather, imagination acting upon a few little facts and coincidences, and perhaps a little fraud too. Do you know the way, if you're jealous or irritable, the way in which everything seems to fit in? Every single word the person you're suspicious of utters all fits in and corroborates your idea. It isn't mere imagination: you have real facts, of a kind; but what's the matter is that you choose to take the facts in one way and not another. You select and arrange until the thing is perfectly convincing. And yet, you know, in nine cases out of ten it's simply a lie! . . . Oh! I can't explain all the things, certainly. I can't explain, for instance, the pencil affair – when it stood up on end before Laurie's eyes; that is, if it did really stand up at all. He says himself that the whole thing seems rather dim now, as if he had seen it in a very vivid dream. (Have one of these sugar things?)

'Then there are the appearances Laurie saw; and the extraordinary effect they finally had upon him. Oh! yes; at the time, on the night of Easter Eve, I mean, I was absolutely certain that the thing was real, that he was actually obsessed, that the thing – the Personality, I mean – came at me instead, and that somehow I won. Mr. Cathcart tells me I'm right – Well; I'll come to that presently. But if it didn't happen, I certainly can't explain what did; but there are a good many things one can't explain; and yet one doesn't instantly rush to the conclusion that they're done by the devil. People say that we know very little indeed about the inner working of our own selves. There's instinct, for instance. We know nothing about that except that it is so. "Inherited experience" is only rather a clumsy phrase – a piece of paper gummed up to cover a crack in the wall.

'And that brings me to my third theory.'

(Maggie poured out for herself a second cup of tea.)

'My third theory I'm rather vague about, altogether. And yet I see quite well that it may be the true one. (Please don't interrupt till I've quite done.)

'We've got in us certain powers that we don't understand at all. For instance, there's thought-projection. There's not a shadow of doubt that that is so. I can sit here and send you a message of what I'm thinking about – oh! vaguely, of course. It's another form of what we mean by Sympathy and Intuition. Well, you know, some people think that haunted houses can be explained by this. When the murder is going on, the murderer and the murdered person are probably fearfully excited – anger, fear, and so on. That means that their whole being is stirred up right to the bottom, and that their hidden powers are frightfully active. Well, the idea is that these hidden powers are almost like acids, or gas – (Hudson tells us all about that) – and that they can actually stamp themselves upon the room to such a degree that when a sympathetic person comes in, years afterwards, perhaps, he sees the whole thing just as it happened. It acts upon his mind first, of course, and then outwards through the senses – just the reverse order to that in which we generally see things.

'Well – that's only an illustration. Now my idea is this: How do we know whether all the things that happened, from the pencil and the rappings and the automatic writing, right up to the appearances Laurie saw, were not just the result of these inner powers.... Look here. When one person projects his thought to another it arrives generally like a very faint phantom of the thing he's thinking about. If I'm thinking of the ace of hearts, you see a white rectangle with a red spot in the middle. See? Well, multiply all that a hundred times, and one can just see how it might be possible that the thought of ... of Mr. Vincent and Laurie together might produce a kind of unreal phantom that could even be touched, perhaps.... Oh! I don't know.'

Maggie paused. The girl at her side gave an encouraging murmur.

'Well – that's about all,' said Maggie slowly.

'But you haven't—'

'Why, how stupid! Yes: the first theory. . . . Now that just shows how unreal it is to me now. I'd forgotten it.

'Well, the first theory, my dear brethren, divides itself into two heads – first the theory of the spiritualists, secondly the theory of Mr. Cathcart. (He's a dear, Mabel, even though I don't believe one word he says.)

'Well, the spiritualist theory seems to me simple R. O. T. – rot. Mr. Vincent, Mrs. Stapleton, and the rest, really think that the souls of people actually come back and do these things; that it was, really and truly, poor dear Amy Nugent who led Laurie such a dance. I'm quite, quite certain that that's not true whatever else is. . . . Yes, I'll come to the coincidences presently. But how can it possibly be that Amy should come back and do these things, and hurt Laurie so horribly? Why, she couldn't if she tried. My dear, to be quite frank, she was a very common little thing : and, besides, she wouldn't have hurt a hair of his head.

'Now for Mr. Cathcart.'

There was a long pause. A small cat stepped out suddenly from the hazel tangle behind and eyed the two girls. Then, quite noiselessly, as it caught Maggie's eye, it opened its mouth in a pathetic curve intended to represent an appeal.

'You darling!' cried Maggie suddenly; seized a saucer, filled it with milk, and set it on the ground. The small cat stepped daintily down, and set to work.

'Yes?' said the other girl tentatively.

'Oh! Mr. Cathcart . . . Well, I must say that his theory fits in with what Father Mahon says. But, you know, theology doesn't say that this or that particular thing is the devil, or has actually happened in any given instance – only that, if it really does happen, it is the devil. Well, this is Mr. Cathcart's idea. It's a long story : you mustn't mind.

'First, he believes in the devil in quite an extraordinary way. . . . Oh! yes, I know we do too; but it's so very real indeed with him. He believes that the air is simply thick with them, all doing their very utmost to get hold of human beings. Yes, I suppose we do believe that too; but I expect that since there are such a quantity of things – like bad dreams – that we used to think were the devil, and now only turn out to be indigestion, that we're rather too sceptical.

Well, Mr. Cathcart believes both in indigestion, so to speak, *and* the devil. He believes that those evil spirits are at us all the time, trying to get in at any crack they can find – that in one person they produce lunacy – (I must say it seems to me rather odd the way in which lunatics so very often become horribly blasphemous and things like that) – and in another just shattered nerves, and so on. They take advantage, he says, of any weak spot anywhere.

'Now one of the easiest ways of all is through spiritualism. Spiritualism is wrong – we know that well enough; it is wrong because it's trying to live a life and find out things that are beyond us at present. It's "wrong" on the very lowest estimate, because it's outraging our human nature. (Yes, Mabel, that's his phrase.) Good intentions, therefore, don't protect us in the least. To go to *séances* with good intentions is like . . . like . . . holding a smoking-concert in a powder-magazine on behalf of an orphan asylum. It's not the least protection – (I'm not being profane, my dear) – it's not the least protection to open the concert with prayer. We've got no business there at all. So we're blown up just the same.

'The danger? . . . Oh! the danger's this, Mr. Cathcart says. At *séances*, if they're genuine, and with automatic handwriting and all the rest, you deliberately approach those powers in a friendly way, and by the sort of passivity which you've got to get yourself into, you open yourself as widely as possible to their entrance. Very often they can't get in; and then you're only bothered. But sometimes they can, and then you're done. It's particularly hard to get them out again.

'Now, of course, no-one in his senses – especially decent people – would dream of doing all this if he knew what it all meant. So these creatures, whatever they may be, always pretend to be somebody else. They're very sharp : they can pick up all kinds of odds and ends, little tricks, and little facts; and so, with these, they impersonate someone whom the inquirer's very fond of; and they say all sorts of pious, happy little things at first in order to lead them on. So they go on for a long time saying that religion's quite true. (By the way, it's rather too odd the way in which the Catholic Church seems the one thing they don't like ! You can be almost anything else, if you're a spiritualist; but you can't be a Catholic.) Generally, though, they tell you to say your prayers and sing hymns. (Father Mahon the other day, when I was arguing with him about having some hymns in church, said that heretics always went in for hymns!) And so you go on. Then they begin to hint that religion's not worth much; and then they attack morals. Mr. Cathcart wouldn't tell me about that; but he said it got just as bad as it could be, if you didn't take care.'

Maggie paused again, looking rather serious. Her voice had risen a little, and a new colour had come to her face as she talked. She stooped to pick up the saucer.

'Dearest, had you better—'

'Oh! yes: I've just about done,' said Maggie briskly. 'There's hardly any more. Well, there's the idea. They want to get possession of human beings and move them, so they start like that.

'Well; that's what Mr. Cathcart says happened to Laurie. One of those Beasts came and impersonated poor Amy. He picked up certain things about her – her appearance, her trick of stammering, and of playing with her fingers, and about her grave and so on: and then, finally, made his appearance in her shape.'

'I don't understand about that,' murmured the girl.

'Oh! my dear, I can't bother about that now. There's a lot about astral substance, and so on. Besides, this is only what Mr. Cathcart says. As I told you, I'm not at all sure that I believe one word of it. But that's his idea.'

Maggie stopped again suddenly, and leaned back, staring out at the luminous green roof of hazels above her. The small cat could be discerned halfway up the leafy tunnel swaying its body in preparation for a pounce, while over-head sounded an agitated twittering. Mabel seized a pebble, and threw it with such success that the swaying stopped, and a reproachful cat-face looked round at her.

'There!' said Mabel comfortably; and then, 'Well, what do you really think?' Maggie smiled reflectively.

'That's exactly what I don't know myself in the very least. As I said, all this seems to me more like a dream – and a very bad one. I think it's the . . . the nastiest thing,' she added vindictively, 'that I've ever come across; I don't want to hear one word more about it as long as I live.'

'But—'

232

'Oh, my dear, why can't we be all just sensible and normal? I love doing just ordinary little things – the garden,
and the chickens, and the cat and dog and complaining to
the butcher. I cannot imagine what anybody wants with
anything else. Yes; I suppose I do, in a sort of way, believe
Mr. Cathcart. It seems to me, granted the spiritual world at
all – which, naturally, I do grant – far the most intelligent
explanation. It seems to me, intellectually, far the most
broad-minded explanation; because it really does take in all
the facts – if they are facts – and accounts for them reasonably. Whereas the subjective-self business – oh, it's frightfully clever and ingenious – but it does assume such a very
great deal. It seems to me rather like the people who say that
electricity accounts for everything – electricity! And as for
the imagination theory – well, that's what appeals to me
now, emotionally – because I happen to be in the chickens
and butcher mood; but it doesn't in the least convince me.
Yes; I suppose Mr. Cathcart's theory is the one I ought to
believe, and, in a way, the one I do believe; but that doesn't
in the least prevent me from feeling it extraordinarily unreal
and impossible. Anyhow, it doesn't matter much.'

Again she leaned back comfortably, smiling to herself,
and there was a long silence.

It was a divinely beautiful August evening. From where
they sat little could be seen except the long vista of the path,
arched with hazels, whence the cat had now disappeared,
ending in three old brick steps, wide and flat, lichened and
mossed, set about with flower-pots and leading up to the
yew walk. But the whole air was full of summer sound and
life and scent, heavy and redolent, streaming in from the
old box-lined kitchen-garden on their right beyond the hedge
and from the orchard on the left. It was the kind of atmosphere suggesting Nature in her most sensible mood, full-
blooded, normal, perfectly fulfilling her own vocation;
utterly unmystical, except by very subtle interpretation; unsuggestive, since she was already saying all that could be
said, and following out every principle by which she lived to
the furthest confine of its contents. It presented the same
kind of rounded-off completion and satisfactoriness as that
suggested by an entirely sensuous and comfortable person.
There were no corners in it, no vistas hinting at anything
except at some perfectly normal lawn or set garden, no

233

mystery, no implication of any other theory or glimpse of theory except that which itself proclaimed.

Something of its air seemed now to breathe in Maggie's expression of contentment, as she smiled softly and happily, clasping her arms behind her head. She looked perfectly charming, thought Mabel; and she laid a hand delicately on her friend's knee, as if to share in the satisfaction – to verify it by participation, so to speak.

'It doesn't seem to have done you much harm,' she said.

'No, thank you; I'm extremely well and very content. I've looked through the door once, without in the least wishing to; and I don't in the least want to look again. It's not a nice view.'

'But about – er – religion,' said the younger girl rather awkwardly.

'Oh! religion's all right,' said Maggie. 'The Church gives me just as much of all that as is good for me; and, for the rest, just tells me to be quiet and not bother – above all, not to peep or pry. Listeners hear no good of themselves : and I suppose that's true of the other senses too. At any rate, I'm going to do my best to mind nothing except my own business.'

'Isn't that rather unenterprising?'

'Certainly it is; that's why I like it. . . . Oh! Mabel, I do want to be so absolutely ordinary all the rest of my life. It's so extremely rare and original, you know. Didn't somebody say that there was nothing so uncommon as common sense? Well, that's what I'm going to be. A genius! Don't you understand? – the kind that is an infinite capacity for taking pains, not the other sort.'

'What is the other sort?'

'Why, an infinite capacity for doing without them. Like Wagner, you know. Well, I wish to be the Bach sort – the kind of thing that anyone ought to be able to do – only they can't.'

Mabel smiled doubtfully.

'Lady Laura was saying—' she began presently.

Maggie's face turned suddenly severe.

'I don't wish to hear one word.'

'But she's given it up,' cried the girl. 'She's given it up.'

'I'm glad to hear it,' said Maggie judicially. 'And I hope now that she'll spend the rest of her days in sackcloth – with

234

a scourge,' she added. 'Oh, did I tell you about Mrs. Nugent?'

'About the evening Laurie came home? Yes.'

'Well, that's all right. The poor old dear got all sorts of things on her mind, when it leaked out. But I talked to her, and we went up together and put flowers on the grave, and I said I'd have a mass said for Amy, though I'm sure she doesn't require one. The poor darling! But . . . but . . (don't think me brutal, please) *how* providential her death was! Just think!'

'Mrs. Baxter's coming home by the 6.10, isn't she?'

Maggie nodded.

'Yes; but you know you mustn't say a word to her about all this. In fact she won't have it. She's perfectly convinced that Laurie overworked himself – Laurie, overworked! – and that that was just all that was the matter with him. Auntie's what's called a sensible woman, you know, and I must say it's rather restful. It's what I want to be; but it's a far-off aspiration, I'm afraid, though I'm nearer it than I was.'

'You mean she doesn't think anything odd happened at all?'

'Just so. Nothing at all odd. All very natural. Oh, by the way, Laurie swears he never put his nose inside her room that night, but I'm absolutely certain he did, and didn't know it.'

'Where is Mr. Lawrence?'

'Auntie made him go abroad.'

'And when does he come back?'

There was a perceptible pause.

'Mr. Lawrence comes back on Saturday evening,' said Maggie deliberately.

The Dennis Wheatley Library of the Occult

In this paperback series we propose to include novels and uncanny tales by:

Marjorie Bowen, John Buchan, Ambrose Bierce, R. H. and E. F. Benson, Brodie-Innes, Balzac, Algernon Blackwood, F. Marion Crawford, Wilkie Collins, Aleister Crowley, Dickens, Conan-Doyle, Dostoyevsky, Lord Dunsany, Guy Endore, Dion Fortune, Kipling, Le Fanu, Bulwer Lytton, Walter de la Mare, A. E. W. Mason, Arthur Machen, John Masefield, Guy de Maupassant, Oliver Onions, Edgar Alan Poe, Sax Rohmer, Bram Stoker, W. B. Seabrook, H. G. Wells, Hugh Walpole and Oscar Wilde.

Aslo books on:

Palmistry, Astrology, Faith Healing, Clairvoyance, Numerology, Telepathy, etc.

For particulars write to Sphere Books Ltd, 30/32 Gray's Inn Road, London WC1X 8JL.

Black Magic titles by Dennis Wheatley
published by Arrow Books

THE DEVIL RIDES OUT

GATEWAY TO HELL

THE HAUNTING OF TOBY JUGG

THE KA OF GIFFORD HILLARY

THE SATANIST

STRANGE CONFLICT

THEY USED DARK FORCES

TO THE DEVIL – A DAUGHTER

A serious study of the Occult, fully illustrated
THE DEVIL AND ALL HIS WORKS

If you would like a complete list of Arrow Books, including
other Dennis Wheatley titles, please send a postcard to
P.O. Box 29, Douglas, Isle of Man, Great Britain.

A Selection of Occult Titles from Sphere

Sphere have an exciting list of tantalising books which cover the many theories about man's origins, about the part that alien beings have played and the hidden mysteries they have left behind them and about the unknown powers of mankind. Can he cross the time barrier? Is yesterday really today? Can we predict the future? These are some of the questions posed and answered in these books.

MY LIFE AND PROPHECIES	Jeane Dixon	35p
GODS AND SPACEMEN IN THE ANCIENT EAST?	W. Raymond Drake	35p
GODS AND SPACEMEN IN THE ANCIENT WEST?	W. Raymond Drake	35p
THE BIBLE AND FLYING SAUCERS	Barry H. Downing	35p
BEYOND THE TIME BARRIER	Andrew Tomas	35p

A Selection of General Science Fiction and Science Fiction Fantasy from Sphere

THE SALIVA TREE	Brian Aldiss	35p
REPORT ON PROBABILITY A	Brian Aldiss	30p
PROSTHO PLUS	Piers Anthony	35p
THE FALL OF THE TOWERS	Samuel R. Delany	50p
THE JEWELS OF APTOR	Samuel R. Delany	25p
THE GAME PLAYERS OF TITAN	P. K. Dick	30p
LORDS OF THE STARSHIP	Mark Geston	30p
CANDY MAN	Vincent King	35p
DRAGONQUEST	Anne McCaffrey	40p
THE ICE SCHOONER	Michael Moorcock	30p
RINGWORLD	Larry Niven	40p
THE MEN IN THE JUNGLE	Norman Spinard	35p
CRADLE OF THE SUN	Brian Stableford	25p
CAVIAR	Theodore Sturgeon	30p
DAMNATION ALLEY	Roger Zelazny	30p

New Nutshells

English Legal System
in a Nutshell

AUSTRALIA
The Law Book Company Ltd.
Sydney : Melbourne : Brisbane

CANADA AND U.S.A.
The Carswell Company Ltd.
Agincourt, Ontario

INDIA
N.M. Tripathi Private Ltd.
Bombay
and
Eastern Law House Private Ltd.
Calcutta
M.P.P. House
Bangalore

ISRAEL
Steimatzky's Agency Ltd.
Jerusalem : Tel Aviv : Haifa

MALAYSIA : SINGAPORE : BRUNEI
Malayan Law Journal (Pte.) Ltd.
Singapore

NEW ZEALAND
Sweet and Maxwell (N.Z.) Ltd.
Auckland

PAKISTAN
Pakistan Law House
Karachi

New Nutshells

English Legal System
in a Nutshell

Steve Brandon
Ian Duncanson
Geoffrey Samuel

London
Sweet & Maxwell
1979

First Edition 1979
Second Impression 1981

Published by
Sweet & Maxwell Ltd. of
11 New Fetter Lane, London
Computerset by
MFK Graphic Systems (Typesetting) Ltd., Saffron Walden
Printed in Great Britain by
J. W. Arrowsmith Ltd.,
London and Bristol

ISBN 0 421 25580 3

Series Introduction

New Nutshells present the essential facts of law. Written in clear, uncomplicated language, they explain basic principles and highlight key cases and statutes.

New Nutshells meet a dual need for students of law or related disciplines. They provide a concise introduction to the central issues surrounding a subject, preparing the reader for detailed complementary textbooks. Then, they act as indispensable revision aids.

Produced in a convenient pocketbook format, *New Nutshells* serve both as invaluable guides to the most important questions of law and as reassuring props for the anxious examination candidate.

English Legal System begins with an introduction to the common law and to important areas of English law. There follows a review of the roles performed by judges, juries and magistrates, in courts and tribunals. Questions of access are covered in chapters on the legal profession and the suitability of existing legal solutions, while the work concludes with sections on developments in common law, remedies and reasoning.

Contents

		page
Series Introduction		v
1	Outline of the Common Law	1
2	Some Areas of English Law	3
3	Judges, Juries and Magistrates	11
4	The Courts and Procedures	19
5	Tribunals	28
6	The Legal Professions and Access to the Legal System	34
7	Amenability of Problems to Legal Solutions	52
8	The Development of the Common Law	55
9	Sources, Remedies and Classification of English Law	78
10	Legal Reasoning	96
Index		104

CHAPTER 1

OUTLINE OF THE COMMON LAW

English law is often referred to as "Common Law." Unfortunately, lawyers use this term in four different senses, and it is important to recognise which meaning is being considered.

(a) Common Law and Civil Law

Law in England has developed principally from consideration of speeches made by judges in court. These are known as Precedents. After a judge has considered a case which involves his deciding certain principles, his judgment can be said to have "laid down a precedent." A future judge, presented with a case concerning the same principles may be "bound" by what the original judge laid down, and will follow the precedent (see Chaps 9 and 10).

Thus English law is rather like a tapestry, filled in by the judges over the centuries, making it, to an extent, amenable to change. Many other countries, *e.g.* Commonwealth members, have adapted the Common Law system.

The Civil Law system consists, by contrast, of a body of codified law, *i.e.* its writers attempt to draw up a detailed mass of law, and the judge need only consider the "Code" in order to decide a case, little reference being made to previous decisions. Most continental countries adopt a Civil Law system.

Though much English Law is now statutory, it must be noted that Acts of Parliament generally lay down a framework which is dependent upon the judges for expansion and interpretation (see Chap. 10).

(b) Common Law and Equity

Here we are concerned only with English law. Historically, there have been two systems of courts in England. Originally, there existed the Common Law Courts, principally the Court of Kings Bench. Justice in these courts was, however, far from adequate. Procedure was complex and technical, and local influence could ensure that a deserved remedy was withheld. From the thirteenth century onwards, there developed a new system, known as Chancery, and eventually Chancery courts were set up. The body of law applied here was known as "Equity," which purported to give relief where the Common Law Courts were failing to do so. Eventually, Equity became a strict body of precedent applied by Chancery Courts (see Chap. 8).

This result was obviously inconvenient as a litigant in a case involving both Common Law and Equitable principles would have to visit both courts.

In the Judicature Acts 1873–75, the two systems were fused, and equitable remedies became available to the Common Law Courts also.

The effects of this historical development are still important. The High Court contains, *e.g.* a Chancery Division and a Queens Bench Division. The Chancery Division deals, on the whole, with matters concerning Equity, notably cases of trusts, probate, conveyancing, etc. The Bar likewise may be thought of as being divided into the Common Law and Chancery Bars. Common Law barristers deal with matters of, *e.g.* tort and contract (*infra*) whereas Chancery lawyers deal, once again, with trusts, companies, taxation, *i.e.* the more specialised fields. Certainly in London, Chambers are either Chancery or Common Law, though these strict divisions break down in the provinces.

(c) Civil Law and Criminal Law

This is a rather confusing distinction. Once again we are discussing English Law, and thus we are not referring to the Civil Law systems of the continent, simply by comparing civil law with criminal law, we mean all areas of English law *except* criminal law. Thus we might compare criminal lawyers with those who take cases in contract, or Chancery matters. One further point here is that traditionally, "Common Lawyers" here dealt with areas like contract, tort, etc. Criminal law only became a respectable field for practice in the nineteenth century. It is therefore possible to talk of a common lawyer as a man who deals with such areas and does not take any criminal cases.

The Courts are divided into those with Criminal Law jurisdiction, and those with Civil Jurisdiction, though many hear both types of cases, while perhaps concentrating on one type.

(d) Common Law and Statute Law

Here one is differentiating law made by judges from that made by Parliament. In a sense the distinction is unreal as most "common law" areas have seen statutory intervention over the years. Likewise, a statute requires judicial interpretation, and judges apply precedents in performing this task (see Chap. 9).

CHAPTER 2

SOME AREAS OF ENGLISH LAW

1. Criminal Law

Here the State, or one of its agencies, prosecutes an individual for his actions. We are thus not concerned with claims between private individuals. The majority of criminal law is statutory, though some offences have remained "common law" and not been considered by Parliament. One important example is murder, the requisites of which are almost wholly the work of judges. Theft by contrast, is now covered by a very comprehensive Theft Act which one might have thought almost "codifies" the law in this area. Nevertheless, there have still been many uncertain points which it has fallen upon the judges to clarify.

Liability may be as a principal offender, *e.g.* by shooting a victim, or as a secondary party, *e.g.* by aiding and abetting, or assisting after a crime. A defendant is guilty of an offence even though he does not actually commit a substantive offence if he incites it, attempts it, or conspires with others to commit it.

Burden of Proof

The prosecution charge the defendant, and it is up to them to prove that he is guilty, beyond all reasonable doubt:

> "Throughout the web of English Criminal Law one golden thread is always to be seen, that it is the duty of the prosecution to prove the prisoner's guilt . . . If, at the end of, and on the whole of the case, there is a reasonable doubt . . . the prosecution has not made out the case and the prisoner is entitled to an acquittal."

(*Per* Lord Sankey, L.C. in *Woolmington* v. *D.P.P.* (1935).)

Note that in all cases, it is for the judge to decide the law, but for the jury to decide the facts (see Chap. 10).

Elements of a Crime

(a) The Crown must prove that the accused physically performed that act complained of, *e.g.* that he shot and killed the victim, or stole her handbag. This is known as the *Actus Reus*. If, however, the defendant's conduct was not willed, *e.g.* because he passed out while driving, it cannot constitute an *actus reus*.

(b) Next the Crown must go on to prove that the defendant's state of mind was as required by the crime in question, known as the *Mens Rea*. Generally, this will entail proving that he intended to perform the *actus reus* or was prepared to take the risk. Thus the accused will not usually be guilty where he accidentally causes the *actus reus*.

There are qualifications. Some crimes merely require proof that the defendant was negligent, the most important being manslaughter. Thus the accused is guilty here if he kills a victim as a result of his carelessness, *e.g.* by dropping a hammer from a high building without thinking.

A few crimes do not require proof of any mens rea at all in relation to some element of the crime, and are known as offences of strict liability. If the accused is charged with having unlawful intercourse with a girl under the age of 16, the Crown does not have to prove that D knew that she was under 16 or even that he was careless about her age.

(c) Despite admitting both the *actus reus* and the mens rea the accused may yet deny that he is guilty by setting up a Defence.

Thus he may agree that he killed the victim intentionally, but say that he was acting in self defence, or under duress.

Some defences do not negate liability completely, but reduce the magnitude of the crime of which the accused will be guilty. Thus if D is charged with murder he may raise evidence to show that he was provoked, and should thus be guilty of the lesser offence of manslaughter. D's burden here is not to prove provocation, but merely adduce some evidence to show that he may have been provoked, known as the "evidential burden." The burden of proof, to show that he was not provoked is upon the prosecution, provided that the defendant satisfies this evidential burden.

Occasionally, D must prove a defence, as, *e.g.* if he

claims that he is insane. Here the burden of proof is merely "on the balance of probabilities," and not beyond reasonable doubt.

2. *The Law of Contract*

Here we enter the area of the civil law, *i.e.* concern is with disputes between private individuals and not with the state prosecuting an alleged criminal.

A contract is an agreement by at least two parties which is intended to produce certain future actions by each of them. Each promises to act (or even omit to act) in a certain way. A promises to transfer his car to B on Thursday, and B promises to give A £1,000 on that day. C promises to allow D to move into one of C's houses and D promises to pay C £30 per week in rent.

The importance of promises contained in a contract is that the parties recognise that they are creating legal obligations. Thus if B or D refuse to pay the agreed sum under the contract, A and C will be able to ask the court for a remedy (see Chap. 9).

Generally, therefore, the court merely enforces the agreement that the parties themselves have made, should one of those parties ask it to.

One problem that often arises is that the parties have not catered for every possibility in their agreement. Here the court must seek to discover what they intended, and will often imply terms in the contract that have not been expressly stated by those parties.

The courts also have a role in implying terms which the parties may not even have considered, but which Statute or Common Law require. Thus if A, a dealer, sells B a new car, the court will imply under the *Sale of Goods Act 1893* that it is of merchantable quality. Likewise, the courts will read into a contract of employment the term that a safe system of work will be provided.

Occasionally, the court will go as far as to negate provisions actually laid down in the contract. Thus, under the *Sale of Goods (Implied Terms) Act 1973*, a clause, *e.g.* stating that any condition implying fitness for purpose is to be void, will be struck out "in the case of a consumer sale" (s. 4).

Thus the legislature has limited the ability of parties to contract freely. "Freedom of contract" may have been a meaningful concept when applied to nineteenth-century merchants of substance, but is hardly applicable when considering the lay consumer entering into an agreement with a large finance company. Parliament has reformed part of the Common Law rules in order to protect the consumer, and the employee.

Making a Contract

One party makes an "offer" to the other, *e.g.* A offers to buy B's car for £2,000. This must be distinguished from an "invitation to treat," where one party asks the other to make him an offer, *e.g.* by placing an advertisement in a newspaper saying "car for sale £2,000 or nearest offer." It would obviously be chaotic for the courts to deem an advertisement to be an offer. Otherwise everyone who read the paper could claim to accept it, and be entitled to buy the car. Only when a reader comes along and says "I'll give you £1,900" has there been an offer (but *cf. Carlill* v. *Carbolic Smoke Ball Co.* (1893)).

The offer must be "accepted" to complete the contract. Thus if our advertiser says "No, but I'll take £1,950," he has made a counter-offer, which the reader may then accept. If he says "yes," there is a contract. Note that the contract, generally, need not be in writing. Though the parties will no doubt envisage exchanging a receipt for the £1,950, the "yes" completed an enforceable contract.

The contract is only legally binding if both parties provide "consideration," *i.e.* promise to act in a certain way. The "consideration" need not necessarily be fair. Thus if A agrees to sell his new Rolls Royce to B for £500, this is a binding contract even though A has made a foolish bargain.

Why Might The Court Become Involved?

Necessarily there must be a dispute between the parties. First, the contract may be unclear on certain points, with each of the parties contending a different interpretation. The court will decide between them.

Secondly, one party may refuse to perform, *e.g.* B hands over his £500, but A refuses to deliver his Rolls Royce. A is therefore in "breach" of contract.

Thirdly, a party's breach of contract may be that his performance is inadequate. Thus C delivers a new car to D, but it is unroadworthy. D may claim also that C has misled him, *i.e.* C made a "misrepresentation," *e.g.* he stated that his car had completed only 10,000 miles, but D discovers that it has done 50,000.

What Will an Injured Party Ask For?

The primary remedy is "damages." In the last example, D will ask the court to "award" him (make C pay) the difference between the value of the car sold to him, and the car that he believed he was paying for, with the lower mileage.

The plaintiff may alternatively ask the court to order the defendant to carry out his promise, *e.g.* sell him his house. This is known as "Specific Performance," but is ordered in exceptional circumstances only.

Next, the plaintiff may ask the court to prevent the defendant from breaking the contract, by issuing an "Injunction" to stop him so doing.

Lastly, the plaintiff may ask for the return of his money, or implementation of an agreed "penalty" contained in the contract. (See also Chap. 9.)

3. *The Law of Tort*

Like the law of contract, tort is concerned with relations between individuals. Tort exists to ensure that, in certain circumstances, a person whose interests have been injured by another may find redress. The injury may be to his person, his property, or even his reputation.

Whereas in contract, it is the contract itself which determines the extent of the obligations of each party, and thus the parties have created their own rights and duties, in tort, the obligations are imposed by the law. Tort thus requires a man not to act in certain ways, which may injure other people. If he does, then a remedy may be available to any person who suffers from that wrongful act. The duty is thus cast in relation to many people.

Tort is itself comprised of a number of separate heads, of which the most important is probably *negligence*. The main consideration is with "liability." It is not enough for an injured plaintiff merely to point to the responsible person, he must show that that person is liable to him.

First, he must show that there was some reason why the defendant should have considered him, *i.e.* that he "owed a duty" to him. It will generally be sufficient to show that it was foreseeable that harm might result to the plaintiff if the defendant performed his activity carelessly. Thus if D is driving a car in which P is a passenger, it is foreseeable that if D drives carelessly, P will be injured. D thus owes P a duty of care.

Next, P must show that D "breached" his duty, *i.e.* that he actually was careless. Thus, P would have to prove that D did drive his car in a dangerous manner.

The plaintiff must then show that the harm suffered was as a result of D's conduct. Here, therefore, P must prove that the resultant accident caused his injuries. Lastly, he must show that the harm he suffered was not too "remote." The latter device stops a plaintiff claiming damages for certain kinds of harm. If, *e.g.* a water main bursts and floods a street containing shops, the shopkeeper whose premises are damaged by water may claim compensation. The shopkeeper who suffers no such physical damage but has to close his shop for lack of custom cannot sue, as his damage ("pure financial loss") is too remote.

Generally, the plaintiff will be seeking damages, *i.e.* monetary compensation to put him in the same position as if he had not suffered from the defendant's activity. Occasionally, he may ask the court for an injunction in order to stop the defendant from pursuing a continuing activity which is injuring his interests (see Chap. 9).

The law of tort also protects a person's land (by the action of trespass) and his reputation ("defamation"). His right to use his property is also protected by "nuisance," which, *e.g.* allows him to sue neighbours whose actions prevent him from reasonable enjoyment of his property. In relation to that property, he also has a duty put upon him as the occupier, to ensure that his land is reasonably safe for his visitors.

Throughout this branch of the law, the courts are asked to make value judgments about the reasonableness of a person's conduct. To this end they frequently employ the "reasonable man test."

By hypothesising a person who is as careful and considerate as the average person, the courts are able to apply a standard by which to judge the defendant. It might be worthwhile noting that this is a standard applied by judges, thus the reasonable man is a creation of generations of judicial thought, and has not therefore had his properties discovered by lesser ordinary mortals (see *Fardell* v. *Potts* by A. P. Herbert).

4. *Equity and the Law of Trusts*

It will be remembered that the Chancery and Common Law systems were fused in 1873–75. All Courts now apply both common law and equity, though the latter takes precedence if there is a conflict. The High Court was separated into divisions, one of these being the Chancery Division. It will usually be appropriate for Chancery matters therefore to be brought in that division (see Chap. 8).

The most important creation of equity was the "trust." This is a method of allowing property to be held by one person on behalf of another. Thus, *e.g.* a child cannot legally own land. It will be convenient for an adult (often the family solicitor) to hold the land for him. The adult is thus the *legal* owner, and is known as the "trustee," the land being registered in his name. The child, known as the "beneficiary," is the *equitable* owner. His rights are limited, in that he does not, strictly speaking, "own" the land. His legal remedy, should anything go wrong, is to compel the trustee to act properly in relation to the land.

Trusts are also important in allowing charities to hold property, providing for future generations (by allowing trustees to hold land for X and then X's eldest son) and protecting property from a wastrel. Trustees might be given the discretion to distribute property as they think right among each of several possible beneficiaries, in which case the trust is known as a Discretionary Trust.

Undoubtedly the main use of the trust in recent times has been to help lessen the incidence of taxation. Estate Duty, *e.g.* taxed the passing of wealth on death. A wealthy person might thus have transferred property to trustees to hold for future generations, and thus his death would not give rise to Duty on that property. With the advent of *Capital Transfer Tax in 1975*, the trust is not as useful as in earlier times for tax avoidance, though, if properly handled, it can still provide a fiscal advantage.

CHAPTER 3

JUDGES, JURIES AND MAGISTRATES

The Judicial Role

The role of the judge is to resolve disputes over which he has jurisdiction. Courses in law schools on the legal systems often concentrate on the more formal courts—the High Court and the County Courts on the civil side, and the Crown Court and Magistrates' Courts on the criminal side. But these bodies have not always been and still are not the only, or even the most important adjudicative bodies. There have always been specialist courts: now they are often called tribunals, though they may not be (*e.g.* the Restrictive Practices Court). They may have a judge (*e.g.* the Employment Appeals Tribunal) or not (*e.g.* the National Insurance Local Tribunals, which have chairmen).

Whether or not a judge or chairman has jurisdiction to hear a case in his court or tribunal is largely determined by statute. If the dispute is about questions of fact, the task of the adjudicator is to decide whom he believes. In two or three per cent. of all criminal cases—the most important ones—this task devolves upon the jury. Most disputes are about facts, and their presentation depends upon witnesses' accounts and inferences drawn from circumstantial evidence. What we know about human perception and memory suggests that the impressiveness and clarity with which a witness presents his evidence is not always a guide to the accuracy of what he says.

Some disputes—the minority—are about how existing rules should be applied in particular circumstances. This is not quite the same as saying that there is uncertainty about the *meaning* of existing rules. There *may* be: but it is equally likely that what is being argued is that a rule, clear in itself, should not be applied, or should be applied in a new way to fit allegedly new circumstances. The existing rules may be products of prior judicial reasoning—common law—or statutes, or regulations made by an official who has been given statutory power to make regulations. (See also Chaps 9 and 10.)

The courts have developed fairly minimal standards to be observed by anyone who undertakes a judicial function in the exercise of his duty. These standards of natural justice apply to ministers and—to their chagrin perhaps—to university vice-chancellors. No one must be the judge in his own cause, which has been taken to mean that a reasonable person, apprised of the situation, must not think that there was a substantial possibility of bias: *Metropolitan Properties* v. *Lannon* (1969). Secondly, each side to a dispute must be heard before the decision is taken, and no-one should be penalised where he has not had prior notification of the case against him. This was of course ignored in the Agee and Hosenball episode, for the Home Secretary had obtained for himself statutory powers to act in breach of natural justice rules. Should he be permitted to do this? (see *R.* v. *Sec. of State, ex p. Hosenball* (1977)).

Eligibility for judical posts.

The following are minimum qualifications.

House of Lords judges (Lords of Appeal in Ordinary)—barristers of at least 15 years' standing, or those who have held high judicial office for two years: *Supreme Court of Judicature (Consolidation) Act 1925*.

Court of Appeal (civil and criminal divisions) judges (Lords Justice of Appeal)—barristers of 15 years' standing or those who have been High Court Judges: *Supreme Court, etc., Act 1925*.

High Court (puisne) judges—barristers of 10 years' standing: *Supreme Court, etc., Act 1925*.

Circuit Judges (who sit in the Crown Court and the County Courts)—barristers of 10 years' standing, or Recorders of five years' standing: *Courts Act 1971*.

Recorders (part-timers who must undertake to sit on the Crown Court bench for at least one month per annum)—barristers or solicitors of 10 years' standing: *Courts Act 1971*.

Disqualifications

Judges of the High Court and above hold office during good behaviour, but subject to an address presented to Her Majesty by both Houses of Parliament for their removal: *Act of Settlement 1701; Supreme Court, etc., Act 1925*.

They must retire at 75 unless appointed prior to 1959: *Judicial Pensions Act 1959.*

Circuit judges and Recorders may be removed by the Lord Chancellor for incapacity or misbehaviour. They must retire at 72, with possible extension to 75: *Courts Act 1971.*

Each division of the Supreme Court has a president. In the Family Division, that is what he is called. The Chancery Division is presided over by the Vice Chancellor, and the Queen's Bench Division by the Lord Chief Justice. In practice the Lord Chief Justice rarely sits in that Division, but presides over the Criminal Division of the Court of Appeal, with the Master of the Rolls performing a similar role for the Civil Division. In the House of Lords the Lord Chancellor acts as the president.

The Lord Chancellor is a political figure, a member of the government. Some Lord Chancellors have felt that their party political commitment, and the fact that their judicial capacity is owed to the Prime Minister's governmental priorities rather than to an expert appraisal of their judicial potential, indicates the need for a low profile. Others, on the contrary, have participated heartily in matters judicial, not always, some lawyers think, with happy results.

The Lord Chancellor, Lord Chief Justice, Master of the Rolls, Lords of Appeal in Ordinary and Lords Justice are technically appointed by the Queen on the advice of the Prime Minister. High Court judges, circuit judges and Recorders are appointed by the Queen on the advice of the Lord Chancellor.

When an appointment is being considered from the Bar to the Bench the Lord Chancellor's office customarily takes soundings among the profession. Since the number of practitioners is so small and centralised, and those who are successful form an even smaller group, choosing a candidate generally thought to be appropriate is perhaps not too difficult.

Juries

Juries are rarely used in the civil process. Indeed they are not permitted except in defamation and false imprisonment actions (*Administration of Justice Act 1933*) and then not where the evidence is likely to be of a highly technical nature.

In the criminal process the more important cases—perhaps two per cent.—are tried by jury. There is a right to jury trial generally speaking where the offence is one for which the maximum term of imprisonment exceeds six months, although the *Criminal Law Act 1977* increased the number of offences triable summarily without the option of a jury trial.

Disqualifications

No person of less than 18 or more than 65 may serve, nor any person who has not been ordinarily resident in the United Kingdom for five years since he was 13. Clergy, the insane, and persons who have in the last 10 years been connected with the administration of justice are ineligible. Disqualified are persons who have been sentenced to terms of imprisonment—whether they are excused for life or merely for 10 years depends on the length of their sentence. M.P.s, and medical and service personnel may claim exemption from service as of right.

Otherwise, every person eligible to vote may be summoned for jury service.

The relevant court office selects at random names from the electoral register. He then excludes those whom he considers will be disqualified or ineligible. He is not supposed to make detailed enquiries about individuals, but it is now revealed that at least since 1948 the secret services have had access to the names of those likely to serve in trials in which the services have an interest, and have "screened out" those who are thought likely to be unsympathetic to the prosecution case. The intelligence services maintain secret files on about two million people and record such details as membership of political parties or pressure groups (*e.g.* the National Council for Civil Liberties and the League Against Cruel Sports) so a person might never discover why he or she was never called for jury service. Such a situation subverts the notion of the jury as a random group of citizens, the principle on which the *Juries Act 1974* was based.

Once a panel has been selected from the names picked out, summonses for jury service are sent out. From those who attend court, a jury is selected by ballot in open court. The accused may object to three without showing cause, and more if he can justify his objections. The number was reduced from seven without any very convincing explanation. The Prosecution on the other hand, may ask an unlimited number of people to "stand by" without giving reasons: the occasion for giving reasons is reached only if the right is exercised to such an extent that it is impossible to derive a jury of 12 from the panel.

Members of the jury may take notes. Their number must be 12 to begin with (eight in a County Court) but they may continue in the absence of not more than two members. They must try to reach a unanimous verdict, but if they fail to do so the judge must instruct them to secure the agreement of nine out of ten or of 10 out of 11 or 12 (depending on how many remain on the jury).

The jury is meant to be the judge of fact (see Chap. 10). After the summing-up the judge instructs them upon what legal verdict to record in order to reflect their conclusions on the facts. The jury is also meant to represent lay involvement in the legal process. It is easy to romanticise, to infer mute disapproval by the citizen of the law out of an inscrutable verdict of not guilty, for example. On the other hand jury trials avoid to some extent the charge laid before fully-professional courts, that they are sceptical of the defence, and too apt to believe the evidence of the prosecution.

Jury trial is slow and expensive. Facilities and information for jurors are poor. No doubt they take their task seriously, but many would rather not do the job despite receiving expenses and loss of earnings allowances.

Magistrates

In each area with a separate Commission of the Peace there is an advisory committee of magistrates and there will usually be sub-committees now that the Commission areas are larger. It has a secretary whose identity is known, and who receives nominations from the public and—most significantly—from organisations in the locality for appointment to the magistracy. Each committee's membership is secret. In non-metropolitan counties, the full committee is under the nominal chairmanship of the Lord Lieutenant. It deliberates and forwards names selected to the Lord Chancellor, who will normally endorse the committee's choice by appointing its nominees.

The prospective magistrate will not normally have legal qualifications, but must, as a precondition of appointment undertake to attend training courses. After that he may sit for the area to whose bench he was appointed, generally, at least 26 times a year, and he may sit in the Crown Court with a circuit judge and at least one other magistrate to hear appeals, or committals for sentence from, magistrates' courts.

To hear applications for bail, or to consider whether to commit an accused for jury trial in the Crown Court, he or she may sit alone. A trial in a magistrates' court must be heard by at least two (and no more than seven: the usual number is three).

It is almost certainly cheaper to have lay magistrates try over 90 per cent. of persons accused of criminal offences than to give the job to legally trained judges. Moreover, as with the jury, there is sense in permitting non-lawyers to participate in the administration of law. In no way, however, are magistrates "representative" of the community. Nominations for appointment from political and other local organisations appear to be taken more seriously than other kinds, and are doubtless far more frequent. Perhaps more investigation of the backgrounds of prospective magistrates is needed, to secure a more balanced Bench than is achieved in some areas.

Magistrates may be removed by the Lord Chancellor for misconduct. They must retire at 70, their names then going on to a "Supplemental List."

Stipendiary Magistrates

The Crown on the advice of the Lord Chancellor may appoint a barrister or solicitor of seven years' standing to any commission area as full-time stipendiary magistrate. A stipendiary has, alone, all the judicial power of two lay magistrates.

Urban areas are probably most suitable for stipendiary appointments but there are several problems. Although solicitors are eligible, the bar is the usual source of appointments, and there are not sufficient barristers as it is. Stipendiaries are expensive compared with lay magistrates. The work is tedious and professionals often become bored and stale. There is, it is said, a tendency more marked among stipendiaries than among lay magistrates to become prosecution minded, to be far less critical of prosecution evidence than of defence evidence, although it may be argued that being lawyers, they are more likely to judge the case on the basis of the evidence before them than are lay magistrates.

Bibliography

Jackson, *The Machinery of Justice in England.*
Griffith, *The Politics of the Judiciary.*
Carlen, *Magistrates' Justice.*
Farrar, *Introduction to Legal Method.*
Abel-Smith and Stevens, *Lawyers and the Courts In Search of Justice.*
Blom-Cooper & Drewry, *Final Appeal.*
Street, *Judges on Trial.*
Abraham, *The Judicial Process.*

Chapter 4

THE COURTS AND PROCEDURES

The court in which an action is to take place depends upon whether it is a criminal or civil matter. Some courts deal with both types of proceedings, *e.g.* the House of Lords is the ultimate court of appeal in all English actions. Others are more specialised, *e.g.* the Crown Courts hear very little civil litigation, and the High Court Chancery Division hears no criminal matters.

(a) Criminal Courts

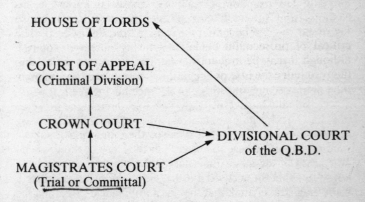

(i) *Magistrates' Court*

The vast majority of criminal cases start and finish in the Magistrates' Courts. Certain offences can only be tried there, and these are known as Summary Offences, *e.g.* parking without lights. Magistrates may also hear more serious offences, which may be tried either by them or in the Crown Court, these being known as offences triable either way (see *Criminal Law*

Act 1977). The Magistrates may decide whether or not such an offence should be heard by them, though the accused must consent to their hearing it. The defendant will no doubt be influenced by the fact that, statistically, he is more likely to gain an acquittal in the Crown Court than he is in front of the Magistrates, although the magistrates have much more limited sentencing powers. (Generally, limited to a maximum of six months imprisonment.) One further disadvantage of electing for Summary Trial is that the magistrates may, upon hearing the seriousness of the offence and the accused's past record, commit him to the Crown Court for sentence, where he will be subject to that Court's sentencing powers.

In a summary trial, the case opens with the Prosecutor, sometimes a senior police officer, reading out the facts of the case. He then calls his witnesses, who generally give evidence on oath. His examination of these people is known as his "examination in chief." After each witness has been so examined, the defendant has the right to "cross examine." If he is represented, then this will be done by his solicitor or counsel. Likewise, the defence will examine its witnesses in chief, and the prosecution will cross examine. Closing submissions may then be made by both sides, the defence having the last word.

Occasionally the defence may wish to claim that the prosecution has not, by its evidence, established a prima facie case against the defendant. If this is so, then they may make a "submission of no case to answer" at the close of the prosecution's case. If the magistrates accept that the prosecution have not shown that the accused may be guilty, the case is dismissed. If the magistrates think that there is a prima facie case, then the defence calls its evidence in the normal way.

In the case of certain minor charges, notably concerning motoring offences, the accused is allowed to plead guilty by letter, thus saving himself the trouble of a court appearance. He is entitled to make a written statement to the court in mitigation of sentence, and only this, together with the particulars of the offence contained in the Summons sent to him, may be read out in evidence.

The magistrates act as arbiters of fact and law. On the latter, they take the evidence of their clerk. The clerk should normally be a barrister or solicitor of at least five years' standing. Nowadays, this often indicates simply a qualification, and not necessarily that the clerk has practised at the bar or as a solicitor. (It not being uncommon for law graduates to enter this service as assistant clerks and take their professional exams while being so employed.) A Stipendiary magistrate, however, is himself a lawyer.

After the defence has made its closing submission, the magistrates may retire, and may reach a unanimous or majority verdict.

If the accused is convicted, or where he has pleaded guilty, the prosecution will read out to the court any previous convictions that he might have. The accused, or his solicitor or counsel, is then entitled to address the court, in order to show why he should be dealt with leniently. This is known as the "plea in mitigation." Lastly, there follows the sentence.

The Magistrates' Court also functions in order to give a first hearing in the procedure leading to a Crown Court trial, here, the hearing being known as "committal." The prosecution is obliged to show that there is a prima facie case against the defendant, and that he should be ordered to go for trial. Often, this hearing is simply a formality and no oral evidence is given, the defence frequently taking the view that it will be better to hold its fire until the trial (see section 1 *Criminal Justice Act 1967*). Under the 1967 Act, the reporting of these proceedings is strictly limited, and only a bare report of the defendant's name, the charge and court's decision may be published. The defendant, however, is entitled to request that reporting restrictions be lifted. In a Joint Trial, such a request by one party allows the evidence against each to be published.

If there is a "section 1 committal," or the magistrates find that after a hearing, there is a case to answer, the accused must be remanded to appear at his trial. Under the *Bail Act 1976*, the accused should be released on bail in the meantime, unless the court is satisfied that the defendant would fail to surrender, commit an offence while on bail, interfere with witnesses, or needs be kept in custody for his own protection. The accused may appeal to a Judge in Chambers against a decision not to grant him bail.

Juvenile Courts

A defendant under the age of 17 should generally be tried by the Juvenile Court. This consists of a panel of suitably qualified magistrates, and must sit in a different building or room from, and at a different time to, the adult Magistrates' Court. At least one of the magistrates sitting should be a woman.

(ii) *The Crown Court*

Where the accused has been committed for trial, that trial will be before a judge (High Court, Circuit Judge or Recorder) and jury, the latter to decide any disputed questions of fact.

Both the accused and the prosecution must be represented by counsel (or in person). Prosecuting counsel will outline his case to the jury, and examine his witnesses in chief, each being cross examined by the defence. Defence counsel may then make his opening remarks and call his witness for examination and cross-examination, though occasionally, the defence may argue that there is no case to answer. If the judge accepts this, he will direct the jury to acquit the accused. If not, the case continues with the evidence for the defence.

The first defence witness should, generally be the defendant. This is because, unlike any other witness, the defendant is present throughout the whole of the trial and, if he heard all the defence witnesses before giving his evidence, he might tell a different tale than if he had not heard those witnesses.

Should either counsel when cross-examining bring up a point that was not dealt with in the examination in chief of a witness, then the other side may make a short "re-examination" on those points.

If there is a disputed point of law, the judge will ask the jury to leave the courtroom. He will then hear argument from both counsel, and usually reach an immediate decision.

After the close of the defence case, prosecuting counsel will make his final speech to the jury, followed by defence counsel. The judge will then sum-up the evidence, and outline any relevant law to the jury. The jury then retire, elect a foreman, and should reach a unanimous verdict. If this is not possible, then, after two hours, the judge may accept a majority verdict, provided at least 10 (or nine if there are, by that stage, only 10 jurors) are agreed.

If the accused is convicted, the prosecution recite his antecedents, and defending counsel makes a plea in mitigation, followed by the sentence.

The Crown Court can also function as an appeal court. Where the accused has been tried before the magistrates and convicted, he may appeal against conviction, sentence, or both. The appeal against conviction takes the form of a re-hearing, though the judge sits with two to four magistrates, and not a jury. Note that here the court may actually increase the original sentence, though within the Magistrates' Court's powers.

(iii) There is an appeal, strictly on a point of law, by either party, from the Crown Court sitting in its latter function (and directly from the magistrates) to the Divisional Court of the Queen's Bench Division of the High Court. Here the hearing is in front of three High Court Judges.

(iv) Appeal from conviction or sentence resulting from a Crown Court trial is to the Court of Appeal (Criminal Division). This will be heard by three judges, of whom at least one will be a Lord Justice of Appeal, and the important cases often come before the Lord Chief Justice. Appeal on a point of law is as of right, but appeal otherwise requires leave of the court.

N.B. The Court will not quash a conviction simply because the judges would themselves have reached a different decision had they been on the jury. The jury's decision must be unsafe and unsatisfactory. The Court is also very reluctant to hear new evidence, especially where it was available at the time of the trial.

As regards sentence, again, it is not enough that the Appeal Court would have imposed a slightly less harsh sentence. As a matter of practice, the judges have developed an informal "tariff" system over the years. Thus there is often a general level of appropriate sentence, taking into consideration the circumstances of the offence, and the accused's past record. Only where the Appeal Court feels that the trial judge was outside that tariff will they interfere with the sentence. (They may not increase it.)

(v) Appeal from the Court of Appeal or Divisional Court, again, strictly on a point of law, is to the House of Lords. The House of Lords will only hear cases after giving its consent, and provided that they are certified as involving a point of law of public importance. Leave to appeal in Criminal cases is given sparingly. (When sitting as the final appeal court considering cases from some commonwealth systems, the members of the House of Lords are referred to as the Judicial Committee of the Privy Council. This also applies to civil cases.)

Where the defendant has appealed to the High Court on a point of law (by "case stated"), appeal is directly to the House of Lords.

If a defendant has been acquitted at a Crown Court trial, the prosecution cannot appeal. Where, however, the Attorney-General feels that the acquittal was based upon an incorrect view of the law, he may refer the matter to the Court of Appeal for their consideration. The Attorney-General's reference does not, of course, affect the acquitted defendant in any manner.

(b) Civil Courts and Procedure

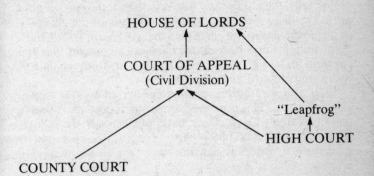

HOUSE OF LORDS

COURT OF APPEAL
(Civil Division)

"Leapfrog"

HIGH COURT

COUNTY COURT

(i) *County Court*

The majority of civil cases are disposed of in the County Court, though some matters, *e.g.* concerning maintenance payments after a divorce or separation, may be heard by magistrates.

A typical County Court's day might include actions for debt, applications from landlords for possession orders, suits for breach of contract by consumers, and negligence actions by motorists.

The limit of County Court jurisdiction is generally £2,000 (*County Courts Act 1959*, s. 39). Either party may be represented by solicitor or counsel, and the action is tried by a single judge.

The proceedings are started by the issuing of a Summons, which must be by the prospective plaintiff himself or his solicitor. On this he will set out the reasons for taking action against the defendant, known as the "Particulars of Claim." These will be sent to the defendant. If he wishes to dispute the claim he must enter a "Defence." There will be a pre-trial review in front of the Registrar, who will attempt to see if the matter can be settled and, if not, precisely what issues will be in dispute at the trial.

Normally, the losing party will have to bear the costs of both sides. The defendant may, however, if he admits the plaintiff's claim in part, pay a lessor sum than that claimed into the Court. Should the plaintiff be awarded damages no greater than the payment in, he will have to bear all the costs from the date of that payment to the end of the trial.

There also exist facilities commonly referred to as the "Small Claims Court." This is misleading, as the procedure is simply that of a County Court action, except that, where the claim is for less than £200 and both parties consent, the case may be tried by the Registrar. If so, neither party will usually be entitled to costs.

(ii) *The High Court*

The High Court is itself divided into three Divisions, Queens Bench, Chancery and Family. Generally, the Queens Bench Division hears the majority of common law cases, concerning contract, tort, etc., and the Chancery Division deals with matters such as trusts, wills, companies and tax.

In the Q.B.D. an action is started by the Issue of a Writ. There then follows an exchange of "pleadings." First, the plaintiff issues his Statement of Claim, which sets out in rather formal language, his claims against the defendant. The latter then, if he wishes to deny liability, issues his Defence. The parties will subsequently attend before a Master of the Q.B.D., who acts rather like the County Court Registrar. He will set down the case for trial, having determined what points will be in dispute.

If the defendant fails to put in an appearance, the plaintiff may obtain a default judgment. Even if the defendant does appear, the plaintiff may still obtain judgment without going to trial, under the procedure laid down in Order 14 of the *Rules of the Supreme Court*. The plaintiff must prove to a Master that he has an unanswerable case. If he does so, he will be awarded judgment. If it is shown that there is a triable defence (though not necessarily that it will succeed) the application under Order 14 will be dismissed, and the plaintiff will probably have to pay the costs of that hearing.

Various matters may arise before the case comes to trial. Orders may be made for "discovery of documents" and examination of evidence. At a pre-trial review, the master will attempt to narrow down the areas of dispute. The defendant may also, as in the County Court, make a payment into court. Again, should a successful plaintiff gain that or a lesser sum in damages, he will have to pay costs from the date of the payment in.

The trial is before a single High Court Judge. Very exceptionally there may be a jury—in cases of defamation, or where there is an allegation of fraud. The judge usually, therefore, decides issues of both fact and law.

In the Chancery Division, many cases are likely to involve solely questions of law, and the interpretation of documents, *e.g.* a will. In such cases, an action will normally be begun by Originating Summons. The party taking out the Summons (who may, *e.g.* be a trustee) will name all interested parties, who are required to "enter on appearance."

At the hearing, evidence is normally given by way of sworn affidavit, rather than oral examination. Counsel for plaintiff and each defendant addresses the Court. Where the case concerns an estate or trust, costs will normally come out of that fund.

The work of the Family Division mostly concerns adoption, wardship and defended divorces.

(iii) *The Court of Appeal (Civil Division)*

Appeals from the County Court are directly to the Court of Appeal, as are the majority of appeals from the High Court. The case will normally be heard by three judges, of whom at least one will be a Lord Justice of Appeal. The listing of cases before the court is ultimately the responsibility of the Master of the Rolls, who naturally tends to hear many of the more important cases himself.

The hearing will normally be by way of legal argument concerning points arising at the trial. Only exceptionally will witnesses be called.

(iv) *The House of Lords*

Appeal lies from the Court of Appeal, on a point of law of public importance. Appeals can also be heard by the House of Lords from a decision of the High Court, provided that such a point of law is involved, and there is a binding authority which would determine the Court of Appeal's decision were they to hear the case ("Leapfrogging").

The hearing will normally be before five law lords, who may decide by majority.

European Court of Justice

If a case before the County Court or High Court concerns interpretation of EEC acts or the Treaty of Rome, the Court may refer the matter to the European Court for a ruling. The Court of Appeal has stated that the ruling must be necessary, and concern a difficult and important point.

CHAPTER 5

TRIBUNALS

As well as civil and criminal *courts*, there are bodies which adjudicate and which are called tribunals. It is hard to find any characteristics they all have in common which differentiate them from courts. Thus, they are specialist bodies, dealing with a narrow area of law designated by statute—but then this is true of the Family Division of the High Court. The "judges" in tribunals generally include a lawyer and two laymen—but then this is true of Admiralty proceedings in the Queen's Bench Division, where two nautical assessors may sit with the judge; equally the County Court judge hearing matters concerned with race relations is assisted by laymen.

The Restrictive Practices Court, set up in 1956, is a superior court, with a very narrow jurisdiction, lay and legal adjudicators and a relatively informal procedure. Moreover it deals with matters of policy and hears evidence of a wide-ranging kind including economic forecasts, employment predictions and so forth, in the course of pronouncing upon the validity of restrictive trade agreements. The Employment Appeal Tribunal and the Land Tribunal are similar, except that, though termed tribunals, their adjudication over policy is narrower.

In truth, tribunals must be seen as courts. There have always been specialist courts simply because the common law and its courts grew up in response to only some of the many kinds of social problems which need to be subject to adjudication (see Chap. 8). In modern terminology, the early Court of Chancery was a tribunal, in the sense that its traditions lie outside the mainstream of common law development: and this may be the nearest we can get to a differentiating characteristic of a tribunal, even if it must embrace some bodies called courts.

Types of Tribunal

The term "administrative tribunal" is unfortunate and misleading. Not all tribunals hear disputes between citizens and government departments, and even those which do are meant to pay heed to the same criteria of impartiality and fairness as courts, while "administrative" suggests amenability to departmental priorities.

(1) *Supplementary Benefit Appeal Tribunals*

They are the least satisfactory tribunals, and show their poor law origins. There is a chairman, who is often not legally qualified, selected from a panel maintained by the Lord Chancellor, a member selected by the Department of Health and Social Security for his relevant knowledge and ability, and a member appointed from among local workpeople—generally this means the local Trade Council Federation. There is a clerk seconded by the D.H.S.S., who is a civil servant and a non-lawyer. Jurisdiction is over refusals to consider claims made in relation to the non-contributory Supplementary Benefit, which is available only to people not in full-time work, and Family Income Supplement, which is available only to persons in full-time work, and with families.

Claimants may be represented, but legal aid is unavailable. The author's experience, confirmed by research conducted by others, is that some tribunals are fair, but others pay scant regard to the principles of due process. A frequent low level of expertise in the area of law in question and an occasional open hostility to claimants who are perceived as scroungers appears to predispose some tribunals to accept the Department's point of view.

There is no appeal from a S.B.A.T. on a point of fact, but appeal lies to the High Court on a point of law, either directly or by requiring the tribunal to state a case for the opinion of the High Court. Given the generally accepted view that S.B.A.T.s are unsatisfactory, it is appalling that no appeal lies on a point of fact.

(2) *National Insurance Local Tribunals*

Appeal lies to these tribunals from an unfavourable decision by a local insurance officer in relation to contributory benefits—unemployment benefit, sickness benefit, etc.—and also the non-contributory Child Benefit. The tribunal has three members, an employer, and employee, and a chairman who is usually—though he is not bound to be—a lawyer, and who is chosen from a panel maintained by the Lord Chancellor.

Unlike S.B.A.T.s the N.I.L.T.s sit in public. Again unlike S.B.A.T. decisions, those made in N.I.L.T.s can be appealed from to a National Insurance Commissioner, who is a barrister of 10 years' standing. Their decisions are recorded and bind subsequent N.I.L.T.s. There is no system of precedent in the Supplementary Benefit field. The advantage of it in the field of National Insurance is that there are clear rules.

(3) *Industrial Tribunals*

A president of the Industrial Tribunals—a barrister or solicitor of seven years' standing—is appointed by the Lord Chancellor. Through regional chairmen also appointed by the Lord Chancellor, the president organises the system generally, though chairmen arrange sittings and choose a legal chairman for each, together with lay members, whose names are on a panel maintained by the Secretary of State for Employment. The laymen must have experience of industry and one is chosen to represent each side, employers and employees. Appeal lies to the Employment Appeal Tribunal, which consists of a High Court judge sitting with two or four lay persons with knowledge of industry, again, one from each side.

The principal jurisdictions of the Industrial Tribunal are over the statute-created unfair dismissal, and discrimination on grounds of sex. Conciliation of matters forming the substance of complaints to Industrial Tribunals is encouraged by the Arbitration Conciliation and Advisory Service set up by the government under the *Employment Protection Act 1975*.

(4) *Rent Tribunals and Rent Assessment Committees*

Under the *Rent Act 1974* Rent Tribunals have jurisdiction over residential contracts of many kinds including tenancies of a dwelling which forms a part of a larger building in which the landlord resides and which is not a purpose built block of flats.

Other tenancies will usually fall within the jurisdiction of the
Rent Officer, with appeal from his decision to a Rent Assessment Committee (R.A.C.s).

Primarily these bodies fix rents—"fair" rents in the case of
R.A.C.s and "reasonable" rents in the case of Rent Tribunals.
Rent Tribunals may also grant limited security of tenants.
Issues may be referred by either the landlord or the tenant, or,
in the case of Rent Tribunals, by the Local Authority—though
this is rare in practice. The panels for both bodies, from which
the membership is chosen by a regional president, contain
lawyers, surveyors and laymen. The lay representative, who is
presumably there to reflect tenants' interests is not necessarily a
tenant and will sometimes be a professional man. Tenants
complain on occasion that although the tribunals seem fair,
little understanding may exist of the problems of being a tenant.

Issues

Tribunals almost always deal with disputes in which the weak
are pitted against the powerful—usually individuals against
government departments. Landlords may be as poor as their
tenants, but often they are property companies.

A relatively inarticulate person who may suffer from a stigma
in applying for state assistance can not usually argue with a
professional representing the other side. It is often argued that,
since tribunals are not formally adversary in procedure, there
are not two "sides," but merely an impartial investigation by
neutral figures. It does not look like this to the participants for
whom, after all, the tribunals exist. Moreover, we have a principle in English law that justice must not only be done, but be
seen to be done.

Thus representation before tribunals would seem to be cru-
cial. Trade unions often act for members before Industrial
Tribunals, and trade union officials may often be the best
representatives there. In social security and landlord and tenant

matters, there is no facility for subsidising representation: legal aid is not available. Solicitors may agree to act for nothing, particularly if they are employed by law centres, but private practice solicitors can scarcely afford to take on much of this type of work.

But the extension of legal aid to tribunals is not cost-effective. The administration of means—and merits—testing is expensive and delays already occur. Where small sums are involved, traditional litigation, using highly-paid lawyers is scarcely justifiable. Yet neither is the abandonment of the claimant to his fate. The best proposal is that of the Legal Action Group, for a paralegal service. Lawyers already use unqualified staff for tasks like conveyancing. They, along with members of local rights groups, tenants' associations, could form a resource from whom tribunal representatives could be drawn, costing far less than lawyers, and probably acting more effectively.

The future of the tribunals as credible bodies probably depends upon a solution being found to this difficulty. If legal aid in the traditional way is extended, tribunals will seem inordinately expensive, and more informal ways of ending disputes will be found: if no representation is made available, as at present, claimants will continue to feel unfairly treated.

Bibliography

Courts and Tribunals:
Barnard, *The Civil Court in Action; The Criminal Court in Action*.
Jackson, *The Machinery of Justice in England*.
Alder & Bradley, *Justice, Discretion and Poverty*.
Farmer, *Tribunals and Government*.
Micklethwait, *The National Insurance Commissioner*.

Chapter 6

THE LEGAL PROFESSIONS AND ACCESS TO THE LEGAL SYSTEM

A picture should be emerging of the legal process as involving, on the one hand, a criminal process, the object of which is the trial of a person accused of an *offence*, and his punishment if he is found guilty; and on the other hand a civil process the purpose of which is to vindicate a right which the plaintiff, the instigator of the action, claims that he has against the defendant.

An accused person is prosecuted in the appropriate criminal courts. An action to vindicate a right is brought in a court or a tribunal. As a general rule if the law is silent about a particular kind of behaviour then it is permissible. If it is not silent then it will label the behaviour as falling within the jurisdiction of a particular kind of court or tribunal. When we are presented with a set of facts and we wish to know which label to pin on it, then we consult statutes and judicial decisions (see Chap. 9).

So if it is alleged that A has intentionally taken B's goods without B's consent, meaning not to return them, the *Theft Act 1968* tells us that an action against A must be commenced in the criminal courts as a prosecution. We gain an idea of how the court will interpret the Act by reading the judgments of previous courts faced with similar cases. If A has promised to sell and B to buy, goods of a particular type, and either fails in his undertaking, the *Sale of Goods Act 1893*, in the context of prior and subsequent case law and legislation, indicates that compensation may be sought in the civil courts. Legislation relating to social security and allied matters specifies to which bodies disputes may be referred for adjudication.

However, not all disputes or alleged offences reach the courts, nor is it desirable that they should do so. The country cannot afford that every crime be solved, or every alleged offender prosecuted. The police, for example, as the main instigator of prosecutions, may decide to concentrate their investigatory resources on crimes that are particularly dangerous, or that cause the most public disquiet. Inevitably this means that resources are not available to detect the perpetrator of every minor offence. And trivial breaches of regulations, such as traffic regulations, may result in a warning rather than a prosecution. Similarly, every victim of a breach of contract or a tort does not launch an action in the courts.

Civil Disputes and the Courts

There are two situations in which the party who considers himself the loser in a civil dispute may not seek a remedy ultimately in a court. The first is where he chooses not to, and the second is where he is ignorant of his rights, or apprehensive of ascertaining or asserting them.

Into the first category came businessmen particularly. They prefer not to use the courts:

(1) Because often they may use their superior economic power to achieve what they want.

(2) Because in situations of economic equality the parties to a dispute can appoint an arbitrator. Arbitration may be cheaper, but even if not it can be quicker, scheduled more conveniently and it is private. The outcome of an arbitration is often more acceptable to foreign disputants, and is more in touch with commercial requirements than a court judgment would be. Of course, since courts operate on the basis of precedent, the fewer cases which are referred to them, the less opportunity there is for putting the law into a close relation with commercial expectations (see *Arbitration Acts 1950–75*).

(3) Associatedly, the risk for both parties of there being established an awkward precedent may be too great for them to contemplate going to court.

Also in this category are the victims of civil wrongs who settle out of court. The settlement may be entirely to their satisfaction, or it may be near enough to make the risk of going to court not worth taking. A defendant who wishes to put a determined plaintiff into a dilemma over whether or not to go to court may do so where the claim is *not* for a specific (liquidated) sum, by paying a sum of money into court. The normal costs rules are that, whilst the judge has a discretion, he will ordinarily order the successful party to pay all or part of the costs of the unsuccessful party. However, if the defendant pays a sum into court and the judge, who will not be informed of the amount, makes an award of damages which does not exceed the payment in, the plaintiff must pay his own and the defendant's costs incurred subsequent to the payment. *R.S.C. Ord.* 62, *r.* 5 (6) (see *Judicature Act 1925*).

Into the second category, of those who refrain from litigation, and even from asserting their rights, come in particular to the poor and the under-privileged. Steps have been taken to provide subsidised advice and assistance for the poor and for middle income people, and to inform people of their rights, as consumers, tenants, social security claimants and accident victims, but nevertheless many claims which may well have been successful are not made.

In order to understand legal aid and assistance, it is first necessary to examine the structure of the legal professions.

Solicitors

Solicitors may practice alone, or they may form partnerships with other solicitors (though not with members of other professions). Alternatively they may be employed—*e.g.* by central or local government, by private or nationalised firms, or as salaried employees of a solicitor's partnership. In that capacity they may do any of the work ordinarily undertaken by solicitors subject to their adherence to the rules made pursuant to the

Solicitors Act 1974 governing the activity in question. If they handle clients' money, for example, they must submit annual audited accounts to the Law Society. They must buy an annual practising certificate—the cost of which enables the Law Society to maintain a compensation fund out of which the victims of solicitors' dishonesty may be indemnified. Insurance must be taken out to meet civil claims, for example for negligence or breach of contract: *Solicitors Act 1974*. Solicitors deal with clients directly and, as a profession are not overly involved in advocacy—though some individual members may specialise in advocacy before the lower courts and, possibly, tribunals. Of the aggregate amount of money earned by the profession, by far the greatest part is earned through the transfer of land—conveyancing—and the property of deceased persons—probate. Indeed, solicitors enjoy a statutory monopoly over the preparation of legal documents for record, and this includes conveyancing documents: *Solicitors Act 1974*, s. 22.

Solicitors and the Law Society

The implications of their professional status is that solicitors control entry to their membership and police professional practices. These goals are accomplished through the Law Society, set up by a Charter of 1845 (replaced most recently by the 1954 Charter), and governed by a council of 65 members. Membership is voluntary but compulsory powers are exercised by the Society over all solicitors, members or not.

The education of solicitors is regulated by the Society with the concurrence of the Lord Chancellor, Lord Chief Justice, and the Master of the Rolls. Presently it involves an apprenticeship (articles) and examinations divided into two parts, each to be preceded by a course of training. The apprenticeship is shorter and exemption from the first part of the examinations may be gained by law graduates. The training institutions are run by the Law Society, but courses leading to the examinations are put on by local authority colleges and polytechnics. Curiously, since the public foots the bill when it grant-aids students and maintains public training facilities, the profession is able to exercise almost complete autonomy over the form and content of its training programme.

The way in which solicitors handle clients' money is prescribed by regulations made by the Law Society under the Solicitors Act, and annual audited accounts must be submitted by each practice. Standard forms for the conduct of business by solicitors are prepared under the auspices of the Society, and whilst they do not have to be used, it is generally convenient to do so, and these, together with refresher courses, pamphlets on new developments and study groups, act to lend cohesion to professional activities. The Society ensures that solicitors act in accordance with professional etiquette, breach of which may result in warnings or disciplinary proceedings.

Additionally, the Law Society acts to protect its members' interests, as a pressure group, submitting evidence to public inquiries justifying current professional practices, and as a public relations organ, explaining to the public what the profession can do for them. An infringement of a statutory restrictive practice by a non-solicitor will normally result in the Law Society's instigating a prosecution.

Perhaps anomalously, since the Society represents only the profession and has no public constituency, administration of the Legal Aid and Advice Scheme is in its hands.

Liability of a Solicitor

A solicitor is liable for breach of contract and in negligence at the suit of his client: *Midland Bank* v. *Hett. Stubbs & Kemp* (1978). However, negligent conduct of litigation by barristers and solicitors is not actionable: *Rondel* v. *Worsley* (1967). He is liable under the criminal law in the same way as an ordinary citizen. He is liable to disciplinary sanctions in addition to civil and criminal liability, and for breaches of professional standards of conduct, before the Solicitors Disciplinary Tribunal.

This Tribunal is constituted by the Master of the Rolls under the *Solicitors Act 1974*, s. 46 from practising solicitors of 10 years' standing and non-lawyers. The Quorum is three, and lawyers must outnumber laymen. Penalties available to the Tribunal include a fine of up to £750, and striking off the solicitor's name from the Roll of those entitled to practice.

Barristers

People who qualify as barristers may use their qualification and expertise in any employment. But they may not practice as counsel, that is, as advocates, available for hire by clients through solicitors, in the courts, unless they occupy a place in chambers. Most sets of chambers are in London. Other metropolitan centres have a few chambers. To open new ones, the consent of one's Inn is required.

Members of chambers are self-employed sole practitioners who employ a clerk and a staff in common. Work is channelled from the public through a solicitor to a barristers' clerk in a set of chambers, and from the clerk with whom the price of the job is negotiated, to a barrister.

Most of the profession's time is spent in advocacy, but a considerable amount is also devoted to advice-giving and the drafting of legal documents and pleadings. The pre-trial work of a solicitor, his instructions, take the form of a brief upon which counsel then bases his pleadings and submissions to court, but a solicitor may also want another view, in a non-litigious matter, or as to whether to take steps toward litigation. He may want a more specialised view, or, if he is a specialist in that particular area himself, he may simply want a second opinion. Sometimes a solicitor may even be seeking a more acceptable or persuasive way of communicating to a client advice he knows will be unwelcome. At any rate, he takes counsel's opinion. Counsel will draft an opinion on the basis of the written instructions which he receives from the solicitor.

The Bar

To become a barrister one must first join one of the four Inns of Court in London. There are, examinations, preceded by a full-time course. Finally, before practising, a barrister must spend one year as the pupil of a practising barrister. The governing body is the Senate of the Inns of Court and the Bar, which regulates and disciplines. There is a Bar Council, representing all of the Bar, which exists to maintain standards and promote the services of the profession. And there is a Council of Legal Education which organises the courses and examinations. The Bar Council, along with the Inns, elects members to the Senate, which contains also the Attorney-General, the Solicitor-General and the Chairman of the Council of Legal Education.

Prior to the English Civil War the Inns themselves had an educational function and attendance at moots and mock trials was necessary. A vestige of this remains in the requirement that before a person can be called to the bar, not only must he attend the training course and pass the examinations, but he must prior to that have attended his Inn (usually) three times per term for two four-term years for the purpose of eating an evening meal.

Rights of Audience

Solicitors have full rights of audience in magistrates' and county courts, before the High Court in bankruptcy matters in tribunals, and in crown courts for limited purposes. Barristers have rights of appearance in all courts, but in all but magistrates' courts they must wear a special costume of a wig, a gown and a winged collar with a white ribbon.

Liability of a Barrister

A barrister, like a solicitor, is immune from a negligence suit in respect of his advocacy, or matters intimately connected with advocacy: *Rondel* v. *Worsley* (1967). Matters more remote from the performance of that task, *e.g* advice about whom to sue, do not involve immunity, *Saif Ali* v. *Sydney Mitchell* (1978).

There is no contract between the client and the barrister, nor between solicitor and barrister. Thus no action for breach of contractually imposed duties can be brought. The clerk and the solicitor normally agree upon a fee for the barrister's performance: only for undefended county court divorces and a few other matters are the fees fixed, though standard fees exist for other matters. Because of the absence of a contract counsel cannot sue if his fee is not paid. His only lever is a communication to the Law Society about the solicitor, or his unique talents, on which the solicitor may wish to draw later. Occasionally barristers do express discontent about the low priority which solicitors occasionally accord to paying counsel, and they may refuse to accept a brief if the fee is not paid on its delivery.

Subject to the acceptability of the fee, which is negotiated by the clerk, the brief's being within the area of his expertise, and his availability, counsel is under a professional obligation to accept a brief. This is the famous "cab-rank" principle. Too much may be made of it, since the above pre-conditions to its operation are fairly comprehensive. Its design is less to justify the barrister's *Rondel* v. *Worsley* immunity than to protect him from any odium attaching to a client whose legal cause he may take on. However, the perspective of the barrister as an "officer of justice" and his symbolic remoteness from the client as a human being—as opposed to a piece of legal pathology—performs this functon quite well enough. And in that case, the "cab-rank" principle is less a high virtue and more a description of a natural enough practice of not turning away business unless there is already too much.

Connected with that, it is often a source of grievance—particularly in London—that a solicitor will arrange for a specific barrister to represent his client, but that at the very last moment the clerk will inform him that that barrister is not available. The case will suffer from the substitute's having had insufficient time to prepare. It is occasionally alleged that since the clerk's income is a proportion of the fees he attracts to the chambers, he will be loath to turn business away even though he may be practically certain that the requested barrister will be unavailable.

Whether or not this is true, the real cause of the problem is the present shortage of barristers. Although the numbers practising rose from 1,000 in 1960 to 4,000 in 1977 (solicitors' numbers rose from 18,500 in 1960 to 31,000 in 1976), the amount of work increased even more. Criminal litigation rose dramatically, not so much because of the rise in the amount of crime (the waves, tides, floods and other nautical imagery of the popular press) but because of the increased availability of legal aid, which enables accused persons to fight—they have advice more readily at their disposal, and they can be represented. Moreover, whilst civil litigation may have declined overall save in the matrimonial area, commercial arbitration, planning matters, industrial conciliation and other similar activities, make extensive use of the services of practicing barristers.

Legal Aid and Advice

An increased demand for lawyers clearly results in part from the availability of public funds with which to pay them. Forty-three per cent. of barristers total incomes is from public funds, though 71 per cent. of solicitors' total earnings was from conveyancing and probate, which do not attract public funds, generally.

However, behind the availability of such funds is a political pressure to make them available. This no doubt because:

(1) The institutional state has extended its functions. There are more regulations to contest, more encroachments to resist or attract by legal means;

(2) People are more aware of having rights to enforce or protect because they are better educated;

(3) Despite the United Kingdom's dismal comparative economic performance there is more wealth in the

community. Individuals clearly buy themselves *into* difficulties of a legal kind—*e.g.* with finance companies—the existence of greater community wealth makes more acceptable the call for subsidised legal services.

Public funds are normally discussed solely in the context of subsidies channelled through individual litigants and persons seeking advice, and this is what we shall discuss. It is worth noticing, however, that public funds also provide work for lawyers that pulls them wholly or partly away for private practice, *e.g.* to advise government and the EEC, to staff government agencies such as the Arbitration, Conciliation and Advisory Service, the Equal Opportunities Commission, the consumer protection services, and so on.

Subsidies to assist those who need legal advice and assistance and representation are made now under the *Legal Aid Act 1974*, and the organisation of them is heavily dependent upon lawyers in private practice. Indeed, the administration of the scheme is largely in the hands of the body set up to represent solicitors' interests, the Law Society, which acts in consultation with the Bar Council and under the general guidance of the Lord Chancellor's Office.

England and Wales is divided into twelve Legal Aid areas, each of which has an Area Committee of practicing solicitors and barristers served by a secretary. Each Area is then subdivided and each subdivision has a Local Committee with a similar composition. The Local Committee considers applications for Legal Aid in terms of their legal merit, and appeal against a refusal goes to the Area Committee. The Area Committee prepares lists of practitioners willing to act under the scheme (practically all practitioners do so), supervises their remuneration under the scheme, and deals with complaints against practitioners' work under the scheme. There is no doubt a case for consumer representation on these committees, which use taxpayers' money and preside over a scheme which exists for the public benefit, but lawyers' commitment to democracy does not usually admit to interference with their own activities.

Advice

Where funds have not already been made available for proceedings in a matter, a means-tested subsidy is available for advice to be given by a solicitor. The solicitor can advise the client whether further legal steps should be taken, and help him or her to apply for legal aid. Services may be given, such as letter-writing and the negotiating of settlements and the drafting of legal documents. It is the solicitor himself who administers the means test, which is based on the earnings of the applicant, with allowances for certain financial commitments. The solicitor may ask the client for the client's assessed contribution (although it is said that he often does not) and claim the balance from the Legal Aid fund. Services up to the value of £25 may be given, hence the scheme is called the "£25 scheme" but with the consent of the Local Committee, an extension of up to £40 may be made. Some committees are more amenable than others.

There are two obvious criticisms. One is that the figures are in need of revision, since they were fixed when £25 had a 1978 purchasing power of nearer £50. The second is that the facility extends only to matters of English law, which seems unduly parochial when there are many people of Commonwealth, Eire, Ulster and Scots origin who may well have problems which involve at least the relation of English law to that of their country of origin.

Legal Aid for Civil Proceedings

Prima facie, a means-tested subsidy is available to cover or contribute toward the cost of litigation before all the courts of civil jurisdiction, and before the Lands Tribunal and the Employment Appeal Tribunal, but not before other tribunals. The applicant submits an application for a legal aid certificate to the

Local Committee for the Area Committee for appropriate proceedings. His means will be assessed by the Supplementary Benefits Commission, and this means that he may be interviewed by a clerk for the Commission (unless he is already in receipt of benefit, in which case he automatically qualifies for free advice and aid so far as the means test is concerned). The legal merits of his application will be assessed by the Committee. Its concern not to waste public funds may sometimes deny the poor the privilege which the rich have of instigating test cases. Thus Distillers enjoyed a double protection against the parents of thalidomide-damaged children. First, even if they had been negligent in marketing the drug, the law as it stood seemed to excuse them since their victims were alive but unborn at the time the injury was caused. Secondly, legal aid seems to have been refused, so that the parents could not ask the courts to consider changing the law in the light of a manifest injustice. Such cases are, arguably, rare. But then, one cannot be certain that one hears of them all. In that case even though the injury was dreadful, public discussion was only sustained by the heroic action of the *Sunday Times* in promoting it.

The response of the Committee may be a refusal on the legal criterion that reasonable grounds have not been shown why the action should be brought or defended. Against this he may appeal and be heard in person. Refusal may be on financial grounds, in which event there is no appeal. A certificate may be subject to a contribution by the applicant, dependent on his means. The figure quoted on the communication to the applicant is the maximum that he could be asked to pay on a pessimistic view of the outcome, but this is not always made clear to the applicant, who may often assume that he will inevitably have to find the sum stated. The certificate may be limited to the obtaining of counsel's opinion as to the likely outcome (which seems a little wasteful since there are barristers on the Committee: if the Committee wished an outside opinion it could surely obtain one in a more streamlined way).

Both the solicitor and counsel who act for a legally-aided client receive their fees from the fund, which then looks to the client for his contribution. It has a limited right to recompense itself out of the damages which may be awarded if the client succeeds. If he loses, he may be asked to contribute to his opponent's costs such amount as may be reasonable in the light of his resources, and his conduct. A non-legally aided litigant who succeeds against a legally aided one may be awarded costs against the Legal Aid fund if costs would be normally made in his favour, and if a refusal in this instance would be to produce severe financial hardship. The rules are to be interpreted to include people of modest means, not only the very poor: *Hanning* v. *Maitland (No. 2)* (1970).

Civil legal aid is not available for defamation actions (which means that only the rich can defend their reputations at law) nor for undefended divorces. Matters relating to custody of and access to children of the marriage and to financial provision, are dealt with under the advice and assistance provisions.

There are two criticisms of the Legal Aid scheme. One is that, again, the means test is too harsh. Only the very poor and the unaided very rich can therefore afford to litigate. A second criticism is that there is no facility for granting legal aid to groups of people with the same legal problem. If there were, then their entitlements could be aggregated and a representative case brought which would settle the law as it affected all of them.

The objection that the procedure is very slow is met to some extent by an emergency procedure, under which legal aid may be granted quickly, subject to conditions.

Criminal Legal Aid

This is administered by the court, and not by the committees. A person may still obtain advice under the £25 scheme, but in order to defend proceedings he must apply to the court in which he is to be tried, or after a conviction, to that court or the appellate court, for Legal Aid for the appeal. An order must be made for Legal Aid where it is in the interests of justice. The question of the contribution is examined afterward, and the means test is much more discretionary and flexible. Contributions are often not collected.

An initial application will usually be to the magistrates' court, since the criminal process always begins here. Where the trial is to be by jury in a Crown Court, in which case the magistrates' court is concerned only with issue of committal to that Crown Court, Legal Aid will almost always be granted.

The court has the power to ask a solicitor who is present in the court to advise an accused person, for example, on how to plead. It may grant a Legal Aid order to enable the solicitor to represent the person who is to be tried in the magistrates' court or who is making a bail application there. There is now a requirement that before magistrates sentence a person to his first term of imprisonment, they must offer him Legal Aid.

Many local law societies now organise a Duty Solicitor scheme to ensure that there will be a solicitor in the magistrates' court upon whose services the court may call, and to give preliminary advice to accused persons. Such schemes are popular with courts if for no other reason than that a properly advised accused makes a coherent plea and does not waste the court's time.

Since each magistrates' court has its own interpretation of when a Legal Aid order will be in the interests of justice for a trial in its own court there is a great deal of variation from one to another. And since defendants can almost never afford to pay for representation themselves, the refusal of a Legal Aid order means that they are denied representation by a lawyer. Some studies have shown that many first-time defendants do not understand what is happening in court, so clearly all is not well. Representation is needed.

Law Centres

There is a century-old tradition amongst lawyers in some big cities of giving free legal advice part-time in poor areas. Since 1968 the number of "legal advice centres" of this type has increased from a few to dozens. There is at least one in every big city, and in many there are several. Most of the work is advisory only, and is done by private solicitors, law teachers and students. If practitioners want to do more than simply advise a client, they may suggest he visit their own offices. This is better than suggesting he or she takes his problem to any solicitor since a preliminary session at the advice centre will often have broken the ice. The individual does not want to repeat his problem to another person.

Because, unlike membership of the Rotary Club or the Golf Club, participation in an advice centre is seen as a form of self-advertisement or touting for business, solicitor-advisors must obtain the permission of the Law Society to refer clients to themselves from there. The consent is generally forthcoming, solicitors do pick up varying amounts of Legal Aid work from their participation at such centres, and the centres do make available legal services to people who would not always have them. They are often in areas of town where there are few if any solicitors' offices, and the services are available in evenings when solicitors do not usually open their offices. Traditional Legal Aid does not take into account that wage-earners who take time off to see a solicitor suffer a loss of earnings, unlike most salary-earners. Moreover, advice centres generally aim to have a less formal atmosphere than conventional offices, and this puts many people at their ease.

Most of the arguments in favour of advice centres apply to law centres, which are similar in location and informality, but which involve full-time salaried lawyers—again usually solicitors. They are a new phenomenon—the first was opened in North Kensington in 1968—and obtain funds from charitable and local authority sources. Additional to lawyers they employ full-time community workers and secretarial resources. Often they have management committees on which local people are represented in order to spread roots in the community and create a tradition, on unfamiliar terrain, of legal advice seeking.

But as well as advice they can and do take on clients just as privately organised firms of solicitors do. Because the legal and paralegal staff are involved full-time with the problems of low-income people—bad and insecure housing, social security and employment problems, wrongful arrests or excess of authority by the police, racial difficulties, etc.—they develop a familiarity with the relevant areas of law which cannot be matched by many private practitioners, and they can provide informed arguments for reform where the law is inadequate to the needs of underprivileged people.

Local solicitors usually view a new law centre with alarm and hostility. Law centre solicitors must obtain a waiver from the local Law Society from the profession's prohibition of self-advertisement in order to break new ground, for their *raison d'être* is that poor people do not know that they have problems that are soluble by law, or where to take them. One local Law Society attempted to stifle a law centre by refusing the waiver. Fears that law centres will unfairly compete with private practice are almost always allayed quite soon. They operate in discrete areas of legal problem. Sometimes there is a spin-off in favour of private practice, for law centres may find that they are overwhelmed with work and refer clients who would not otherwise have gone, to traditional solicitors.

Alternatives

Local authorities and others sometimes provide specialised advice facilities—*e.g.* housing aid centres, consumer advice centres. The most comprehensive is the national network of Citizens' Advice Bureaux, which offers advice and acts as referral agency on a wide range of matters. The Citizens' Rights office offers legal, other advice and sometimes services on welfare law matters, and the National Council of Civil Liberties has expertise in the area of civil liberties. Both of these are privately funded and maintain a precarious charitable status, which gives them certain tax privileges.

The other way in which legal services are made more available is by lowering their cost. This method has the advantage of not calling for extra public funds. Now that undefended divorces no longer qualify for legal aid the County Courts that deal with them must provide procedures that a reasonable person can cope with by himself, or with the advice rather than the performance of a lawyer.

Also within the County Court there now exists a mandatory arbitration facility for small claims. Where a small sum of money is involved, the Registrar adjudicates, and the cost of legal representation is not awarded to the winner against the loser. Self-representation is thus encouraged and the hope has been expressed that the procedure of the arbitration will reflect the fact that those who appear before it will not be professional advocates.

Cases before the welfare state's tribunals are often conducted by the persons involved or by lay representatives. Again, advice can be obtained beforehand, under the £25 scheme subject to the means test. Legal aid is not available for representation either in the small claims procedure in the County Court or in the Welfare State tribunals.

The availability of Legal Aid and thus of legal representation is not necessarily a good thing. In defended proceedings, a poor person is often not skilled in the techniques of presenting his own case, whilst his opponent—who may be the legal advisor or representative of a large organisation in the County Court, the agent of a landlord before a Rent Assessment Committee or Rent Tribunal, and a civil servant in many other tribunals—is often highly skilled.

Lay representation is perhaps to be encouraged for tribunals, on the grounds that lawyers are not cost effective: the sums at issue are often relatively small. Where they are large, perhaps Legal Aid should be available, though there is then the risk of creating two classes of litigants in tribunals.

Where Legal Aid is denied for trials in magistrates' and county courts there is a discretion available to the court to permit lay representation: *O'Toole* v. *Scott* (1965); *Simms* v. *Moore* (1970) (magistrates' courts); *County Courts Act 1959*, s. 89 (county courts). Courts generally resist lay representation on the rational ground that it is less skilled than professional representation, and wastes time. This objection disappears, of course, if professionals have been ruled out by the denial of Legal Aid.

Lay *help* may be given in any court to a person conducting his own case, provided the helper confines himself to the activities of quietly advising the litigant in person: *McKenzie* v. *McKenzie* (1970).

Bibliography

Zander, *Cases & Materials on the English Legal System*, 2nd ed.
Zander, *Legal Services in the Community*.
Byles & Morris, *Unmet Need*.
Jackson, *The Machinery of Justice in England*.
Freeman, *The Legal Process*.
Abel-Smith, Brooke & Zander, *Legal Problems and the Citizen*.
Bankowski & Mungham, *Images of Law*.
Abel-Smith & Stevens, *Lawyers & the Courts*.
Abel-Smith & Stevens, *In Search of Justice*.
Farrar, *Introduction to Legal Method*.

CHAPTER 7

AMENABILITY OF PROBLEMS TO LEGAL SOLUTIONS

It is almost certain that our behaviour and our attitudes are heavily influenced by the existence of legal rules. If we do not know in many instances what the law is, we are generally willing to be guided by those—officials and others—who say that they do. The people who live under one government form very many, often interlocking, groups with different values and aims. The content of the law cannot possibly represent them all because many of them conflict. Since our society seems to be an advanced industrial and business organisation it is fair to assume that whatever our personal preferences the rules that govern us when we come into conflict with them will reflect those priorities. Our lives must fit in with rules that govern employment and buying and selling and owning goods.

The extent to which we can be protected from the possibly evil consequences of these priorities is in the end limited by the degree of affluence which the organisation produces. We can expect to be compensated for injury at work, or by the use to which others put their ownership of goods only if employers have profits out of which to compensate us directly, or by the establishment of funds from which compensation is payable, or if owners of goods are sufficiently affluent to pay us damages, or take out insurance. We cannot expect laws which contradict these societal priorities. Laws which attempted to do so would fail.

Nor can we reasonably expect that laws which represent one view of how things should be, will be enforceable against those who strongly hold some opposing view. There is nothing magically persuasive about law, and certainly nothing about it which renders it morally compelling. If a group powerful enough to secure the enactment of a law nevertheless does not persuade those affected that they should adhere to it the ineffectiveness of the law is a sign of the group's miscalculation, not a sign of impending social disaster.

Laws, then, are limited by the type of social organisation, within fairly wide boundaries, in which they are situated. They should also reflect, or be capable of producing a broad agreement about what ought to be done, or, again, they will fail.

Within government, general, prospective, policy-making laws are considered to be the task of legislation, while detailed adjudication arising out of disputes within such laws is left to administrators who specialise in that function. The most prestigious of those are the judges. Whether they can approach the legislature in the scope, generality and power of their lawmaking really depends on the place assigned to them by the constitution. Judges in the United States do so to a greater extent than English judges.

Most disputes in criminal and civil procedures are about fact. The more significant ones, from a legal point of view, concern the interpretation and applicability of legal meanings. Judges are responsible for incremental change, for the legislature lacks the time either to consider the application of its products to individual cases, or to adapt and shape the law in the context of every social change. If judges avoid this responsibility, or cope with it clumsily, more work will be given to other officials, which is what is occurring. We may gain in efficiency from this trend and we are unlikely to lose much in terms of civil liberties since judges are not very protective of these; legislative scrutiny and political awareness are the citizen's best defence here.

Disputes high in politically controversial content cannot be satisfactorily resolved by courts. Disputes of almost any other kind, perhaps, can be, but subject to other considerations. For example, if all citizens do not have the same access to the courts, if some cannot afford to litigate, then the law will operate to create or maintain inequalities. A solution to this problem, that of subsidising litigation is expensive if it is sufficiently thoroughgoing. One of the ways around this difficulty may be to reduce the area of dispute, as we have done by permitting parties to agree to divorce each other. In the provision of compensation for personal injury we may be able to save money by a scheme that does not require the injured party to prove that another has been negligent (*cf. Pearson Report* (1978) Cmnd. 7054).

Traditional litigation is probably best suited for the task for which it was intended—disputes between businessmen and people of property, who have equal access to legal services, and criminal matters, public concern over the fairness of which at higher levels has made funds available to equalise the battle between prosecutor and accused.

In the criminal sphere, where a person's liberty may be at stake, and possibly his reputation and future job prospects, there seems to be no cheap alternative to the expense of an exhaustive trial. The issue between the parties cannot be reduced to compromise. Proper assessment of the conduct of litigation in criminal courts requires a recognition that, whatever the pre-trial difficulties of the prosecutor in locating possible criminals, prosecution resources always exceed those of the defence. If we abandon safeguards that balance this, in order to secure a conviction of the unmeritorious, we undermine our own liberties. To paraphrase Thomas More's warning in Bolt's "A Man for All Seasons," if we fail to give the Devil the benefit of the law in our pursuit of him, when the Devil turns on us in a new guise, what shall we shelter behind—the laws being knocked flat by our own earlier zeal?

Bibliography

Boyle, Hadden & Hillyard, *Law and State*.
Kluger, *Simple Justice*.
Scarman, *English Law—A New Dimension*.

CHAPTER 8

THE DEVELOPMENT OF THE COMMON LAW

Introduction

One of the main obstacles facing the newcomer to the common law system is that an understanding of the present can only be achieved via an approach from the past. Modern English law is firmly rooted in its historical tradition.

This historical tradition reflects itself in several ways. First, in respect of classification. English lawyers have traditionally thought in terms of remedies rather than rights—except perhaps where property is concerned (*cf. Hubbard* v. *Pitt* (1975))—and this has led not only to the divisions of law being centred around various types of action (*e.g.* debt, trespass; below Chap. 9) but also to the operative level of the system's being fixed at a low point of abstraction. Secondly, the historical conflicts between the judges and the executive have led to a particular attitude on behalf of the English judiciary: this attitude is probably best exhibited in the approach taken towards interpreting legislation (see Chap. 10). Thirdly, the relationship between procedure and substance. The Forms of Action may well be dead, but they have bequeathed a powerful thought process that still exhibits a dialectical tension between procedural form and factual substance: the way in which facts are interpreted and the appropriate law applied exhibits a mysticism that is perhaps one of the main fascinations of the common law (see Chaps. 9 & 10). Fourthly, of course, the whole courts' structure still reflects—faintly—the very early beginnings in the Norman *Curia Regis*.

The modern common law system has its roots in three main institutions: (i) the *Curia Regis*; (ii) the Court of Chancery; and (iii) the Law Merchant. Though it should be said at once that this is not to deny the important influences of other institutions like the ecclesiastical courts and the Court of Star Chamber.

Curia Regis *and the Early Common Law*

Before the arrival of the Normans in 1066 English society, such as it was, was a society with no central administration. This meant that any system of courts and law was strictly on a local basis; as yet there was no "common law." However, there were the beginnings of Feudalism. This was a social, political and economic structure which was later to conceive and nurture our early pattern of legal institutions and legal thinking; the modern common law still bears traces of this medieval social system.

Feudalism used land as its central *physical* feature. But as its central *conceptual* feature it constructed a positive pyramidal network of obligations which had at its head the owner of a large estate. In return for loyalty and certain services, the owner of land would grant part of his estate to tenants who in turn might grant portions to other tenants who in turn might grant small portions to serfs; in this way the landlord consolidated his own economic position, which he could protect by calling upon tenants and serfs to take up arms, and, for their part, the tenants and serfs were less vulnerable to roaming invaders.

The first aim of the Normans after their invasion of Britain was to establish a strong central government; and William I set about achieving this by appropriating *all* the land to himself, extending feudalism to the whole country, and then granting holdings to his most important followers. However, this is not to say that there were any direct changes in local administration or local justice; indeed feudalism as a system actually confirmed the local court approach in that one of the duties of a tenant-in-chief and Baron was to hold a "seignorial" court for the tenants below them.

The changes made by the Normans were ones of standardisation. In their plan to centralise government under strong Royal authority they created conditions in which a uniform and central law could be established: thus in the local courts bishops were removed (to be put in a separate system of ecclesiastical courts) and local magnates were discouraged from attending. In turn this led to an increase in the importance of another local official, the sheriff; and he was a Royal appointment. Furthermore the local courts also came under the supervision of the *Curia Regis*—a private council of advisors which the king brought with him to England.

The function of the *Curia Regis* was threefold—executive, judicial and legislative; "In the narrow sense [the *Curia Regis*] was primarily composed of what might be called great ministers of state and ... working civil servants" (Radcliffe & Cross, p. 26). However, as land was the main focal point of the social and economic system the *Curia Regis* developed a special interest in not only the revenue which such land provided, but also any disputes which might affect the regularity of the taxes arising from such property. Thus Royal authority gradually began to take control over serious breaches of the peace; fines and confiscations, of course, also helped the coffers.

As a result of this interest in revenue one of the first "departments" to develop within the *Curia Regis* was the Exchequer. This "body" took control of all fiscal matters and soon developed an increasingly exclusive jurisdiction over disputes arising in respect of taxation. Furthermore under Henry II there was established the "General Eyre." This was the name given to Exchequer commissioners who travelled the country with the object of seeing whether any Royal revenue had been missed; however, these commissioners not only assumed the role of auditing accountants. By taking a great interest in all disputes which might result in profit for the crown the General Eyre also assumed the role of travelling court.

It was not long before Exchequer needed a permanent home from which to operate—for king and *Curia Regis* were often on the move. Thus Exchequer, with its increasing jurisdiction to hear pleas of the king's subjects, became one of the first royal "departments" to settle in the Palace of Westminster. And this "establishment of a stationary royal court, which suitors knew where to find notwithstanding the king's whereabouts, marks the origin of the traditional judicial system of this country" (Baker, p. 23).

The next development in the function of the *Curia Regis* was to involve itself with pleas beyond those supposedly concerned with revenue matters and feudalism. And here there was no shortage of consumers for many of the king's subjects distrusted local justice with its local prejudice and bias. The problem with the *Curia Regis*, however, was not that it lacked the officials capable of dealing with such disputes but that it lacked a static base: parties who wanted their dispute settled by royal officials (*iusticiarii*) often had to chase around the country after the king. However, with the anchoring of one "department," the Exchequer, in Westminster the idea soon developed that other justices of the king's court (*coram rege*) could also remain for a while in one place (*in banco*); indeed during the reign of Henry II this was often necessary as the king spent frequent periods abroad.

Towards the end of the twelfth century the practice of a number of justices of the *Curia Regis* remaining fixed in one place had become accepted. Thus a distinction developed between the king's own court (*coram rege*) and the court of justices *in banco residentes*; but this did not mean that the powers of the latter were in any way inferior. However, when *coram rege* was in session it did tend to consume most of the *in banco* work thus undermining the concept of a fixed court of royal justice. But by the *Magna Carta 1215* the idea of a fixed court was "given a new statutory form and force: 'common pleas' were no longer to follow the king, but were to be held in some fixed place. The fixed place was usually Westminster Hall" (Baker, p. 24).

At this point in time the courts of the *Curia Regis* were literally royal courts in the sense that the king himself often sat with the judges and thus exerted considerable influence. Indeed it was not until the fifteenth century that this habit became obsolete. However, with the "common pleas" justices permanently residing at Westminster the *Curia Regis* gradually began to develop two more judicial "departments" alongside Exchequer: there were the common pleas justices themselves and the justices who continued to follow the king. By 1224 these two judicial "departments" had become separate courts with their own records: the *coram rege* became the court of King's Bench and the justices *in banco* the Court of Common Pleas. Thus by the end of the thirteenth century three courts of common law, each with their own professional judges, had emerged out of the *Curia Regis*: Common Pleas, King's Bench and Exchequer.

Henry II and the Writ System

Mention must be made of two important factors during this period of the "split up" of the *Curia Regis*: the influence of Henry II and the development of the writ system.

The reign of Henry II (1154–89) has "a good claim to be considered the most important of our legal history" (Radcliffe & Cross, p. 30). For Henry, with his love of administration and jurisprudence, made far-reaching changes in the legal machinery set up by William I. These changes fall into three areas.

First, Henry tried to curb the strong influence of the ecclesiastical courts by the *Constitutions of Clarendon*. This document attempted to settle jurisdictional issues between the lay and ecclesiastical courts over feudal land, as well as attempting to settle the question of the lay jurisdiction over clerics. Perhaps Henry might have been more successful in his aim if he had not resorted to murdering Beckett who, as Archbishop of Canterbury, had resisted Henry on these legal matters; as a price for reconciliation with the pope Henry had to concede the right of "benefit of clergy." The ecclesiastical courts as a result were to remain very influential until the Reformation.

Secondly, changes were made with regard to the criminal law. The *Assize of Clarendon 1166* and the *Assize of Northamp-*

ton 1176 laid the foundations of what later became known as the Grand Jury (which survived in England until 1932)—an institution consisting of 12 local representatives charged with bringing felons to justice. Furthermore the General Eyre, together with the travelling justices which had become accepted procedure under Henry, established the beginnings of the modern judicial circuits.

However, it is in the third area, land, that Henry's most important changes were made. In order to discourage self-help over land disputes new possessory remedies were introduced known as Possessory Assizes: these speedy remedies, perhaps modelled on Roman possessory remedies, consolidated the idea that a possessor (as opposed to owner) had certain rights in property. Furthermore Henry introduced important changes with regard to disputes over land ownership: although such issues were normally tried in feudal courts, royal authority was exercised over these disputes by means of a *Writ of Right*. Simply, a writ was an order from the king which was needed to initiate the court proceedings in respect of the land dispute; the writ of right contained a threat to the local court that if they did not settle the dispute quickly then the case would be removed to a royal court.

But the writ as an administrative procedure was to have a far-reaching effect on the common law. For it became established that a royal writ issued by the chancery was required before any court proceedings—including those in Common Pleas—could be commenced; and although all manner of writs were probably available during Henry II's reign this was not to be true of the thirteenth century. "In the middle ages [the system of writs] hampered the expansion of the common law by restricting the kinds of claims that could be brought before the court"; for "the formulae of the writs, mostly composed in the thirteenth century to describe the claims then commonly accepted, slowly became precedents which could not easily be altered or added to" (Milsom, p. 25).

The development of the common law from the thirteenth to the seventeenth century is dominated, first, by the jurisdictional struggles between the common law courts themselves and between the common law courts and "outsiders" like Chancery and Star Chamber. And, secondly, by the writ system—which gave rise to a particular kind of rigid legal procedure—which in turn generated its own kind of legal thinking—known as the Forms of Action (see Chap. 9).

During the thirteenth and fourteenth centuries the court of Common Pleas (*in banco*) and the court of King's Bench (*coram rege*) probably functioned side by side in harmony. In both courts the development of a professional body of judges and advocates was underway although in the case of King's Bench it was by no means easy to distinguish court sittings from the ordinary council work of the *Curia Regis* until the end of the fourteenth century. Indeed in 1366 the council attempted to reverse a decision of Common Pleas (for the *Curia Regis* and later King's Bench saw themselves as, amongst other things, a superior court) but in fact this met with little success as the judges by now were beginning to regard themselves as a professional élite outside the executive.

The jurisdiction of Common Pleas was much as its name implied: as a court of original jurisdiction it dealt with disputes arising between subject and subject. However, the court, as supervisor to the local courts, also became a kind of appeal chamber to which cases might be transferred from the provinces; and two weapons which helped Common Pleas in this pursuit were the writs of prohibition and habeas corpus. This latter writ is still used today to challenge the legality of an imprisonment, although modern courts are rarely ready to question the executive (*R. v. Sec. of State, ex. p. Choudhary* (1978)).

The jurisdiction of King's Bench was in many ways similar to that of Common Pleas. Broad distinctions can possibly be made—for example that King's Bench was more concerned with trespass, Common Pleas with debt and detinue (see below, Chap. 9); or that King's Bench dealt with criminal cases, Common Pleas with civil (above, Chap. 1)—but this may give a misleading picture. Perhaps a more important function of King's Bench was as an appeal court dealing with jurisdiction in *error* to correct mistakes on the records of other courts (*cf. R.* v. *Northumberland Compensation Appeal Tribunal, ex p. Shaw* (1952)); for it was this jurisdiction that became the basis of our modern appeal system. However, error must not be confused with our modern appeals because a case could not be retried as such; only an error—however, trivial—on the record of the case could be considered and this meant that from quite an early period lawyers were distinguishing between questions of fact and questions of law (see below, Chap. 10).

Another important aspect of King's Bench was its supervisory jurisdiction. By the use of a variety of writs—habeas corpus, certiorari, prohibition, mandamus, quo warranto—the court was able to compel a lower court to carry out its duty or prevent such a court acting in breach of its jurisdiction. Many of these writs (now known as orders) are still in use: *R.* v. *Electricity Commissioners* (1924).

Exchequer, as we have seen, was concerned mainly with matters of revenue. Nevertheless it had jurisdiction as a court (with its Barons becoming accepted as judges under Elizabeth I) in respect of all matters of taxation and finance. Furthermore by an extension of its *Quominus* jurisdiction (a creditor who could not pay his taxes could use Exchequer to sue his debtor(s)) involving the use of a fiction of indebtedness to the crown, Exchequer was able to encroach upon the jurisdiction of Common Pleas.

In the sixteenth century the jurisdiction of Common Pleas was also being encroached upon by King's Bench. This again was achieved via a fiction. In order to secure for example a debtor's appearance in court it became the practice to issue a fictitious writ of trespass so that the debtor could be arrested by a sheriff (for trespass involved a breach of the king's peace), and once in court the trespass fiction would be dropped and the real claim pursued. King's Bench adopted this method—via the *Bill of Middlesex* which alleged that a defendant had committed a trespass in the county, *viz*. Middlesex, where the court had now settled—in order to be able to deal with claims like debt that normally could only be started in Common Pleas. Once a person was in the custody of its court King's Bench claimed exclusive jurisdiction over all matters. Although Common Pleas attempted to resist these encroachments by adopting fictions of their own and by later appealing to Parliament the damage was done: the courts of Common Pleas and King's Bench "became in practice, in matters of private law, parallel courts of exactly co-ordinate jurisdiction, and thus they were destined to remain until the Judicature Act 1873" (Hanbury, p. 74). Accordingly the jurisdiction of Exchequer, Common Pleas and King's Bench, "originally distinct, gradually merged to produce a coherent body of law, the common law" (Weir, para. 90).

The use of fictions in order to achieve goals of substance illustrates the common law's obsession with form. This was particularly true of the writ system which, as has been indicated, was "an administrative routine which came to govern the end it had been created to serve" (Milsom, p. 22). By the time of Henry II's reign legal actions required a royal writ before they could be commenced; at first these writs were produced to fit each plaintiff's claim. However, by the beginning of the thirteenth century the process had become fossilised: standard form writs only were available for common claims like, *e.g.* debt, trespass, nuisance, covenant and trover; if there was not a writ to fit a person's complaint then he would have no remedy. This writ system gave rise to a procedural process known as the Forms of Action: a process that, as we shall see (Chap. 9), was to mark itself indelibly on the common law thought process.

The Court of Chancery

Obsession with technical form was not the only defect of the common law during the fourteenth and fifteenth centuries; delays, bribery, corruption, acute conservatism and the failure to recognise new writs meant that many plaintiffs never received justice at the hands of the common law courts. Indeed perfectly good actions could be lost by a mere technical slip; even fictions (*i.e.* lies) had to be said correctly. Furthermore the common law could only offer one main remedy, that of damages; and they refused to recognise new institutions or concepts like the use, forerunner of the trust (see Chap. 2).

During this period people who were disgruntled as a result of these defects took to petitioning the king who, as the "Fountain of Justice," would either review the cases himself or, as became the norm, hand them over to his Lord Chancellor: "and chancery slowly changed from a royal office to a royal court, retaining, however, a preponderance of officials over judges" (Weir, para. 90). The law that was administered in this court of Chancery became known as *equity* (see Chap. 1).

Equity never set out to make a frontal attack on the common law; instead it tried to supplement it by going to the substance of matters rather than to the form. Indeed early Lord Chancellors regularly sought the advice of common law judges not only as to points of strict law but also as to the equitable principles upon which relief should be given. What the Court of Chancery set out to achieve, in theory at least, was "to support and protect the common law from shifts and crafty contrivances against the justice of the law. Equity therefore does not destroy the law, nor create it, but assist it" (Lord Cowper in *Dudley* v. *Dudley* (1705)).

In its attempt "to soften and mollify the extremity of the law" (Lord Ellesmere) the Court of Chancery offered litigants a number of distinct advantages over the common law courts. The process was much less technical and during the early period unhampered by procedural form and precedent. New remedies such as specific performance and injunction were recognised. Furthermore in looking to the substance of the case matters such as fraud, duress and unconscionability—matters which were, of course, "against the king's conscience" (of which the Chancellor was keeper)—could be taken account of and might even be a basis for prohibiting a plaintiff from enforcing (or, in civil law terms, abusing) a right at common law: see *Lloyds Bank Ltd.* v. *Bundy* (1975) for a modern example.

The harmonious relationship between law and equity was not to last, however. The common law judges grew increasingly disgruntled at the loss of litigation—and thus loss of fees—from Chancery injunctions and prohibitions; and matters were probably not helped by Chancellors such as Wolsey who "displayed complete contempt for the whole common law system and openly expressed a preference for continental systems" (Baker, p. 43). The conflict between the common law courts and the court of Chancery came to a head in the seventeenth century: Sir Edward Coke, Chief Justice of King's Bench, barraged Chancery with habeas corpus and prohibition writs, finally declaring that to go to equity was a criminal offence under the statute of *Praemunire* (*Earl of Oxford's Case* (1615)). The dispute was then submitted to James I who was advised by his council to support Lord Ellesmere and the Court of Chancery, which he duly did. Where rules of equity came into conflict with rules of common law, equity was to prevail: confirmed by the *Supreme Court of Judicature Act 1873* s. 25 (11).

From 1616 onwards equity was free to develop, which it did under the guidance of Lord Chancellors such as Nottingham (1673-1683), Hardwicke (1737–1756) and Eldon (1801-1806, 1807–1827). Nevertheless by the eighteenth century Chancery had become in its practice little different from the common law courts: rules, precedents and rigidity were hardening the arteries. And it is only in recent times, under the guidance of Lord Denning, that a certain flexibility and sense of purpose has been rediscovered: see, *e.g. Central London Property Trust Ltd.* v. *High Trees House Ltd.* (1947); Denning, Part V.

Although law and equity were administered in separate courts until the latter half of the nineteenth century, the two systems were not entirely insensitive to each other's influences. Imaginative common lawyers like Lord Mansfield—Chief Justice of King's Bench 1756–1788, and a "Scot with a natural sense of principle" (Weir, para. 137)—recognised the value of some of the equitable approaches (see, *e.g. Moses* v. *Macferlan* (1760)), and so while it is still possible to classify areas of law exclusively to equity (*e.g.* trusts) or common law (criminal, tort), the jurisdiction of the two systems are now often mixed (contract, unjust enrichment).

The Courts Merchant and Maritime

Although Lord Mansfield never achieved his aim of breaking down the barriers between law and equity, he was successful in his attempts to extinguish the gulf between common law and the law merchant.

Widespread travel not being the norm meant that the "position of merchants and mariners in the medieval period was peculiar" (Potter, p. 183). For merchants and mariners, almost literally, were men of the world and thus, like Sindbad, would often put to sea "Voyaging many days and nights from isle to isle and from shore to shore, buying and selling and bartering whenever the ship anchored" (Penguin ed., Dawood, p. 115). For such people "the early common law was wholly unsuited, dominated as it was by rules relating to land, disputes about which need not be swiftly resolved" (Weir, para. 137). A more suitable system of justice was provided, at first, by local courts:

the courts of piepowder, and later courts of Staple, would spring into existence at fairs and markets to settle disputes both swiftly and, because juries were composed of merchants of all tongues, sympathetically. The *Statute of the Staple 1353* prevented interference into the jurisdiction of these courts of Staple towns by common law judges, and appeals lay to the King in Council.

This sytem of local courts was not to last, however. For in the fourteenth century there was developing another court around another official of the king's council, the Admiral. The expansion of the Court of Admiralty—which dealt with matters of sea as opposed to land—came to encompass in the fifteenth and sixteenth centuries the law merchant; this is hardly surprising given that sea and mercantile law were both international in outlook so that the disputes of merchants were well within the competence of the civilian orientated Admiralty judges. But the court of admiralty was not to have the resilience, or perhaps luck, of the court of chancery: the attacks made by jealous common lawyers led by Coke virtually stopped the court from carrying on and, although a compromise was effected, the political upheavals proved deadly. By the middle of the seventeenth century Admiralty had been stripped of most of its commercial jurisdiction.

However, this victory by the common law was hardly to be viewed with enthusiasm by the merchant community. For the ways of the common law courts, more used to entertaining disputes about property rights, were most unsuitable for the mercantile law with its equitable and international flavour. But the position was drastically altered when Lord Mansfield appeared in 1756: he appreciated the difficulties facing the mercantile community and set about adopting the common law for their needs. Thus mercantile custom was recognised as law, advice was taken from the merchants themselves, foreign legal principles were not ignored and juries were packed with men of commerce. Furthermore the action on the case (see Chap. 9) was by now proving flexible enough to lay the foundations of a law of contract (see Chap. 2). Thus "in a majestic series of excellently reported decisions the principles of commercial law, of bills and notes, of insurance and of charterparties" (Weir, para. 137) became part of the common law which today is handled by the commercial court of the Queen's' Bench Division: *Administration of Justice Act 1970*, s. 3.

Council and Star Chamber

From what has been said so far it might almost be imagined that the only conflict to be experienced in Britain was that between Coke and his adversaries. History as seen by lawyers can sometimes reflect their unreal world. During the Tudor and Stuart period the country was quite often in a state of political upheaval as Parliament and monarchy struggled for supremacy; this struggle in fact had important repercussions upon the development of English law. First, after the Wars of the Roses, there had been a general revival of the judicial power of the king's council (witness the Court of Chancery); in its attempt to maintain strong government and royal power this council resorted, via conciliar courts, once again to its judicial functions. Secondly, associated with this revival of conciliar jurisdiction went a renewed interest in the civil law—for this was a system that best suited the monarchist claim. Thus the Court of Requests, a kind of local royal court of equity dealing with small claims, became a court of civil law, although "it is not easy to say how far, if at all, it contributed to the development of equity as a body of legal principles" (Potter, p. 170).

By far the most famous of the conciliar courts was that of Star Chamber. It is difficult to trace the actual creation of this court, but the *Act of Camera Stellata 1487* confirmed the council's jurisdiction to hear cases not easily dealt with at common law—*e.g.* cases of bribery, perjury, etc., or cases where the defendant was a particularly powerful figure. Although the court had some civil jurisdiction (usually via the fictitious allegation of a riot), its main importance was in respect of the criminal law: as a court closely associated with executive power it developed crimes like riot, conspiracy, attempt, criminal libel and perjury—crimes which were (and still are) most effective against political dissenters. Indeed it was this close association with royal power that, with the victory of Parliament, was to be Star Chamber's downfall. But although the court was formally abolished in 1641, it bequeathed its criminal jurisdiction to King's Bench, the influence of which can still be felt today: *Shaw* v. *D.P.P.* (1964); *R.* v. *Lemon* (1979).

Ecclesiastical Courts

It was not only within the conciliar courts that the civil law had its influence. The system of ecclesiastical courts set up by William I, and which survived both Henry II and Henry VIII, also administered law that was very international in its outlook.

Before the nineteenth century the jurisdiction of the ecclesiastical courts was much wider than it is today: it covered not only people in orders but also matrimonial and succession matters. Because of the international flavour of canon law the judges of the ecclesiastical courts became associated with the judges of the Court of Admiralty—forming the Doctors' Commons—and it is from this historical association that there sprang the Probate, Divorce and Admiralty Division of the High Court: but see now *Administration of Justice Act 1970*, s. 1.

The Legal Profession

One of the main reasons why civil law made little more than marginal headway in England was due to the structure—indeed the existence—of our legal profession. On the continent the rediscovery of Roman law in the eleventh and twelfth centuries led to a renaissance in jurisprudential studies within universities and this had an important practical effect on the development of legal thinking and procedure. In this country, however, it was the common law institutions themselves that fostered the profession of lawyers and judges needed to staff and operate the legal system; and this had a profound effect upon common law thinking. For the legal practitioners "did not aim ... to produce reasoned structures but rather lists of ... actions which would be useful in practice because they suited the typical and recurrent particular needs of litigants" (Max Weber).

In the early *Curia Regis* judges as a separate professional body could not really be isolated until Henry II established Commissioners to handle the increasingly complex matters of royal government; but even then the commissioners' role was as much administrative as judicial and, being ecclesiastics, they often had little legal training. In the later medieval period, when the courts had established greater independence from the council, the judges were drawn from a body of eminent court advocates known as sergeants-at-law; and the advocates themselves were becoming a distinct profession from another group of court officials known as attorneys—who acted as representatives rather than advocates—and thus gradually the pattern was set for the modern division of duties between barristers and solicitors (see Chap. 6). Furthermore the practice of appointing judges from the ranks of professional lawyers is still adhered to today with the higher judicial posts still going to advocates (*viz.* barristers).

Although the actual profession of sergeants waned their role was continued by other advocates who had in the fourteenth century established themselves in four Inns of Court; and these Inns—which still exist today (see Chap. 6)—took control of both legal practice and legal education. Thus from an early age the common law was to be a professional skill rather than an academic science. The attorneys for a time were also involved in the world of the Inns of Court, but a growing elitism amongst advocates led to their exclusion at the end of the sixteenth century. The attorneys later formed a separate organisation, the Society of Gentleman Practisers, which became the forerunner of the modern Law Society (see Chap. 6).

Exchequer Chamber and House of Lords

Before the nineteenth century, as we have seen, the main machinery for appeal was by writ of error. This lay from Common Pleas to King's Bench and from there to the House of Lords; Exchequer had its own Court of Error, Exchequer Chamber (1), which had been set up in 1357—from which there was also an appeal to the House of Lords—and consisting of the Treasurer and Lord Chancellor with justices to assist them. A statute in 1585 set up a Court of Error, Exchequer Chamber (2), to hear appeals from King's Bench in certain cases like debt, detinue, covenant, trespass and case; this court consisted of Common Pleas justices and Exchequer Barons. Furthermore, in the middle ages the judges of King's Bench and Common Pleas often met in an informal court, Exchequer Chamber (3), to discuss legal problems of particular difficulty; if a judge was faced with a problematic case he would adjourn the hearing, seek advice from his brethren in Exchequer Chamber (3), and then return to give judgment. However, this procedure had died out by the eighteenth century, although not without leaving an impression on English law.

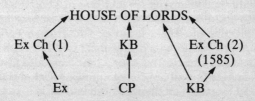

In 1830 the whole of this system was swept away and a new appeals procedure was established. A new appeal court, Exchequer Chamber (4), was set up to hear appeals from all the common law courts; and from Exchequer Chamber (4) there was an appeal to the House of Lords. This new court of Exchequer Chamber consisted of judges from any of the common law courts except the one from which the error was brought.

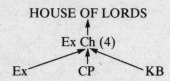

Although the common law judges had made strong objections to the House of Lords' claim that it could be a court of first instance, they never seriously disputed its right to sit as the highest Court of Error (*Shirley* v. *Fagg* (1675)). The reason for this willingness to accept the House of Lords was probably due to the fact that the common law judges recognised the body as representing the King in Council; in other words the appellate jurisdiction of the House of Lords is a hangover from the ultimate judicial functions of the royal council itself. Originally this appellate jurisdiction was seen as part of the ordinary work of the House of Lords and thus lay peers could insist on taking part and voting (see, *e.g. Bishop of London* v. *Ffytche* (1783)); however, by the nineteenth century the opinions and votes of lay peers were being ignored (is this why there is no third judgment in *Rylands* v. *Fletcher* (1868)? *cf.* (1970) 86 L.Q.R. 160) and today the law lords must be legally qualified: *Appellate Jurisdiction Act 1876*.

The Nineteenth Century

By the nineteenth century the economic, social and political structure of England had changed from feudalism to capitalism.

Yet the structure of the legal system was still firmly rooted in its medieval ways: the higher courts were complicated and there was little co-operation between them; there was no consistent system of appeals; no system of courts to try small civil cases; no adequate organisation of the lower criminal courts; and the actual procedure in civil cases was still firmly tied to fictions and the writ system. Furthermore the reputation of the courts—especially Chancery—for slowness was itself giving rise to fiction (Dickens, *Bleak House*). In short the legal system was quite inadequate for the new bourgeoisie.

With some guidance by writers and scholars like Jeremy Bentham (1748–1832), Parliament was induced into making the nineteenth century an age of legal reform. The *Uniformity of Process Act 1832* dispensed with fictions like the Bill of Middlesex and the *Real Property Limitation Act 1833* simplified the procedure for the recovery of land; the *Civil Procedure Act 1833* attempted to simplify pleadings but this was not really achieved until the *Common Law Procedure Acts 1852–1860*. These last mentioned acts finally abolished—in theory at least—the forms of action (see Chap. 9) as well as making it possible for judgment to be given in default of appearance by the defendant.

The Court of Chancery also attracted the attention of the legislature. The *Court of Chancery Act 1850* provided a speedier method for settling points as to the construction of documents like wills and the *Court of Chancery Procedure Act 1852* simplified actual proceedings in court. The *Chancery Amendment Act 1858* (Lord Cairns' Act) empowered the Court of Chancery to give damages in lieu of an injunction, which saved a defendant who failed to get an injunction from having to go to the common law courts: for a modern example see *Wroth* v. *Tyler* (1974).

However, the main restructuring of the legal system followed a report of the Judicature Commissioners in 1869: the *Supreme Court of Judicature Act 1873* (see now *Supreme Court of Judi-*

cature (Consolidation) Act 1925). A new court was created, the Supreme Court, and this operated on two levels—first instance and appellate—with the old common law courts being consolidated into divisions, and a new Court of Appeal replacing the Exchequer Chamber.

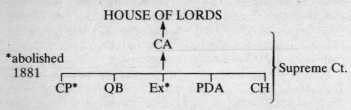

In 1881 the Exchequer and Common Pleas divisions were abolished—their jurisdiction being assumed by Queen's Bench—but the other divisions, along with the House of Lords (which was nearly abolished in the 1873–75 period), survived until the minor reorganisation of the High Court in 1970: *Administration of Justice Act 1970*, ss. 1–3 (see Chap. 4). Greater co-operation was introduced between the divisions by the consolidation of jurisdictions—especially between law and equity which the 1873 legislation "fused" into a single body for the purposes of administration in any court—although this is not to suggest that there is today no difference between legal and equitable remedies (see, *e.g. Miller* v. *Jackson* (1977)) or that jurisdictional problems were to become extinct (see, *e.g. Edwards* v. *Quickenden* (1939)).

Another major defect of the legal system which attracted the attention of the nineteenth-century reformers was the gap left in small claims jurisdiction by the abolition of the conciliar courts. Attempts had been made at the end of the eighteenth century to revive the old County Courts of Middlesex and extend the system to the whole country, but a proper system of local courts to try small civil cases (especially debt actions) was not established until the *County Courts Act 1846*. This statute divided the country up into districts and in each of these districts was established a county court grouped into circuits and having their own judge and Registrar. These courts were small local versions of the high court but with, at first, only moderate jurisdiction; since 1846, however, the jurisdiction has been progressively widened owing to the popularity of the courts, the decline in the value of money (for one of the main limitations upon jurisdiction was, and still is, financial: see Chap. 4) and the increase in welfare legislation.Today the county courts derive their authority from the *County Courts Act 1959*.

The three main institutions of the criminal law—*viz.* travelling justices, juries and justices of the peace (all with histories stretching back to the twelfth century, although the functions narrowed with the establishment of local government and police)—survived the nineteenth century. Changes were made with regard to the conduct and procedure of criminal cases, and magistrates' courts were given formal regulation *via* the *Summary Jurisdiction Act 1848*. Also, statutory recognition was conferred upon an informal criminal appeal court which was not unlike the old Exchequer Chamber (3), the Court for Crown Cases Reserved, although this only survived until 1907, when it was replaced with a Court of Criminal Appeal which lasted until 1966. With respect to major changes in the area of criminal law the twentieth century will be of greater significance than the nineteenth.

The nineteenth century also saw the establishment of a semi-official body of law reporting, the Incorporated Council of Law Reporting. This body, regulated by the Inns of Court and the Law Society, was given the task of producing comprehensive reports from all the major courts; today the judgments are of great accuracy as they are revised by the judges themselves before publication. Before the Council was established in 1866 law reporting was in the hands of private individuals whose reports, at least before the eighteenth century, tended to be unreliable because reporters only attended some cases and even then tiredness and heavy lunches could impede accuracy. The Incorporated Council did not put an end to private reports (which had improved in the eighteenth century), but today the *All England Law Reports* published by Butterworths are the only comprehensive non-specialist private law reports to survive. Although the *Times Law Reports* were discontinued in 1952, *The Times* actually continued to carry law reports until suspension of the newspaper last year; it is to be hoped that the reports will continue if the paper reappears as they sometimes carried details of decisions not easily available elsewhere.

Conclusion

Perhaps one conclusion that could be drawn from this brief historical survey is that the common law survived not so much as a result of intellectual and social prowess, but more because the minds of those who staffed the institutions were, with only few exceptions, extraordinarily narrow, inflexible and riddled with petty jealousies. Perhaps the chief ideal of the judges of the middle ages was, for reasons of self-interest, to expand their own sphere of influence; and while on occasions this expansion might involve a challenge to an executive institution like Star Chamber, it might be wrong to view such a challenge as having a firm foundation in some legal or moral principle. For the common law judges not only knew when not to challenge the executive (just as they do today: *Liversidge* v. *Anderson* (1942); *R.* v. *Secretary of State for the Home Department, ex p. Hosenball* (1977)) but also they were quite happy to assume and continue Star Chamber's criminal jurisdiction with its questionable "crimes" like conspiracy and criminal libel. What the common law seemed to offer to an executive was a bureaucratic and administrative machine whose thinking never ventured beyond the metaphysical bricks it constructed to handle disputes which at first centred around land but later came to embrace people, things, money and, in more recent times, intangible "property" like confidential information.

Of course this is not to underestimate the power of the metaphysical thinking of common lawyers. The concepts of "property," "debt" and "trespass"—nurtured in formal and highly conservative royal institutions—established powerful thought patterns whose usefulness was to extend beyond feudalism to form a solid foundation for developing capitalism. And it is to this metaphysical side of the common law that we must now turn in the following chapters.

Bibliography

Radcliffe & Cross, *The English Legal System* (6th ed. by Hand & Bentley, 1977).

Baker, *An Introduction to English Legal History* (1971).

Milsom, *Historical Foundations of the Common Law* (1969).

Weir, "The Common Law System," *International Encyclopedia of Comparative Law*, Vol. II, Chap. 2 (1977).

Potter, *Historical Introduction to English Law* (4th ed. by Kiralfy, 1958).

Hanbury, *English Courts of Law* (4th ed. by Yardley, 1967).

Kiralfy, *The English Legal System* (5th ed., 1978).

Zweigert & Kotz (trans. Weir), *An Introduction to Comparative Law* (1977), Vol. I, pp. 189–226.

David & Brierley, *Major Legal Systems in the World Today* (2nd ed., 1978), pp. 286–308.

Harding, *Social History of English Law* (1966).

Denning, *The Discipline of the Law* (1979).

Chapter 9

SOURCES, REMEDIES AND CLASSIFICATION OF ENGLISH LAW

Introduction

When one talks about the metaphysical side of law one is really talking about the whole mass of rules—often referred to as The Law—which form the intellectual (and ideological) grist used by the courts for the settlement of the disputes before them. In many of today's cases the relevant rules are to be found in the form of printed statutes (legislation), but for some disputes the appropriate rules are not to be found in such a concrete linguistic source. They are to be elucidated from the record of a previously decided dispute and/or from a factual reality of society or part of society (case law, custom). However, whatever the source of the grist there is the problem that before the relevant part can be applied it must be discovered; and in a complex society there may be so many rules that only a sophisticated system of classification will facilitate discovery. Much of the metaphysical side of law thus consists of the sources, discovery and classification of rules.

Sources
The sources of English law must be divided into three areas—legal, factual and information. The first area represents the actual procedure by which rules become law; the second contains the motivating facts that generate law; and the third deals with the publications in which the rules, once validly made, can be found.

Legal Source
In the United Kingdom today there are three legal sources by

which law can be generated: (i) legislation, (ii) court decision, and (iii) custom.

Legislation is the passing of rules by a competent authority of government and in the case of the United Kingdom the highest competent authority is now Parliament (although before the seventeenth century such power lay in the monarch). In this country legislation is "written" law and so, as we shall see (Chap. 10), the courts have power to interpret the language and application of legislative rules; however, the courts do not have power to declare properly passed legislation as invalid except in one situation. That situation is in regard to delegated legislation. Parliament can pass an Act empowering another body or person (see, *e.g. Consumer Safety Act 1978*) to make rules of law but if that body or person exceeds the powers conferred upon it, or attempts to legislate beyond the scope of the enabling Act, a court has power to declare any such delegated legislation as *ultra vires* and void: see, *e.g. Roberts* v. *Hopwood* (1925); *Prescott* v. *Birmingham Corporation* (1955).

Modern legislation takes the form of a printed statute divided into sections and often containing schedules. Since 1963 the "chapter numbers assigned to Acts of Parliament ... shall be assigned by reference to the calendar year, and not the Session, in which they were passed; and any such Act may, in any Act, instrument or document, be cited accordingly" (*Acts of Parliament Numbering and Citation Act 1962*, s. 1). An Act of Parliament becomes law, not when it is published, but when it receives Royal Assent.

Legislation is now the most important source of English Law and its purposes are diverse. Statutes may be designed to amend or alter aspects of the common law (see, *e.g. Animals Act 1971*) or previously passed legislation (*e.g. Theft Act 1978*); or they may be enacted to rationalise whole factual areas of difficulty where for example legal control was formerly piecemeal (*e.g. Consumer Credit Act 1974*). Legislation may also be designed to deal with particular kinds of unsociable

behaviour with the hope of encouraging social harmony (*e.g.
Race Relations Act 1976*); or it may be passed just to codify (*e.g.
Sale of Goods Act 1893*) or consolidate (*Fatal Accidents Act
1976*). In times of economic and political instability—or in
times of war—legislation may be passed to deal with problems
of public order and emergencies (*Public Order Act 1936; Pre-
vention of Terrorism (Temporary Provisions) Act 1974*); or it
may be passed to attempt to handle more indirect forms of
dissent (*Industrial Relations Act 1971*, repealed by a subsequent government).

For the purist, however, the most important source of
English law are the law courts themselves. Indeed legislation in
"classical theory . . . is only a secondary source of law, a series of
errata and *addenda* to the main body of English law formed by
the decisions of the courts" (David & Brierley, p. 355). But in
order to understand how the decisions of the courts become law
one must be familiar with the hierarchy of the courts (Chaps. 4
and 8), the law reports (Chap. 8) and the concepts of *ratio
decidendi* and *obiter dictum* (below and Chap. 10).

For the purposes of binding precedent (*stare decisis*) "it is
necessary for each lower tier, including the Court of Appeal, to
accept loyally the decisions of the higher tiers" (Lord Hailsham
L.C. in *Cassell & Co.* v. *Broome* (1972)): thus the High Court is
bound by decisions of the Court of Appeal and in turn the Court
of Appeal is bound by decisions of the House of Lords; the
"Judicial Committee of the Privy Council is technically not an
authoritative tribunal in the English hierarchy, but as its personnel is normally identical with that of the House of Lords, its
judgments will at least be read with respect" (Fifoot, p. 24).
Both the Court of Appeal and the House of Lords were originally bound by their own decisions, but this is no longer true of
the House of Lords (*Practice Direction (Judicial Precedent)
(1966)*); the Court of Appeal can only depart from previous
cases where (i) there is a conflict between two previous decisions or (ii) there is a decision which cannot stand with a House

of Lords decision or (iii) one of their decisions was given *per incuriam* (*Young* v. *Bristol Aeroplane Co. Ltd*. (1944); *Davis* v. *Johnson* (1978)).

It is not only important to know who binds but also what binds. For this purpose the common law has developed two conceptual tools: *ratio decidendi* and *obiter dictum*. "In its simplest form [the *ratio decidendi*] may be said to be the principle or principles, deduced from authority, on which the Court reached its decision; or, negatively, the principle or principles *without which* the Court would not have reached the decision that it did reach" (Allen, p. 259). However, as Devlin J. observed in *Behrens* v. *Bertram Mills Circus Ltd*. (1957): "A judge may often give additional reasons for his decision without making them part of the *ratio decidendi*; he may not be sufficiently convinced of their cogency as to want them to have the full authority of precedent, and yet may wish to state them so that those who later may have the duty of investigating the same point will start with some guidance." This latter reasoning is described as *obiter dicta*—things said by the way. Thus a previous decision is only binding if the *ratio decidendi* of the case covers the situation arising in the instant dispute; but what amounts to the *ratio*—as opposed to mere *obiter dicta*—of a previous decision is a problem that lies at the very heart of common law reasoning (see Chap. 10).

The third source of English law, custom, is generally regarded as being of minor importance today; custom as a source of law was really of greater relevance in the more formative days of the common law and at stages like the absorption of the law merchant (see Chap. 8). Furthermore it can often be difficult to distinguish between custom and judicial decision as the source of a legal rule (see, *e.g. Sagar* v. *Ridehalge* (1931)) and this is particularly true where the custom—*e.g.* "negotiable instrument," "reasonableness," "trade usage"— has become part of the central law. Custom may also be important as generating local variations to centralised law, but in order to do so the custom must satisfy stringent conditions of antiquity, certainty, reasonableness and notoriety.

Factual Source

Custom, of course, can be seen as either a legal or factual source of law—for the law is really just formally recognising a factual reality of society. However, in the field of legislation—where the legal source is *only* the written language of the formal statute (see Chap. 10)—one must actually look behind the statute itself in order to identify the real source of any particular rule or set of rules. Accordingly some legislation might result from agitation by public pressure groups or from election pledges of a political party; other legislation may be generated by some sociological research or by a report from a government commission. Thus the *Consumer Credit Act 1974* resulted from the *Report of the Crowther Committee on Consumer Credit* (Cmnd. 4596, 1971) which in turn considered a wide range of evidence from a variety of organisations and individuals.

In 1965 a permanent body, the Law Commission, was established for the purpose of promoting law reform. The function of the commissions is "to take and keep under review all the law with which they are respectively concerned with a view to its systematic development and reform"; and this includes "the codification of such law, the elimination of anomalies ... and generally the simplification and modernisation of the law" (*Law Commission Act 1965*, s. 3 (1)). Accordingly since 1965 some legislation owes its origin to the researches, efforts and recommendations of this Law Commission which itself received evidence from those who responded to its Working Papers (see, *e.g. Animals Act 1971*). In the field of criminal law a Criminal Law Revision Committee was set up in 1959 to examine and make recommendations as to law revision; the *Theft Act 1968* is an example of legislation resulting from one of their reports (Cmnd. 2977, 1966).

The factual sources behind the rules generated by the courts themselves are often less easy to identify and may for example depend upon the factual evidence produced in court (see, *e.g. Roe* v. *Minister of Health* (1954)). Some judges—and this is particularly true of Lord Denning M.R. (see *The Discipline of the Law*)—will be more open as to the social and factual reasons for adopting a particular course, but often it is left to the academics to speculate (see, *e.g.* Griffith, *The Politics of the Judiciary*). Nevertheless it must always be remembered that with a great case like *Donoghue* v. *Stevenson* (1932) the importance of the decision lies not only in the establishment of some new legal principle: such a case is also important because it represents the law's recognition of a factual reality like the relationship between manufacturer and consumer. At the present time the courts are locked in a controversy as to whether the rules of the law of tort ought to take account of the factual reality that many classes of defendants are covered by insurance; the House of Lords, unlike the Court of Appeal, remains unimpressed: *Morgans* v. *Launchbury* (1973).

Information Source

The main information sources of English law are the publication of statutes (HMSO) and the Law Reports. Unlike some other countries, England does not have an official Statute Book (although there is now an attempt to compile a *Statutes in Force*), but copies of many Acts of Parliament are individually available from Government Bookshops and comprehensive collections—often annotated—are available in private publications like *Halsbury's Statutes* or *Current Law Statutes*. Law reports as we know them today (*viz.* accurate and comprehensive) are a relatively recent phenomenon whose rise (see Chap. 8) and importance is closely tied to the whole development of *stare decisis*; before the appearance of reliable law reports much of the knowledge of the common law was to be gleaned either from the court records (Plea Rolls, Year Books) or from early commentators like Glanvill (twelfth century), Bracton (thirteenth century) and Littleton (fifteenth century).

Much law is also to be found in the increasing number of tomes and tomettes being published by academics. Some of these works are aimed specifically at the practitioner (*e.g. Chitty on Contracts*) while others are written with law students in mind (*e.g.* Cheshire & Fifoot, *Law of Contract*)—although this is not to suggest that the latter are not utilised and appreciated by both barristers and judges. The learned periodicals like the *Law Quarterly Review* (L.Q.R.), *Modern Law Review* (M.L.R.) and *Cambridge Law Journal* (C.L.J.) contain monographs on law and also have notes on the latest decisions; other journals like *Public Law* or the *British Journal of Law and Society* have a subject or academic bias. Over the last 20 years—probably as a result of the case-method approach from the United States—collections of edited legal materials (cases, statutes, articles, notes, etc.) have appeared on various subject areas of law; as well as being useful portable libraries these casebooks can sometimes contain many stimulating comments and questions by the compilers.

The Structure and Divisions of Law

According to Gaius, a Roman jurist who lived in the second century A.D., the "whole of the law observed by us relates either to persons or to things or to actions" (*Institutes* I. 8, trans. de Zulueta)—a classification that operated "with respect to the subject, or with respect to the object, or with reference to the machinery of enforcing it" (Pound, p. 952). In fact this pragmatic way of classifying Roman law was adopted for teaching purposes only; and so in the *Digest* one finds many other distinctions—public law is distinguished from private, *ius civil* from *ius gentium*, contracts from delicts and ownership from obligations. Some of the patterns of this thought process have found their way into the common law: thus, while the English lawyer does not make the same rigid distinction between actions *in rem* (property) and actions *in personam* (obligations), the idea that one can have a legal relationship not only with another person but also with a thing does find considerable expression (in, *e.g.* the law of mortgages, or hire-purchase; see also *Willis & Son* v. *British Car Auctions* (1978); *cf. Law Reform Committee, Eighteenth Report* (Cmnd. 4774, 1971) para. 13). Furthermore metaphysical institutions like "contract" and "fault" (*culpa*) have also found their way from Roman to English law and so the common law has, to some extent, developed structures which would be familiar to the Roman jurist: see, *e.g.* Lord Diplock in *Moschi* v. *Lep Air Services Ltd* (1973) ("law of obligations") and in *Gouriet* v. *Union of Post Office Workers* (1977) ("the difference between private law and public law").

But what makes Roman law of particular interest to the common lawyer is that both systems—unlike the modern codes of Europe—take as their starting point of classification legal remedies as opposed to legal rights. For the "very similar ways in which litigation was initiated led legal practitioners in Rome and England to think not so much in terms of rights as in terms of types of action, and to interest themselves more in the concrete *facts* which fell within the various actions or writs rather than in elaborating the substantive law into a *system* based on some rational method" (Zweigert & Kotz, p. 195). And a system that thinks in terms of remedies rather than rights is likely to have that thinking distinctly coloured by the *procedure* for obtaining those remedies.

The Forms of Action

The influence of procedure is particularly true of the early common law whose actions formulated themselves around the administrative process of the writ system. As we have seen (Chap. 8), by the thirteenth century there had developed a series of standard form writs covering most of the common types of claim—debt, detinue, covenant, trespass and nuisance.

These types of action came to represent not only a procedural method for obtaining a remedy but also a conceptual method for classifying claims; if a plaintiff sought a remedy for which there was no writ it came to be thought that the law, at both a procedural and metaphysical level, could be of no service. Thus for trespass to lie the damage had to be *directly* caused; if the damage had occurred indirectly—*e.g.* the defendant, instead of hitting the plaintiff with a log (direct damage), had left it in the road for him to trip over—the old lawyers came to find it difficult, at least in the royal courts, to grant a remedy. For causation became a focal point—both in practice and in theory—by which the good claim was to be distinguished from the bad; and it required a change of procedure to lead to a change of thinking.

The change occurred in the fourteenth century and for some is to be attributed to the *Statute of Westminster II 1285*, c. 24. Whether this legislation actually led to the development of the Action on the Case is now in doubt, but by the middle of the fourteenth century the chancery clerks were issuing writs analogous to the established ones. Thus, in the trespass example above, the plaintiff who had suffered damage indirectly might now have an action on the case for trespass.

The action on the case was of major importance to the common law in that, by making the procedure for obtaining a remedy more flexible, the way was paved for more creative development at the metaphysical level. And it was during this period (*viz.* post fourteenth century) that the concept of trespass—"that fertile mother of actions" (Maitland, p. 39)—became particularly important: for trespass on the case as a remedy for damage caused by indirect "invasions" was to prove one of the most elastic of concepts. All that was needed was a motive for such development and this was supplied by the voracious appetite of King's Bench (see Chap. 8); indeed in 1602 this royal court even managed to interpret an offshoot of trespass on the case—*assumpsit*—as covering debt (*Slade's*

Case)—one reason why debt is subsumed today under a contract theory while its sister, detinue, remained alive and independent until the *Torts (Interference with Goods) Act 1977*, s. 2 (1).

Nevertheless the action on the case did not lead to any revolution in procedural thinking—a plaintiff right from the very beginning still had to attach a label to his action and if he chose the wrong writ, or sued in trespass when he should have claimed in case, then this could be fatal to the whole action (*Reynolds* v. *Clarke* (1726); *cf. Scott* v. *Shepherd* (1773)). Indeed it was exasperation with such formal technicalities that drove some plaintiffs into the arms of the Lord Chancellor (see Chap. 8). However, by the nineteenth century many new forms of action had emerged as offshoots from older ones and newer, more abstract, theories of liability were developing to meet the needs of capitalism; thus at the substantive level concepts such as contract (see Chap. 2) and negligence (Chap. 2) were cutting across the traditional patterns of liability based upon kinds of harm.

The forms of action were finally abolished by the *Common Law Procedure Act 1852*. All that a plaintiff now had to allege were the facts plus a cause of action; however, for a long period after the act—indeed even today to some extent—these "causes of action" just followed the old writs. Thus, for example, trespass with its requirement of directness (see *Harnett* v. *Bond* (1925)) survived to become the tort of trespass, and detinue, right up until 1977, remained a different cause (*viz*. form) of action from conversion (*General & Finance Facilities Ltd*. v. *Cooks Cars (Romford) Ltd*. (1963)). Even debt, although incorporated into contract, retained its independence from an action for damages (*Overstone Ltd*. v. *Shipway* (1961)). Nevertheless the abolition of the forms of action did allow the courts to make revolutionary shifts in the metaphysical classification of remedies: in the law of tort, for example, the basis of liability for physical injury caused by defective chattels was shifted off the thing that did the damage and on to the behaviour of the defendant (*Donoghue* v. *Stevenson* (1932)) and once behaviour was established as a focal point of liability new heads of complaint could be recognised without coming up against the traditional procedural restrictions (see, *e.g. Hedley Byrne* v. *Heller & Partners* (1964)). Of course this is not to suggest that vestiges of the old procedural approach cannot still be found amongst the modern judiciary (see, *e.g. Esso Petroleum* v. *Southport Corporation* (1956))—indeed even amongst the law reformers (see, *e.g. Animals Act 1971*).

Causes of Action

"A cause of action," as Diplock L.J. pointed out in *Letang* v. *Cooper* (1965), "is simply a factual situation the existence of which entitles one person to obtain from the court a remedy against another person." However, as the judge went on to explain, "it is essential to realise that when, since 1873, the name of a form of action is used to identify a cause of action, it is used as a convenient and succinct description of a particular category of factual situation which entitles one person to obtain ... a remedy." And to "forget this will indeed encourage the old forms of action to rule us from their graves."

The idea that the forms of action still rule from the grave is often on the lips of contemporary lawyers—and this is hardly surprising. For the common lawyer often gets frustrated with the historical tradition of his subject which he wrongly thinks was repudiated with the change from forms to causes of action. But as Diplock L.J. implies, the notion of a cause of action still involves a remedies approach to liability via "a particular category of factual situation" and so rather than accuse the forms of action of being an anachronism it might be nearer the truth to argue, as Weir does, that they "actually ... have quite a modern flavour" (C.L.L.R., p. 16).

The problem facing the modern lawyer is to understand a basic clash of approaches. The forms of action "provided a remedy for typical fact-situations" (Weir, *supra*) which had little interest in organising themselves to conform to some highly abstract rational theory of legal rights, while the nineteenth century was busy eschewing such pragmatism in favour of concepts that reflected the new philosophies of liberalism. Thus, blissfully insensitive to the fact that the forms of action were hardly in a position to bequeath a schematic and rational system of law at a high level of abstraction, the nineteenth century legal architects stopped thinking in terms of trespass and debt and started to classify in terms of contract and tort—categories that are now being discarded in favour, once again, of a fact-based approach to liability: see, *e.g. Midland Bank Trust Co.* v. *Hett, Stubbs & Kemp* (1978).

What are the factual situations which now give rise to a civil remedy? In order to answer this question it is once again necessary to look back into the past and examine the "interplay between two simple ideas from which the common law started ... the demand for a right and the complaint of a wrong" (Milsom, p. 211). The main difference between these two ideas is essentially one of emphasis: "rights" emphasise a theory of remedies from a plaintiff's point of view—the focal point being the invasion or entitlement of the plaintiff; "wrongs" on the other hand emphasise a theory of remedies from a defendant's point of view—the defendant ought only to be liable if he has caused damage by his own irresponsible behaviour. This difference of emphasis was loosely reflected in the dichotomy between original writ actions (debt, detinue, trespass, etc.) and case (where negligence or deceit became important requirements); today the difference is reflected in the concepts of "fault" and "property"—the notion of "promise" (or contractual "right") often falling midway between the two (see, *e.g. Beswick* v. *Beswick* (1966) C.A.; *cf.* (1968) H.L.).

This dichotomy between remedies for rights and remedies for wrongs still pervades the modern causes of action. In the law of tort for example interference with property can still be actionable without proof of fault, while accidental invasions leading to physical injury normally requires "wrongfulness" (*Fowler* v. *Lanning* (1959); *Dymond* v. *Pearce* (1972)); thus the modern causes of action broadly involve the protection of rights of property and the remedying of harm wrongfully caused. The Continental lawyer might be tempted to see this as a reflection of the old Roman distinction between actions *in rem* (property) and actions *in personam* (obligations) but this division must be treated with caution in England. For much of what a Roman lawyer would see as problems of property are in fact dealt with by the common law under the obligation headings of Contract and Tort: see, *e.g. Ingram* v. *Little* (1961); *Willis & Son* v. *British Car Auctions* (1978); *Law Reform Committee Twelfth Report* (Cmnd. 2958, 1966) and *Eighteenth Report* (Cmnd. 4774, 1971); *Torts (Interference with Goods) Act 1977*.

Whether a set of facts give rise to a cause of action, then, depends just as much upon how a common lawyer categorises those facts as upon any rules of law applicable. The skill of a lawyer lies not only in interpreting the law but also interpreting the facts; before the law can be applied the facts must be categorised—but, of course, in order to categorise the facts the law must be applied (see Chap. 10). What the common lawyer must do is to present the facts to a court in such a way as to indicate that they disclose a cause of action—that is that the facts fall within a recognised category like Property, Contract or Tort (see, *e.g. Ex Parte Island Records* (1978)); although this is not to suggest that the causes of action are mutually exclusive (*Esso* v. *Mardon* (1976)).

Remedies

Causes of action really represent a rationalisation of remedies—a guide to the judges as to when they can and when they cannot grant the particular remedy claimed. But while the study of causes of action gives an excellent overview—or map—of English law, it gives little insight into how the law actually goes about granting relief: to understand this aspect one must turn to the main remedies themselves.

At common law the main remedy is an award of money. But this can take two forms—debt and damages. The former is a liquidated, specific sum of money usually arising as a result of a contractual transaction (*White & Carter (Councils) Ltd.* v. *McGregor* (1962)) but available also to prevent unjust enrichment (*Moses* v. *Macferlan* (1760); *The Aldora* (1975)); the latter is an unliquidated sum which has to be assessed during the trial and itself may be the subject of an appeal (see, *e.g. Lim Poh Choo* v. *Camden Health Authority* (1979)). From the historical angle the difference between debt and damages is reflected in the different remedies of debt and trespass and, originally, the former writ was much closer to the law of property; today, however, debts tend to be associated with the law of obligations: see Lord Diplock in *Moschi* v. *Lep Air Services Ltd.* (1973).

Although the early law was centred around property, the common law courts themselves found it difficult to think in terms of remedies other than monetary awards. It was the Court of Chancery that generated most of the developments with respect to specific restitution. The common law could grant restitution of land by the remedy of "ejectment" but when it came to chattels the actions of trespass, detinue (now abolished) and conversion allowed the defendant the option of paying the value rather than making restitution. This position was not properly remedied until the *Common Law Procedure Act 1854*, s. 78 (and see now *Torts (Interference with Goods) Act 1977*, s. 3).

This limitation of common law remedies, in the field of private law, to money judgments was one reason why some litigants of the past were driven to the Court of Chancery (see Chap. 8). And in order to fulfil the objectives of equity the Court of Chancery felt bound to provide a range of alternative remedies—although these were designed to complement rather than usurp the common law ones. Thus positive orders could be made via specific performance and mandatory injunction; negative orders by prohibitory injunctions. Transactions could be set aside by the remedy of rescission; written documents corrected by rectification. Furthermore the Chancellor, by using the doctrine of estoppel, could prevent a prospective common law plaintiff from abusing his rights at law; while abuse of power might be avoided by the trust device or by granting relief against penalties. From the cause of action point of view many of these equitable remedies were motivated by principle: for example rectification, rescission or, indeed, the trust device might all be used to prevent the common law's method of justified enrichment—*viz.* contract—from becoming, because of fraud, duress, misrepresentation or mistake, an instrument of unjust enrichment.

However, this is not to suggest that the common law remained insensitive to equity. In the eighteenth and nineteenth centuries, having previously been unable to beat the Chancery judges, the common lawyers went part of the way in joining them: debt actions plagiarised notions of the trust (the action for money had and received) and were utilised to reflect the equitable notion of unjust enrichment (*Moses* v. *Macferlan* (1760)); the idea of "tracing"—whereby a plaintiff could assert his "property" right in money possessed by the defendant—was adopted in *Taylor* v. *Plumer* (1815). Today the common law happily uses equitable remedies to give greater definition to its property and other rights: *Ex Parte Island Records* (1978); *Beswick* v. *Beswick* (1968).

One major difference between common law and equitable remedies must be mentioned. And that is that the latter are only available at the discretion of the court. So, for example, if a defendant commits the tort of nuisance the plaintiff will be entitled to damages as of right (although these might only be nominal: see, *e.g. Constantine* v. *Imperial Hotels Ltd.* (1944));

an injunction to stop the defendant from continuing the nuisance will only issue if the court thinks fit: *Miller* v. *Jackson* (1977). Also, under the *Chancery Amendment Act 1858* a court has power to give damages in lieu of specific performance or injunction (see *Shelfer* v. *City of London Electric Lighting Co.* (1895) *per* A. L. Smith L.J.).

In the field of constitutional—or public—law the courts have inherited a selection of remedies (see Chap. 8) for controlling executive departments and tribunals. Mandamus is available to order a statutory body to perform its public duty; certiorari can challenge a decision from a body which has failed in its duty to act judicially. Prohibition is still available (see Chap. 8) to restrain a public authority, which has legal authority to determine the rights of subjects, from taking further action; habeas corpus can be used to challenge an unlawful imprisonment. Nevertheless these remedies are not truly confined to the field of "Public Law" (see, *e.g. Barnado* v. *Ford* (1892)) anymore than the private law remedy of damages for say negligence or defamation is confined to private persons or bodies (*Dutton* v. *Bognor Regis U.D.C.* (1972); *Bognor Regis U.D.C.* v. *Campion* (1972)).

Of almost equal importance in the field of public law—although by no means confined to that area—is the ability of the court to issue an opinion—or declaratory judgment (see *Rules of Supreme Court*, Ord. 15, r. 16). In many ways these judgments are rather alien to the tradition of the common law which has always eschewed the world of hypothetical and academic questions in favour of actual concrete disputes. Thus before a court will grant a declaration the "question must be a real and not a theoretical question; the person raising it must have a real interest to raise it; he must be able to secure a proper contradictor, that is to say, someone presently existing who has a true interest to oppose the declaration sought" (Lord Dunedin in *Russian Commercial and Industrial Bank* v. *British Bank for Foreign Trade Ltd.* (1921)). In the field of criminal law by virtue of the *Criminal Justice Act 1972*, s. 36 reference may also be made by the Attorney-General to the Court of Appeal for an opinion on a matter arising out of an actual case where the accused has been acquitted but the Crown wish for a point of law to be resolved (see, *e.g. Attorney-General's Reference (No. 3 of 1977)* (1978)).

Conclusion

The problem of how the common law should be classified is not just a problem of pragmatism and convenience: classification can influence the way in which we think about law on the metaphysical level. Accordingly the whole question of the structure and divisions of law has important intellectual overtones and this is one reason why Roman legal philosophers spent time and energy on the subject.

But in trying to describe the sources, classification and divisions of English law one is faced with an almost infinite number of approaches: fact-based classifications like Labour or Consumer law can be opposed to abstract divisions like Public, Property or Crime; causes of action can be opposed to remedies. Family law or Shipping can be opposed to liability for Personal Injury or Interference with Goods; liability for acts or statements can be opposed to liability for negligence. Law can also be structured by the metaphysical devices it establishes: thus Contract, Hire-Purchase and Trusts can be opposed to an historical classification like Equity or Land Law. The pragmatic nature of English law with its traditional emphasis on procedure means that the common lawyer is really a person who thinks with his feet rather than his head—though this is not to suggest that, for much of the time, he is not sure-footed—and so English lawyers have never really found it necessary to have as a starting point some comprehensive rational and schematic plan.

Nevertheless the lack of a coherent structure in some aspects of English law can on occasions prove troublesome. In the field of public law, for example, the emphasis on remedies, as various writers point out, has led the courts away from important policy issues lying behind the facts of the cases before them; similarly in the area of personal property the emphasis on the forms of action has meant that English law has not really worked out any rational legal plan as to the relationship between persons and things (see, *e.g. Ingram* v. *Little* (1961)—property problem treated as a contractual one; *Moorgate Mercantile* v. *Twitchings* (1976)—"perennial failure of English law to develop a proper method of charging movable property").

Bibliography

Weir, "The Common Law System" (above, Chap. 8).

Weir, "Abstraction in the Law of Torts" [Michaelmas 1974] *City of London Law Review* 15 (C.L.L.R.).

Allen, *Law in the Making* (7th. ed., 1964).

Cross, *Precedent in English Law* (3rd. ed., 1977), Chaps. III and V.

Zweigert & Kotz (above, Chap. 8), pp. 260–284.

David & Brierley (above, Chap. 8), pp. 308–367.

Lawson, *Remedies of English Law* (1972).

Wilson, *Cases and Materials on the English Legal System* (1973), Chap. 7.

Maitland, *The Forms of Action at Common Law* (1909).

Milsom (above, Chap. 8).

Pound, "Classification of Law" (1924) 37 Harvard L.R. 933.

Jolowicz, *Lectures on Jurisprudence* (1963), pp. 191–380.

Jolowicz, *Roman Foundations of Modern Law* (1957), Chap. VIII.

Jolowicz (J. A.) (ed.), *The Division and Classification of the Law* (1970).

Fifoot, *English Law and its Background* (1932).

CHAPTER 10

LEGAL REASONING

Introduction

In the last chapter we saw that the skill of a lawyer lay not only in the handling of the "law" but also in the handling of the "facts."

Categorisation of Facts

Interpretation and classification of facts is not only important in respect of the actual dispute before the court; when it comes to interpreting previous cases for the purposes of precedent, how the judge views the facts of a previous decision may be of the utmost importance. For example in *Grant* v. *Australian Knitting Mills* (1936) in order to discover whether a rule laid down in a previous case, *Donoghue* v. *Stevenson* (1932), was applicable it was first necessary for the court to decide whether the fact that the wayward product in *Donoghue* was a bottle of ginger-beer was of relevance. In other words how was the chattel in *Donoghue* to be factually described and classified—as a "product" or a "bottle of ginger-beer"? If the court was to decide that it must be classified as "ginger-beer" it would then be possible to hold that a rule formulated to deal with such a "fact" was hardly applicable to the "facts" of *Grant* where the cause of complaint was a contaminated pair of underpants; if on the other hand it was classified as a "product," then the rule might well be relevant.

Findings of fact are also relevant where legislation is concerned. Thus it is of importance to discover for example whether certain kinds of activity amount to "insulting" behaviour for the purposes of the *Public Order Act 1936*, s. 5 (*Brutus* v. *Cozens* (1973)); and sometimes these findings of fact may in themselves be questions of law in that once decided they become binding on lower courts. Accordingly it might now be true to say (*cf.* Cross, *Statutory Interpretation*, p. 53) that as a rule of law the word "insulting" does not necessarily include behaviour that evinces contempt of other people's rights. Furthermore, in "the context of the doctrine of precedent, the question whether a particular matter is one of law or fact is itself a question of law" (Cross, *Precedent*, p. 223).

Finding the Law

Having discovered and categorised the facts the next task of the judge (with help from counsel) is to discover the law—*i.e.* the appropriate "rule" to cover the facts that he has just classified. If the relevant rule is to be found in legislation then the judge, prima facie, need look no further than the appropriate printed statute, although of course he may have to turn to the law reports in order to seek guidance and clarification on the meaning of a particular word or phrase. If the relevant rule is to be found in court decisions then the judge's task will be to discover the rules from the cases cited to him by counsel; a task that involves the judge in seeking out the *ratio decidendi* (see Chap. 9) of one or more of the previous cases so that he can discover the rules that are binding upon him.

Ratio Decidendi

How does a judge go about determining the *ratio* of a previous case and distinguishing it from mere *obiter dicta*? The answer to this question largely depends upon one's epistemological standpoint in understanding the judicial process. To the lawyer, as indicated, the process is one of distillation: "[the *ratio decidendi*] is almost always to be ascertained by an analysis of the material facts of the case—that is, generally, those facts which the tribunal whose decision is in question itself holds, expressly or implicitly, to be material" (Lord Simon in *F.A. & A.B. Ltd.* v. *Lupton* (1971)).

Interpretation of Statutes

If the relevant law is to be found in a statute rather than the cases, then the judges must indulge in a different exercise of interpretation: an analysis of the actual printed words of the appropriate legislation. English judges, unlike those of the American Supreme Court, recognise now that they do not have the power to declare an Act of Parliament invalid, for Parliament is seen as the supreme law making authority; nevertheless the judges consider themselves as a body independent of the executive, one of whose functions is to act as a check upon abuse of power. Thus they have reserved the right to "interpret" the law handed down from Parliament and this in effect means that the law contained in a statute is only what the judges—on final appeal, the House of Lords—say it is.

Such an attitude has, on occasions, led to some curious situations. In *Fisher* v. *Bell* (1961) a Divisional Court held that the words "offers for sale" in the *Restriction of Offensive Weapons Act 1959*, s. 1 (1) must be interpreted in accordance with the law of contract; thus a shopkeeper in Bristol who displayed in his shop window a flick-knife was held not to have committed an offence as goods displayed in shop-windows are not contractual "offers." Although such a decision plainly frustrated the intention of the legislature, the courts nevertheless claim that the main test for statutory interpretation is to discover the intention of Parliament.

What then are the tools of the lawyers when it comes to interpreting statutes? First, there is the legislation itself: this may often contain a definition section and so for example if a defendant's hinnie tramples upon a neighbour's chrysanthemums the relevant rule applicable will be section 4 of the *Animals Act 1971* because section 11 of this Act defines "livestock" as including the defendant's trespassing animal. Furthermore the *Interpretation Act 1978* provides a number of general definitions (*e.g.* "person" includes a body corporate) as well as consolidating a number of statutory provisions (*e.g.*

words importing the masculine gender shall include females; and words in the singular include plural, etc.: s. 6).

Secondly, the courts themselves have formulated various rules, principles and presumptions in respect of statutory interpretation. Traditionally it is said that there are three "rules" of interpretation: (i) the Mischief Rule, (ii) the Golden Rule and (iii) the Literal Rule. The source of the Mischief Rule is to be found in *Heydon's Case* (1584) where it was "recognised that there are, in connection with the interpretation of statutes, four questions to be considered: (1) what was the common law before the making of the Act; (2) what was the mischief or defect for which the law did not provide; (3) what remedy Parliament had provided, and (4) the reason for the remedy" (Viscount Dilhorne in *Black-Clawson* v. *Papierwerke* (1975)). The judge should then adopt a construction that will suppress the mischief. "It is, in other words," said Lord Simon in *Maunsell* v. *Olins* (1975), "a positive and not a negative canon of construction; it enjoins a liberal, and not a restrictive, approach." At the other end of the scale is the Literal Rule which stipulates that the words of a statute must be interpreted according to their literal meaning and sentences according to their grammatical meaning; the fact that this might result in an absurd interpretation appears to be irrelevant for the "Court has nothing to do with the question whether the Legislature has committed an absurdity" (Lord Esher M.R. in *R.* v. *The Judge of the City of London Court* (1892)). Between these two approaches lies the Golden Rule which seems to take as its basis a literal approach "unless that construction leads to a plain and clear contradiction of the apparent purpose of the Act or to some palpable and evident absurdity" (Alderson B. in *Att.-Gen.* v. *Lockwood* (1842)). The Law Commission criticised the literal approach in that it assumed "an unattainable perfection in draftsmanship" and ignored "the limitations of language" (Law Com. No. 21, para. 30); they appear to favour the Mischief Rule although they made the sharp observation that

Heydon's Case is "somewhat outdated in its approach" and "reflects a very different constitutional balance between the Executive, Parliament and the public" (para. 33; see also Lord Diplock in *Black-Clawson* v. *Papierwerke*).

Besides these "rules," the judiciary have also formulated presumptions in respect of the interpretation of statutes. Thus there is a presumption that criminal statutes will not operate retrospectively and that they will require *mens rea* (*Sweet* v. *Parsley* (1970)) as an element. Also there is a presumption that "in the absence of any clear indication to the contrary Parliament can be presumed not to have altered the common law farther than was necessary to remedy the 'mischief'" (Lord Reid in *Black-Clawson* v. *Papierwerke*).

Another curious feature of the common law's attitude towards legislation is in respect of the admitting of extrinsic materials (*e.g.* reports of Parliamentary debates, Royal Commissions, etc.) in aid of interpretation. As a general rule such materials are not admissible (*Ellerman Lines Ltd.* v. *Murray* (1931); *Assam Railways* v. *I.R.C.* (1935)). Nevertheless there do appear to be occasions where the judges have made use of external materials (see, *e.g. Salomon* v. *Commissioners of Custom & Excise* (1967); *James Buchanan* v. *Babco* (1977) *per* Lord Wilberforce) but this has been justified by the argument that the judges were only trying to find the "mischief" for the Mischief Rule (*Black-Clawson* v. *Papierwerke*).

Applying the Law

Having discovered the facts and the law the next task of the judge is to apply the latter to the former—although it should be said at once that to divorce this process from the interpretation of facts and the discovery of law is misleading in that the earlier exercises are often guided by this last task. Thus a certain "fact" and a particular element of a "rule" may both be stressed during the discovery and categorisation stage so as to facilitate an application that will lead to a desired result.

For example in *Read* v. *J. Lyons & Co.* (1947) a woman injured by an unexplained explosion in a munitions factory was denied recovery ostensibly on the ground that factually there had been no "escape" of a dangerous thing so as to bring the case within an element which the judges had decided to stress of the rule of *Rylands* v. *Fletcher* (1866)—*viz*. "likely to do mischief if it *escapes*" (Blackburn J.). In order to arrive at the desired result—*viz*. denial of liability—it was necessary to interpret the facts so as to stress that this was an injury *on* (as opposed to off) the defendant's premises and to interpret Blackburn J.'s rule in such a way as to indicate that it applied only to persons injured off the defendant's land. Thus the application of law to the facts—especially when it is a common law rule being applied—may actually just be a formality, the real issues having been decided at one of the earlier stages. Furthermore it is worth noting that *obiter dicta* can sometimes be just as influential in respect of the final outcome of a subsequent case as any *ratio decidendi*.

Nevertheless the application process can assume importance where the rule itself appears quite widely drafted or stated. In *R.* v. *Peart* (1970) the hirer of a motor-van took the vehicle further than he promised and the question arose as to whether this amounted to an offence within section 12 (1) of the *Theft Act 1968* which stipulates that "a person shall be guilty of an offence if, without having the consent of the owner or other lawful authority, he takes any conveyance for his own or another's use." The Court of Appeal (Criminal Division) thought that the facts did not fall within the rule for otherwise the 1968 Act "would in effect be inventing a fresh crime—obtaining possession by false pretences—an offence unknown to the law except when accompanied by intent to deprive the owner *permanently* of possession."

In *Peart* the rule was adjusted so as not to be applicable to the facts, but sometimes it is the facts that can be adjusted to facilitate application of a rule. In *D.P.P.* v. *Ray* (1973) the respondent and three others entered a restaurant and ordered a meal, all having the intention of paying; however, once the food had been consumed, they changed their minds and ran out of the restaurant without meeting the bill. The respondent was charged under section 16 (1) of the *Theft Act 1968* for "dishonestly" obtaining by "deception" a "pecuniary advantage" and the House of Lords upheld this conviction even though there was no specific finding that the waiter was *deceived* or that the respondent intended to deceive the waiter. What the majority did in this case was to interpret the facts in such a way as to come to the conclusion that the waiter was in fact deceived, thus facilitating application of section 16 (1).

Tools of Reasoning

As the previous cases indicate, given the nature of language and the flexibility of many of the judicial devices there will be numerous occasions when a court has a choice as to whether it arrives at one decision or another; and so the question arises as to what kinds of reasoning the judges will use to justify the approach finally decided upon. Undoubtedly one of the main tools is that of logic: for "no system of law can be workable if it has not got logic at the root of it" (Lord Devlin in *Hedley Byrne* v. *Heller* (1964)); and logic has the further advantage of perpetuating the idea that law is a politically and socially neutral process. A good illustration of the working of logic can be found in the case of *Partington* v. *Williams* (1975). In an attempt to steal money a pickpocket lifted a wallet that turned out to contain no money; she was caught and prosecuted for attempted theft. Her defence counsel argued that anyone who attempts a crime that is impossible to commit is not guilty of an offence (see *Haughton* v. *Smith* (1975)); the pickpocket, by lifting an *empty* wallet, could not have physically succeeded in the crime, and thus she could not be guilty of attempt. The defence was upheld.

Associated with the logical approach is reasoning by analogy (see Lord Simon in *F.A. & A.B. Ltd.* v. *Lupton* (1971)), and this is a tool much used by the common lawyer, being especially useful for novel factual situations. Thus the tort of negligence has been extended to new situations by analogy: if a manufacturer of ginger-beer is liable for putting into circulation a defective product why not the builder—or indeed, inspector—who puts (or allows) into circulation a defective house? (See *Dutton* v. *Bognor Regis U.D.C.* (1972); and see now *Defective Premises Act 1972* s. 3.) On the other hand the judges can sometimes specifically refuse to be guided by analogy. In *Read* v. *J. Lyons & Co.* (1947) counsel for the plaintiff urged that the employers should be liable because they had undertaken a dangerous activity and ought therefore to bear the risk of injury; an analogy was drawn with the dangerous animal cases (see now *Animals Act 1971*, s. 2 (1)). But Lord Macmillan rejected this type of reasoning: "the emphasis now is on the conduct of the person whose act has occasioned the injury and the question is whether it can be characterised as negligent"; and he concluded "such an exceptional case as this [*viz.* the dangerous animal one cited by counsel] affords no justification for its extension by analogy."

Index

Appeal, 22 *et seq.*
Arbitration, 35

Bar, The, 40
Barrister, 39
  liability of, 40–42
Burden of proof, 4

Cause of Action, 88
Committal, 21
Common law, 1 *et seq.*, 55 *et seq.*
  courts of, 59
  development of, 55 *et seq.*
Contract, 6–8
Court,
  Appeal, 24, 27, 74
  Chancery, of, 69, 73
  civil, 25–28
    county, 25
    High Court, 26
    process in, 35
  Common Pleas, of, 61
  criminal, 19
    crown, 22–24
    magistrates', 19
    process in, 34
  ecclesiastical, 59, 69
  European, 28
  juvenile, 22
  King's Bench, 62 *et seq.*
  maritime, 66
  merchant, 66
  Restrictive Practices, 29
  small claims, 50
  Staple, of, 67
Criminal law, 3 *et seq.*
Curia Regis, 57 *et seq.*

Damages, 91

Equity, 2, 10, 11, 92
Exchequer, 57, 71, 72

HMSO, 83
House of Lords, 24, 28

Injunction, 92

Inns of Court, 40, 75

Judge, 11–14
Jury, 14–16, 75
  Grand, 60

Law,
  application of, 106
  classification of, 86
  finding of, 97
Law Centre, 48
Law Commission, 82
Law reposting, 75
Laws, 52 *et seq.*
  sources of, 78
Law Society, 37, 75
Legal Aid, 42 *et seq.*
  civil, 44
  criminal, 46
Legal profession,
  development of, 69–71
Legal publishing, 84
Legislation, 79
  interpretation of, 98

Magistrate, 17, 18, 75
  stipendiary, 18
Mens Rea, 5

Precedent, 80, 96
Public law, 93

Ratio Decidendi, 80, 97
"Reasonable man," 10
Roman law, 84, 85

Solicitor, 36
  liability of, 38
Star Chamber, 61, 68
Statute law, 3

Trial,
  summary, 20
Tribunal, 12, 28 *et seq.*
  issues before, 32
Tort, 8–10